after

Engine Books
PO Box 44167
Indianapolis, IN 46244
enginebooks.org

This is a work of fiction. Names, characters, places, and incidents are either the product of the author's imagination or used fictitiously.

Also available in eBook formats from Engine Books.

Printed in the United States of America

10   9   8   7   6   5   4   3   2   1

ISBN: 978-1-938126-22-2

Library of Congress Control Number: 2013935830

after

a novel

KRISTIN WATERFIELD DUISBERG

Engine Books
Indianapolis

ALSO BY KRISTIN WATERFIELD DUISBERG

THE GOOD PATIENT

For Grace and Henry

"One cannot divine nor forecast the conditions that will make happiness; one only stumbles upon them by chance, in a lucky hour, at the world's end somewhere…"

— *Willa Cather*

Part One

Spring 2003

one

A BEGINNING, AND AN end: Nina Baldwin was in the shower when she found the lump in her breast. She was in a hurry, but making good on the self-exam she assured her doctor—far too cavalierly, and not at all truthfully—she performed every month; her skin slick with soap, she ran her hands over both breasts at the same time. On the left, her fingers made out the familiar geography: sloping upper half, the spongy terrain of nipple, the full swell where breast curved down to ribs. (Champagne cups, a guy she had dated in college had once called the shape of her breasts; she'd pictured the insulting, udder-like elongation of champagne *flutes* and they'd broken up not long thereafter.) On the right side, though, the pads of her fingers rode over a bump just above her nipple, slid on, and then stopped. Reversed. Nina put both hands to her right breast, and there was no disputing it: a distinct lump, hard and round as a pearl, lodged beneath her skin.

For a minute, she wasn't quite sure what to think. After all, in more than one morbid moment she'd imagined this: the uninvited rise and fall beneath her fingers, the desperate decoy of gooseflesh, the way the lump would form a scornful knot beneath her puckered skin. She'd felt the shower's heat beating down on her, heard the eerie submerged echoes of the tub, knew the way the steam would catch her breath and the world would freeze for a heartbeat into a perfect, crystal *oh*. That her first thought now was something more like *huh* seemed an embarrassment, the revelation of some sort of character flaw that she couldn't even for this, of

11

all things, be serious.

Her fingers felt with more intent: she could almost roll the lump, pick it up inside her skin, and yet—there was a strange sense of it, almost the *idea* of tugging, as if the object underneath her skin was something attached absolutely to the deepest part of her chest. An image came into her head: a boat buoy, one of those bright orange balls that bobbled on the surface of Charlotte Harbor, where she'd spent her childhood summers, mooring the furled-sailed boats to the rocky bottom with an eye-bolt and an algaed tendon of rope. It made no sense; that was the problem. She looked down at herself and frowned. The upper curve of her areola was drawn in slightly, her nipple canted upward like a lazy eye. Her fingers smoothed the skin absently, futilely. *Huh.*

In fairness, Nina had real reason to suppose there was nothing to worry about: her medical history was distinguished by nothing more than a string of oddities. Near maladies that proved to be harmless; well-that-was-close type good outcomes that had conditioned her to greet each successive aberration with more and more bemusement about the peculiar sense of humor her body so clearly poooooood. At seventeen, a throbbing pulse in her abdomen had occasioned emergency ultrasound—an aortic aneurysm, her doctor was sure, in danger of blowing any minute—later, the same doctor had ordered a colonoscopy when she complained of blood in her stool only to discover (indignity upon indignity) hemorrhoids. Blinding headaches in her twenties had been an allergy to artificial sweeteners; an infected hangnail looked like staph, but wasn't. And then there was the thing that had started it all, when she was twelve years old, a strange bulge in her femur that, in the days before CT scan and MRI, had looked for all the world like bone cancer; she'd actually been wheeled into an operating room with the expectation that she'd wake up with her leg amputated up to her thigh. Three decades and change later, Nina still felt a pair of distinct emotions when she fingered the neat scar on her left quadriceps: gratitude that the growth therein had been benign, and a deep shame at having stirred up such a frenzy of panic in her family, all for naught.

Even Nina's experience with pregnancy—that had survived *two* false alarms: a day of bright red blood during her ninth week, then a triple-screen result in her second trimester that raised the threat of Down syndrome. Well. Audrey had celebrated her seventh birthday a month ago, lovely and intense and high-minded in a way that was a mystery to Nina. High-minded was actually Nina's best term for it; there had been experts who had advanced other, less positive descriptors with which, in weaker moments, she had concurred. Anxious. Obsessive-compulsive. Atypical. Nina fought the labels, but it didn't cost her too much to concede that her daughter took on even the standard pleasures of childhood—throwing stones into the oval pond at the end of the street; galoomphing around the backyard by herself, pretending to be a sheep-herding border collie—with a sort of grave dedication that was *almost* a problem. Her daughter, she supposed; her husband's daughter, absolutely.

Eventually, after the visit to the doctor, after the mammogram and the ultrasound and the first meeting with her Boston medical team, what would come was the response Nina had thought, upon that first moment of discovery, she *ought* to have: the cold clutch of her stomach, the curl of terror that lodged itself at the back of her throat. *What if—?* For now, however, she just stepped out of the shower. Rubbed the mirror free of fog and inspected herself. In reflection, the lazy-eye effect was more plain to see: the upper right side of her areola was pulled in as if someone had taken a purse-string stitch to the underside of her skin. She put her finger to it. The dented skin was bumpy and slightly coarse, stippled as if with cold.

Nina went to the bedroom for the telephone and dialed her husband's office. Martin was a doctor, a cardiologist, emeritus chief of cardiac medicine at St. Serafin Hospital. It was not exactly his domain, a breast lump, but at least it was geographically proximal.

Martin's secretary picked up on the first ring.

"Hi, Elaine, it's Nina. Is Martin available?"

"Nina, hi. No, I'm sorry." Elaine had been the department receptionist before she'd moved to the back office; her voice still executed the requisite dealing-with-the-public slide from delight to sympathy effortlessly. "Martin's in a procedure right now."

"Of course he is. I forgot. It's Tuesday, isn't it?"

Martin spent Tuesdays in the cardiac catheterization lab—the cath lab, as he referred to it, or the calf lab, as Audrey had once thought. Nina had always loved her daughter's childish understanding of her father's work, loved the thought of Martin moving among a herd of velvety calves in a lab coat and rubber gloves, rubbing wet noses, scratching the bristly undersides of jaws. It could hardly be farther from the truth of how her husband spent his days, and yet the image stuck with Nina, conferring a sort of softness onto what she knew was otherwise strictly cerebral work.

"It looks like he has a break between cases around ten or so," Elaine said. "I'll have him call you then, unless it's urgent. He's off-pager now, but I could always have someone run across the street."

Was it urgent? Nina returned to the bathroom and looked at herself in the mirror, her nude body a portrait still framed by fog. She watched her pointer finger tap the indentation, then press the lump, just slightly north. How could she have missed it before? It was as screamingly obvious to her now as a bull's-eye tattooed on her skin. On the floor behind her, the workout clothes she'd sweatily shucked after her walk with her friend Jenny lay in a heap: Lycra pants and a moisture-wicking shirt, a windbreaker, a jogging bra. The two women had joked before about what sadism must have gone into the designing of sports bras, which smashed their chests as flat as a couple of boys'; maybe the bra was to blame now. An old milk duct, finally sufficiently aggrieved. A pimple, one of those cyst-like ones, with Nina's luck. That would be appropriate: flirting with menopause on one hand, and yet still battling the quintessential teenage affliction in only its strangest form on the other.

"No, Elaine. Not urgent. I just had a question." (And what question was it she'd ask, actually? Martin sweetheart, I have a lump in my breast. Can you tell me, over the telephone, just what it is?) Maybe she'd call Dr. Raab, her primary care physician. Dr. Raab was always reassuring. She'd probably tell her that everybody has lumps these days, what with the hormones in milk, the pesticides sprayed on every vegetable and piece of fruit, all the dioxins leaching from microwaved plastic. Yes, Dr. Raab. Her office opened at nine.

"I'll have him give you a call."

"Thanks. On my cell, though." Nina picked her watch up off the counter. It was eight-fifty now. She had grocery shopping to do this morning; she'd volunteered for the book fair at Audrey's school and had to be there by twelve.

"I'm writing him a note right now."

Elaine read Nina's cell phone number back to her. He should have it, but both women knew that while he could glance at an echocardiogram and spot the merest nick in an ST-wave to identify a patient's heart attack, Martin wasn't able to hold on to even the most fundamental piece of household data—his and Nina's anniversary, say, or the code to the house security system, which was the same as Nina's birthday. It was one of the concessions she had made early on: making sure he had the information she needed him to know rather than waiting for him to disappoint her. Probably advice she'd read in some women's magazine, but—whatever. It worked.

"That's it," Nina said, "thanks. How's everything going with the wedding?" In the mirror, she made a face at herself. Elaine was getting married in June, and she was, as Martin put it rather unkindly, pathologically obsessed with the details. Why on earth was Nina making small talk now? She tucked the telephone against her ear with her shoulder and reached for her toothbrush. At least she could do that while she listened.

"A complete disaster, actually. First of all, my dress isn't going to be in until *much* too close to the wedding, Paul and I can't agree on a first-dance song, and even if we do I'm not sure we'll survive his two left feet. And then there's the cake—" Friends had insisted Elaine check out a particular bakery, and now that she had her heart set on rolled fondant, the baker said he couldn't deliver to their reception site. Nina got it, even if she couldn't necessarily relate to any of the specifics. She and Martin had been married in a civil ceremony at City Hall.

"I think we may skip the wedding," Elaine said, "and go straight for the divorce."

Nina spat as quietly as she could into the sink. "If it's any consolation, a friend once told me it's easier to *be* married than to *get* married."

Elaine laughed. "Well, I think it has to be."

Nina hung up the telephone feeling strangely better, deflected reassuringly into the plane of the norm. So she had a lump in her breast. So? There were still weddings to plan, songs to haggle over, cakes to taste. Nina buckled her watch to her wrist. There were still groceries to buy and school activities to serve. She did some quick mental math. Twenty minutes to the store, forty-five to shop, half an hour, at least, to unload the groceries and put away—how could it be she got up at six every morning but was still badly behind three hours later? If her job—running the household, raising Audrey—were a real one, like those she used to evaluate candidates for on a daily basis, her reviews would mention poor time management and lousy judgment in evaluating the scope of project work. She took a quick scan of the bathroom: the heap of her workout clothes merely previewed a much larger pile waiting in the laundry room. Martin's faucet dripped, a regular *blip-blip-blip*, leaving a ring of lime around the drain. She had thought about hiring a cleaning lady. Why hadn't she called the plumber yet? Because it had to be something she could fix herself with a monkey wrench and a roll of plumber's tape. She gave the telephone, face up on the counter like an overturned beetle, an almost apologetic glance. She'd call Dr. Raab from the road, or in the afternoon.

WAS IT EASIER TO be married than to get married? Nina thought about this as she pushed her cart through the aisles of Watson Brothers Grocery. It was a statement she'd taken—and repeated—without much reflection. She remembered the surprisingly bitter guffaws of several older women when she'd heard the pronouncement made at a coworker's bridal shower years ago; she noted, with some interest, that she hadn't particularly claimed to represent her own position in saying it to Elaine on the phone.

In some ways, Martin was extremely easy to be married to: he was stable and intelligent, he was an excellent provider; at almost twenty-two years her senior, it was hard to argue that he was anything but mature. And of course, it wasn't particularly difficult to get along with a husband who was rarely there. Though Martin had reached retirement age in March, he still insisted on a full schedule and patient load: at the hospital by seven-thirty, infrequently home by dinner. His hands were still steady; he was as adept with balloon angiography as any thirty-five year old. He'd remarked more than once, disdainfully, that he would never be one of those older physicians who kept an office and showed up just to read their journals long after they were able to perform real work.

And it wasn't as if he was *never* home. On Sunday mornings, Martin cooked elaborate brunches: shirred eggs and sausages, raised German pancakes with confectioner's sugar and red currant jelly, the menu one of the rare nods he was willing to make to his Prussian childhood. He had a rather sly, dry sense of humor. He was an earnest father—serious about his attentions to his serious daughter. And even now he was handsome. Not handsome *for his age;* just handsome. Still lean from daily bike rides and five-mile runs. A full head of iron gray hair. A wide, sensual mouth, often screwed up in an inscrutable smirk.

Nina and Martin had met at a ribbon-cutting ceremony at his hospital, eight years earlier. He had been fifty-seven years old, divorced; she was a month away from her thirty-sixth birthday and just getting comfortable with the idea that she might never have a husband or a child. Just like that awful *love is like a butterfly* sentiment, she'd joked to one of her college girlfriends, ten years married by then and living out in Ann Arbor, ferrying children to kindergarten and second grade. What had attracted Nina was that Martin was so utterly unlike anyone else she'd ever dated: stern, arrogantly knowledgeable, not even vaguely interested in saving the world, notwithstanding his choice of career. He had a certain remoteness that had, however perversely, appealed to her. She'd wanted so much to please him, to impress him, and yet revealing the depths of her thirty-five-year-old soul often netted her either his condescension or—surprisingly—sadness. He had been a challenge, and she knew the Freudians in the crowd would have plenty to say about that. He was, after all, *old.* Nina's father was dead; killed in a car accident along with her mother six years earlier.

Martin wasn't too old, however. Nina had gotten pregnant, and they'd gotten married—in that order, and within six months of their first meeting. Martin had three sons in their twenties from his first marriage and an ex-wife who regularly called their house late at night and hung up. Though Martin and Beth had been divorced for years, and at Beth's instigation, when he and Nina met, it still had been an outrage—Nina cast in the part of the young and fertile strumpet—and there was some shameful, private part of her that had thrived on the sheer density of the drama. Romance, pregnancy, a wedding, threats of miscarriage and birth defects, all set against the backdrop of Beth Winzer's covetous fury.

But lately…Nina had to admit to a small, mean fear that maybe that had been all the excitement she got, and she'd used it up in what, in retrospect, was rather an ill-considered burst. She was in a place in life she knew she was supposed to enjoy—well married and well mortgaged;

mother to a brilliant, obedient child; gifted with the sort of financial flexibility that allowed her to spend much of her time as she liked. Finally, it no longer felt like everything was a struggle: long behind her were the relentless angst of her teenage years and the painful haze of her parents' deaths; distant too the creeping unease of being in her thirties with her life arranged not at all as she'd imagined. It was a grace period, the calm before the storm of Audrey's adolescence, her own legitimate claim to middle-age, and—morbid to say this, yes, but—Martin's desuetude and sure predecessive demise. And yet she was dogged by a sense of stasis. There were days she watched Audrey's school recede in her rear view mirror and thought *now what?* She'd go for her walk—forty-three and she could almost still shimmy into the jeans she wore in college—weed the garden, again consider all the other things she could, should do. Join the parent committee at school. Work the county soup kitchen regularly, rather than when her conscience occasionally chastened her. Volunteer for the Read-to-a-Resident program at the Cabot nursing home.

Standing in the middle of the Watson Brothers Grocery, though, Nina found herself confronted not for the first time with how meaningless even those so-called accomplishments seemed to her. Would organizing the school gift-wrap fundraiser actually bestow on her a greater sense of purpose than, say, figuring out the week's dinner menu did? (Easier said than done; Audrey was a picky eater with an ever-changing list of foods that were off limits; whether Martin would be home on any given night was often anyone's guess.) Would turning the last page on the latest cookie cutter legal thriller—her throat reduced to a rasp from reading not only out loud but loud—inspire a greater sense of accomplishment than remembering everything she needed at the store without resorting to a list, paying the bills and calling the handyman about getting the deck power-washed and repainted, and throwing a load of laundry in the washer with time to spare before she had to leave again to claim Audrey from school?

It was a little deflating, to put it mildly, to consider any of these options her highest and best use, the sum worth of all her struggles and second chances and *almost-but*s. And it wasn't just the what of Nina's life that occasionally troubled her. There was also the *where*—the surprising sense of shame she felt at finding herself living back home in the suburbs of Boston, raising Audrey in the same town she'd grown up in and left some twenty-five years earlier, her closest friend a classmate from high school.

As a teenager, there had been no more pressing goal for Nina than that of getting out of Cabot, a smug and affluent college town half an hour's drive from the Massachusetts coast. She'd chosen a college in Michigan for reasons as geographic as academic and spent a semester in England feeling worldly and urbane and safely *removed*. Summers and holiday breaks had been a source of perpetual misery, every store and every street imbued with the particular humiliation and despair of being sixteen— the time she'd lied about sneaking into a Cabot College party and gotten caught, the time she'd thrown herself at one of her ex-boyfriend's pals and been turned down. And yet somehow, upon graduation, she found herself taking a job back in Boston, listening to the same radio stations and cheering for the Red Sox, loading up her VW Golf with dirty laundry on Saturday mornings to wash in the same avocado-green washing machine her mother had used since she was in elementary school.

That she was back in Cabot proper now was only partly happenstance. Martin's hospital was two towns northeast of it; he and Beth had raised their boys in an even smugger and more affluent town on the North Shore, and Martin had rightly perceived that mixed in with Nina's disdain for her hometown was a grudging admiration for its postcard houses and white-steepled churches, the vast acres of open land that still surrounded certain old farmsteads. Five years ago they had bought a beautiful house in a beautiful development, a house that bore much closer resemblance to the Cabot of inherited country club memberships, split-rail horse pastures, and shimmering, private ice-skating ponds she had always envied than the faculty neighborhood of split-levels where she had grown up (gone now; razed a decade earlier when Cabot College had put in a new athletic complex). On the arm of her doctor husband—trusted cardiologist of half the town's retirement-age population—she felt protected from the self-satisfaction that had suffocated her when she was younger and still lingered like a fog above certain Cabot gatherings. The Cabot College faculty musical, any wedding at the Briarwood Hunt Club. David and Milly Crawford's annual Robert Burns dinner, an event Nina's parents had attended faithfully for years, her father's legs pale and hairless beneath an actual kilt.

What Nina feared most, perhaps, was the possibility that her life choices betrayed a decided lack of imagination: back in the same zip code where she grew up while her college peers sent missives to the alumni magazine from San Francisco and Chicago and New York, steering her SUV down the roads on which she'd learned to drive her mother's station wagon, past the same houses and the same landmarks, the same, the same. Even her friendship with Jenny Rutherford, genuine though it was, bore the markings of automatic behavior. She had recognized the familiar face on Audrey's first day at a Gymboree class; Jenny had pointed out her daughter, Willow, as the ponytailed brunette circling a dozen seated three year olds while a chipper instructor had introduced herself to the class; over a string of Tuesday mornings, they had visited while the girls ran underneath rainbow-colored parachutes and jumped into foam-ball-filled pits, feeling their tentative way from 1978 to 1999. Like two pieces of a puzzle, they had connected on all the critical points: a shared history, common job and marital status, raising daughters less than a month apart in age.

Jenny had two older children, a son in fifth grade and another daughter in third, and Martin and Jenny's husband, Jim, were as different as hammers and a string quartet. But the overlaps had been enough, Jenny's equanimity about living in Cabot reassuring, her greater experience with parenthood a lifeline on days when Audrey left Nina despairing. Jenny was, Nina had eventually realized, the walking, talking rebuttal to an argument a boyfriend had offered once, a rationalization of his inability to stay monogamous, no matter how hard he tried, that for a time had shaken Nina with its apparent, irrefutable, hopeless truth: that human beings were conditioned for adversity and change, hardwired not to be happy with their lot in life.

Nina hadn't thought about that boyfriend in years, but she dusted off his old rationalization as she finished her shopping, got her groceries home and stowed in their proper cabinets and shelves, and turned around again to drive to Audrey's school. Maybe unhappiness wasn't a truth for the human race in general, but maybe, just a little bit, at least, it was for her. As she drove, Nina slipped her left hand beneath the collar of her shirt. Her fingers found the lump right away, still there, the little dip an obvious script to her fingertips. *Drama*, that was all it was. A self-indulgent need for drama, conditioned by all those earlier experiences, the need, perhaps, to connect to the most relatable of female tragedies. It was the number-one health threat to women, wasn't it, breast cancer? Or number two, perhaps, after heart disease. Martin could tell her that.

Well, then. In her head at least, for the first time Nina had said the words. Breast cancer. *Not that it was necessarily*— *Not that it was even statistically* likely *to be*— Her fingers rolled the lump over and over. She thought of an unripened blueberry, a little glass bead. A bulb of onion grass, its filamented roots reaching deep into loamy soil.

two

WHEN MARTIN WINZER WAS in medical school at Queens University in Ontario, back in 1962, a classmate once remarked that medicine was the perfect career for someone with a dissociative disorder. The classmate was the son of a psychiatrist, an Austrian analyst who had actually trained under Freud, and he was already sure in their second year that psychiatry was the path that he would follow, too. Martin bore that in mind; here was a fellow who was going to see everything about the world through a certain lens. It was the argument with which he protected himself any time he feared the other man had been pointing to something specific in him. They had been in Autopsy at the time, working on pathology slides, and while his classmate busied himself applying more and more Vick's VapoRub to his upper lip, Martin had made exquisite cross-sections of brain. Here the lovely shell-pink of healthy tissue, there the graceless calling card of dendritic plaques. It had been extraordinary: dementia made flesh!— and Martin had felt the sweet, poetic thrill of absolute certainty in the diagnosis. There wasn't anything dissociative about that. The ability to see a body as an organism, a set of systems, was a crucial skill. His job was to find disease and eradicate it, a pure intellectual exercise. Adding emotion to the equation would only weight him, dull with *feeling* what he *knew*.

Martin saw his old classmate's face flicker before him, his weak little chin and his cold green eyes, on the Tuesday evening he examined his wife's right breast. Nina lay flat, her arm raised above her head, her nipple involuntarily tightened by exposure or anxiety. She made some sort of self-mocking come-hither comment but Martin was focused on her flesh: the obvious asymmetry of the areola, retraction of the skin directly above. He palpated the breast lobe and his fingers found the lump immediately: hard and well defined, restrictedly moveable in the spongy tissue around it. In a milk duct, he surmised, based on location. Two millimeters, perhaps; three at most. He squeezed the nipple and a serous fluid welled.

"Did you call Laurel Raab?" he asked.

"No." Nina cleared her throat. "Not yet. I was going to do it this morning after I talked to Elaine but I didn't think her office was open until nine. Then I had bad cell reception, and then I had Audrey with me and then—I just ran out of time."

Martin's hands probed the rest of the breast—benign—and moved toward Nina's armpit, checking the lymph nodes. Good, and good. One in the crease of her armpit was swollen, a small, hard bladder. Further up, another. Positive nodes in axillary levels two and three. "When was your last mammogram?"

"I've only had one. Right after my fortieth birthday. It was October, I think."

So, three and a half years ago. That was meaningless. "Well, you're going to need a diagnostic, of course. And ultrasound. Have you checked your left side?" He lifted Nina's other arm as she shook her head negatively.

"Jesus, Martin," she said.

For a moment, Martin felt a flare of annoyance, the same flare he felt whenever a patient came in, morbidly obese, dissolving in tears as Martin delivered a diagnosis of coronary artery disease. They would sit there, these patients, hands resting on thighs too large to bring together, wheezing out their distress, and Martin would wrestle his disgust. Did these people truly believe that a lifetime habit of fatty food and no exercise wouldn't have a price, or were they just hopeful that Martin could wave his magic wand and perform some sort of miracle, a medical absolution, perhaps? Most of these folks came in with a predictable handful of co-morbid conditions: lung disease, diabetes, deterioration of their knees and hips and backs. He wanted to lecture that the body each of them inhabited was only theirs; their survival was their and only their obligation; he knew they didn't see it in that light.

How long had Nina's breast been that way? How could it be that she hadn't noticed it before? The dimpling of the skin, the inversion of the nipple, they were as classic a clinical red flag as one could get—Martin realized with a searing start he had to ask the same question of himself. After all, he surely spent more time looking at her naked breasts than she did, albeit not necessarily through clinician's eyes. They had made love last—when had it been? A week ago Sunday, after dinner at Steve Boucher's. The lights had been off; had he even caressed Nina's breasts? Aah, yes. She'd kept on her brassiere, the black satin one with the wide shoulder straps; he remembered the base, priapic thrill of sliding his hands over those full, satin mounds, the material slick and erotic under his palms. Shame on him now; shame on him. He'd slipped his hands underneath the bra from the bottom, his thumbs rubbing her hard nipples like a teenage boy.

"So what's the verdict, Dr. Winzer?"

Martin felt all the way up his wife's left armpit, across her clavicle, and down the sternal crease. That breast was negative, as were all the lymph nodes. That was something, at least. "The left breast feels clear."

"The left breast," Nina repeated. She stressed *the* just slightly, and Martin knew that was a reproach. *Her* left breast. *Your* left breast. "What about the right?"

"Well—" He pinched his lips together with his thumb and forefinger, an automatic tic, doctorly. "There's clearly something there. I'm not a surgeon, Nina, but—"

"—But it could be anything, right? A cyst. One of my college roommates used to get those, and she'd have to have a needle stuck in them and have them drained. Or what about a plugged milk duct? Those stupid, sweaty jogging bras—"

"Well," Martin said again. He steeled himself. Nina was not looking for a medical opinion. He knew the words for what she was asking for: love, reassurance. They were as unnatural to him as the world in which he moved surely was to her. Objectivity. Differential diagnosis. Gently, he lowered Nina's arms and helped her sit, wrapping her robe back across her chest. He couldn't do this with that breast staring at him, a dozen Bayesian questions churning madly through his head. *What percentage of upper outer quadrant masses were malignant? What were the survival rates for ductal versus glandular lesions? Did involvement of lymph nodes necessarily signify metastasis?*

"It could be a lot of things. A cyst, yes. Ultrasound would tell. Many, many breast masses turn out to be benign. We'll get you into town, right away. I'll find out who the right person is to see you there. There have been wonderful advances, they're doing remarkable work—" It was the best he could do. He couldn't bring himself to give shape to the lie, *I know you'll be absolutely fine.*

Nina lapped the sides of her robe over her throat. "I walk three miles every day. I eat a lousy green salad for lunch, for Pete's sake." She laughed just a little. "I'm young. I'm healthy. Martin—"

Martin closed his eyes and breathed in sharply through his nose. This was the place the conversation couldn't lead: to the terrible shoals on which his medical knowledge would meet his heart. Yes, Nina was young and healthy. Young enough to play host to an aggressive tumor, a tumor that would fuel its helter-skelter growth off her hormones. And what about her personal history? Her parents had died in an auto accident when Nina was in her late twenties; she had two older brothers, Roger and Neal, who both lived on the other side of the country and with whom, by any account, she wasn't close. Her father had been a professor of zoology at Cabot College; her mother had been a homemaker who had been in her late fifties when she died. In good health, Martin assumed, though he'd never thought to ask. He hadn't supposed that was the sort of thing spouses queried about, holding hands across a candlelit table. Had your mother reached menopause before she died? Any problem with breast lumps or cysts? Martin didn't even know when his wife had begun menstruating, nor had he heretofore imagined it was information he had any need or desire to know. Yet he worried Nina would hold him blameful for that, as if the comprehensiveness of one's catalogue of data were the true measure of a marriage. If that were the case—it was what Martin knew about his patients: facts about grandmothers, sisters, aunts. It was the first-degree relations that were paramount, and that code to Nina's history was buried, irretrievable at least in one way.

Martin exhaled. Enough. He knew how to banish his brutal knowledge, how to put it in a concrete-lined box with a bank of locks and no key. It was a trick he'd learned long ago, visualizing the dark, basement-level rooms in his mind, marching facts and emotions off through separate doors like naughty children caught up by the collar, hearing the echoing boom of windowless cubes slamming shut. Indeed, it had long been the secret to his *own* survival—holding his personal past at bay, pretending his life had begun the day he received his medical degree. It had to be enough, even through the many dark hours when it was not.

But there was something else Martin knew how to do, too. He knew how to make his eyes soft and warm, how to broadcast calm reassurance with a smile that engaged cheeks and forehead. Patients, drowning in the sudden terror of their confronted mortality, needed to look in your eyes, needed humanity. They'd throw away everything else to cling to the confidence and understanding held there.

Nina was looking at him. The fear was there, yes, but there was something else, too, hard and challenging. Hostile. *Good for you,* Martin wanted to say. He cupped the side of his wife's head and pulled her to him. "Yes, Nina," he said. Young and healthy. "Yes, you are."

three

THREE DAYS LATER, NINA sat in the office of a doctor she'd just met, a radiologist named Marcus Hughes, looking at a dispirited spider plant behind his desk and the strange, oddly sexual movement of his beard-fringed lips as he spoke words that at first would simply not compute. "I'm sorry, Ms. Baldwin," he was saying, "but it's cancer."

It had been a week for building panic, starting with the call to Dr. Raab. When Nina had called on Wednesday, the receptionist had been warm but blasé at the word lump—Dr. Raab was awfully booked, one of the nurse practitioners would be able to get her in tomorrow or by Friday at the latest—less so when Nina mentioned the pulled-in nipple and swollen lymph nodes. Lauren Raab herself had called Nina back to tell her to come in at six that night, after office hours; she'd sat at her secretary's desk to put in an urgent page to Susan Tredway after she finished Nina's exam. "The very best breast surgeon in New England," Dr. Raab had explained—a statement less reassuring than it surely was meant to be—"and also a friend from medical school. She's a breast cancer survivor, and she really knows her stuff." Then there had been blood tests, two of them—the tech hadn't drawn enough blood the first time around—and finally another miraculous hole in another impossibly busy calendar, this time at Boston Metropolitan Hospital's Breast Imaging Center.

Nina didn't know if it was Martin or Dr. Raab who'd pulled strings to get her into the Boston center, but it had been clear to her the moment she walked through the door that this was the place for serious mammograms, and not the just-roll-your-eyes type of baseline screening she'd endured with some humor three years earlier. (The way the machine had squashed her breasts into pale, pulled ovals of vanilla taffy, comically visible through a clear plastic tray! The praise she'd gotten, oddly, for pectoral muscle visible on the film, forensic evidence, apparently, that for forty she was in pretty good shape.) This center was brand new, full of earth-toned upholstered blondwood chairs and tiny bubbling rock gardens, professionally feng shui'ed, possessed of the newest technologies. There was a wall of magazines that appeared largely undisturbed by the women who sat around the room solo or in huddled pairs; there was a tray of complimentary coffee and pastries, tiny cherry-cheese danishes, blueberry scones, chocolate and butter croissants in frilled paper wrappers. Nina had admired the optimism implicit in this particular nicety, the suggestion that anyone with a need to be here might have an appetite.

Jenny had insisted on driving and staying, flipping though an outdated *Newsweek,* Nina imagined, while Nina stood in a darkened room for six different pictures of her breast. Halfway through the series (frontal view, and then a side, then an x-ray with a smaller plastic tray that pressed flat the upper-third of Nina's breast), the technician's easy chatter had fallen away and she had told Nina she was going to have to wait until the radiologist had a chance to review her results, he might want to send her down the hall to have an ultrasound, and after nodding obediently and buttoning her shirt with fingers that had trembled just slightly, Nina had returned to the waiting area to dispatch her best friend to pick their daughters up from school. It was nothing, she was sure. If the mammogram showed cancer, why would they do an ultrasound? She could call Martin to come and be with her if she needed to. It was after one o'clock already and she was more anxious about making sure Audrey didn't get left waiting than whatever the tech was seeing on her films. It was three o'clock, pick-up time precisely, when Dr. Hughes had pivoted his computer monitor to show Nina her mammogram and the grainy, unfathomable ultrasound films.

When Nina had the lump in her leg when she was twelve, the doctor had stuck the X-ray up on a light board for her and her mother to see. For the most part, her femur had looked like a child's drawing of a bone, a straight stick with a double-bulbed bottom and top. The middle, though, had swelled grossly, in a way Nina knew wasn't normal, wasn't even possible, and her mind had flashed to a photo she had seen in *National Geographic* of a python that had swallowed a dog whole. Now, on Dr. Hughes's computer screen, the arc of her breast looked like the western bowl of the African continent, an image captured by satellite at night. Most of the orb gave off a muted, mottled glow, filled with ropy, netlike striations of light and dark. Two distinct areas, however, glowed like cities, teeming with life. Dakar and—what? The only West African city Nina could think of was the capital of Senegal. The one spot, toward the top curve of the breast, the nipple-lump Nina could feel, was almost perfectly round, as if someone had slipped a lighted BB underneath her skin. The second, however, anchored to a swath of white that Nina recognized as her in-shape pectoral muscle, was ragged and irregular, tailing out in a trail of scattered dots.

For a moment, the room was silent, as if Dr. Hughes were giving Nina time to absorb the news. Then Dr. Hughes fingered the image, pointing to the two cities, and cleared his throat. "This and this," he said. "These two bright spots. It's extremely clear."

Numbly, Nina nodded. Dakar and what? Algiers? Casablanca? "Two cancers, you mean."

"Possibly." Dr. Hughes propped himself against the corner of his desk, his hands folded across the tops of his thighs. "Not likely, though. Chances are it's one cancer in two different spots."

"I don't think I know the difference."

"There are lots of different types of breast cancer. Intraductal and intralobular are the most common, but there are also others—medullary, mucinous, Paget's disease. When a mammogram shows us more than one spot it's typically the same cancer in more than one location, what we call multicentric or multifocal disease."

Nina stared at the computer and shook her head. "Mucinous," she said. Now there was an ugly word. "What type is that?"

"Based on the location, the highest likelihood is intraductal. You'll have to have a biopsy, though, and then your oncologist will be able to tell you for sure."

Despite the presumption that she had an oncologist already, Nina nodded again. "I'm seeing Susan Tredway next Wednesday."

"Dr. Tredway's terrific. But you do know she's not an oncologist, of course. She's a breast surgeon."

"A breast surgeon," Nina repeated. "Not an oncologist. Do I have to have both?" Immediately, she winced. What a stupid question to ask. Back in the fall, Audrey had fallen from the see-saw at school and needed X-rays of her arm. She had been stoic about the pain but had fallen apart at the sight of the X-ray machine and the tech had asked Nina to stay in the room while he took the films. As he handed Nina a lead apron to wrap around her torso, he'd asked her if there was any chance of a pregnancy, and Nina had replied in confusion, "Who, me or her?" Good lord, the girl had been six!

"Oh, God," she said now, "Never mind. Of course I do. A surgeon for surgery and an oncologist for everything else. It's just that I wasn't expecting—" Her voice trailed off. "My husband's a doctor. A cardiologist. He was supposed to come meet me but there was some kind of patient emergency. He works at St. Serafin. Martin Winzer."

There was a standard explanation that usually followed this revelation of out-of-character feminism, and Nina pressed her lips together hard to keep from launching into it now. Dr. Hughes didn't care that she had kept her own last name when she and Martin married because her parents were gone, or that she'd considered hyphenating but didn't like the stuttery repeated syllables of Baldwin-Winzer.

"Mrs. Baldwin." Dr. Hughes leaned forward from his desk perch, his hands now earnestly gripping his knee. "I have been doing this job for twenty years, and telling a woman that she has cancer is news that never gets any easier to break. But your treatment options are excellent and they keep getting better all the time. More effective chemotherapies, and better drugs to mitigate their side-effects. Reconstructive procedures for mastectomy—"

The word *mastectomy* jerked Nina from the strange, almost pleasant murkiness into which she had been sinking. She had been so focused on the lump in her nipple, so sure of its piddling size and her own good medical luck that the thought of mastectomy hadn't even crossed her mind. Now she looked again at the mammogram behind Dr. Hughes, the tailing city to the right of the computer screen. "Am I going to lose my breast?"

Dr. Hughes shook his head. "Again, that's not for me to say."

Nina was, at once, bitterly, explosively angry at this man—square-fingered and offensively bearded—at the child drawings on his walls, at the coffee mug on his dusty window ledge: *radiologists make no bones about it*. She hated him for the ease with which he had tossed around the word cancer, as if he was saying dandruff; the seal-clubbing bluntness with which he had pronounced his verdict, without determining first whether it was news Nina was ready to hear. Right or not, she had always assumed there was a widely held protocol for breaking of cancer news: a decorous procession of visits and tests and reassurances, bad news parsed into acclimable increments, disclaimers of uncertainty attached to all delivered results. *It might be— It looks like— We won't know until—* Dr. Hughes had catapulted himself right over all those mincing steps, yanking her along by the hair. An hour earlier, she hadn't had cancer; she'd had a lump in her breast, a cyst. That she had cancer now had to be somebody's fault.

"But surely, with all your years of experience, you have some sense." Nina waved her hand in the air, encircling the room. "You must have some idea."

"Mrs. Baldwin, I can't tell you how very sorry I am. If you'd like, I can call Dr. Tredway when we're finished and let her know I've made a positive diagnosis."

Nina stood. "So is this what you actually do all day? Tell women they have cancer and then send them on their way?"

Dr. Hughes had the decency to look chastened. "I won't presume to say I know how you feel, but I do understand what you are going through. Days like this are terribly difficult. I'm much more looking forward to the one when I can read your mammogram and tell you that your cancer's gone."

As Nina exited the Breast Center and made her way through the hospital, she moved cautiously, looking at all the wheelchaired, johnny-ed, IV-ed patients: they're sick. We're sick. She saw white-coated doctors grouped in twos and threes, fiddling with stethoscopes slung sideways around their necks, checking beepers and putting them away. She felt a fleeting rage for their indifference, a wash of regret for her own former smugness. That had been one of the things that had attracted her most deeply about Martin when they first met: the medical uniform he wore, and the cold bravado with which he wore it.

Outside, valets with clear raincoats over their black jackets moved busily, waving cars through the hospital's main turnaround, opening cab doors and proffering blue and white striped Boston Met umbrellas for patients, wheelchairs for those too weak to walk through the glass doors by themselves. *Will that be me soon?* Nina wondered. She entered the cab queue numbly, gave the driver her home address before remembering her car—and her daughter—would be at Jenny's house. This morning she had rolled her eyes like a teenager when Jenny had insisted on driving; Jenny had said Nina would need the designated driver when her mammogram was fine and she drank half a bottle of champagne to celebrate. "Something fabulous, like vintage Tattinger," she had suggested. "How about something cheap and horrible, like André?" Nina had countered. Now, that exchange felt like it had happened years ago.

"Sorry," she said to the cabbie, "I gave you the wrong address." The man nodded—*not a problem, madam*—and she leaned her head against the cracked vinyl of the seat, closing her eyes.

So, *cancer*. The word was a drumbeat across Cambridge Street and onto Storrow Avenue, two taunting syllables that throbbed in time to the windshield wipers. *Can-cer. Can, sir. Cancer.*

When the cab slowed for the Allston tollbooth and entered the Mass Turnpike, Nina opened her eyes, reaching for her purse to unearth her phone. No call from Martin, though she'd left a message with Elaine between her mammogram and ultrasound; just a voicemail from Jenny letting her know she had made it to school with plenty of time. *I'm sure everything is going to be fine, I'm prepared for you to make fun of me for being such a little old hen, Audrey did just fine with the change in plans.* Nina had heard the false heartiness in her friend's voice. Though she was as comfortable with Jenny and Willow as anyone in the world, Nina was sure her daughter had reacted to the news that Jenny and not her mother would be taking her home from school with suspicion at best. At worst—Nina couldn't think about that just yet.

As she squeezed the phone tight against her hand and stared forward through the rain-streaked windshield, Nina's attention was caught by a flash of color up ahead. On the overpasses that carried local traffic into

Newton and Wellesley, a series of rusty bridges leading to the most pristine of towns, someone had stuck red, white, and blue plastic drinking cups through the cyclone fencing, forming patterns that created messages to be read from below: "Good luck, Sgt Jiminez," the first bridge said. "♥U, Marianne, Kayla + Kevyn," said the second, and the third: "Bring them home alive." Nina had seen similar messages before, sending soldiers off to battle in Iraq or much less frequently welcoming them home, and wondered how the recipients felt about them, if they even saw them at all. The public declarations had always seemed to Nina to be odd homage, a strangely industrial *cri de coeur*. As Sgt. Jiminez's message flashed above her, however, she suddenly knew how those soldiers, waiting to go off to war, must feel: like travelers from a different place and time, just unable to grasp the customs and preoccupations of an almost-familiar world.

four

PERHAPS THE ARGUMENT NINA had meant to make with herself the day she found the lump in her breast was that her life craved a *different* sort of drama.

Almost four years earlier, at Audrey's three-year-old physical exam, her pediatrician had raised the question of whether she might be autistic. More precisely, Dr. O'Donnell had wondered, tapping a thoughtful finger against his lips as Audrey launched into her then-standard recitation of the nine planets and all their moons, if Audrey might just have a smidge of autism. The word had rankled Nina for its insouciance, its whimsy—*smidge*, as if a life-changing disorder were a surprise ingredient that some feckless baker had tossed in with all the sugar, spice, and everything nice that Audrey was otherwise made of—and it was for that reason that when the pediatrician suggested Nina take Audrey for a full developmental evaluation, she had not done anything more than fold the piece of paper that the receptionist had handed her along with her updated vaccination booklet and her copay receipt. A list of developmental specialists with offices in the greater Boston area, photocopied so many times over the names were slightly fuzzy around the edges.

It had been true that Audrey was different—quieter than other children her age, loath to make eye contact, given to hysteria if certain aspects of her routine were to change. But Nina had reasoned that her daughter was shy, an only child with two older parents, a toddler of such startling intelligent precocity that playing with other boys and girls her own

KRISTIN WATERFIELD DUISBERG

age was all but impossible. At three, she eschewed the dolls and cartoon characters that so engaged other kids; she was enchanted with the solar system and had an almost encyclopedic knowledge of the planets. *Mercury is the closest to the sun, a hilly, hot planet that gets smashed with meteorites all the time.* It was her unfailing bedtime ritual, to name the planets from Mercury out to Pluto, indicating orbits in the air with her hands as she recited each planet's particular description. *Jupiter is the largest planet, fifth from the sun. It has four moons all its own: Io, Europa, Ganymede, and Callisto.*

It was, too, this particular proficiency that Nina had expected Dr. O'Donnell to marvel at during Audrey's office visit: a three-year-old who knew the planets! A three-year-old who knew, for heaven's sake, the number of days it took for Neptune to orbit the sun! When he'd instead put his hand on Audrey's head in mid-recital and turned to Nina with a list of questions about Audrey's diet, her sleep patterns, her motor skills, Nina had at first been annoyed: it was rude, was it not, and what kind of pediatrician would turn his back on a child who was so clearly trying to impress? As she answered more and more of Dr. O'Donnell's questions, however—yes, Audrey had food texture aversions (rice made her gag and she reacted to oatmeal as if being forced to eat glass shards); yes, she liked to rock herself; no, she hadn't napped since before she turned two—Nina's irritation had turned into a much more complicated thing. Fear and guilt and grief and confusion all jumbled up together in a sloppy structure buttressed, to Nina's great surprise, by an indiscriminate rage.

Worst of all, Nina felt herself turning to her own daughter, the blond, blue-eyed Hummel child she had heretofore seen only as extraordinary and exquisite, with a feeling that was entirely, unwelcome-ly new: a stomach-squeezing shame. It was true: even as Nina and Dr. O'Donnell had been talking, Audrey had rattled on, through Saturn, Neptune, and Uranus, her round eyes fixed unseeingly in front of her. *Pluto is the farthest planet from the sun, 3.6 billion miles. Somebody else just found something out after Pluto, called Sedna, but I don't think it's really a planet because it doesn't have an actual orbit. I think it's maybe only a moon.*

Nina hadn't mentioned her conversation with the pediatrician to Martin—Martin, who had raised three sons and so surely would know if there was something wrong with his child—and for several months, the square of paper with the list of developmental experts had remained at the bottom of her purse, collecting graham cracker crumbs and goldfish dust in its many folds. It was fall when she finally dug it out, called in to preschool by a teacher concerned that two months into the school year Audrey still preferred her own company while all the other children were coming together in twos or threes for games of dress-up and ice cream store and blocks. The first three places she called were scheduling appointments more than a year out, but there was a group in Worcester that had a cancellation the day after Thanksgiving no one on their waiting list wanted to take.

The same instinct that had kept Nina from telling Martin about her conversation with Dr. O'Donnell led her to keep the appointment in Worcester a secret. Even so, when she returned with her head spinning with words and possibilities, she had not been prepared for the bluntness—the absoluteness—with which he rejected it all. The team of experts had been extremely thorough. For the occupational therapist, Audrey had drawn circles and balanced on wobbly boards and kicked balls rolled toward her (Nina had cringed inwardly when Audrey swung her foot *after* the ball rolled past); for the speech therapist, she'd named objects and played games with plastic figures—or at least watched the therapist play, regarding the woman's manipulation of tiny dolls and animals in a pretend birthday party with puzzled curiosity. She had clamped her hands against the sides of her head and screamed *NO!* when the pediatrician asked to look in her ears with his otoscope; she'd performed years above age level on sentence-recall for the psychiatrist, but had sat immobile and unblinking as the woman built a little train out of wooden cubes, choo-chooing it across the table and encouraging Audrey to do the same with her own pile of blocks.

At the end of the afternoon, tinkling Muzak versions of Christmas carols playing in the background, the team members had relayed their impressions with a terrible, pitying kindness. She was too young for them to diagnose for sure, but they thought there was a good chance Audrey's characteristics put her on the spectrum for autism. She was bright, yes— she was surely bright; her grasp of detail, wow—But she had performed below age level for expressive and receptive speech—what she said and understood—for motor skills, for emotional responsiveness. The good news was that if she *was* "on the spectrum" (a phrase Nina would in very short order learn to despise) it was at the very high end, and there were lots of things Nina and Martin could do to help their daughter. Hold bright objects next to their faces while they spoke to encourage eye contact. Play "conversation games," coming up with a topic other than the planets for Audrey to discuss, passing a ball back and forth between speakers to signal each person's turn. Play dates, speech and occupational therapy; when school time came, a classroom aide. The Winzers were lucky to live in Massachusetts, the developmental pediatrician said. He saw families from Connecticut and New York all the time who were simply on their own.

Nina fought tears on the way home, a two-hour crawl on which Audrey insisted on hearing only "Frosty the Snowman" from the CD of Christmas songs Nina had put on to distract her. She let them fall that night, sitting at the kitchen table, when she told Martin—finally—about her day, and about her conversation with Dr. O'Donnell from six months earlier.

"They said she had low affect, Martin, and it's true. She does. I mean, I always thought, well, okay, she's shy and that's why she never smiles at anyone. But it's more than that. It's like she doesn't even know they're there half the time. She spent forty-five minutes with the psychiatrist and when the woman started talking to her in the reception area afterwards she just gave her this blank look, like she had no idea who she was.

"They said she had echolalia, that the parroting thing she does isn't just normal echoing. And you know the way she's practically memorized every book she's read and video she's seen? They said she produces lots of speech, all right, but she has no idea what she's saying half the time. The speech therapist showed Audrey a knife, a fork, and a spoon, and she couldn't even tell her which thing you used to cut. I said, well, you know, it's not like she cuts her own food up, so maybe—" Nina had hiccupped, wiping a tear off her cheek. "They said no; had she never seen me cut her food? *Poor prosody,* they called it.

"I'm just so confused right now. I went down there completely prepared to hear that Dr. O'Donnell was some yahoo who didn't have the first clue what he was talking about, Audrey was just some superchild, and now—I've got to admit there were a couple of things that gave me pause. Like when Audrey was with the occupational therapist. You should have seen her, Martin. She covered her face when the woman tossed a ball. She actually fell over trying to stand on one foot. I always thought she was just a little clumsy."

At that, Martin had finally nodded. "So the bottom line is, tight-rope walker is out as a career option."

Nina's whole body jerked. "This isn't some kind of joke, Martin. The bottom line is, her vestibular system—"

Nina's husband had interrupted her. "Of course it's a joke. It's preposterous. I can't imagine what you'd want me to say. This kind of testing, on a three-year-old. It's irresponsible. And to do it behind my back, without telling me. Why would you choose to go looking for trouble like that?"

Nina swallowed and spoke softly. "This is exactly why I did it without telling you, because I knew this is how you'd react."

"Well, of course this is how I'm going to react!" Martin had slapped his hands flat against the table. "You—you—*ambush* me with this story about taking our child off to see this group of doctors who tell you she's defective and then you expect me to say 'well isn't that interesting, thank you for looking into it?' You set me up for this, Nina. I didn't have a chance of reacting otherwise!"

Nina's throat ached and tears coursed down her cheeks. This wasn't the point; it wasn't the point at all. "They didn't say she was defective," she whispered.

"Didn't they?"

"If there's something wrong with Audrey, we can help her now. Everything I've read says the sooner you get to these kids the better off they are in the long run. Dr. O'Donnell said—" Nina reached back in her brain for the metaphor the pediatrician had used six months earlier, an image so benign and trite that Nina had found it at once insulting and a comfort. "Dr. O'Donnell said it's a lot like having a broken ankle or something. We can fix it now and she'll be just fine or we can ignore it now and she'll spend the rest of her life with a limp."

Martin stood up. "We're ending this conversation," he said curtly. "I'm a doctor, and I know my own child." He stared at Nina coldly. "*Fix* it, Nina? Fix her, fix our child, like she's some broken ankle? My God. There's nothing wrong with Audrey other than people who don't understand how her mind works."

He walked out of the kitchen, but for a moment, he had paused at the kitchen door, his back to Nina. "Please," he said. His voice had been hoarse, and briefly, Nina thought he'd been apologizing, preparing to confess how torn up he, too, had been about Audrey's strange fixations, her intensity, her lack of friends. "For all of us, find a hobby other than our daughter to fill up your free time."

NINA HAD TRIED. THAT Christmas she had bought Audrey a baby doll—a bald-headed creature with startled blue eyes that clicked mechanically when they opened and shut—a stack of dress-up clothes, and a Playmobil farm with pigs and two Holstein cows; in January, she signed Audrey up for the Gymboree class where they met Jenny and Willow Rutherford. But the baby doll had received only some obligatory Christmas Day curiosity (Audrey had thumbed her visor-like black eyelashes, frowning, removed her pink sleep suit to inspect the anatomical inaccuracy of the cloth body beneath), and Audrey had howled at the scratchiness of the princess dress' purple tulle skirt and the plastic stiffness of the firefighter's jacket; had given the Holsteins and the pigs just a few rides on the moving hay lift before shutting all of the animals and the farmer into one of the faux-wood stalls and returning to her well-worn solar system book, and Nina had quickly fallen into studying her daughter with a vigilance that even she recognized bordered on unhealthy. But she couldn't keep herself from doing it any more than she could help suspecting Audrey's problems were her fault.

At the age of thirty-seven, she'd entered into motherhood with brazen confidence, one hundred percent certain there was no one more capable of raising her daughter than she was, but now every decision she had ever made seemed to hold the potential to be disastrously wrong. Had the parent-directed feeding philosophy she had followed, nursing on a strict schedule, imprinted her daughter with a certain inflexibility? Had the Ferber approach to sleep she had embraced, putting Audrey in her crib awake so she could learn from the beginning how to soothe herself, taught her not to need her mother or anybody else? Nina had been amused and slightly baffled by the peers who bought every Baby Genius DVD in the toy store and traded their tailored suits and Caesar salads for Disney-character-embroidered overall shorts and peanut butter on white, as if the secret to being a good mother was becoming childlike again yourself, but maybe that had been the point, exactly; maybe these mothers had understood something essential that she hadn't. Martin had been impressed by her competence as a mother, and that had mattered to Nina; it had mattered terribly. Had she cared about winning her husband's approval at her daughter's expense?

When Jenny approached her at that initial Gymboree class, Nina's first instinct had been to withdraw, not wanting the other woman to notice the differences between their daughters. The friendship between Audrey and Willow had come about through sheer force of will, achieved with an amount of practice and ritual that ultimately proved enough to overcome its less-than-promising start. The first few times they met at the playground, Nina could almost hear the voices of the doctors in Worcester who had enumerated Audrey's social shortcomings. While Willow would leap from one pursuit to another (sliding down the slides, pushing herself, belly-down, on the swings, climbing the jungle gym, where she would inevitably encounter another little boy or girl eager to play) Audrey would sit in the sandbox looking for pieces of mica, which she would then lay out in order of size. No amount of coaxing or prodding could convince her to abandon this activity in favor of whatever Willow was doing ("look, Audrey: Willow's mom is helping her do the monkey bars. Wouldn't you like to try that, too?"); the few times Willow had tried to join in on the mica hunt, she'd quickly abandoned the effort, discouraged, Nina imagined, by Audrey's lack of reciprocation to her constant chatter, Audrey's not-infrequent rejection of *her* pieces of mica as not good enough.

Without fail, Jenny Rutherford had met Nina's dismay over Audrey's behavior with reassurances: Audrey was an only child, of course she was more comfortable playing by herself; Willow's big brother, Silas, had been just like Audrey at the same age. When Nina finally, hesitantly, told her friend what the Worcester team had said about Audrey, the terrible news had been met with little more than a shrug.

"So she's quirky," Jenny said. "Silas is quirky, too. Every kid is different. Believe me, I've seen it." Before her own children were born, Jenny had been a middle school English teacher, and with the girls in the next room eating a snack of Goldfish crackers and applesauce she had let loose on an educational system bound and determined to pathologize every classroom disruption, to assign a diagnosis and a label to any child who wouldn't sit quietly at a desk for hours on end. Did Nina know that metro Boston had the highest and fastest-climbing autism rates of any region in the entire United States? She didn't buy it; it was the diagnosis *du jour.* "The last time I checked," she said, "we were raising children and not sheep."

It had been Jenny who had pointed Nina toward the Goldengrove School, a private pre-K-through-eight where her two older children went, set on an old farm in Cabot's historic Back River district. Cabot had an excellent public school system, but Goldengrove offered a much more individualized approach, small classes with music and French lessons as early as kindergarten, sewing and cooking and pottery as integral elements of the curriculum, voluntary homework and tests all the way through grade eight. Nina had fallen in love with the place as soon as she had seen it—cathedral-ceilinged classrooms painted in soothing pastels, an organic garden where even the youngest children took turns watering and weeding and picking, long hills the headmistress said were for sledding in winter and rolling down in spring and fall—and Audrey, too, had felt immediately at home. She and Willow had been placed together in the four-year-old class, and it wasn't long before Willow established herself as the classroom leader: the architect of recess games, the authority on what the right songs were to sing and what class subjects were fun, the undisputed decider of when it was time for snacks. What had come as a pleasant surprise was Audrey's willingness to be led. After one of the only Goldengrove events Martin had ever attended, a Halloween party in the school atrium that first year, he had taken umbrage at the interactions between the girls: "It's like the queen bee and her drones. That little brunette bosses Audrey and everyone else around, and Audrey just does whatever she says." He'd failed to see the larger point. Nina was immensely grateful for the way Willow would drag Audrey into games of Wedding Day or Restaurant, teach her the jump rope rhymes and clapping songs Nina remembered from her own childhood. From the first moment Dr. O'Donnell had wondered if Audrey might just have a *smidge* of autism, Nina had reassured herself that Audrey would eventually find her crowd, join forces with a couple other brainy oddballs who had recognized the benefit of strength in numbers; she'd soothed herself with mental cinema, replaying the victories wrought by hapless heroines in every teen movie she'd ever loved. Once there was

Willow, however, there was cause for actual hope. With Willow's hand in hers, Audrey looked just like any other little girl on the playground, and the concerns voiced by the teachers at Audrey's previous preschool were rendered moot—*Audrey seems not to have made any connections with her classmates. Even when the other children invite her to join them she prefers to play by herself. On the playground, we've noticed, she will spend the entire playtime spinning herself in circles. Have you noticed her doing anything like that at home?*—and now, there were long stretches of time when Nina would once again dare to hold up to the light what had become her homely, abeyant hope for her daughter's life: that she would grow up to be just like everyone else.

Indeed, as she watched her daughter evolve, it struck Nina how truly daunting the task of finding your place in the world really was, especially when finding your place meant finding someone else. Was there ever a time it had *not* meant that? It seemed to Nina the answer to was no, and yet how did two people ever find each other to love and be loved by in return, exactly the way that they were?

·

THANK GOD IT'S NOT her. Thank god it's me and not Audrey. Thank god it's not her.

On the drive from Dr. Tredway's office to the Rutherfords' house, and then from the Rutherfords' home, Nina clung to that thought, repeating the two sentences to herself over and over like a chant. Audrey, in the back seat, was immersed in a book, seemingly both oblivious to her mother's turmoil and uninterested in learning why she had gone home from school with Jenny and Willow again. There was some mercy in that, at least; though it had been a full two weeks since she had found the lump in her breast and eight days since her diagnosis, Nina had yet to tell her daughter she was sick, and nothing about her out-of-the-ordinary comings and goings had prompted Audrey's curiosity. She couldn't imagine having the conversation with her seven-year-old, couldn't fathom finding a way to start it. Soon, though. Among the packet of papers she had slid into her purse an hour earlier was a brochure that had been handed to her by Dr. Tredway's nurse practitioner, describing various support groups for children with parents who had life-threatening illnesses. Surprised by the sheer number of offerings—there were special groups for teens and others for adolescents; there was a group that was exercised-based and a group open only to minorities—Nina had been tempted to ask if there happened to be a group for children on the autism spectrum, but the question had been gallows humor, and the strain in Martin's expression made it clear the appointment had already been hard enough. *I'm sorry,* she had caught herself thinking. *I'm so sorry I'm doing this to all of us.* Thank god it was her.

The appointment with Dr. Treadway had turned out to be not just a consulation with the surgeon, but a meeting with an entire cancer team. There had been Iris Kennett, Nina's oncologist; Harald Olsen, her radiation oncologist; Maria Thorpe, her oncology nurse practitioner. They were all *her* doctors, as if Nina had won some sort of marvelous prize; they had each introduced themselves by their first names, Iris and Harald and Maria, as if they were gathered not to talk cancer but to enjoy a cocktail party. It had taken Nina a minute to get over Dr. Tredway herself—petite and blonde, with a pixie cut like Mia Farrow circa *Rosemary's Baby* and pale pink lipstick that suggested Bonne Bell more than Estee Lauder, she had looked too young to be a doctor of any stripe, never mind a cancer surgeon. When she had turned to Nina's mammogram, however, any protective, motherly doubt Nina had felt fell away. Circling the tumor on Nina's chest wall with the cap of her pen, Dr. Tredway had pulled no punches. "I don't like the looks of this at all," she said. "I won't know for sure until we get inside, but from these pictures it looks as if this tumor has actually started to infiltrate the chest wall."

Nina had nodded, feeling oddly chastened, as if the tumor's ragamuffin ugliness was somehow her doing. "Does that mean you won't be able to do a lumpectomy?"

Dr. Tredway had looked her in the eye when she explained that lumpectomy was out of the question. Because she had two tumors, and because of the location of the deeper one, in the very best case she'd be looking at a modified radical mastectomy. Martin had asked for the worst case, and it seemed to Nina that Dr. Tredway winced faintly before explaining that the worst case would involve removing all of the breast, lymph nodes, and chest wall muscle.

"So a Halsted procedure," Martin said.

"Not a Halsted, exactly, but in essence, yes. Worst case is a bridge I don't like to cross before I come to it, however."

Dr. Tredway had smiled reassuringly, but Nina had still struggled to focus as Dr. Kennett took her turn, telling her about chemotherapy, and then as Dr. Olsen described the radiation that would follow it. A fragment of a joke she wanted to make flitted through her head, something about the absurdity of a mastectomy being both *modified* and *radical,* but it failed to cohere. After the three doctors had finished, shaking Nina and Martin's hands the same way they had when they'd first introduced themselves, Maria Thorpe had taken them to a different room to schedule Nina's needle biopsy for the following week. They'd set a tentative date for her mastectomy, April 24.

At the Rutherfords', Jenny had protested. "April 24? But that's spring vacation week!"

"Apparently not for Dr. Tredway it isn't."

The other woman bit her lip, and Nina knew she was struggling not to cry. *Please don't,* she thought. She herself hadn't cried, not yet, and she didn't want to start. Not here, not now. "Audrey can stay with us for as long as you need. Willow will be thrilled. I'm going to line up all kinds of daytrips. We were already planning on going to that new indoor water park in Avon Mills one day and Calla wants to spend a day at the Isabella Stewart Gardner museum. Maybe if it's really nice we can go to Newport. Or up to Portsmouth, Strawbery Banke—"

As Jenny ticked off the ideas on her fingers, Nina had nodded silently, grateful, sure the prospect of an extended play date with Willow would ease whatever sting was to come. For a fleeting moment, she wondered if it might be possible to avoid telling Audrey about her surgery at all, to present the stay with the Rutherfords as a vacation treat in its own right. It was absurd, of course—she'd heard enough at the appointment with Dr. Tredway to know she'd leave the hospital bandaged and drained, only a couple of days into what would be a multi-week healing process, and even Audrey wasn't *that* oblivious. But the thought was tempting…

Pulling off the Rutherfords' street and onto the road that wound around the Cabot country club, Nina gave a quick glance to the rearview mirror. On the passenger side, Audrey reached for her backpack and pulled out a hardcover book, spreading it open on her lap.

"What have you got there?"

Audrey silently raised the book. In the mirror, Nina saw the dark yellow cover, the picture of a brown-furred rabbit in profile, and added another item to her list of worries. *Watership Down;* was there another first grader out there who would voluntarily pick up a 400 page novel about talking rabbits? Nina herself had slogged through it in high school, goaded on by an older brother (she couldn't remember anymore which one) who had disdainfully assured her she wouldn't get the human metaphor—which, if she had, she certainly no longer remembered.

"Wow. That's heavy reading. What made you choose that book?"

Audrey gave a 'dunno' shrug and folded back the crease she'd made to mark her page. "We had library today and Mrs. Donovan said I could look in the Upper School section. It looked interesting."

Nina twisted, and the car gave a little drunken swerve as she over-turned the steering wheel. "I read *Watership Down* when I was in high school. Isn't there some kind of rabbit language that a bunch of it is written in? I just remember having to flip to a glossary in the back of the book that defined all the rabbit words and how hard that made it to really get into the story."

If Audrey heard her mother, she didn't answer, and for a few minutes, they drove in silence. Turning onto Route 20, Nina glanced back at her daughter again, feeling a pang of pure, anguished love for the way Audrey's lips moved as she read her book.

"So what else did you do today, besides go to the library?"

Audrey shrugged.

"Nothing? You spent all day at the library?"

"No," Audrey said, drawing the vowel out disdainfully. "We had Spanish. And I did some math."

"Math, wow," Nina said automatically. "Multiplication? Division?" She was, she realized, desperate to keep her daughter talking. In the silence between them, the two sentences in her head drummed relentlessly, but as long as she was still here, in the car with Audrey, she was just a mother—a *concerned* mother—looking for information about her daughter's day at school. Today was just like yesterday, when she believed she would keep her right breast, and like a month ago, when she didn't have cancer at all.

"Mom, do you mind? I can't exactly concentrate when you keep asking me so many questions."

Nina nodded. "Sorry, sweetie. I just wanted to catch up, is all."

Audrey sighed and closed the book, her finger sandwiched to mark the page that she'd been reading. "Here," she said, pushing a crumpled sheet of yellow paper into the front of the car for her mother. "You can read this. John Henry's mom says we haven't signed up yet."

"What is it? I don't want to try to read it while I'm driving."

"It's a reminder about the spring concert. We're supposed to bring a healthy snack for the reception."

"The spring concert," Nina echoed. Her mind was a complete blank. "When is that?"

Audrey sighed again. "Mom, it says right on the paper. Next Thursday."

Of course it was. Thursday was the day after her biopsy. *Crap.*

"We *are* going, aren't we? I have to be there. The whole class has been practicing since January."

A thin current of panic ran through Audrey's voice and Nina hastened to reassure her. "Of course we are. I'd just forgotten which day it was. We'll put it on the calendar when we get home."

"Good." Audrey flipped her book back open. "Speaking of snacks," she said, not looking up, "I'm hungry."

"Didn't you eat a snack at the Rutherfords? Jenny said she fed you when you got there."

"I'm still hungry."

Nina opened her mouth to make the rational argument, but instead she put her blinker on at the next intersection and reversed direction for the local mall. There was a food court and a handful of kiosks spread across the two floors of shops. A cookie store, a pretzel stand, even an Orange Julius, a place Nina hadn't been to herself since she was probably in junior high. In the parking lot, Audrey asked her, puzzled, what they were doing, and as lightly as she was able to Nina told her they were shopping, of course.

Audrey unbuckled herself and frowned. "What for?"

A car drove by, music pouring from its open windows. Though it was almost four-thirty, the sun was still warm on Nina's face and arms, and she smiled at her daughter as she felt around the sheaf of papers in her purse for the case to her sunglasses.

"Summer clothes. You're getting so tall." Nina meant *you're growing up,* and she tried to hold to the thought. That was all she meant. She didn't mean *I wonder if— Will I be there to—* "We'll get a snack first and then hit the stores."

Audrey shrugged, but then she smiled a little, and she let Nina hold her hand as they walked, and that was enough. With all her might, Nina concentrated on the warmth of her daughter's fingers, the slight stickiness of Audrey's palm against hers.

five

MARTIN WAS HUNGRY. IN this dream he was always hungry. And cold. There was no fire on—all the coal was gone—and the sweater he was wearing was an old one belonging to one of his sisters, yellow and full of holes, cashmere, too light to provide any warmth. This time, he was bored, too. Always bored! He missed his toys, his little dog, his bicycle, his own room with the shelf of tops and blocks and the little wooden man Papa could make dance on a stick. Here, there was nothing. Two rooms, no rugs on the floor; Hedy and Brigid had books but Martin couldn't read. He could scribble and play with his stuffed bear, he could pace and pace until Brigid scolded him to stop. He used to set traps for the mice with a hatbox and bits of cheese, but now, even that— Martin's stomach growled and he felt sick. He heard the *knock, knock* of leather shoes on the stones below and lifted the heavy shade to peek out at the streetway. Mutti, coming up the *Strasse* with bags over her arm.

Even Brigid leapt up from her chair. "Hello, children," Mutti said, kissing each of them, slicking Martin's bangs from his face. "Mother went to the marketplace." She was wearing her mink coat, the one that tied with a belt, and her hair was done in stiff finger waves that smelled of—what? Fish. Men's cigars. "Look."

One bag was full of fruit, apples and oranges perfect in their skins. Whole walnuts and hazelnuts, milky round cheeses with dusty rinds, a cake of pure white butter. The other bag held sausages—fat, lovely, white sausages, two loaves of hard brown bread, a tin of paté, a packet of Mutti's cigarettes. Martin's hands shook with panic, desire. There was a *clink!* and his mother pulled a bottle of cold milk from beneath her coat. She urged Martin to eat, and he did, standing elbow to elbow with his sisters, stuffing hunks of meat and cheese into his cheeks faster than he could chew. Mutti laughed and pulled on her cigarette: *eat. Eat!* Martin chewed faster, hunger now replaced with dread. It would all be gone; it was all gone; they should save some, the bread, at least. They wouldn't eat again for three days, for a week.

Where was the milk? Martin couldn't find it. "I'm thirsty, Mutti," he said. His mother's face clouded and she loosened the belt to her mink. Beneath the coat, she was naked, dressed only in heels. Her hipbones jutted like fossils, the spread of her ribs like a birdcage beneath her drooping, deflated breasts. *Trinken,* Mutti said, drink. She held one breast forward and aimed it at Martin's mouth, *here.* Martin felt a sudden, springing terror; her nipple had become a blackened eye. His mother shook the breast insistently and it came loose in her hand. She put one hand behind his head and forced the detached breast toward Martin's screaming mouth: *Trinken!*

MARTIN HEAVED HIMSELF UP off the sheets, gasping for breath. *God in heaven.* It had been a year, at least, since he'd had one of these dreams, and—why now? Well, he supposed he knew why now. In the dark, he looked around the room: still his armoire and Nina's dresser, its mirror opaque with pre-dawn light. Still the ceiling fan, lazily stirring the air, still the valet at the foot of his bed, holding the morning's clothes. As was his ritual, he touched what he could reach: the comforter across his legs, the glass of water at his bedside table, his reading glasses, all real. He would make himself lie back down. He looked at Nina: Good, he thought; he hadn't awakened her. She blinked, and he saw the liquid glint of her open eyes.

"Bad dream?" she asked. She didn't look at him, but straight up, her voice quiet but as clear as if she'd been awake for hours.

Martin nodded and cleared his throat. "Yes."

"What was it about?"

"It was nothing. Same as always. I don't remember."

after

The dark room vibrated with the turning of the ceiling fan, the animate hum of some system—the sump pump or central humidistat—engaging two floors below. Martin heard Nina sniff. "Right," she finally said. Wordlessly, she rolled away from him.

What could Martin say? That his mother pulled her own breast off and tried to push it down his throat? That he was a little boy again, cold and hungry and bored? It had been a *dream*, for heaven's sake; not even historically, biographically accurate, and Martin had no interest in either dissecting the lurid scene his subconscious had amused itself in assembling or defending himself against what he was certain would be Nina's painfully sympathetic reaction to the undigested recounting.

The inviolable blank of Martin's past had always been an ocean between the two of them, and it had been a long time since Nina had asked. Martin thought it was something they had agreed to during their courtship—tacitly, at least: the very inviolability of that blank. He'd clashed with Beth too often over what she had termed his "refusal to share himself" and knew enough the second time to make his limits clear. But that, if anything, was Nina, always pushing, always renegotiating; it was part of what he loved her for even when it worked against his own best interests. And now, he supposed, if anyone had a claim to changing the rules— He'd seen it happen many times in patients, a certain steel, a directed fury that gave shape to the fight of their disease. It was good for her, a touch of belligerence. Martin had to keep that in mind. None of this was about him, an observation he would endeavor to apply to his subconscious workings, as well.

The clock on Martin's table said 4:53. He leaned over and touched the back of Nina's hair. "I'm going to get up."

In his closet, Martin patted the shelves for his running clothes without turning on the light. The dream had jarred him, left him awake in an unpleasant way that vibrated all the way to the tips of his fingers and that could only be sweated back out. If he didn't get his run in, a restlessness would haunt him for the rest of the day. It had happened before, and Martin had regretted the way it made him short-tempered with his staff and indifferent to his patients.

There are easier ways, Nina had said to him once, not a fight but an appeal, and he'd pretended he didn't know what she meant. Easier ways to medicate himself, easier ways to subdue his demons than wearing them out, but for all his being a physician, Martin didn't believe in medicine for *that:* a physiologic crutch. Nina, he knew, had taken an antidepressant after her parents died, and that was well and good for someone who cried so much she couldn't get out of bed. But for Martin—no tobacco, little alcohol; he didn't even drink coffee and couldn't help but feel a slight superiority over his colleagues who did, yawning their way through seven a.m. committee meetings with Styrofoam cups in their hands. *Wimps,* that was the word his sons would have used when they were teenagers; by seven a.m. Martin would have run for an hour or put in twenty miles on his bike. "You should give it a try," he'd suggested to more than one fellow—they were clinicians, after all, and they should, wasn't it the phrase, "walk the talk"? They all had their excuses: long hours, family obligations, arthroscoped knees, golf.

Martin couldn't run as fast now as in his thirties and forties, but speed had never been his concern: the point was to head out the door and keep moving until his legs turned to lead. He loved the power he felt, the hypnotic *thock* of his footfalls, the sure way his cardiologist's heart thrummed in his chest. Other runners said that was when they did their best thinking, on a run, but for Martin the point was to empty his brain of everything, to sink down inside the scraping of his breaths and the ache of his legs. *Thock-thock, thock-thock*, nonsense words would sometimes attach themselves to the rhythm in his head: *Happy-happy, happy-happy; beetle-beetle, beetle-beetle; eight-nine, eight-nine, nein.*

When his sons were young, Jonathan and Peter in early grade school, Christian still in diapers at home, Martin had begun running marathons. Beth had resented it—him—tremendously; the boys barely saw their father as it was and now he was going to take Sunday mornings for fifteen-mile training runs? But at the time it hadn't felt like a choice. He simply *needed* the feeling—not just the runner's high that kicked in after mile five or six, a floating effortlessness that felt like his legs could keep moving, machinelike, forever, but too the inevitable crash. The burn of lactic acid in his quadriceps, the goring pains in his solar plexus, the disjunctive churn of the failing, struggling machine. Let Beth think he was selfish. Better that than risk a breach of the concrete box inside his head.

The sky was just beginning to silver as Martin made his way down the street and out of the neighborhood. It was a new development, a series of branching cul-de-sacs full of two-and-a-half-story stone-front Colonials with three-car garages and swimming pools. The early morning air smelled of cocoa-shell mulch and the first lawn mowings of the season. For a mile, the only signs of life were streetlights and an occasionally spotlit front door. A tiger cat skittered across a driveway and disappeared around the side of a house. As Martin headed toward the long, rolling stretch of road that led to downtown Cabot, more windows glowed around the edges of still-drawn shades. He passed a woman being pulled along by a large, heaving dog and another power-walking, her elbows pointed out. A man in Jockey shorts raised his hand in greeting as he retrieved his newspaper from his front yard. In a glassed-in sunroom, Martin saw a woman about Nina's age, with Nina's long auburn hair. She had one hand to the window, the other across her mouth as if pressing back a scream.

Martin looked away, but too late; the words from Dr. Tredway he had struggled to push out of his head all week, the words he'd tried so hard to objectify, rationalize, negate, rushed in: *hyperdense, spiculated masses; a belligerent neoplasm; evidence of architectural distortion.* As a young medical student, the language of medicine had been the first thing about his chosen vocation to truly romance him. Though it seemed counterintuitive— he had to translate twice, in a way, from German to English and from the medical vernacular to the everyday—the words had thrilled him for their devastating, metaphorical accuracy, their ability to take a molecular, physiological process and thrust it with terrible clarity into the concrete world. A patient with abdominal pain might be suffering an incarcerated bowel; one who presented with skin and muscle stripped away had a degloving injury. Though Martin suspected Nina was hoping Dr. Tredway couldn't be 100 percent certain it was cancer until she'd completed the biopsy and the tumor cells were typed and staged, the words the surgeon had used told him everything he needed to know. Spiculation and infiltration, architectural distortion. Dr. Tredway was not only sure it was cancer, she was sure it was an aggressive and advanced form.

For a moment, Martin's legs went heavy, the cold terror that had churned steadily against the walls of his defenses for two weeks now finding a weakened spot. With effort, he swung his arms harder, hastening his foot turnover. How preposterous, he told himself. The woman in the sunroom was surely just yawning as she waited for her coffee to perk.

six

Up at the front of the Goldengrove School auditorium, Audrey walked across the spotlit stage, bowing soberly out at the darkened room before taking her place at the back of the U of xylophones. None of the other children, Nina noted, had bowed, and as a current of laughter rippled around her she tensed. Were *adults* actually laughing at her daughter? Jenny Rutherford put a hand on her knee and pointed: three instruments down from Audrey there was a boy wearing a Batman costume, complete with cape and pointed rubber ears. Nina relaxed, and the two women exchanged a look. *And you think you've got problems,* Nina could almost hear her best friend joking.

Miss Morosini, the Goldengrove music teacher, twitched her little plastic baton in the air, and in almost perfect union the U of first graders raised their hands, xylophone mallets fisted. The song that began was familiar, but just barely, a jerky, hollow version of a song that was on one of the Raffi cassettes Nina had thought Audrey might like as a toddler. Audrey played capably but without pleasure, her expression fixed into an almost-frown. Nina wasn't going to worry about that, however; with a few exceptions all the children looked serious—some even anxious—glaring down at their instruments. Audrey's position on the stage was just to the left of an overhead light, emphasizing her high forehead and her broad Slavic cheeks, and Nina couldn't help but think—pettily, and not for the first time—how much more attractive her daughter was than most of the other girls. There were a few small mercies, at least.

The song ended, and after some whispering and fidgeting, a few renegade xylophone notes competing with the perfunctory parental clapping, another began. Nina carefully rearranged her arms, rotating her wrist to look at her watch: 6:40. The kindergarten class had gotten the evening off to a late start; it would be another forty-five minutes, at least, before all the grades had completed their performances. Nina slumped a little lower in her metal folding chair, ready for the Vicodin she had taken in the gymnasium bathroom to cast its gauzy spell.

A morning earlier, Nina had dropped Audrey off at school as if it were any other Wednesday, then drove to Martin's office and let him take the wheel the rest of the way to Boston Metropolitan. At a quarter after nine, the hospital's day had been in full swing, one of the two parking garages already full, the main entrance lobby teeming with people and wheelchairs, white coats and pastel-colored scrubs, busy ambassadors in maroon jackets answering phones at the central information desk. "Onion, ugh," Nina had whispered to Martin as the two of them passed the first floor coffee shop; the burnt-bagel smell was heavy in the air, churning her empty stomach. At the breast center, she had been greeted by the receptionist as if she were a regular already, and was led directly to the same small locker room where she'd changed into an identical sea foam green hospital gown some two weeks earlier, naked to the waist, open at the front.

Dr. Tredway had explained the biopsy procedure at Nina's team meeting, her pointer finger the hollow needle that would extract tumor samples *here* and *here*. An interventional radiologist would numb her breast and find the tumors with ultrasound; Dr. Tredway would be able to take samples from both sites with a single stick. It wouldn't hurt, it wouldn't take more than ten or fifteen minutes. The only evidence would be a Band-Aid and a deep, black bruise that might take a while to fade.

Martin had held Nina's left hand as the surgeon raised her right arm, turning her head away to face a poster-sized profile diagram of a cancerous breast. The ultrasound wand ran cold over her skin as she studied the magnified lobules and the yellow fat, the volcano nipple that stood optimistically erect in spite of the cellular mutinies going on just beneath it. A pinch now, Dr. Tredway had said, and less than an hour later, Nina had left with a pair of prescriptions she had strict instructions to fill, regardless of how she *thought* she felt walking out the door.

After Audrey was home from school, she had taken the first Vicodin, a big, chalky tablet that she'd had to spit out twice before she got it down. The result had been worth the effort, though: as she had puttered around the kitchen—unloading the dishwasher from the morning's dishes, left-handedly sweeping graham cracker crumbs off the table—she had become aware that she was floating, her mind swaying gently as if her brain sat on a waterbed inside her skull. She'd taken another pill at bedtime, one when she awakened this morning; she hadn't thought about medicating herself again until she and Audrey pulled into the Goldengrove parking lot an hour earlier and her fingertips had encountered the amber cylinder of pills in her purse. In the Goldengrove bathroom, she'd debated with herself: was she truly still in pain, or did she just want the floaty feeling again, a little something to get her through the tedium and potential anxiety of another school event? She'd decided it was the former, washed down the pill with a handful of lukewarm tap water and only the smallest twinge of guilt. Maria Thorpe had cautioned her about driving while taking it, though she had allowed that most people did just fine. It was easy enough to see how anyone might get hooked.

On stage, Audrey and her classmates finished their third song, a tentative, error-riddled version of "This Land is Your Land." Nina watched as her daughter carefully laid her felt mallets lengthwise across her xylophone's keys, then stood, looking uncertain about what she was supposed to do next. The U of xylophones was split in half, and, with Miss Morosini's help, the children pushed the instruments away from the center of the stage, the boy in the Batman costume and a girl whose sneakers flashed purple and pink moving around the still-standing Audrey as if she were merely a part of the scenery. At the back of the stage, the row of children linked hands. Nina lunged forward, ready to—what? Hiss directions to her daughter? Implore Miss Morosini to help her out?— just as Willow crossed over to the spot where Audrey stood, leading her by the hand to take her place at the left end of the row. More or less together, the first grade took a few steps forward, and this time everyone bowed. Applause and a few whistles filled the room, and once again Nina checked her watch. 6:45.

An hour later the concert was over, and Nina found herself in the school atrium, leaning against a folding table laden with fruit and veggie plates, multiple variations on hummus and pita, and three different bowls of snack mix all proudly declaring themselves nut-free. A plastic cup of water in one hand and a half-drunk box of apple juice in the other, she was making slightly woozy small-talk with another first grade mother, Carolyn Hadley.

Carolyn picked up a carrot stick. "So what's Martin's excuse for not being here tonight?" she asked Nina. "Ted's is a box seat at Fenway—first home game against the Yankees. God knows we couldn't miss out on *that*."

Nina smiled and shook her head. "Nothing that interesting. Just work, as always."

Carolyn grimaced sympathetically and looked around the room. "Aah, yes. Work." She sighed. "The Mom-to-Dad ratio at these things."

Nina had noticed, more or less, but she looked around again. The room was populated with what Martin would have somewhat scornfully called the usual suspects. Mothers grouped in the same clusters of three or four they formed at every Goldengrove event, dutiful grandparents sitting against the wall in folding chairs, a couple of fathers in suits, arms folded across their chests as they talked. On the far end of the atrium, Nina spied Audrey and Willow. Out of habit, she watched her daughter for a minute, comparing Audrey's stiffened back and arms-at-her-sides posture with Willow's constant, animated motion. As other children moved around them, Willow shifted her weight back and forth, occasionally bouncing up on the balls of her feet or pointing her toes in a quick ballet position. She swooned in toward Audrey to say something close to her ear, then spun away again, her head thrown back in laughter. Audrey laughed, too, and Nina felt her own shoulders relax. Another student from the girls' class— Heather Moran, Nina noted to herself—ran by, and Willow reached out to her, grabbing Heather by the shimmery sleeve of her silver blouse.

Nina took a swallow from her cup of water then nodded at Carolyn Hadley. Her brief survey of the room had confirmed what she'd observed before: mothers outnumbered fathers at least three to one; the majority of the males in attendance were students, siblings, or grandfathers.

"Remarkable, isn't it? How do you suppose they all pull that off?"

Carolyn shrugged. "Same as yours and mine, I guess. Better places to be. Except for that one, there."

Nina looked where Carolyn pointed, to a tall, good-looking man wearing a t-shirt and sun-bleached baseball cap she'd skimmed over without notice on her first sweep of the room. Surrounded by a cluster of upper school mothers, the majority of whom had at least a decade on him, he chatted with apparent ease, rubbing his chin in thoughtful consideration of a comment by Ginny Mansfield, scrutinizing the spine of a book Lisa Pulsifer produced from her handbag. Bonnie Mason, treasurer of the Goldengrove board of directors, grabbed his forearm with her manicured fingers and he grinned at her almost flirtatiously, a dimple like an errant apostrophe revealing itself in one cheek.

"Who is he?" Nina asked. "I've never seen him before, I don't think."

"Todd Slocum. New this year. His daughter Juliette is in the sixth grade. The dirty blonde with the braces who played the handbells for the second song?"

Nina shrugged apologetically. Carolyn's older child—a son, Nina thought—was in the sixth grade with Calla Rutherford. By that part of the concert Nina had tuned out entirely, giving herself over to the blissful swells of the Vicodin. "So he's what, Mister Mom?"

"Close enough. Retired, I think, is the socially acceptable term. He does woodworking or something like that." Carolyn waved her carrot stick in tiny circles. "His wife's the big breadwinner, a venture capitalist in Boston."

Nina lifted her plastic cup to her lips again and discovered it was empty. When had that happened? She pantomimed swallowing, feeling foolish. The fact was, though she was intensely critical of her daughter's social interactions at school, Nina really couldn't blame Audrey for whatever discomfort she might feel about her Goldengrove peers; she often felt decidedly out of place herself. There was no reason that she should—she looked the same and dressed the same, she drove the right kind of car—and yet she sometimes felt it was all a big dress-up game where everyone was waiting for someone else to throw her hands in the air and cry uncle. She would go to the Monday morning socials and nod along to conversations about the new playground budget or the eighth graders' petition to allow flip-flops and spaghetti-strap shirts, as if these were burning topics on her own personal agenda, all the while fighting the urge to elbow the woman next to her and say, "Oh, come on. Do you really give two shakes about any of this?"

Her fellow parents couldn't possibly all be so noble, so secure in their conviction about all things Goldengrove. A glance around the atrium right now, for example, was enough to rebut the widely accepted belief, inculcated from Audrey's first day of school, that Goldengrove students preferred healthy snacks to sweets. Platters that at the beginning of the reception had held store-bought cookies and cupcakes were empty; the three takeout pizza boxes brought by an unsuspecting kindergarten mother to the disapproving scowls of the Goldengrove elders had been picked clean of their last shreds of cheese. The multiple veggie plates and hummuses on the table behind Nina and Carolyn, however, remained largely intact, patronized by far more Goldengrove parents than their supposedly cucumber- and celery-loving kids. Even this very conversation—Nina perceived that Carolyn felt a genuine, indignant ire as she expounded on Susan Slocum's snubbing of Goldengrove's earnest productions. What did it matter?

As a child, spying on the cocktail parties her parents had thrown for her father's Cabot College zoology department colleagues, Nina never imagined that any of the women chatting with her mother might have been lonely, in spite of the gold hoops in their earlobes and the plates of Swedish meatballs in their hands. She'd envied those women their puffy perms and their frosted pink lips, their wraparound skirts and their white sandals that showed off their painted toenails. Had one of them listened to her mother holding court on hanging wallpaper and explaining her secret for making perfect salmon croquettes, feeling a stunned sort of disbelief that this was her life? Had another smiled at the tedious recounting of one of Nina's or her brothers' childish antics, hoping the drink in her hand would hurry and soften the agglomeration of griefs at the base of her stomach? Nina had nothing against Carolyn Hadley, but it hadn't crossed her mind to confide in the other woman about her cancer, even as the first dull ache in her breast pushed its way through the light fog of Vicodin. She supposed the news would get out—it was inevitable in a school of Goldengrove's size—but first things first: there was telling Audrey, and then Audrey's teacher, Mrs. Roy, and the Goldengrove head of school, Mrs. Chisholm, and then all assurances of discretion to the contrary, the rumor mill would go to work. Overhead, a massive mobile hung from the atrium's cathedral ceiling, its discs of colored glass throwing shards of ruby, turquoise and indigo light around the room. *It's all about timing.*

"What's about timing?" Carolyn asked.

Nina started, realizing she'd spoken her last thought out loud. She laughed a little, rattled now, and made a dismissive wave with her left hand. "Don't pay any attention to me," she said. "I'm talking to myself again. Do you think she minds? Juliette, I mean, that her mother isn't around for these things. Such a pretty name. Her father seems comfortable enough with the arrangement."

Nina glanced over to where Todd Slocum was still talking with Bonnie Mason and company. As she watched, he lifted the baseball cap from his head, quickly running his free hand over his head before he resettled the hat. Beyond him, she spied Audrey, yawning prodigiously now while Willow bent her head close to Heather Moran's. Nodding automatically at Carolyn's response—a snide observation about whether or not Juliette Slocum had a choice in the matter—she made what she hoped was a graceful enough exit from the conversation and signaled Jenny that she and Audrey were leaving. Clearly, it was time for the Baldwin/Winzer girls to go home.

On the drive across town, Nina tried to get her daughter to talk. "So, I liked the performance," she said. "Did you have fun being up there?" She glanced in the rear-view mirror to see Audrey's face.

"Yeah." Audrey shrugged. "It was fine."

"Everyone did a really great job, I thought. Three songs seems like a lot to learn."

Audrey frowned. "Brandon Melcher was really bad. He kept messing up and distracting me."

"Was he the one in the Batman costume?"

Audrey answered affirmatively, her voice dark, and Nina waited for what else she might have to say on the matter. When she realized Audrey was finished, she continued. "I'm surprised Miss Morosini let him wear that up on stage, aren't you?"

Audrey shrugged again. "Not exactly. He's obsessed with Batman. He has a Batman notebook and Batman sneakers. He's even got all these Batman Happy Meal toys he brought in for his class share one day."

McDonald's, Nina thought to herself; yet another Goldengrove sacred cow brought low.

"He said they were collector's items," Audrey added. Nina heard her daughter shift in her seat. "Mom, what's eBay?"

"eBay? It's on the internet. It's an on-line auction house, I guess you'd call it, where people can sell things to each other. I don't know too much about it."

"Brandon said his dad bought some of the Batman toys for him on eBay."

"That's nice."

"I don't think so. I think it's stupid. Batman is for babies."

"How do you know?" Nina asked her daughter. "You've never seen it, have you?"

"Heather Moran has."

Nina lapsed into a silence she knew her daughter would not be the one to break, and suddenly, desperation clutched at her. eBay and Batman? Happy Meals? Twelve days and counting, and she still hadn't come close to telling Audrey about her upcoming surgery. Every time she thought about it she was utterly stymied by the *how* of it. Was there a segue, an obvious opening? Was it wrong to tell her daughter in the car? More than once, Nina had thought about the way Audrey would sometimes write her notes rather than talk to her when she had something difficult to share ("Dear Mom, I wasen't happy when you threw away my Merrell shew box when I tolled you I wanted to keep it, love Audrey."), wishing it wouldn't be too cowardly for her to do the same.

At the meeting with her cancer team (*her cancer team, her cancer team,* a phrase that had gone through her head so many times now it no longer shocked her with its bizarre mundanity), just before Maria Thorpe had presented Nina with the brochures about Boston Metropolitan's support groups for children of parents with cancer, Dr. Kennett had offered to set Nina and Martin up with a social worker who could help them figure out how to talk to Audrey about Nina's disease. Nina had declined, and not just because of the look of—it had been more than disapproval; panic, perhaps—on Martin's face. It had seemed at the time that if she couldn't do this for herself then she had a bigger problem than just being sick.

Now, however, it didn't seem so absolute, so tidy. From about the age of four, Audrey had been fixated on death, wrestling with questions that Nina had struggled to answer well. "What happens when you die?"

"Where do you go after you die?" "Will I ever have a chance to live again?" (*Good grief*, Nina remembered thinking. Why couldn't Audrey fear all the things she herself had at the same age—lockjaw and rattlesnakes and scorpions, the astronomically remote possibility of stumbling into a pool of quicksand in her own backyard?) At the nadir of her daughter's anxiety, a stretch of weeks when she had stayed awake half the night sobbing over everything from being put in a box in the ground to the fact that her mother was *old,* and would therefore die before other mothers did, Nina had found herself promising her daughter that she would do her best to live until she was a century, at least. Even at the time she had known it was an ill-advised promise to make—the child who remembered every license plate in the neighborhood was unlikely to forget that her mother swore she'd help her blow out sixty-three candles on her own birthday cake—but she'd thought she'd have at least several decades before she had to do her backtracking.

Just before the turn that would take Nina and Audrey to Weston Road and then to home, Nina saw the glowing red and white sign of the Cabot Friendly's restaurant and checked the clock on the dashboard—it was 8:15, after Audrey's bedtime, but her daughter seemed wide-awake now. When Nina had had her childhood cancer scare, she'd heard the news at the doctor's office, the wrench of nausea in her stomach forever linked to a room with peach walls and a framed print of Picasso's *Hand with Flowers.* Perhaps Audrey would develop an aversion to family ice cream shops, but there were worse things, weren't there? Better that than to see her mother's cancer in the cushions on the living room sofa or pineapple posts at the end of her bed. Nina eased her foot off the gas and turned her left blinker on.

"Where are we going?" Audrey asked her.

"To Friendly's. I thought maybe we'd stop and get some hot chocolate."

Nina turned into the parking lot. Audrey leaned forward, straining against her seatbelt. Her face was tense. "I don't want to."

"You don't want to?" Effortfully, Nina made her voice sound casual. "Why not?"

"I already had a sugar food at the reception, a chocolate cupcake. I have school tomorrow."

"Well, maybe we'll play hooky."

"Not from school!" Audrey's voice was shrill with alarm. "We're having Earth Day. I got picked to do recycling! Someone's coming to talk to us from Keep America Beautiful."

Nina sighed. She had turned the engine off, but her hands still gripped the steering wheel.

"I don't want to go," Audrey repeated.

"Sweetie," Nina said, "There's something I need to talk to you about and I thought this might be easier. You could help me out, okay? I thought this might even be fun."

Audrey shook her head harder, her hair lashing from side to side. "I'm not going in," she said. "I don't want to and you can't make me."

Nina backed out of the parking lot. For the remainder of their trip home, neither she nor Audrey said a word, though she several times opened her mouth to say something—anything—only to find herself unable to speak. As they made the final turn onto Vaughn Circle, Nina could see the silhouette of their house at the back of the cul-de-sac, a hulking black square against the outlines of a dozen budding trees and the blazing lights of the neighbors' windows. Martin was at the office. Still.

Inside, she flicked lights on room by room, suddenly so angry she was shaking that Martin had left her and Audrey to come home into darkness. True, he'd taken half a day for her biopsy and was double-booking patients so he could be home after her surgery, but all the same—at eight-thirty? He wasn't seeing patients at this hour; he never got that far behind on his dictations. He wasn't at home because he didn't want to be.

Silently, Audrey headed upstairs, and silently Nina followed her. Halfway up, however, Audrey paused and turned around. "Mom," she said. Her voice was quiet now. "I know what it was you wanted to talk to me at Friendly's about."

Nina swallowed. "You do?"

Gravely, Audrey nodded. Her eyes filled with tears and she took two sudden steps downward, ramming her lowered head into Nina's stomach as she wrapped her arms around her mother in a fierce hug. "Please, Mom," she said. "I'm begging you. Please don't make me leave Goldengrove."

"Leave Goldengrove?" Nina repeated. For a minute, she felt disoriented, staggering with the sudden weight of Audrey against her abdomen and her wholly unexpected words. What train of thought had led Audrey to that place? "Honey." She stroked Audrey's silky hair. "Nobody's going to make you leave Goldengrove."

"You promise?"

Nina unlaced Audrey's arms from her waist so she could tilt her daughter's chin up and look her in the eyes. "I promise."

"Because I thought that was what you were going to tell me."

"Well, I wasn't." Nina trailed her fingers across her daughter's forehead and around the apple-curve of her cheek. "Whatever gave you that idea?"

"Heather Moran said so. Well, not exactly. She said I'm probably going to be leaving Goldengrove."

"She did?" Nina shook her head. "Why?"

"Well, you know how Heather's family is going to go on a Disney cruise for vacation week?" (Nina did not, but didn't think it mattered.) "She said it's because her family's rich and they can afford things like that whenever they want them. I told her we weren't going anywhere so I guessed that meant we weren't rich and she said that was right."

"I see." Nina gave herself a moment. "And that relates to having to leave Goldengrove how?"

"Because Goldengrove is expensive, and if you and Dad aren't rich then we probably can't afford it. Heather said that was why Kyle Lowry had left, because his parents couldn't afford to send him to private school, and if we aren't rich then you probably weren't going to be able to either."

"Well." Nina gave a small, harsh laugh. "Nice as it is of Heather to be concerned about our finances on your behalf that's a subject matter she can leave to me and your dad."

She shook her head again to stop herself. She was perfectly sure the sarcasm was lost on Audrey, but still, there was no need for her to stoop. Heather Moran was just a child, a seven-year-old, the same as Audrey. "We certainly have enough money to send you to Goldengrove."

"But not to go on vacation?" Audrey pressed. "Abby Shapiro's going to Florida and Callie Burke has a timeshare. Brandon Melcher's going to Washington, D.C. and we aren't even doing that."

Slowly, Nina sank down onto the stair next to Audrey's feet. Her heart was pounding and she felt nauseated; so this was how it was going to be. One shaky hand patted the tops of Audrey's shoes. "Sit, honey," she said, "right next to me." In front of her was the picture her mind would frame, hold, indelibly print: the Oriental stair runner, a pattern of maroon and olive and gold; the half-moon hallway table, half-visible downstairs. A long strand of spider web ran from one wall to the opposite corner of the ceiling; there was the powdery carcass of a long-dead moth in the bowl of the first floor hallway light.

Audrey sat, and Nina put her arm around her daughter's shoulders. For a moment, she rocked her from side to side. "Sweetheart," Nina began, speaking around the lump in her throat. "About that. You're right, we're not going anywhere on school vacation week." She kissed the top of Audrey's head, breathing in the baked-bread smell her daughter had given off ever since she was very little. "That's the thing I need to tell you about."

seven

"MRS. HEBERT? I'M DR. Winzer."

Martin pushed on the door of exam room seven, his eyes on the chart he held open with his thumb, greeting his second-to-last patient of the day as he took in quickly what he needed to know about her: eighty-nine years old, six days post subendocardial infarct of the right ventricular wall subsequent to ischemic heart disease. History of pneumonia and osteoporosis; both hips replaced in the 1980s. She'd had a small skin cancer removed from her nose about ten years ago and a complete hysterectomy in 1976.

After nearly forty years, the routine was automatic to him—the knock on the half-open door; the greeting; the rapid, dispassionate inventory of the body's fallibility—and Martin often had to give himself a beat or two, the pause after the inquiry into the patient's current health, to connect his job and purpose with a living, breathing organism. It was a strange thing about medicine: so many doctors got into it because they wanted to help people (a cliché so threadbare Martin was tempted to reject out of hand any resident candidate who offered it) and yet to do the job well one really had to look at the human body separate from the person, as a set of systems—and in his particular line of work a set of systems afflicted with a grave error. For Martin, at least, it took a tremendous leap to bridge the space between ST-segment depressions and ejection fractions and percentages of lumenal narrowing—the currency with which his world dealt—and the lipstick-crooked smile on a patient's face or the tremble in her age-spotted hands.

Rita Hebert, sitting on the exam table in front of him now, looked the same as two other patients Martin had seen today, and perhaps a dozen more he would see this week: an age-mapped face with pink-rimmed, lashless eyes; a fragile, folded body overwhelmed by a one-size-fits-all examining gown. One might have unstable angina; another congestive heart failure, perhaps secondary to emphysema and a decades-long two-pack-a-day habit. There were mitral regurges and diabetic hypertensives. There were ventral septal defects, valve insufficiencies, stenoses. There were coronary artery diseases *out the wazoo*, as Nina would say. The MI Martin had seen this morning had also come in following a heart attack, but that one had been a large, transmural infarct, the third the patient had suffered in as many years. Though she'd been younger, in her mid-seventies, the other patient's outlook hadn't been as good as Mrs. Hebert's was now.

"Dr. Winzer," Rita Hebert repeated, as if testing Martin's name, affirming it. "Good to meet you."

"I'm very sorry you had to wait." Martin offered a smile to his patient, but he did not put out his hand. Over the years, he had developed a sense for which patients expected a handshake and which did not, and even without the cues offered by her age and gender, Mrs. Hebert didn't strike him as the hand-shaking type. Her white hair was long, held up in an elaborate crisscross of braids on the top of her head; there was a broadness to her wrinkled face that called to mind for him an Old World *grossmutter*, a woman who baked her own bread and cleaned her windows with newspaper dipped in vinegar. It was because his dreams were back, no doubt, but for a moment Martin was unsettled to catch in his patient a flash of his childhood cook.

A heavy-set man, Mrs. Hebert's son sat in a chair to her right, and Martin turned to greet him as well. Martin's own age or perhaps half a decade younger, his forearms were thick and scaly with psoriasis. "Richard and his wife, Linda, take care of me," Mrs. Hebert said.

"At home?" Martin asked.

"Mom was in a nursing home in Florida after Dad died, but she was miserable, so we brought her up when all the kids were out of the house," Richard Hebert explained. "My sister's in upstate New York and she's got a place on Lake George Mom goes to in the summer. Not this year, though."

"Not until we've gotten you a little better stabilized," Martin agreed.

He fitted the earpieces of his stethoscope into his ears and lifted the bell toward his patient, rubbing the cold plastic of the diaphragm against his palm. "Let's take a listen." He looked from his patient to her son. "I assume you would like Richard to stay in the room?"

Martin breathed inward as he bent his head down toward Mrs. Hebert's chest, listening for the robust *lub* of her atrioventricular valves snapping shut, the deeper *dub* of the pulmonic and aortic valves doing the same. For Martin, the evaluation represented an act of extraordinary intimacy—leaning in so close you could tell what your four o'clock patient had eaten for his lunch, displacing breasts to locate the apical impulse along the midclavicular line, then feeling their strange, familiar weight against the back of your hand like an indolent dog—and it very often happened within minutes of meeting a patient you might or might not ever see again. Face to chest with bony sternums, Martin had been subject to the most inappropriate, personal exchanges. Patients made disparaging remarks about their bodies; they passed gas; they held rigidly still with their eyes screwed tight, huffing coltish breaths through their nostrils. They remarked on Martin's thick head of hair, his warm hands, the pleasing scent of his aftershave.

Mrs. Hebert was a watcher. As Martin moved the scope across her thin chest, she studied him silently, her hands gripping the sides of the examining table. He knew other doctors who would be talking to her right now, perhaps explaining the clear, late diastolic atrial gallop he could hear from her MI, but the approach was not one Martin liked to take. More than likely, Mrs. Hebert would have questions, he would fail to answer them in any way that made sense, and the exam would take that much longer because Martin would be unable to hear what he needed over the rumble of words coming from her chest. Indeed, the need for silence was an excuse he often exercised to end the stream of commentary from patients who squirmed and shifted against the table's papered top.

Martin rolled Mrs. Hebert toward him and slid his stethoscope across her back. She smelled of *old*, a combination of body odor and infrequently washed hair, exacerbated by the unforgiving trap of nylon fabric. When he sat her upright, he flipped through her chart. All her notes were faxed; she'd suffered her MI at a wedding in Maine and had been treated at the medical center in Portland. "Mrs. Hebert," he said, "when you were

71

in the hospital up in Portland, did Dr. Kwon talk to you about putting a pacemaker in?"

Martin watched his patient's lips form a thin, unhappy line. "He did, and I say to you the same thing I said to him, Dr. Winzer, thank you and no."

"No?"

"No. I am too old already. I don't want anyone cutting me open and putting a battery inside to run like a toy for a child."

"I see." Martin unhooked his stethoscope from around his neck and tucked the instrument in his lab coat pocket. "Did Dr. Kwon explain to you the way a pacemaker works?"

"He did not."

Inwardly, Martin sighed. Talking to patients about their illnesses in a way that made sense to them was a challenge for him—a desecration of the soaring, gorgeous language he loved so much—and he'd long ago recognized that he wasn't a natural teacher the way so many of his colleagues were. (More than once, in fact, his first wife had suggested that he should have cast his lot with pathology, rather than dealing with living, breathing humans. Cell samples and corpses, she had said. Those were the patients for him.) The very moment was an excellent case in point; Martin's only pacemaker analogy was to a car's electrical system, a concept he suspected Rita Herbert would find of little relevance. Still, he had to try.

As he spoke, Mrs. Hebert seemed not to be listening. Toward the end, however, she closed her eyes as if in terrific concentration.

"If you're worried about the rigors of the procedure, you're in excellent shape. Complications are possible, but relatively uncommon. It takes about an hour to put the pacemaker in and we'll keep you in the hospital just one night, as a precaution. You'll be able to go home the next day and up to Lake George before you know it."

Rita Hebert opened her eyes again. "And I will die if I don't have the operation?"

"Your tests show an irregular pattern of electrical messages going into your right ventricle, the lower right part of your heart. It's not possible for me to be one hundred percent certain. But right now you are a good candidate for having another heart attack."

An expression of almost pleasure—relief?—crossed her face. "Then that is God's will, doctor. I am ready. Eighty-nine years is already too much time. You know this."

Martin frowned. "I'm sorry. I don't think I do."

Every day, Martin dealt with people who had learned that life was provisional, and that theirs in particular could be taken with a certain brutal suddenness. They came to him angry or scared, and always with the same terrible need: that *he* be the one to save them, to restore their hope in the seventy or eighty years they'd always believed they had. Sometimes, he was able to. All too often, though, the only role he could play was that of informed witness to death, unable to realign the mismatch between the mind's will and the body's capacity for work. And now, even as his wife counted down the days to her mastectomy, here sat this patient, a healthy eighty-nine year old in need of only the simplest fix. He was surprised by his own need for her to recognize the gift she seemed entirely ready to hand back.

"Mrs. Hebert, you have an eminently manageable condition here and a pacemaker could very well give you a number more good years with your children and grandchildren. I would be very sorry to see you make an unfortunate choice. Perhaps if you could tell me what you're worried about, I could reassure you. Surely your son, here—"

Martin turned to Richard Hebert. The other man folded his scaly arms across his chest and shook his head. "Mom," he said. "We've talked about this so many times. Remember the question Linda asked you: what if what God wants is for you to live?"

Rita Hebert pressed her lips tight. "Then I will live, if He wants me to suffer, just like I answered you the last time." Turning to Martin, she added, "Please, Dr. Winzer, you can tell me this. Is sixty years not punishment enough?"

"I am sorry, Mrs. Hebert. I'm afraid I don't understand."

For a moment, Mrs. Hebert stared at Martin, her expression unreadable. Then she took Martin's hand and patted it, like a teacher counseling a recalcitrant boy. Martin told himself he was imagining the hard, calculating gleam that had come into her eye, the crafty edge to her smile. "I apologize to you, Dr. Winzer. Even after so many years, my English is not so good."

Martin jerked his hand away, picked up his pen again and started to write. At first, it was just scribbles—the circles that started a balky ballpoint going, the jags and dashes rendered by a four year old pretending to sign his name. He was marking up his patient's official chart, however, so he forced himself to think in words. *Tangents,* he wrote; *tangential thinking = cognitive issue?* Perhaps he had misread Mrs. Hebert after all, and she wasn't in nearly as good health—mentally at least—as he had first surmised; perhaps her resistance to such a simple procedure was evidence of an established dementia. *Alzheimer's disease;* he wrote, *neurology consult; TIAs?* He traced his question mark heavily, his eyes running up and down the page.

Shaking himself, Martin made a couple of quick notes—*patient refuses pacemaker AMA; will attempt beta blocker/medical management*—and then he turned to Richard Hebert, explaining that it wasn't possible for him to treat his mother against her will. He would prescribe a couple of medications; if Richard could encourage his mother to take them regularly, he would suggest she come back in two months to see if there had been any improvement in her heart function. Martin dashed the prescriptions off angrily: Warfarin, atenolol, elanapril. He was late now for his last patient; he'd spent considerably more than the ten minutes Mrs. Hebert's HMO reimbursed for conducting a fruitless conversation with a *non compos mentis* patient—that was the excuse he made to himself as bid the Heberts a brisk good-bye. Quickly, he walked down the hallway and to his office; quickly he shut the door. It wasn't his job to talk his patient into a surgery she didn't want. He would leave that to the nurses when Mrs. Hebert was hospitalized with her next MI. It wasn't his job to understand.

But even as Martin picked up his final patient's file, taking a few deep breaths to steady himself, there was this: a minute earlier, as his eyes had frantically coursed Mrs. Hebert's chart, they had fallen upon something, a slight but meaningful error he had made in his end-of-day fatigue. For the time he had been in the exam room with her, he had been calling his patient Rita Hebert, had been thinking of her as Rita Hebert, but the imprint from her insurance card said otherwise. Ruta. She was Ruta Hebert; and finally, as she had patted his hand (mockingly? consoling?), he had placed the accent his preoccupied brain had missed. She had called him not Doctor Winzer, with the blunted, lazy consonants of an American patient, but *Doktor* Winzer, hard with the bitter, palatal *C*s and *D*s of a forgotten—forsworn—world. Polish? Hungarian? Goosebumps prickled

Martin's arms and the back of his neck. He *had* understood Ruta Hebert's question, much better than he wanted to, and what he'd shut the door on was the idea that she had known he would.

•

MARTIN HADN'T EVER WANTED to be a doctor, not really. He had the brain for it but not, so to speak, the heart. If he had had dreams as a little boy of what he did want to be, he didn't remember them—*wouldn't* remember them. His right to have dreams for himself was as lost to him as everything else that had been his life in Germany.

The facts of Martin's life were these: he had been born in Berlin in 1938, in the early days of World War II; his family had remained there until the city fell to the Russian army; he had left the country, alone, in the late autumn of 1946 and had never gone back. In some ways, medicine felt like just another something that had happened to him, a redefinition of his existence as volitional as bidding farewell to his home and then his family and finally any sense he'd ever had of being a good person, living a worthwhile life. First, his father had killed himself; then the Russians had taken over, forcing Martin and his mother and sisters to flee with little more than the clothes on their backs. He had lived in an internment camp, then a refugee settlement, then a bleak, cold apartment far away from his mother and sisters, with relatives who resented the very air he took up with his breath.

From the age of eight until he graduated university, Martin had lived in England, in the Cumbrian town of Penrith, housed by his father's cousin's family in rooms above a chemist's shop. As a teenager, to earn his keep and fill his hours, he had worked in the shop, first as a janitor and stock boy of sorts—sweeping the wide stone steps that led to the street, washing the gilt-lettered window, *Arthur A. Foulds and Son, Chemists,* carrying boxes of supplies from the delivery truck up the narrow side aisle to the back room. Later, and very privately, he'd helped Mr. Foulds himself. He'd measured liquids into brown glass bottles and tapped the stoppers into the tops, folded paper envelopes by the dozens to hold powders and pills, printed dosing instructions in his best English schoolboy block print.

In its predictability, in its monotony, the work had been strangely soothing. Martin had grown to love the biting, bitter smell of the medicines and the glow of sunlight through green jars ranged across the pharmacy counter, the thrilling wealth of wooden tongue depressors and cotton and gauze. Mr. Foulds dispensed advice and peppermints alongside prescriptions; as he counted out pills or tilted a bottle of sludgy-looking liquid he would keep up a steady stream of conversation that he often simply continued with Martin after a customer left. "The thing about a fever is," he would counsel an exhausted looking mother with a flame-cheeked child, "it's your little one's body working to drive his infection out. You give him the penicillin, of course, but don't be afraid to let the fever do its work."

To a grim and disfigured veteran, hobbling one-legged into the shop on a wooden crutch, he would sigh and shake his head. "The body remembers pain, you know, as much as your brain tries to talk it out of it." He would measure out the dose of Veronal with a tiny spoon and wrap the powder in a paper envelope, hand it to the wordless veteran, who would hobble away. "Sleep is the only cure for a pain like that. You dream, and your body heals by remembering itself whole."

When it was just Martin and Mr. Foulds, Martin would ask questions: exactly how did the Veronal work? Were there any other choices or other treatments? Why would a leg that was no longer there cause pain? Mr. Foulds would give him answers, and also books to read—*The American Materia Medica, Therapeutics and Pharmacognosy; Gray's Anatomy.* Martin had devoured the texts the way other boys devoured comic books. He had done well in school, excelled at maths and science, and won a full scholarship for university. Canadian tuitions were good, and so when it was time, he had written away to a handful of medical schools in Canada. Dalhousie University, McGill, Queens…Queens' envelope had arrived first. Queens University it had been.

That was the truth on one level, at least. On another, medicine had been a deliberate choice, made for one clear reason: amends-making; propitiation; the sins of the father paid by the son. To anyone who ever asked, Martin said that his father had been a businessman in Germany, a white-collar worker for a company that collapsed with the rest of the economy at the end of the war. The description was true, but only partly so, and only in the way that a description of Adolf Hitler as Chancellor of Germany during the years 1933-1945 fully captured the man. Martin's father, Josef, had been a member of the *Partei*; he was chief financier for an oil company that made enormous profits in the early years of the war. There were an infinite number of ways to be a German criminal in World War II, and Martin felt as tainted, as implicated, by his father's privateering as if he had been personally responsible for the suffering of every gypsy, homosexual, and Jew. It wasn't until well after the war had ended that Martin understood he had lived in comfort long after the lives of his fellow countrymen had plunged into nightmare; it was later still when he realized that by managing the operations of a company that filled Nazi pocketbooks and literally fueled the tanks and planes that were the Nazi war machine, Josef Winzer had been one of the men who had made World War II *possible*.

Early in their relationship, Martin and Nina had fought about his unwillingness to share his past. At one point, Nina had grabbed Martin's wrist, twisting it over as if looking for the tattooed numbers there. "Not at all, my dear," he'd told her stiffly. "I'm sorry to say you're on the wrong side of that line entirely."

He'd watched her expression change as she'd made the mental leap from *Holocaust victim* to *executioner* without attempting to correct his wife's misconception; after all, to what American did *Nazi* not mean SS officer, Hitler's rank and file? In truth, he had felt more relieved than aggrieved by Nina's stereotypic rush to judgment: There they were at last, on the *terra cognita* of his shameful past. Indeed, what had troubled him had not been his wife's imagining his faceless father decorated with a *Gruppenführer's* chevron, goose-stepping and *Heil Hitler*-ing at every turn, but the sequence of emotions that ran across her face as she did: shock, of course, and then the inevitable repugnance; but then, ultimately...*beguilement*.

There was no word in the English language that carried the visceral, moral, emotional charge of *Nazi*, and yet Martin was as utterly incapable of explaining to a non-German the profundity of the shame rooted into the label as he was of understanding the American fascination with the same. When his boys were young, they had been enamored of that aspect of their history, often scheming to dress as S.S. officers for Halloween or playing war in the backyard and arguing over which one of them would get to be Hitler. ("None of you will be Hitler. Find someone else to be. Be Idi Amin."). Once Martin had overheard Jonathan bragging to a neighborhood friend that his family was all Nazis and Martin had nearly dislocated the boy's shoulder pulling him into the garage to demand that he never say such an atrocious thing, not to any one, for any reason, again. The boy had sobbed, "But why, Dad? They think it's cool. I didn't say that *you* were a Nazi."

The black and blue marks on his son's upper arms had lasted for weeks, but it had taken much longer than that for the hollowed-out, breathless terror Martin felt to subside. He had been found out. He would be reviled. There would be bricks through his windows and burning swastikas on his lawn. There never were, and what gradually had become more horrific was the strange, distant respect his history conferred on him by the few people who found out. Everyone who stopped to consider Martin's birth date and place wanted to ask about it, had no hesitation to push their fingers in the runnel of the wound.

At Queens, Martin's instructors and classmates were mercifully incurious about his past, many of them also accented fellows with their own stories not to tell. In his residency, however, he'd started courting Beth, and the questions had begun. What had brought him to Canada, she had wanted right off to know; where was his family; had he suffered in the war. Naïve, starry-eyed with brand-new love, she'd declared she wanted to go to Germany with him, so she could see the world through his eyes, share in what he had felt. Martin had shrugged. "There is nothing left, and I feel nothing for it, so—" He'd forced himself to smile. "I'm afraid it would be a brief and disappointing trip."

For Nina's part, once she had made the adjustment to the notion of her husband as a young Nazi, she pushed him on the subject—much harder than Beth ever had. Less than a week after their first (and Martin had expected, last) conversation about his past, she had come back at him. "But everyone knows what happened to the Germans," she said. "Especially in Berlin, right? And you were only a child."

Martin had been jarred by her brazenness, the arrogant assurance of *everyone knows*. "Well, if everyone knows," he'd replied, "then there's no need for me to tell you, now is there?"

Nina's face had looked shocked, as if Martin had slapped her. "I mean I took World History in high school. I listened to Eddie Schwartz give an oral report about the Nuremberg Trials. I don't have the first idea about what happened to you, except it was so awful you still have nightmares about it and all your family is gone. I'd like to think that's something you could share at least a little with me, that I know something about. I mean, okay, I was a grown-up when I lost my parents, but that doesn't mean it didn't hurt, that my life wasn't completely upended."

"My father was a criminal," Martin said quietly. "He killed himself rather than pay for his crimes, which he left the rest of us to do. It's different."

"But it wasn't your *fault*. It's not like you're responsible for the crimes that someone else committed."

"Who is, then?"

"Well," Nina stammered, "Adolph Hitler, for starters. All those men who were convicted at Nuremberg."

"The dead ones, you mean?" As much as he hated the conversation, Martin had felt oddly calm. "Or the little old men in Argentina who claim mistaken identity, it wasn't them? I think you mean to say the Nazis are responsible. Who's left to be held accountable if not me?"

The truth was, Martin was no longer sure that what he remembered of his childhood wasn't itself a dream, as distorted and symbolic as the vivid, imprecise show of pictures that still heaved him from his sleep on far too many nights. He was quite sure he had not taken a shovel at the age of eight to bury dead at Sachsenhausen, but had he really lingered at the closed door of a farmhouse in Sievershagen, a thick gob of spit still warm on his cheek, the words of the frau who had issued it echoing in his head? *Not as much as a single egg for you, you filthy beggar boy.* He was fairly certain he had spent the winter of 1945 at an internment camp in Wolfenbuttel, huddling up against his sister Hedy for warmth on a prickly bed of hay bales, plugging his ears against the cries of fellow refugees dying of cholera and hunger. He thought he had, but he could no longer be sure.

Even if what he remembered was true, it was impossible for Martin to explain to Nina the complexity and the—the *expedience* of his suffering, the way it felt to be implicated by blood for the worst crime committed against humanity in all of history. Too young to actually join the Hitler

Youth, Martin had worn a miniature version of the costume he so coveted, hand-stitched for him by his nursemaid. He had lived in a sprawling half-timbered house behind a high stone wall; there had been pear trees in front and a little finger of the Spree River behind. Though Martin had erased most of his German memories, he remembered this: sitting cross-legged on that wall, the collar of his *Hitlerjugend* costume still wet with pear juice, glaring ferocious four-year-old daggers at an elderly man with a yellow star sewn to his shirt. It had been late summer 1942; that night or another like it, Martin had overheard his parents talking on the patio, glasses of a ruby-colored liquid in their hands. *That's the last of them, I think,* his father had told his mother. *I was by the Putlitz Street station today and they were loading them onto freight cars.*

Martin didn't want Nina's sympathy, her absolution. What he had experienced was as different from losing your parents in an auto accident at the age of twenty-eight as the cold, dead moon was from the sun.

Only momentarily stymied, Nina had changed her tack. "You know," she said, "I think it's arrogant. I don't think it's that you think you haven't suffered, or aren't deserving. I think it's that you think you've suffered in such a terrible way that nobody else could possibly fathom, so what's the use in sharing it?"

Martin was fine with leaving it at that. He had always been suspicious that the unfilled blanks of his past were actually *what* Beth had loved him for, the romantic possibilities of mystery and tragedy, and he had no desire to repeat the pattern with Nina. The problem with Beth had been that what came along with that particular "romance" was the expectation that there was more to Martin, something richer and deeper that simply needed to be plumbed, and when there hadn't been, she'd been more than merely disappointed. She'd been bitter, she'd been betrayed. It was, in some ways, the most fundamental problem with his past: the way people would give him latitude he neither welcomed nor wanted, just because of the sufferings they assumed they knew.

Martin had never been the kind of person to go around making excuses for himself. Nobody wanted to hear about a little Nazi boy.

eight

MARTIN STOOD IN THE shower, his eyes closed and his head bowed down. He was hiding, and he was aware of it—he had gotten home late again, past Audrey's bedtime, and he had been in the shower twenty minutes at least, long past the point of productive cleaning—but he felt that it would send the right message to Nina (reassurance, routine) if he stuck with the norm. Almost every work night, Martin gave himself ten minutes before he went to bed to rinse away the last few remnants of his day: patients with sniffles and coughs and halitosis, the cloying stink of the antiseptic scrub he used in the cath lab. He hadn't shared this with Nina, of course, but he'd already showered at the hospital, following a much-needed evening run. His legs had ached and the chilly spring air had hurt his lungs, but the exertion had stilled the shaking of his hands, captured a more authoritative rhythm for his pounding heart.

For a rare, unwelcome moment, Martin was feeling his age: tired and fallible. He despised uncertainty in himself, and for two weeks now he'd been tiptoeing around inside his own life, unsure of what role Nina needed him to play. Was it rock, reassuring in the face of everything? Was it physician? Protector? Lover? He didn't want to get it wrong, but he had recently become aware that, in an effort to not be the wrong thing, he had ended up being nothing at all. Gone before seven in the morning, back as late as nine or ten, busy on the weekends, using Audrey as a sort of shield. The silences between him and Nina were not of the comfortable variety, and he knew that with every passing day the divide between them grew. It frightened him, and yet how could anything he might say to her make a difference? There were no consolations, no magic words.

The water that had been punishingly hot when he started was turning cold. Martin soaped his chest and beneath his arms one final time, rinsed, then willed himself to twist off the taps. In the bedroom, Nina was sitting up in bed, leaned forward with her arms around her drawn-up knees. Her eyes were puffy, but only slightly, as if mere allergies were the sum total of her woes; there was a horizontal crease, like a sleep mark, across her left cheek.

"Nina," he said. "You're still awake."

"So it seems."

Martin crossed the room and kissed his wife's forehead. She smiled up at him—grimaced, really, and asked him, "How was your day?"

For an instant, Ruta Hebert's face flashed in front of him, her accented English echoed again in his head. "No complaints, I suppose. It was an office day, one of those Fridays when everyone is in a panic about getting their prescriptions refilled before the weekend. You know how much I relish those."

"That I do." Nina nodded to herself for a moment, then put a hand up to her head, twisting a section of hair between her index and middle fingers.

"How about you?" It seemed an absurd question to ask, an impossible question not to ask. *Did you do anything fun today? Watch any good television? Feeling any better about that breast cancer of yours?*

Nina flipped the section of hair between her fingers back and forth. "I was going to get my hair cut this morning, but I chickened out. I know I have to. Everything I've read says do it before you start chemo so you don't wake up one morning to find it all stuck to your pillow. Might as well do it while it seems like something I'm choosing. I was going to, but— Do you remember? When we were at Dr. Tredway's office, Dr. Kennett said something about one of these places that can make a wig for you out of your own hair. She mentioned where, but my brain was so full at that point I just completely blanked. I was thinking I might go that route, ease the sting."

Martin walked around the bed to his dresser, buckling his watch back onto his wrist. He pushed in the drawer that held his black and charcoal work socks, still slightly agape from where Nina earlier had been putting laundry away. "On Newbury Street. I didn't think to take down the address." Dr. Kennett *had* mentioned it, yes; in the context of telling Nina that her assignment was to get herself a wig before she had surgery, but she had also said she didn't recommend a "real" wig over one that was synthetic. For one thing, human hair wigs were expensive; for another, they were hard to care for, and the last thing most women who were sick from chemo wanted to do was fuss with a wig. Martin wasn't going to remind Nina of that now, however. If Nina wanted a wig of her own hair she could have it, whether or not she ever wore it. It was only a couple hundred dollars, money well spent.

"Newbury Street," Nina repeated. "That's an interesting choice, don't you think? Probably right between Burberry and Giorgio Armani." She frowned down at the lock of hair and said, "I don't know, though. If I'm gonna go through all this I might try my hand at being a blonde. See if it's true blondes really do have more fun."

"Not in my experience it's not."

"Right." A dozen questions—possibilities—flickered on Nina's face. "Just look at poor Audrey."

Audrey, it was true, had Martin's coloring: wheat blonde hair and ice blue eyes. That she did had been a triumph of recessive genes; Nina was brown and brown, as had been Beth, as were all of Martin's sons. It was at least one way in which his daughter took overwhelmingly after him. He folded back his side of the comforter and slid into bed.

"Poor Audrey? How so?"

Nina sighed, a deep, alveolar release of regret. "I told her about my surgery last night, and she barely even reacted. She just said okay, just as long as it didn't mean she had to leave Goldengrove. I told her I had something called cancer and that it wasn't making me sick yet but that it would if doctors didn't get rid of it so I was going to have an operation and then some medicine that would make me tired for a while but after that I'd be better. I said I was having the operation on the twenty-fourth and would have to be in the hospital a couple of days so the good news was she was going to get to stay at Willow's for vacation. I told her I might lose my hair, but it would grow back again and I could wear a wig or something if she thought I looked too funny without any hair at all, and she just nodded and said okay."

For a minute, both Nina and Martin were silent. Then Nina shook her head. "*Okay*, from a kid who asks questions like, 'How do people know what shape atoms are if they can't actually see them?'" Nina turned to Martin. "You know what she asked me the other day? She asked me how CPR can work if the air you're blowing into the other person's lungs is already deoxygenated. I told her I had no idea." She laughed a little bit. "When I had the scare with my leg the first thing I did was look up cancer in the encyclopedia. Granted, I was twelve at the time, but I wasn't Audrey.

"I didn't know what to do, if I was supposed to push it more. I mean, I'm not sure she even heard what I *was* saying." Nina sighed again. "Part of me was just so relieved not to have to say any more."

Martin didn't know either if Nina should have pushed more; he would not have felt any differently about the conversation than she did. If talking to his wife was out of his ken, then what help could he possibly be, advising on how to handle the subject with a seven-year-old child? *His* seven-year-old child, though that perhaps made it worse; he knew he was often guilty of seeing Audrey from much too narrow a remove. She was very much like him, though: rigid, serious, intellectual. Were it up to him, what he would give his daughter was the facts. Just data; no interpretation; no emotion. That was what comforted him, absolutes. That Nina had cancer was an absolute. That she would have surgery, chemo, and radiation were absolutes. That she would lose her hair, suffer, die from this disease—those were not.

"Well," Martin said. "It sounds to me as if you did just fine. You did just what I do with patients, tell them what they need to know in terms that are appropriate, and then give them a chance to ask questions. Overwhelming them with too much all at once is as much of a mistake as not telling them enough."

Too late, he recognized the fallacy of the argument: this was his child they were discussing, not some post-infarct senior citizen. He braced himself for Nina's anger and was surprised instead to see her nod her head.

"Kind of like that old joke about the birds and the bees, I guess."

"I don't think I know it."

"This little boy comes home from school and asks his mother where he came from, so she launches into the whole thing about the birds and the bees. He gives her this horrified look and says, 'no, I just meant did I come from California like my friend Johnny?' I guess the message is not to apply adult assumptions to child thinking, or something like that."

Martin shifted himself a little closer and placed his hand on Nina's bent leg. "I must be better at that than I would have thought. That's about the level of discussion about sex I ever had with my boys, I'm afraid. 'You came from Deacon-Davis Hospital. Any more questions, ask your mother.'"

"Somehow, hearing that doesn't surprise me at all." Nina smiled a little, then laid her cheek on top of her knees, rocking herself. After a moment, she lifted her head again and looked at Martin. Her smile had vanished. "Jesus, Martin," she said. "I have cancer." Her voice was quiet, but full of grief and wonder, and Martin knew precisely what she meant. A hundred times a day at least, it surprised him. Nina had cancer. His wife had *cancer*. How could that have happened? How could that be possible?

"I know, sweetheart. I'm so sorry."

Nina's whole body shuddered, and Martin thought that she might start crying, but when she spoke again her voice was clear. "Do you trust Dr. Tredway?" she asked. "I mean, mastectomy…Even after that stupid Dr. Hughes was so blunt with me, I never thought— There's this weird thing that I've been trying to do."

"What weird thing is that?"

"I guess it's trying to psyche myself out. I keep trying to imagine my breast as this terrible thing, this poisonous, rotten *something*, like a bad piece of fruit, that my body just has to get rid of as fast as it can. I bought this tape of affirmations yesterday, guided imagery stuff Dr. Tredway said some patients use to get themselves through surgery. She said there was this one about imagining yourself as the sky, something that needles and scalpels and whatever couldn't touch, and I really liked the idea, but—"

Martin put his arms around his wife carefully, his eyes fixed on a baby photo of Audrey on her dresser. It was one he had never particularly liked. Hairless and naked, it looked like a picture of any baby, except Audrey's face wore the slightest hint of a scowl, an unexpected look of accusation that Martin couldn't help imagining was about what an ugly business all of it was, this world. "Is it helping?"

Nina shook her head. "Not really. Isn't it ridiculous, though, to mourn this thing that really is so awful, just a *part* of myself? I mean, if I don't get rid of it, it really is going to kill me."

"It's not ridiculous." There was more that needed to be said, but Martin struggled for the words that would come next. "But it doesn't change things, Nina. The surgery, I mean. To me, you'll still be beautiful."

"We'll see." Nina smiled unhappily, cupping her hands over her biopsied breast. "You haven't seen it yet. We'll see how beautiful you think I am when I'm some kind of lopsided circus freak."

"It's just tissue, Nina. It's just fat and skin." Martin didn't believe it, himself, but he shared the single thought of consolation he'd been able to come up with over the past two weeks, an image that had come to mind in the middle of one sleepless night, a sepia-tone picture of a Grecian urn from one of his secondary school texts. "You'll be an Amazon, a Greek warrior. Amazon women would cut off one breast for better aim with their bows and arrows, Andromache and Phoebe and Ainia, who fought at Troy."

"It isn't *just tissue*, Martin. It's my womanhood, my sexuality, and now you're belittling it. It's not enough that I have to worry about dying, about being cut apart. Now I have to be ashamed about how shallow I am, too."

"I'm sorry. I didn't mean it that way."

"It wouldn't be *just tissue* if it was your penis we were talking about, would it?"

"No, it wouldn't." Martin paused and said again, "I'm sorry."

Nina tipped her head back against the bed, her eyes squeezed shut. "No, *I'm* sorry," she said at last. "I think I'm trying to pick a fight. It's just—I'm crawling out of my skin. I want this to happen now, I want it go away. I could hardly expect you to understand the way I feel when I don't understand it myself. I'm so turned around I don't even know what I think.

"What do *you* think, Martin?" she continued. "We haven't really talked at all. Am I weak? Am I frivolous? Are you angry with me? I'm angry with me. Do you think this whole thing is my fault?"

Martin's mouth was dry. "Of course I'm not angry, Nina. How could I be? Cancer is—" He paused. "I suppose there are some cancers you could argue certain people bring on themselves. Some of the lung and liver cancers, for example. But breast cancer is a biological roulette wheel, a cellular signal gone haywire. It isn't something you did. You had no more control over this than you did the color of your eyes."

"I could have found it sooner, though. I could have actually *done* monthly breast exams, instead of just saying I did."

I could have noticed it, too, Martin thought. "Maybe, or maybe not. Dr. Tredway and Dr. Kennett both said it was a fast-growing cancer. Who knows how quickly it developed?"

"Jesus," Nina said quietly. "Do you think Dr. Tredway will be able to—" She opened her eyes and looked at Martin. "Martin, I want you to tell me. What do you *think?*"

Martin held his wife's gaze and breathed deeply, then answered the question Nina had started to ask, the answerable question of whether he thought Dr. Tredway would get her cancer out. He explained to Nina the correlation between the number of surgeries a doctor like Susan Tredway did and how well her patients fared; he discussed the many advances that had been made in oncology. There wasn't just chemotherapy and radiation; there were all sorts of high-tech treatments—proton beam, biological and immunological therapies, tumor antiangiogenesis…

He kept on talking, even though he knew he wasn't answering the question Nina really wanted to know. He knew what his wife was asking from him: the slippery, shapelessness of the stuff—the nameless, primeval stuff—that churned in his guts, a messy *thing* he could pull out with his bare hands and offer up to her. But how could he do that, when sitting in Susan Tredway's office a week earlier, the overwhelming feeling he'd experienced had been not rage or fear or sadness—any of the acceptable emotions he had expected—but something strangely akin to relief, a simple, undecorated moment of *yes?* Staring at the ugly, tentacled image of Nina's mammogram, he had been unable to shake it, no matter how selfishly shamed he was, no matter how hard he tried. At long last, there it was: the sword that had hung over Martin for so many years had finally declared itself, and he had realized at once that it was something he had known all along. Of course it was Nina. Of course he would lose her. The foolish thing had been thinking he had ever had a right to the happiness he felt in his life with her.

ALMOST EIGHT YEARS AGO, Martin had been standing as close as possible to the door of St. Serafin Hospital's brand-new Nuclear Cardiology and

Stress-Testing Center, wearing a tuxedo and a frequently checked watch. He'd been pressed into taking the chief of service's place at the center's ribbon-cutting—last-minute family obligations; it would be good for Martin to make nice with some of the hospital administrators—and had used up his store of small talk and patience hours before. A young woman with long auburn hair (stunning, lovely; young enough to be his daughter) had come over to him and introduced herself. She'd asked if he was on staff; he had asked the same; he soon knew that she was the human resource manager for the construction company that had built the center, and she that he had spent three decades at St. Serafin successfully avoiding these sorts of things. For the past two hours, she'd been dodging the mournful architect she'd recently ended things with. This was the first time he'd been in formalwear since his divorce.

When the conversation reached its natural end, they'd stood side-by-side, both rattling empty glasses, him nervously, and then she had turned to him with a wicked smile. "So what time *is* it, anyway?"

Something about the moment had emboldened Martin—Nina's playfulness, the way her smile lit her face, the very sense he had that this incandescent young creature was drawn toward him. She had gotten new drinks for both of them, and when they'd finished, he had suggested that a new Italian restaurant walking distance from the hospital made desserts far more appealing than the sodden éclairs and pecan tarts borne by the waiters circling them. Nina had given him her arm and a stream of lively conversation over coffee and tiramisu. On the walk back to St. Serafin, however (hours after the end of the reception, and Martin's self-imposed ten o'clock bedtime), she'd grown silent—suddenly awed, Martin had thought solicitously, tenderly, no matter how ridiculously, by the momentous *thing* that was talking place between them. In the parking lot, he saw despair beneath her glibness as she said perhaps they'd do this again the next time St. Serafin opened a nuclear cardiology and stress-testing center, and, in a moment that hadn't been Martin—not ever, not before or since—he'd taken her into his arms and kissed her. Her mouth was hot, slightly flavored with mint. She wore bracelets, which fell down her arm like music as she wrapped herself around him. In high heels, she almost matched him for height and he had to close his eyes against the heady pleasure of her hips meeting his, her breasts pressing up against his chest.

after

Eight years later, when Martin thought back to that night, what came to him first was a memory of Nina's hair. How he'd slid his fingers through it, the feeling somehow reminiscent of the pull of sand beneath his feet as waves washed backwards around his ankles. The way, covertly, guilty as a little boy, he'd breathed in the smell of it, a scent of ripe melon and sunshine. How he'd awakened at dawn the following morning in an unfamiliar room, his head on an unfamiliar pillow, and seen the dark locks of it tumbled around Nina's sleeping head, like ribbons on the most extraordinary gift, wonderful and undeserved, he'd ever unwrapped.

Even then, he had thought to himself, *No. I cannot.* He would awaken her—he would not skulk away like some twenty-two year old—apologize for his unseemly forwardness, wish this lovely young lady all the very best. It had been for him a remarkable evening, a memory he would take with him and get great pleasure from revisiting, and that would be that.

nine

THE OPEN PARKING SPOT in front of the hair salon had to be a sign.

For more than a week now, Nina had been steeling herself daily to make an appointment with her regular stylist to cut her hair off, but she couldn't get herself to complete the call. Half the time she only dialed the first couple of numbers before she put the handset down; twice, she had hung up on the receptionist in the middle of her affected-British *Thank-you-for-calling-Davis-Hairdressing* hello. She'd been going to Ingrid as long as she and Martin had been in Cabot, and didn't want to have to explain why, after five years of "just even it up," she was cutting her hair short; she didn't want to run into anyone she knew and have to explain the same—mothers from school in for facials or cherry-red manicures in the downstairs spa, older women she'd known from childhood in for their weekly shampoo and set.

With an hour to kill between dropping Audrey off at school and her scheduled arrival at the Rutherfords' house to walk with Jenny, she had come through downtown Cabot with a handful of potential errands mind...*if* the light rain speckling the windshield didn't turn into a full-on shower; *if* she could find a spot on one of the side streets where the parking was free. When the little green Volkswagen pulled out half a block ahead up Center Street, she assumed one of the cars in front of her would swoop into the space; when she pulled in and saw not only that there was still almost two hours left on the meter but that the space was right in front of a little hair salon, the name *Sheryl's* pasted to the door in hardware store letters, she asked herself: Why not? It was a place she had noticed before with some pity, a homely shop on a block of gilt and etched *Bellavisos* and *Golden Doors*; inside the empty salon, she could see a single hairdresser—Sheryl herself, presumably—straightening rows of shampoo bottles and folding towels. She checked her watch, deliberating; Jenny was making meals for her surgery and had the day scheduled so they could walk while something particular (a lasagna? A casserole?) was baking. Then she grabbed her purse. The pathology report from Dr. Tredway had arrived on Monday, the final, fleeting possibility of a false positive diagnosis firmly squelched. The words were there in black and white now, irrefutable, infiltrating ductal carcinoma, right upper outer quadrant, HER2/neu negative, tumor grade 3. Dr. Tredway's voice on the telephone had been filled with warmth and regret. She needed to do this. It was time.

The salon smelled of eucalyptus and tinkly, New Age-y music played from overhead speakers. Sheryl, a young, streaky blonde with heavy black eyeliner, looked up from her folding and gave Nina an anxious smile.

"Good morning," she said. "Can I help you with something?"

Gesturing behind her to the *Walk-Ins Welcome!* sign in the front window, Nina said, "I was hoping you might have time to do a haircut."

The hairdresser moved the stack of towels and looked around her shop. The small space was immaculate, with a manicure table and shampooing station, a corner walled off with purple curtains to create a laundry room/business office. The stylist's voice was good-natured but a little rueful when she answered Nina. "I think I can fit you in. Give me just a second to put this stuff away."

In the chair, Sheryl combed through Nina's hair with her hands, her fingers sliding in behind Nina's ears, massaging her scalp. Nina watched her hair cascade around her mirrored reflection, a shimmering brown collar on top of the black vinyl cape. So this was it, then? She was sorry she hadn't known that when the alarm clock had gotten her up three hours earlier. What kind of useless ritual of mourning might she have performed, shampooing her hair over and over, brushing it with a ritualistic 100 strokes, sobbing over the loose hairs she normally swept into the trash without a second thought?

"Beautiful hair," the stylist said. "What did you have in mind?"

Nina extracted a hand from beneath the cape and held it against the side of her ear. "Something like this."

"Seriously?" the other woman asked.

"Seriously. I decided it's time for a change."

The stylist came around to the front of Nina's chair, leaning against the counter while she studied her from the front. Her tight jeans made sharp lines across the tops of her thighs. "Were you thinking about donating it to charity? Back in the fall, I did a bunch of donation cuts for one of the sororities. They had a member who had cancer, so they did it for a moral support kind of thing then donated all of it to Locks of Love. One of those places that makes wigs for little kids."

Nina nodded. "I was thinking about doing something like that."

"I'll cut it dry, then, take most of the length off. After that, we'll give you a wash and you can tell me what you had in mind for a style."

Sheryl combed Nina's hair back and then plaited it into a long, thick braid. When she was finished, she raised her silver scissors for Nina to see. "You're sure about this, now?" she asked.

Nina nodded. "Go for it."

The scissors bit into Nina's hair with a crunching sound. She couldn't suppress the quick shudder that gripped her, the memory of the last time she'd cut her hair short, as a teenager, in the thrall of newly crowned Olympic gold medalist Dorothy Hamill. Wearing braces, her skin red and pimply, she had sobbed to realize the haircut had not endowed her with the skater's elfin beauty, her gleaming white smile. Escorting her weepy daughter from the hairdresser's shop, her mother's only comment had been to remind her she'd said beforehand she didn't think Nina would be happy with the cut. "I hate it," Nina had sobbed hysterically. "I look like a boy!"

Now, a few grinding cuts and it was finished; two decades of ponytails and elegant updos over in a matter of seconds, the hair that had been part of Nina, part of the image of herself her mind's eye had for so long held, suddenly something entirely separate, dull, inert. Sheryl held the braid in the air so Nina could see it.

"There it is," she said. "No turning back now."

Nina touched the back of her head, the empty space. In the mirror, she was surprised to see she still looked like herself. "No, indeed."

She shook her head, shivering at the sensation of hair brushing against the line of her jaw, the cool rush of air on the back of her neck.

She watched as the stylist coiled the hair then slid it into a plastic bag. On her lap, it weighed almost nothing at all, and in an instant it was decided. The price tag for a custom wig could run easily into the thousands. What if she hated it, found it uncomfortable? She might decide it was easier to wear a baseball cap or scarf. Real wigs worked for children because it was their parents—their mothers—who washed and styled them; Nina could imagine a little girl with long hair the color of her own wrapping the hair around her finger, laying a swath of it across her upper lip to smell as she curled up in her bed.

The plastic bag crackled as Nina picked it up and set it on the counter in front of her. "You wouldn't happen to have the address for Locks of Love, would you?"

AT THE RUTHERFORDS', NINA gave the front door a perfunctory knock and then let herself in without waiting for a response. She wasn't terribly late—less than half an hour—but the house already smelled of oregano and sautéed garlic. Jenny's voice came from the kitchen. "Nina?" she called. "I'm in here."

Jenny was at the stove, stirring a wooden spoon around a sizzling pan. "Don't be mad," she said, without turning. "I have a very ambitious day of cooking and baking planned, so I got started without you. I'm almost done with the lasagnas and I did the turkey-rice casserole. Yesterday, actually. I'm thinking chicken pot-pie, and since I'm already making crust, strawberry-rhubarb. I found some berries in the freezer from last summer but they're double-bagged so they still should be pretty good."

"Wow," Nina answered. She crossed the room to kiss her friend on the cheek. "I should get cancer more often. Sorry I'm late."

Jenny turned, her mouth opened to respond, then stopped. "Nina!" she said. "Your hair. It's—"

"Gone," Nina interrupted. "Tell me about it." Sheryl had taken great care with Nina's final cut, even though Nina had told her she didn't need to work too hard on it. Nina had been more pleased than she had expected with the results.

"Not that. I was going to say, I don't know. 'Great.' Or maybe, 'cute.' When did you cut it?"

"Just now. You're the first person to see it."

"Why didn't you tell me you were doing it?" Jenny wiped her hands on her apron. "I would have gone with you. I was thinking that I might get mine cut, myself. You know, for moral support."

"And get me in trouble with Jim for letting you turn yourself into Little Orphan Annie again?" Nina ticked her chin at a photo on the refrigerator of her friend holding an infant Silas. In the photo, the younger Jenny's hair was a bushy mass of copper curls, her shoulder-length waves having been recently chopped in a fit of new-mother pragmatism. Jenny had confided once that Jim hadn't gone near her sexually for four full months after Silas was born—a dry spell she attributed more to the haircut than any lingering shock over anything her husband might have witnessed in the delivery room. "No thanks."

Nina told Jenny about the parking space on Center Street, the little hair salon with the hardware store lettering. "I actually didn't know I was going to do it until I walked through the door. And anyway, you've already done more than plenty here."

Jenny's countertop was crowded with tomato cans and noodle boxes, a cutting board with several mounds of chopped herbs, mixing bowls piled with meatballs and ricotta. Nina picked up a wrapped triangle of Parmesan cheese, then set it back down. "Haven't you heard of the frozen food department? This is way too much work."

Jenny reached for the mixing bowl with the ricotta and cracked an egg against the side. She shook her head. "Not too much work." With a fork, she whipped the egg and ricotta, her body jerking with the effort. Nina watched her add two of the little mounds of herbs, then grind salt over everything. "It's the least I can do."

For a while, the two women worked in silence. While Jenny assembled her lasagna, Nina sat at the kitchen table, trimming rhubarb and drinking a cup of green tea Jenny had insisted she have. As she worked, she tucked the longer front sections of her new haircut behind her ears. One piece slipped out and she smoothed it back again, making a huff of exasperation as it once more swung forward, grazing her cheek. Jenny watched her.

"Seriously, Nina," she said, "That cut looks great on you. I've never seen you with short hair. You should keep it like that."

Nina resisted responding *I'd be happy if I could keep it at all;* from

Jenny's expression she could see that her friend had gotten to the same place herself. "I don't know. I think I kind of look like I'm trying for a Ghost-era Demi Moore, only without the gorgeous face and the deep, husky voice."

"Ha," Jenny answered. "Demi Moore should be so lucky. You look about twenty."

"Wouldn't that be nice."

"What, being twenty again? I don't remember it being so great the first time around."

"Really? I loved it. All that freedom and no responsibility. All those boys, all that sleep—"

Jenny made a face. "I was fat."

"Really?" Nina repeated herself, only half-listening. There were still times it surprised her to realize she *wasn't* twenty any longer. Like everyone else, she often found herself publicly shaking her head over how much faster time went by now that she was older, but privately, she wasn't sure if that was true. When she thought about her life generally, as a *thing*, it seemed remarkably long (forty-three *years*? It was nearly endless), but if she were to think back on any single, specific event—her high-school graduation, for example, or her parents' funeral—it didn't seem as if it had happened long ago at all. It felt to Nina that the amount of time that passed between events was not absolute but relative, as if her life traveled some sort of elasticized path that could be stretched or contracted at *somebody's* will, if not her own, and she wondered aloud to Jenny when they had stopped being twenty. Shook her head at her friend's response: about twenty years ago.

"Isn't that—" Nina paused, "*incomprehensible?* I have no idea how I got to be a grown-up—a parent—a person in charge. There are days I look at Audrey and I think, *are you kidding me?* It makes me wish I could apologize to my mother. When I was a kid, I used to get so mad at her when she'd tell me she wasn't perfect, she didn't have all the answers, she was just a person, because I always thought, What do you mean? *Of course* you know everything. You're a *mom*."

"You mean she didn't? We don't?" Jenny laughed. "Just wait until Audrey is Silas's age. Neither of you will harbor any illusions about how little mothers know."

Again, as soon as the words were out of her mouth, Jenny looked stricken. This was the part that Nina hated; the awkwardness that she had feared. Was there any topic that wouldn't threaten with landmines? Quickly, she asked her friend, "I know this is a totally clichéd question, but if you could go back, would you do anything differently? I mean, seriously. Would you?"

Jenny had finished her second pie crust, sandwiched it in waxed paper and put it in the refrigerator. She wiped her pastry board with a sponge, scraping scraps of dough into her cupped hand and brushing them into the garbage. She had taken her rings off for baking; now, she reached for them again. Nina watched her friend's hands as Jenny put on her wedding ring, corkscrewing the gold band around her knuckle with effort.

"I don't know," Jenny said. "I guess I might be a little more aggressive about going back to work again once Willow was in school. It seemed like every year there was a reason not to—somebody or other was having a hard time, then my mother died, then before I knew it, boom. Ten years with nothing to put on my resume but PTA positions."

Nina nodded. Jenny asked her, "What about you?"

"Well," Nina said, "I don't have any regrets about work. Reading job applications and explaining health care benefits to high school grads isn't quite as noble as teaching seventh-grade English."

"Eighth-grade English," Jenny corrected her. Jokingly, she added, "Please."

"What about—" Nina waved her hand "—other stuff? You know, Jim, the kids, living here."

Jenny looked around her kitchen. For a moment, her smile was small and pleased. "No," she said. "I've always loved it here."

Nina envied her friend's equanimity. Jenny and Jim's house had once been Jenny's parents', bequeathed to Jenny by her father after her mother died. Growing up, it had been the kind of place that had awed Nina—a baronial stone cottage set on one of Cabot's meandering back roads, the sort of place where a groundskeeper in Wellington boots and a Barbour jacket wouldn't look out of place, driving a flock of stout sheep into their pen. Jenny graciously disparaged her house's shortcomings—her kitchen was older than she was; every day, another of the floor boards acquired a squeak or popped a nail; she would trade the solitary boxes of her first floor rooms for Nina's great room any day—and Nina knew it wasn't false modesty, but after all these years, she still couldn't pull up to the tree-lined turnaround without feeling a little insecure.

Would she feel the same as Jenny if she'd lived in her best friend's Cabot? She supposed she would. In high school she had dated boys who had shared Jenny's calm assurance about their place in the world—boys whose parents poured them wine at dinner before they were old enough to drive; boys who just assumed that you'd have sex with them, not because they thought you were easy, but because it was part and parcel of the sense of entitlement with which they had grown up.

"You're lucky," Nina said. "Me, I guess I'd have slept around a lot more."

"What?" Jenny's eyebrows shot up disapprovingly. "Nina—"

"Oh, please. Don't go getting all Catholic on me, Jenny. I mean, come on. If I had known that this was going to be it, I would have put my boobs out there a lot more when I still had the chance. If I had known they had an expiration date—" Nina trailed off.

Jenny closed her eyes, covering her face with her hands. "God, I'm such a jerk. I'm sorry."

"No, you're not. You don't have to apologize. To tell you the truth, I'm kind of glad to know that you're not looking at me and thinking *cancer, cancer, cancer* every second."

"I am, though." Jenny opened her eyes again. "So maybe that's why I'm sorry. I just keep looking at you and thinking, Why is this happening to you? Why? It must be driving you crazy."

The truth was that Nina had gotten over her inclination to ask *why* a long time ago, a question that carried with it the implied belief there might actually be an answer, a god. People were born, they lived their lives, they died. Nothing Nina had experienced to date—not her parents' deaths, not Audrey's struggles—had compelled her to find human existence more complicated than that. She had wondered from time to time if her acceptance of her life's smallness suggested that she was too simple, her cognitive capacity for the big questions insufficient, but as far as she had been able to tell, life was very much a sequence of actions and consequences, impulses and thought-out decisions that were acted upon and that intersected with the impulsively undertaken and well-thought-out actions of others. She had acted and things had happened. Others had done things and their actions had affected her. Her father had insisted on keeping a dinner date in the middle of an ice storm, driving his old Lincoln instead of her mother's new Camry with the airbags and anti-lock brakes. When the knock had come at her door well after midnight—*Nina's* door, because her brothers both lived on the other side of the country; because her mother's handbag lay against the window of the overturned car, still zippered tight, Nina's name printed on an emergency contact card inside—no particular piece had fallen into place; in the months and years that followed, she'd gained no perspective from it all, no light bulb over her head.

As a child, she had believed. Most Sundays, the Baldwin family had taken its well-scrubbed place in the balcony of the Episcopal church in downtown Cabot, and along with her Sunday school classmates Nina had acquired a mental model for the bearded man in the clouds, the wrathful Bible God who sent plagues and darkened skies and offered mercy only at a very high price. She had believed in God through her first medical scare— surely He had delivered her then, when she'd prayed she'd try harder in math class, stop arguing with her mother about so much, if only He'd make it so she didn't have cancer. It had been a few years later when doubt had entered; Nina had been a teenager, watching a grainy, silent, documentary film of the Hindenburg disaster in her American history class. The part that had shaken her had been not the explosion of the zeppelin itself, but the footage that preceded it: crew members on the ground, wrangling docking ropes; eager passengers peering from the basket, waving; the swaggering captain, spliced-in images of him debarking from a successful 1936 flight. They were doomed, they all were doomed, and none of them had the faintest clue. Nina found it excruciating to watch their foolish innocence, to know about them what they did not, to be helpless to watch as their tragedy played out. Strangely, when the Hindenburg had finally gone up in flames it had come as almost a relief; finally, the people on the screen had equal knowledge of the horror that had been lying in wait for them.

If there was a god question at all, it seemed to Nina that it wasn't *why?* but *how?* How could there be a god with the capacity to simply *regard* each and every human life, knowing not just that a catastrophe was coming, but what the specific catastrophe was? It wasn't that she didn't want to believe; she truly didn't believe that there was a God out there somewhere who had flipped through His giant cosmic rolodex, come across her card, and thought *hmmmm, Nina Baldwin, maybe a little breast cancer to shake things up.* At her cancer team meeting, Dr. Kennett had said it was possible that everyone had little cancers growing in them all the time, exploratory mutations the immune system was able to squelch before the rogue cells could form any grand ideas. One had gotten by her, maybe when she had been fighting off a cold or worrying about Audrey. She was going to be treated by one of the best cancer teams at one of the best cancer centers in the world, and there was no place for *why* in that. If God had something to add to the equation, a degree from Harvard Medical School, Nina wasn't aware of it.

What she *was* aware of was that she didn't want to continue following this particular line of thought with Jenny. She wanted things to be normal, for the two of them to be able to talk like it was any other Thursday morning when they would complain about their husbands and their children and the endless list of house-related tasks they were each ignoring, in a joking sort of one-upmanship. If she allowed it to, the subject of cancer would coil itself around her like a python, squeezing tighter each time she took a breath.

She nodded in agreement with her friend. "In any case," she said, "you're right. It's not like wishing I'd slept around more is some kind of noble goal."

Jenny shook her head. "No, I'm not right. I didn't mean to sound like such a priss. You do know, don't you," she added, her expression proud and at the same time sheepish, "Jim and I were— Jim's the only man I've ever been with."

Nina and Jenny had had this conversation before. "Martin, on the other hand, is not."

"Right," Jenny said. She turned toward the dishwasher, her back to Nina, a signal, Nina figured, that the conversation was done.

ten

Dr. Tredway reached across her small maple conference table, squeezed Nina's hand, and smiled. "Now, then," she said. "What questions can I answer for you?"

Though the surgeon had been the one to call this meeting, Nina's pre-op appointment, Nina felt obligated to respond—if only she could get one of the million snippets of thought caroming through her head to cohere. In less than twenty-four hours, she would be back here at Boston Met for her mastectomy, and in spite of the crowd out in Dr. Tredway's waiting room—women Nina's age wearing business suits or blue head-scarves and matching toenail polish, older women in warm-up suits and pristine white Keds, one girl who looked like she couldn't even be thirty—the surgeon had taken her time in talking to Nina, describing the surgery and its aftermath. On a pad of graph paper with the name of a medicine printed across the bottom, she had drawn pictures: a bull's-eye breast, a Mona-Lisa-smirk-scalpel-line, a tidy envelope like a coin purse in the place that had once been Nina's right breast. Once Nina was asleep, she would make incisions like *this* and *this* to remove the breast tissue; if possible, she would leave the skin (but not the nipple—that was breast tissue, too) to leave open the option for reconstruction if Nina decided that was something she wanted to have. Samples would go to pathology during the surgery to be sure all the margins around both tumors were clean; she would be doing a sentinel lymph node biopsy while pathology worked, and with any luck only a few of Nina's lymph nodes would have to

101

come out. The whole procedure would take a couple of hours; Nina would stay in the hospital that day and the next; if all went according to plan, she would be back home again within 48 hours. "But only if you're ready for it," Dr. Tredway had emphasized. "I have no qualms whatsoever about going toe-to-toe with any insurance company. I don't do drive-through mastectomies, and my patients don't go home until they're ready to."

Underneath her lab coat, Dr. Tredway was wearing a pink sweater set and a string of pearls, a gray skirt and black loafers that made her look like her next obligation was not another patient but perhaps a Talbot's catalog photo shoot. Nina couldn't quite imagine her ferocity, arguing with some faceless insurer about a patient's length of stay. She liked her, though; her questions to Martin notwithstanding, Nina trusted Dr. Tredway to take care of her. Dr. Tredway had trained at Boston Met. She was a breast cancer survivor herself.

Extracting her hand from the surgeon's, Nina made a helpless gesture and said, "I'm sorry. I think I have a million questions, but I can't come up with any of them this second. I should write them down next time, I guess."

"It's a good idea." Dr. Tredway nodded. "Lots of people also find it helpful to bring someone with them to their appointments, a second set of ears. That way, you can compare notes afterward and make sure you both were hearing the same thing."

Nina didn't think Dr. Tredway was levying an accusation, necessarily, but she felt the need to defend Martin nonetheless. "I know," she said. "I'm sorry. I'm the one who told my husband not to come. He'd shuffled around his schedule so much to do the surgery on the twenty-fourth and then when we had to cancel it—"

Nina trailed away. Three days before her planned mastectomy date in April she'd awakened with the bronchitis Audrey had brought home from school the day before spring break; the surgery had been postponed until May 2. It was May 1 now, May Day in a host of European countries, a day for children in pinafores and Peter Pan collars skipping around a ribboned pole.

"I'm sorry," she said again. "I guess I'm not particularly used to the idea of being a patient just yet."

"Don't apologize." Dr. Tredway smiled. "It's my hope you don't have to get too used to being a patient at all."

Nina's mouth was dry. There was only one question she wanted to ask: Did Dr. Tredway really think she could beat this cancer?

Dr. Tredway had hazel eyes, with flecks of gold around the irises. They studied Nina now, as if weighing whether to answer her candidly. "As we talked about in our first meeting, you've got a lousy looking tumor back by your chest wall. I'd be so much happier if we were just talking about the spot at the top of your breast."

In spite of herself, Nina laughed. "I'd be so much happier if we weren't talking about any of this, at all."

"Of course you would. I'm going to tell you what I tell all of my patients, and what, frankly, I myself live with every day. Don't stop living your life. Live *with* this cancer, but don't live it."

Nina thanked Dr. Tredway and stood. The surgeon picked up a business card and the pen she'd used to sketch out Nina's bullseye breast. "If you have any questions before tomorrow—anything—call me at any time. I mean that."

Dr. Tredway handed the card to Nina. She'd added two phone numbers to the three already printed across the front of it, the three Nina had gotten at her initial cancer meeting, her cell phone number and home. Martin didn't carry a cell phone (he kept his in his car, for emergencies only) and Nina was confident he'd never given his home number to a patient in his life. Their home number was unlisted—Nina assumed Dr. Tredway's probably was as well—and Martin had hesitated to include it even in the Goldengrove directory, a point on which Nina had teased him. "What?" she had said, "you think Goldengrove parents are going to break out the handbook and look you up every time they have a chest pain?"

Driving home, Nina turned on the radio, grateful for the small distraction it offered. A song she recognized from a children's movie came on and she flipped over to one of the college stations, a tiny act of rebellion; when she drove with Audrey, she could listen only to the local "soft rock" station. Her daughter paid far too much attention to song lyrics and the last thing Nina needed was to try to explain Nine Inch Nails or to justify why she thought the Beastie Boys' rapping about needing a girl to clean their room and do their laundry was funny. (She wasn't even sure she could explain that one to herself.) WBMB was doing its lunch-hour flashback, playing a song Nina remembered from high school. She turned the volume up and was surprised by a rush of pain, the feeling of something inside of her folding in half.

The song was not one that had had any particular meaning for her— no first kiss, no slow dance in the sweat-sock-smelling high school gym. It was something that had been popular the summer she'd turned seventeen, one of those songs that seemed to be playing every time she turned the radio on, in the bathroom in the morning, on the ride to Pennock Pond with her girlfriends, when she walked into the air-conditioned cool of the Watson Brothers Grocery store. Now, it conjured up a memory of driving home from Sally Scoops, the ice cream parlor where she'd worked, her scooping arm achy and her legs tired. It was night, the sultry air was full of insect noises; earlier in the day, a Cabot College guy had flirted with her. Nina hadn't been interested, but she'd flirted back anyway, thrilled by the possibility. Next year, she'd be going to college herself, getting out of this burg. The world stretched out in front of her like an endless expanse of green.

Was it over already? The thought took Nina's breath away.

eleven

THE NIGHT BEFORE HER mastectomy, Nina shut herself in the bathroom after Martin climbed into bed, only to emerge moments later in a black silk negligee. Martin knew he must have looked startled—he was; he'd assumed Nina had gone into the bathroom to have a long cry and hadn't been sure if he should wait, tap on the door, or fall asleep—and she gave him an almost-embarrassed smile.

"I thought we might as well both enjoy them one last time."

Shamefully, Martin felt himself respond instantly, the first ache of an erection stirring in his groin. "Is that what you want?" he asked.

"I suppose so." Nina's smile faded slightly. "I guess I thought you'd want— Well, I'm not looking to force myself on you or anything."

It wasn't that; it was, if anything, the opposite. Martin and Nina hadn't made love since she had found the lump, more than a month before, but he had dreamed about it almost every night. Smelling her skin, devouring with his eyes and mouth her glorious, heavy breasts—it had been a source of great shame. Since Nina's diagnosis Martin had felt an almost constant, insatiable appetite for his wife, and the terrible truth was that mixed in with the choking fear he felt when he thought about Nina's cancer diagnosis was a selfish, ignoble mourning for what *he* was going to lose: her physical proximity, the comfort and release of their sexual relationship, her beautiful breast.

In his first marriage Martin had had what he would have considered a normal sex drive—he and Beth made love once or twice a month, and it had been perfectly adequate. From the start, making love with Nina had been something else entirely: a mutual, consuming *want*. If they had sex at bedtime, he was ready for her again upon waking, if they made love in the morning he would daydream about it, fantasizing about when—and how—he would have her again. After Audrey was born, her desire for him had waned, replaced by explanations and apologies he remembered all too well: she was still sore, the baby had kept her up all night, she was nursing and conflicted about sharing her breasts. Eventually, her appetite had returned, but Martin had retained the sense that something—a something that was important to him, that he *needed*—had been taken from him. Even now, if Nina had made an overture every night, every night he would have been ready for her. And for the most part, he did feel that he needed to wait for her overture, like some Freudian little boy afraid of being flung back into the trauma of his infancy if he were to reach out to her and be refused.

Now, he searched his brain for the right thing to say. "I should think you already know force is never required. I just want to be sure you're doing this because you want to, and not because you want to please me."

Nina had recovered herself. She raised her eyebrows at him and said, "Au contraire, my love. I fully expect for you to please me." She crossed the room to his side of the bed and pulled the covers back. "It's not contagious, you know."

"Of course it's not. It's not that I don't want—"

"Then just play along with me, please, if you could be so kind." Nina ran her fingers through Martin's hair, running the tips along the backs of his ears and the side of his neck in a way that made him shiver. Her new haircut framed her face; it had taken almost two weeks, but Martin had finally stopped doing a double-take whenever he saw her. He had loved his wife's long hair; yet another of the many things he could not admit. "I'm not dead yet, after all."

Martin pulled himself abruptly upright. "You're not going to be dead at all."

Nina smelled of talc and the cedar closet where her nightgown had hung. She smiled a small smile and said, "Well, now, Doctor Winzer, you of all people have to know that simply isn't true. We all have to die at some time."

"At some time," Martin repeated. "When you are very old, one of those stubborn old ladies who come in and put up a fight about giving up their cigarettes because they've made it to eighty-five in perfect health and why should they change that now?"

Nina climbed across the mattress to straddle Martin's stomach, her smile a little softer now. "Okay, then. When I'm a very old lady, smoking Marlboros and drinking bourbon and still in possession of a pair of stunning, stripper-worthy silicone double-Ds."

Nina and Martin needed to be at Boston Met in the morning at six o'clock. Jenny Rutherford had taken Audrey for the night. Martin slid his hands up his wife's sides, feeling the thrilling cool of silk and Nina's curves. Firm buttocks, the inward turn of waist, the outward spread of ribs, and then those soft, glorious, full mounds. The slip rode up, clinging to Nina, and underneath it Martin discovered the humid warmth of her skin. She had no panties on. She pressed her body around Martin's, gripping his now insistent erection with her thighs. "Martin—" Nina breathed.

Martin wanted to taste her, smell her, to lay her naked on the bed and witness her every goose bump and fist clench, every arching of her back (taut-nippled breasts thrust for the sky) and flaring of her nose as he ran his tongue from her instep, around the lovely curve of her calf, past her knee and along the silky skin of her thigh. He would open her with his hands and then his mouth, probe every slippery, briny groove, proud of and humbled by his fleetingly held power to center and distill a monumental, animal need. Nina had always climaxed fiercely, a swift, almost aggrieved release of pleasure so closely guarded as it built that her orgasms often took Martin by surprise. When she cried out—he imagined it, a single, agitated *oh!*—he would take her hips and pull her to him, push himself inside her like a teenage boy.

Martin froze, reeling with the disgrace of his lust. In the morning his wife was going to lose her breast, and his stomach ached with the need to be inside her, plunging blindly toward some unformed goal. And yet: he pulled back with every shuddering fiber of self-control and Nina gave him a look of sheer incredulity. She kissed him hard and pushed him backward onto their bed. She rocked her hips, riding his bared stomach so that he felt her pulling, slippery wetness as she slid her arms through the straps of her camisole and let the fabric pool around her waist.

You goddamn fool, her eyes said. *Look at me. Get your fill.* He raised his hips to remove his pants and she lowered herself down on him, leaning her body back, reaching to grip his buttocks from underneath. He said her name and she said his back, a declaration of victory. *Love me like I'm whole,* her eyes demanded.

In spite of himself, he did.

twelve

NINA WAS GOWNED AND capped, premedicated and IV-readied, her teeth rattling with cold despite the two warmed blankets covering her. She was sitting up on her gurney, which was parked just outside the operating room, trying not to notice the way the undersides of her braless breasts pressed against her chest, trying not to imagine the difference she would feel in a matter of hours. Would her chest be bound like a Puritan teenage girl's? Would her cancerous breast be stuck in a plastic-zippered bag and discarded in a Boston Metropolitan trashcan? Six weeks ago, she had been worrying about a varicose vein on her left calf and the robust foothold a new crop of gray appeared to have established in her hair, and now she was in an antiseptic green holding room that felt miles away from the crystal May morning outside, saying good-bye to her right breast, good-bye to her old life.

Nina had thought on a day like today she might be turning over her garden with Audrey, telling her daughter about the way, when she was a girl, she would help her mother do the same job, pouncing on the blue-bladed spade with both feet, digging furrows for some of the early growers: green leaf lettuce and Swiss chard, the small red beets her mother would make palatable with a sugar and vinegar sauce. She thought she might be baking banana bread or chocolate chip cookies, arranging her schedule with Jenny's so Audrey and Willow could have a play date after school. Instead she was in the middle of a very different sort of play date of her own, about to boot the greedy internal houseguest she'd been playing hostess to for who knows how long. Every cell in her body rebelled against the knowledge of what was about to happen, screamed *don't do it!* and yet—that was exactly the point, wasn't it? A goodly portion of those cells needed to be brutally shown to the door. Nina wouldn't feel sorry for herself, not yet. After she and Martin had made love last night Nina had gone back into the bathroom and folded both hands over the right side of her chest. It wouldn't be so bad, she'd told herself. It would be just like that. She pictured Martin in the surgical waiting room in his neatly pressed khakis and button-down shirt, alone.

The anesthesiologist came out of the operating room and asked Nina how she was doing; did she need some Valium now? Nina shook her head—she was fine. The frowning doctor glanced from her to the monitor attached to the top of her bed, every line of which bore testament to her lie. "Mrs. Baldwin," he said, "I hate to argue with you."

The guided imagery tapes Nina had bought on Dr. Tredway's recommendation had instructed her to imagine herself in a place from her childhood that made her happy, and as the anesthesiologist pressed his fingertips into her wrist she tried, her brain ping-ponging from her house on Hamel Drive to her best friend Christie's bedroom to her grandparents' shingled cottage on Aggamassic Reach, in Charlotte Harbor, Maine. Nina had spent every summer from the time she was six until she was twelve in Charlotte Harbor, and for a moment she clung to it, trying to picture her grandmother's kitchen, swallowing hard to force her hammering heart back down from where it had climbed at the top of her throat. A brown refrigerator. Chairs with Band-Aids on the corners of their backs so they wouldn't gouge the soft-pine paneling of the kitchen walls. At lunchtime, it was Nina's job to dry the dishes. A little crank with a knob that always fell off opened the window above the sink that faced out toward the ocean. A steady breeze would blow, bringing in the sound of the waves and the smell of salt from the air.

"The thing is," the anesthesiologist continued, "we're running a little behind, and it isn't okay for you to suffer." The scrub-clad doctor pulled a syringe from his shirt pocket. "You're just going to have to trust me on this. Give it just a minute or two and I guarantee you'll feel a whole lot better."

Nina leaned forward, half-intending to protest. The anesthesiologist put his hands on her shoulders and said again, "Trust me. This isn't the time to prove how tough you are. Take some deep breaths, think some relaxing thoughts, and let the Valium do the rest." Nina inhaled the sharp smell of alcohol as the anesthesiologist swabbed off the top of her IV port. The needle went in, and Nina waited.

Beneath his heavy gray eyebrows, the doctor's blue eyes held hers.

"Your eyes match your scrubs," she said.

"'Atta girl." The scrub-blue eyes twinkled at Nina, then shifted over to a nurse Nina was fairly certain hadn't been standing there a minute earlier. "Stay with her for a few minutes, please, if you would," he said. "I gave her a full dose."

Nina wanted to ask, *How much is that?* but her tongue felt large and clumsy and her eyes were starting to droop. A wave rolled over her and the green walls started to sway.

Aggamassic Reach. Charlotte Harbor.

•

AGGAMASSIC REACH WAS SOME fifteen miles north of Bar Harbor and Acadia, one of a cluster of islands comprising Charlotte Harbor, attached to one another and the mainland by a rusty chain of bridges. A quarter mile separated the first of the islands from Schoodic Point on the mainland, and if you needed to you could walk across the last bridge and minutes later be in town, buying groceries at Shop n' Save or filling the gas can for the lawnmower at Arvin's Garage, and yet to Nina the island felt like the remotest, romantic-loneliest place on the planet. The island boasted only half a dozen houses and Nina's grandparents' was the easternmost, aimed out at the savage sweep of the Atlantic. The weathered houses facing the island from neighboring McKittrick Rock, close enough Nina could see shadows and light inside and the occasional flickering television when she rounded the southern point to gather blackberries, the red-hulled sailboats and the lobster boats bobbling in the harbor itself—none of them existed for her unless she wanted them to.

In the mornings, Nina helped her grandfather set his lobster traps and her grandmother hang out heavy loads of wash that would snap and blow in the wind until they were dry. Sometimes her father would wake her up before dawn, when the air was still so chilly she needed to wear a coat and pants, and the two of them would walk over to the mainland and back. He would tell her about all the marine life surrounding the island and share stories from when he was a boy. (One winter, he didn't go to school for the entire month of February because it was too dangerous to cross the iced-over bridges. A different summer, he had tried to run away by stowing himself in a fishing boat he'd never seen on the island before, figuring it was on its way to Canada or Cape Cod. The boat had been a new acquisition of one of their neighbors, of course, and he'd been not only found out but punished.) He would point north, in the direction of Lubec, and show Nina the first place in America to see the sun rise every day. On the Fourth of July Nina would bring a plastic shopping bag to Schoodic Point to collect the candy thrown out by the fire brigade in the annual parade; even without tasting it, she would vote for her grandmother's chowder in the Down Easter Chowder-Off. Nighttimes, she would go to bed early, lulled by the waves and the sound of voices coming from the first floor.

Looking back, Nina marveled at the extent to which her parents had simply turned her loose on the island. True enough, there were only dirt roads on Aggamassic Reach, the cars that traveled them too slow to inflict significant harm, and—when she was younger, at least—on most days she tagged along after her brothers, who occupied themselves with harmless pursuits. They held beach plum races; they dug clams from the mucky tidal flats with their sneakered feet; they threw pebbles at the omnipresent, hovering herring gulls. But there were days her father and brothers went out fishing with her grandfather, and she would grow fidgety helping her mother and grandmother thin carrots and knead loaves of bread. As young as eight or nine, she was given permission to venture out by herself. "Just stay out of trouble," her mother would tell her. There was a beach, a rocky-bottomed cove that on hot days beckoned with its icy-cold navy water, and all around the granite margin of the island was the raging Atlantic. From the northeast side, Nina could have slipped on a seaweed-covered rock and been gone in an instant, smashed to pieces or dragged out to sea.

The rules were simple: Stay on the island. Always keep something on your feet. (There were crushed mussels and razor shell clams everywhere, sharp enough to slice open Nina's foot.) Stay out of the woods—a dense square of scrubby pine—don't even think about going to the cove to swim without a grown-up. Stay away from the windswept outcropping where the seagulls nested.

For five summers, the worst thing that happened to Nina was a deep cut on her left knee, sustained while running, squealing, from her brothers. Every year, she returned home to Cabot brown with sun, her hair full of surprising yellow streaks. She would lie in her bed, back in her dormered room, and continue to hear the gargling cry of the seagulls and the sloppy boom of waves throwing themselves against the rocks. She'd close her eyes and see the blue of the endless sky, the point at which it met the endless ocean, and feel certain if she opened them up again it would all still be right in front of her. Charlotte Harbor and Cabot might as well have been on separate planets, so different was the way she felt about her two homes. On Aggamassic Reach she felt completely free, as sure and as wild as the elements that lashed themselves around the island; in Cabot she was plain old Nina Baldwin: an awkward girl with the wrong clothes and crooked teeth and a house that was just barely on the right side of the Charles River. She would hold her arms across her face and her skin would still smell of the sea.

The last summer Nina was at Charlotte Harbor was the summer she got her period. She was not quite twelve, and she was completely horrified. At home, she had seen her mother's supplies in the cabinet beneath the bathroom sink—the stretchy white strap of a belt, the fat pads with their long tails—and a few months earlier her mother had sat down with her to explain menstruation. Though her mother had said it would still be another year or two, and though the ugly, brick-brown smudge in her underpants looked nothing like the tidy tablespoon or so of bright red blood she had had imagined from her mother's words, when Nina pulled her underpants down she knew at once what it was. It was *gross.* Her stomach twisted with dull, heavy cramps. For a long minute she'd stared disbelievingly at the glaring evidence on her underpants, stretched out between her knees, then wadded up a handful of toilet paper. She'd tucked the paper between her legs and pulled her shorts back up. She wasn't going to have her period. Not yet.

For the rest of the day she had kept toilet paper in her underpants, flushing away one wad when it got dirty and folding up another in its place. Overnight she began to bleed more heavily, and the following morning she woke up to find a staccato of stains on her bed sheets and a corresponding circle of blood on the back of her nightgown. Her mouth dry with fear, she brought the balled-up sheets downstairs, where her mother and grandmother were at the counter making breakfast and her father and grandfather were sitting at the table, drinking coffee and disagreeing about President Nixon.

"Um, I think I need to wash my sheets." Nina sidled up to her grandmother, who was slipping poached eggs onto waiting pieces of toast, cracking new eggs into the skillet of simmering water, and spoke as softly as she could.

"Your sheets?" Her grandmother repeated. "No you don't. I just did that wash two days ago."

"Yeah, but I got them dirty again."

Nina's mother had crossed the room with an armload of plates and silverware. She set them on the table in front of Nina's father and crossed back to Nina again "Dirty how?" She held her hand out to Nina. "Let me see."

Nina cringed as her mother unfurled the sheet. At the table, the men continued to talk. Nina's brothers were still upstairs, asleep. "I think I cut myself or something. I had a bug bite I was itching."

Nina's mother frowned at the stains, then scratched at one with a fingernail and lifted the sheet up to her face. She took another step toward Nina and then sniffed audibly. "Honey," she said, "are you having your period?"

Nina felt her face burning. She couldn't answer. Her mother said, a little louder this time, her voice ringing with surprise and maybe happiness, maybe amusement, "Nina, sweetheart, you're having your period."

Quickly, unintentionally, Nina glanced over at her father. He had heard. He had stopped talking about Mao Zedong and his hands, which had been gesturing and thrusting toward Nina's grandfather animatedly, now lay posed on the table, like objects that no longer belonged to him. She looked at him and he looked at her and she saw in his eyes a myriad of things she didn't understand: sadness, hesitation, embarrassment, a little fear. He smiled quickly and then looked down at his lifeless hands and

Nina bolted out the door.

The northern tip of Aggamassic Reach was a seagull breeding ground, a bare plateau of granite that drew biologists from as far away as Cornell University and Woods Hole, Massachusetts; there was a species of seagull not normally found in the northeast, Franklin's gull, that had begun building nests there a few years earlier. Why anyone would care whether or not some group of seagulls settled on Aggamassic Reach was beyond Nina—they were nasty, belligerent birds; Neal, whose hair was light blond, had to wear a baseball cap all summer long or risk donating a clump of hair (and chunk of scalp, usually) to some bird or other's nest— but she'd always obeyed without question the rule that she had to stay away. Though the outcropping loomed at least a dozen feet above the reach of the incoming waves, the rocks were perpetually slick with spindrift, and as Nina's running feet took her toward them it was the wildest rebellion she could imagine. She would storm across the rocks, scattering the new mothers and their chicks. She would stomp on nests. She wouldn't stop moving until she reached the very edge of the outcropping. The treads on her sneakers were worn flat and if she slipped— So be it.

Nina was panting by the time she climbed the rocks, ribbed and crevassed and striped with seagull droppings. Gray-winged ring-bill gulls clucked at Nina angrily and rose a few wary feet in the air when she lunged at them. Nests woven with sticks and bits of yarn and ribbon held clutches of brown-spotted, tan-colored eggs or screaming gray chicks with black beaks and black eyes. Nina saw sections of the same waxed-paper wrapper in three different nests. She kicked the closest nest, overturning it with her sneaker. She bent over a second, her hand hesitating above a clutch of eggs before she turned.

Nina walked the entire length of the point. Between large crevasses, she could see kelp slapping along with the eggbeater rhythm of the ocean. Sawgrass grew out of smaller cracks and magenta-petaled beach roses bobbled constantly with the blowing wind. Nina's hair lashed across her face, sticking to her lips and eyelashes. An enormous, gnarled branch of driftwood lay not far from the water's edge, flung up from a storm after being worked over by the waves, and Nina sat down on it, wondering where it had come from. Schoodic Point, or farther away? Canada maybe? The toilet paper in her underpants had shifted to the back, and she scooted it forward.

Her heart still pounding in her ears, Nina thought again about her father and the way he had looked at her. Back in the spring, she'd gone with a couple of her friends to the Cabot College library to do some research for a school report and seen her father walking across the campus. Flanked by two pony-tailed Cabot coeds, he had passed right in front of Nina and her friends where they sunned themselves on the library steps. He hadn't seen her, and she hadn't called out, watching him recede with a mixture of sadness and guilt. When one of her friends had asked if that had been her father Nina denied it. The older girls had been flirting with her father in a self-assured, almost patronizing way, calling him Professor B., touching his arms, veering against him with their shambling, easy strides. He had walked with both hands gripped around the straps of his shouldered backpack, the expression on his face that of someone who wished he could be anywhere else. Nina understood her father's discomfort had been with the girls' easy sexuality, the way their breasts swung beneath their shirts, the roundness of the hips they'd bumped against him. She'd wanted to defend him; she had wanted to compete. Just wait until *she* was a woman. She'd walk right up to those girls, she'd take her father's hand—

Nina shivered and lifted the hem of her t-shirt to wipe her face. She wasn't crying but her nose was running and a fine salt spray had settled on her skin. She stretched the shirt, tenting it over her doubled knees, and rocked herself, wondering what to do next. Her stomach growled and she remembered her missed breakfast; poached eggs on her grandmother's homemade toast was her favorite. She wasn't sure how long she'd been gone but knew she'd missed her chance, regardless; she'd made a scene and run out of the house, slamming the screen door behind her, and her mother would be mad.

The first summer they'd spent at Aggamassic Reach Nina's father had helped her and Neal and Roger make messages in bottles and send them adrift from the southern end of the island, where a strong current ran all the way to the bicep curl of Cape Cod. They'd put their names and address on pieces of paper folded and sealed into sandwich bags—*Please tell us where and when you found this message!!!*—then rolled the bagged messages into narrow scrolls they'd stuffed into glass cola bottles. They'd never heard anything back, though Nina had held out hope much longer than either of her brothers, who'd argued over whose scenario for the bottles' fate was more likely. Neal thought they had probably broken on the rocks. Roger figured they'd washed up on Schoodic Point and been thrown away by someone who took their senders for a bunch of idiots. Nina hadn't thought about the bottles in years, but she did now as she heard footsteps approaching. Without looking, she could tell it was her father.

"Why did you let us make those messages in a bottle in the first place?" She scowled down at her shirted knees as he sat down next to her. "You knew they weren't actually going to go anywhere."

Nina's father shrugged. "The same reason I let you make parachutes out of garbage bags and jump off the porch, I suppose."

Nina snorted. "I never did that."

"Didn't you? I know your brothers did."

"Well, I didn't. I tried to make ice cream once with ice cubes and powdered milk and chocolate syrup."

Nina's father nodded absently, slowly rubbing his palms together. "And anyway, I'm not ready to say just yet that I've given up on those bottles. If the Labrador Current got hold of them they could be halfway around the world. Who knows? Maybe whoever found them is busy learning English so he can send you a postcard."

"Yeah, right. And maybe Susan Dey is planning to be Roger's date at his senior prom."

"Maybe so," her father agreed.

Nina shook her head, disgusted. "Do you even know who Susan Dey is, Dad?"

"I think I've heard the name. A girl from school?"

"She plays Laurie Partridge. You know, as in the Partridge Family? Tuesday nights, on channel four?"

Nina's father chuckled. "Well, then, maybe not."

For a minute, neither one of them said anything else. Most of the gulls Nina had perturbed were settled now, picking their way among the nest-covered rocks or churning skyward as they set out to fish. A bunch of fishing boats were out and the seabirds circled them in packs, eagerly awaiting toss-backs and dropped chunks of bait. Nina couldn't wait any longer to ask. "So is everyone out looking for me?"

"Nope. Just me. Mom and grandma went into town and grandpa's reading the paper. Your brothers are still in bed, I think. Your mom said I should leave you alone, but if I found you, to tell you that she's sorry."

"Sorry for what?" For the first time since he'd sat next to her, Nina looked at her father. "Why couldn't she tell me she's sorry herself?"

"That," he said, "is something that's between you two girls." Nina's father ruffled her hair and smiled but she saw on his face again the expression that had sent her running from the kitchen earlier. "You're growing up, sweetheart. I know it's not always easy between mothers and daughters."

Panicked, Nina quickly stood. Zoology professor or not, there was no way she was having a conversation about puberty with her father. Indeed, when they had had their menstruation talk, her mother had lectured her about the importance of keeping her body's shenanigans private— wrapping her used maxi pads in toilet paper and pushing the bundles down to the bottom of the wastebasket, not leaving blood-stained underpants, which should be soaked in cold water, lying around where her brothers or father might see—as if she would! Tears Nina hadn't needed to cry earlier crowded against the back of her throat.

Once again, the handful of birds closest to Nina erupted, filling the air with their angry screaming. Nina's father stood, too, shielding his eyes with one hand and pointing with the other. "Right there. That one and that one. See the gulls with the black heads and the black legs? That's a couple of Franklin's gulls right there." Nina's father scanned the rock plateau, looking for nests. "They both must have a clutch of babies around."

Nina nodded wordlessly. Her moment of terror was over, leaving in its place relief and, for some reason, a vague sense of disappointment. She looked the direction her father pointed and then at her feet, the rubber toe caps of her sneakers gravel-scarred from where she'd dragged her feet to stop the swings at recess when she was in a hurry. She'd made an idiot of herself, just like she had the day she'd stomped up to Sean McDeavitt to tell him she didn't have a crush on him and she never would. He'd looked at her completely baffled; whoever had told Nina that Sean had a crush on her had obviously been wrong.

"You know of course," Nina's father continued, "why we're all supposed to stay away from the breeding grounds."

"I know," Nina said quietly. "If the seagulls smell human scent on their eggs or their chicks they'll abandon them, and then they'll die."

"That's what the folks from Woods Hole say. Personally, I'm not all that convinced. For one thing, birds in general have a pretty unremarkable sense of smell, with the notable exception of the turkey vulture. And for another thing, as you well know, these sea gulls here have absolutely no compunction about taking a person on, if a little bit of hair might make an attractive addition to their nest. I find it hard to believe a little eau de Tom, Dick, and Harry in their house might drive them away."

Nina's father smiled, squinting, relaxed, and in that moment she loved him more than she ever had before. His mustard striped shirt and his denim-blue double-knit pants, his enormous watch with the braided leather strap. His crooked teeth, the top row almost hidden by his mustache, his thinning head of hair, shaggy and mousy brown. If they had been sitting, she would have wanted to crawl into his lap and smell his aftershave, hear the rumble of sound coming from his chest as he sang a song to her the way he had at bedtime when she was little.

"But most of all, I just don't buy it. It's not a biological imperative, not for any species, for parents to abandon their young." Nina's father hugged her, but carefully, as if there were some invisible force around her body that took up twice the space she actually did. Nina pressed her face against her father's shirt. She could hear his crashing heartbeat through the scratchy fabric, *kaboom, kaboom.* It felt good. It hurt.

•

"MRS. BALDWIN?"

Nina lifted her heavy eyelids. A woman in a blue outfit and a blue papery hat was stroking her hand. For a moment, she was confused—where was she? why was her mother there?—and then she remembered. It was time. She was having a mastectomy.

"Dr. Tredway is ready for you now."

Nina nodded and felt the gurney moving, herself borne through a pair of silver doors and into the operating room. She squinted against the painful brightness. More people in blue outfits moved around the room; a tray draped with a cloth of matching blue, folded over like it was hiding a present inside. The overhead light looked like the underside of a spaceship, clusters of tiny glowing circles orbiting a larger ring.

How much did you give her? One voice asked.

Ten milligrams, said another. Her vitals were through the roof. Mrs. Baldwin, we're moving you onto the operating table.

Hands moved Nina's arms and legs, arranging them, and another warm blanket was laid across her body.

"Okay, Nina?" Dr. Tredway herself loomed over Nina, her hazel eyes serious above her surgical mask. "Let's get this over with. I'm asking Dr. Finneran to start the anesthetic now."

Nina tried to nod once more, but she was sinking again. *Good-bye, me*, she thought as coherently as she could. Good-bye. She knew she wasn't supposed to swim in the cove all by herself and she willed herself to lie back in the icy water and float on the churning waves. Charlotte Harbor had been before *Jaws* came out and yet Nina had never been able to let herself float for too long, even in the protected curve of the cove, her imagination too easily hijacked by thoughts of what thing might come at her from under the water. She had to swim! Her brothers, on the shore, laughed and lashed at each other with seaweed ropes. Her mother was a blackened figure, lit all around with a halo of white, one arm lifted to shield her eyes against the sun.

"Nice and easy," she heard her father's voice say from far away, "Just like that. In a few seconds you're going to be fast asleep."

Fall 2003

thirteen

ONE TIME WHEN AUDREY was younger, she had asked her mother why she leaned up against the wall every time she got into an elevator. Her mother had said it was because she didn't like elevators, which didn't answer Audrey's question at all, or make any sense, for that matter. Why would you lean up against something you didn't like, which would only make you be closer to it? Audrey's mother had then said she didn't like the way elevators made her feel when they started to move; going up or down made her feel like she might fall over, and Audrey had nodded her head to that. That made much more sense to her; that had been what she wanted to know. It seemed to Audrey she was always getting yelled at for leaning on things ("sit up straight in your chair, Audrey"; "Don't lean on your neighbor during circle time, Audrey"), and the chastisement was unfair, bitterly so. She felt like she might fall over, like the ground was going up and down beneath her, just about all of the time.

What Audrey liked were corners, clean and hard up and down spaces where she could fold herself into a square if she needed to, and these days she needed to a lot. The second grade was starting out much harder than she had counted on, with movement first thing in the morning and math right before lunch, when her skin was so itchy from the press of her desk against her thighs and belly and elbows that just looking at all those hard black numbers on paper felt like stabbing her eyes with sticks. Griffin Edgerly had the desk next to her, and every day he smelled like bacon. Mrs. Usher-Alderbeck, Audrey's new teacher, said if Audrey was going to read different books than everyone else then she had to do oral reports for her, just so she could be sure Audrey's choices were *comprehension appropriate.* Audrey liked to repeat those words to herself, liked the way they felt in her mouth, but she didn't like doing oral reports and she didn't like the name *Usher-Alderbeck,* which sounded like how it would feel to be swept down a river and then hit your head on three rocks in a row. Audrey didn't much like her own name, for that matter, the menacing points of the A and Y, and she didn't particularly like Mrs. Usher-Alderbeck. Audrey's mother was sick with cancer. She was taking a medicine called AC-T chemotherapy, which stood for adriamycin, cyclophosphamide, and taxotere, names as sharp as glass shards when you said them. Last summer, Audrey's father had shown her a fallen tree in the town forest that had been eaten by termites from the inside out. He had pressed his foot down on it and it had collapsed in a puff of reddish dust, which had made Audrey cry, "Stop, Daddy, please don't step on it!" If the AC-T didn't kill all the cancer in Audrey's mother's body, the cancer would eat her up her insides just like the termites had eaten the tree.

Right now, the hospital room where her mother was staying had a perfect space for being square, a space that almost made up for everything else that was wrong about the room. Along the outside wall with the window, there was a little bumped out place—a jog, her father had called it—where the heating duct ran up from the basement to the roof of the building. The jog was close to, but not right up against, the corner where the outside wall met the wall that backed up to Audrey's mother's bed, and it made a space that was almost exactly as big as Audrey's hips were wide. When Audrey's mother had first been in the room, to make the space seem like it was there for some good reason, somebody had parked a silver IV pole in it and then put a chair with a turquoise vinyl cushion across the front. The first time Audrey had come to see her mother she had moved the pole to the bathroom (and yes, she had looked first; it *wasn't* the one her mother was connected to) then dragged the chair back into its place. When she crawled beneath the chair legs and came out into that little rectangle, her body almost immediately felt the right size again, as real and sure as the space it occupied. If she closed her eyes and pressed her hands against her ears and squeezed her teeth together until it made her face hurt, she could feel herself again, the edges of her shoulders and the bumps of her spine, and she could lose herself inside a place where there were no terrible smells or scary bursts of sound or people asking her if she was doing all right today.

For the most part, Audrey liked her mother's nurses, and not just because it hadn't taken them long to figure out she wasn't playing a game of hide-and-seek or asking to be coaxed from her corner. They wore pink or blue matching shirts and pants that were called scrubs and in spite of the crinkly plastic gloves they were always taking on and off, most of them had a smell Audrey liked, like soap and baby powder. They all were nice to Audrey's mother, bringing her ice chips and pillows and telling her not to worry every time she apologized for asking for something else. They'd tell her not to be ridiculous (though Audrey didn't think her mother was being ridiculous at all); what were they there for if not to take care of her? That made sense to Audrey; if *she* were the one in the hospital bed she'd be pushing the little button that called the nurses' station all the time. The medicine and the hospital were there to make her mother better and so far it didn't seem to be working. Audrey's favorite nurses were the one with the short, black hair—her name was Debbie—and the one with the long, red ponytail whose name she would turn over and over in her mouth like an ice cube: Siobhan. *Shavonne,* she'd whisper against her cupped hands, smushed in her corner. *Chivonne.*

Audrey's mother was in the hospital because of the cancer, but also not because of the cancer. Over the summer, she had started taking the AC part of her medicine, and everything had happened just the way Audrey had been told it would. Her mother got tired and threw up a lot. After a few weeks her hair started to fall out even though she'd already cut it short, like what a man would wear. When her mother had shaved her head, she had brought Audrey to the hairdresser with her—"just so you can see it's still going to be me, okay?" but Audrey had decided it was better not to say anything about that. Of course she knew it was her mother; she knew her mother by her hands, the shape of her body, the little shiny scar in the trapezoid-shaped dip at the bottom of her neck; her getting rid of the spidery brown hairs she was leaving everywhere was a relief. They were ugly. They stuck to the back of her clothes and the couch, they collected on the floor; they hung from her hairdo, around her face, like her whole body was beginning to come apart. Two weeks ago, right before Halloween,

Audrey's mother had slipped on a clump of wet leaves coming down the front steps from the house and gotten a cut on her shin that was shaped like a fishing hook. She got stitches and another medicine, and when the cut still didn't heal she skipped a week of AC-T and started wearing a funny white sock that went all the way past her knee and left little crossed-up lines all over her skin but even then the cut just got worse. Finally, she got a fever and Dr. Kennett said she had to come into the hospital for IV antibiotics, and Audrey's father said it was because of the cancer.

"So she has more cancer, now, that cut on her leg?" The first night they had been alone, Audrey and her father had sat at the kitchen table, drinking milkshakes from McDonald's as he explained to her why her mother hadn't come home after her doctor's appointment in Boston. It was a little weird, it being just the two of them, but it wasn't awful. Audrey had a question, however. Though she hadn't wanted to see the scars just yet, she knew her mother's cancer was in her breast and that she'd even had to have a breast removed (a phrase that, every time someone said it, made her imagine a skin-colored half sphere with a square of Velcro on the back, something that came off and on as easy as a pot lid). Unless the cancer had spread, hadn't all come out, how could it now be causing a problem in her leg?

"No, the cut on her leg is an infection that can't heal because of the cancer medicine, the chemotherapy. Everything in your body is made of cells, correct?"

"Correct," Audrey had replied.

"Well, the thing about the cells in your body is, some of those cells grow faster than others. Cancer cells grow very fast, and chemotherapy works on fast-growing cells. The problem is, it doesn't know how to find *just* the cancer cells, and so it kills all different kinds of cells that grow fast, including the white blood cells that fight infection and skin cells that heal cuts. Also including hair cells, by the way. That's why the chemotherapy makes your mother's hair fall out."

Audrey had nodded and sucked on her chocolate shake. She'd had it for a while now and it was getting easy to drink; she liked it when her father talked to her like this. Her father had an explanation for everything, words that made her think about real *things*, like cells and hair and skin, blocks she could see in her head and line up in just the right order.

126

Chemotherapy killed cells that grew fast, and skin cells that healed cuts grew fast, so Audrey's mother's cut leg couldn't grow new skin cells and heal. If she didn't have cancer, then she wouldn't need the chemotherapy that was killing the skin cells, and so cancer was to blame for her infection. She lined the blocks up for her father and he had nodded, yes. If Audrey's mother didn't have cancer, this cut wouldn't be such a problem.

"You could also say the cancer's to blame because the chemotherapy made her lightheaded and so she fell, though that one's a little more arguable," he said. "That one you could also blame on Mother Nature, or the fact that we live in Massachusetts, where the autumn means wet, slippery leaves, or on your father for not doing a better job of clearing off the front steps." Audrey's father had smiled, though nothing he had said was funny. "Cuts on legs can be difficult to heal, because we're always moving, and we're always putting pressure on those injured tissues."

"Right," Audrey had said. "Like walking or running."

"Exactly."

When Audrey was talking with her father, she felt every bit as real, as *there*, as she did when she squished herself into a corner. When she looked at something, she believed that what her eyes saw was right in front of her—a chocolate shake, a stripey straw, bubbles of water on the yellow "M" on the cup. She didn't feel, the way she so often did, like she was some tiny creature peering out at the world through eye-socket spaces that could fit a hundred of her whole entire body, that there were an impossible number of things to pay attention to—the pattern on her father's tie (rhombuses with lopsided ovals in the center of them), the reflection of the kitchen light off the silver teakettle, the words written in handwriting she didn't recognize on a piece of paper on the countertop, the always-running hum of the refrigerator, the annoyingly quiet tick of the clock. Audrey just knew, without ever discussing it with him, that her father saw things the same way she did. Instead of talking about things, everyone else always wanted to talk about what things *might* be, or how things *felt*, words that made Audrey's head feel fuzzy and loose.

For the four days Audrey's mother had been in the hospital, there had been school and a string of play dates and babysitters, and everywhere she went there were people who treated her like *she* was the one who had something wrong. They got too close to her and tried to hug her or to pat her hair; they either spoke to her in big, exaggerated voices and small words like she was stupid or—even worse—they talked to each other about her like she wasn't even there. They said she was brave; they called her a poor lamb or a poor thing or a poor dear; they talked about how she was eating and sleeping and doing in school like she was two years old. Even Jenny Rutherford, Willow's mother, had done it to her, right in front of Willow, and Audrey had been so embarrassed she'd had to run out of the room.

Yesterday, when one of her neighbors, Mrs. Reynolds, had picked her up from home to visit her mother in Boston, another neighbor, Mrs. O'Bryan, had walked across the lawn to put her head inside the sliding door of Mrs. Reynolds' van. "She's doing so well with all of this," Mrs. O'Bryan had said to Mrs. Reynolds. "I just wasn't sure what to expect, what to think." Mrs. O'Bryan tilted her head to where Audrey sat in the very back of the van, her arms holding open the sliding door alongside the second row seats. "Well, you know."

Audrey *did* know, and she had wanted nothing more than to slam the door shut on that nasty Mrs. O'Bryan's hands, on the hands of all the mean old Mrs. O'Bryans in the world. The truth was, for a long time now, Audrey had known that she was somehow different from the other kids, but for the most part it didn't matter. Wasn't everyone different from each other? Some of the things her teachers made a big deal about seemed just plain idiotic to her: why should people sometimes say things that were the exact opposite of what they meant, and why should Audrey care if they did? It was just a dumb way to be. Why should Audrey do things she didn't want to, like cursive writing, and definitely why should she do them without complaining? Last year, Mrs. Roy had told her it had to do with getting along, with being a *citizen of Goldengrove*, but if being a citizen of Goldengrove meant playing wedding day with Callie Burke and Molly Hadley all recess long and listening to Heather Moran sing the same stupid song seven times in a row—Audrey had counted—then Audrey didn't really care if she was one or wasn't.

Only when her mother had talked to her about it had it mattered, and then it had been scary and awful. They had talked after the worst school day Audrey had ever had, a Thursday Willow had packed up her lunch box and gone to sit at a table with another group of girls after Audrey said her sandwich smelled like dog food. Her mother had taken Willow's side and it had been worse than unfair; it had been confusing. Why shouldn't she have said that when it had been true? Willow had brought a tuna fish sandwich.

"Because you hurt Willow's feelings," she'd said, "that's why."

"But she asked me why I wasn't eating my lunch and that was the reason, because of the smell."

"But don't you think it would have hurt your feelings if Willow had said your lunch smelled bad?"

Audrey guessed so, but at the same time, it was an answer that would have made sense to her, especially if she had packed something as disgusting as a tuna salad sandwich. Her mother had said she'd teach Audrey about something called a little white lie and then told her it was something people sometimes did for onc another, as a way of being kind. Audrey hadn't understood and her mother had said it was just one of the ways human beings related to each other. By pretending? Audrey had asked. By lying?

Her mother had sighed. "I know it's really hard to understand, sweetheart, but you'll just have to trust me," she said. "You'll work your way through it in time. The thing that makes people different from animals is our ability to use words to communicate and sometimes that means we're not always straightforward. We play with words, or we fake it just a little. But somehow we still all understand what we mean."

"Well, I don't," Audrey had replied. All at once, she'd felt her throat hurt and her eyes sting. She was about to start crying. She didn't want to cry. She had thought what her mother was saying was about the stupidest thing she'd ever heard.

"I know you don't, sweetie. I wish it wasn't so hard for you."

"Well, *I* wish I was an animal. Animals tell the truth."

Audrey's mother's arms had rocked her back and forth. "Most of the time," she had said.

"No, all the time," Audrey had insisted. "I wish I was a dog. If I was a dog then I wouldn't even have to try."

On that Thursday, she'd let her mother hold her and rock her, and she'd let herself cry and cry for a sadness she didn't quite understand. All at once, it had seemed like the world was nothing but things she didn't understand. How could she know so many things but not understand anything at all? She knew her multiplication tables through the thirteens, she knew the birthday of every kid in her class and the kind and color of every car driven by every grown-up in her neighborhood, she knew all the parts of an atom and which was the heaviest element, number 108, Hassium. She knew a million things nobody else did, but she didn't even understand why being with her mother always made her feel stirred up inside, like all her bones and muscles and organs were being mixed around, and why still she was the only one who could make her feel okay again just by hugging her.

Audrey hated that her mother was sick. She knew she wasn't supposed to be angry at her for it, but still, there were all these things that were happening and her mother couldn't help her with any of it. *Let your mother rest, Audrey. Your mom isn't feeling good right now, Audrey. Sweetheart, I'm sorry, but Mommy can't hug you with both arms because of the surgery. Would a left-side hug be good enough?* No, it wasn't good enough at all. Mr. Seaton had made them play dodge ball in gym today and Brandon Melcher had thrown a ball right in her face, even though it was completely against the rules, and then he'd laughed copying the way her arms had closed around nothing and she'd fallen down. Mrs. Usher-Alderbeck had said that was sometimes how boys showed that they like you, by doing things that seem mean, but then she'd punished Audrey when Audrey had walked up to Brandon at recess and kicked him in the leg. Audrey *hated* Mrs. Usher-Alderbeck! Last week she'd said it wasn't nice for Audrey to tell people her mother had become a Buddhist nun and that that was the reason she didn't have any hair left, and that saying that didn't count as a little white lie, not at all, Sir. One of Audrey's teeth was really, really loose and it was terrible! She hated the way it felt but she couldn't make her tongue stop pushing it and she was sure it was going to come out any minute and *then* what would happen? Yesterday she'd cried in her mother's hospital room when she bit a chocolate caramel that bent her tooth almost all the way back but she wouldn't tell her mother what she was crying about, no matter how many times she asked or how long she held her arms out; what was her mother going to do about it? Even if Audrey told her mother about the tooth right now she would probably be too sick to help her by the time it got around to actually falling out. By the time Audrey's tooth got around to actually falling out her mother would probably be dead.

That was something else Audrey *did know* that none of the grown-ups around her seemed to think she did: she knew that her mother could die from her cancer, and if she died she would be gone forever.

There was nothing that made Audrey feel more like she was falling than to say those words to herself; saying them was like forcing herself to stand on the very edge of a cliff that would drop her straight down if she even took a breath. People seemed to think she didn't get it, talking about the *what ifs* when she was right in the same room, but what if was something she understood entirely. When she was younger, she'd worried about dying all the time, and she could still make herself feel the out-of-breath terror she'd felt the first time she tried to grasp the blocks of the thought that she *would,* absolutely, some day be gone from the world. Every day she was growing older, a happening she could no more stop than she could will off the pumping of her heart. She would grow up, she would die, she would be put in a box in the ground. She would be gone. She wouldn't eat or breathe or see and she would be—*erased.* It was much too big and too slippery a thought and it made her cross her arms across her body and squeeze.

Was that another thing that other people were different about, was it easier for them to talk about being dead and gone and never coming back again? Sometimes now, Audrey would practice it. This will be the last time I see a sunset, the orange and pink and purple streaks of the sky. The last time I eat a bowl of ice cream, see the sign for Joseph's Coffee House, the puzzling one that says "Not just your average [cup of] Joe," the last time I ride my bike or take a bath. The last time, forever, I hear my mother's voice saying *I love you.* Forever. When Audrey said those words to herself, she folded her arms, dug her fingernails into the squishy skin above her elbows, and held on.

Part Two

Spring 2005

fourteen

NINA LIFTED HER HAND to her forehead, shielding her eyes from the glare of the late morning sun. Far up the beach, she could still make out Martin, an upright figure moving briskly among the hand-holding couples and sandcastle-building children who heavily populated the dark strip of sand where the ocean met the shore. Though there was a concrete path that ran the entire length of the beach, Martin was determined to run on the sand, and even from this distance, Nina could almost feel her husband's exasperation at navigating this human obstacle course.

On the four mornings prior to this one, Martin had gotten up early to take his exercise, lacing his sneakers and kissing Nina's forehead while their room was still a deep, inky blue. By the time Nina awakened—still sunrise, thanks to the six-hour time change and her lingering jet lag—Martin would be back and showered, his newspaper already read, a room-service fruit plate and Nina's coffee at the ready, the latter covered with a saucer to keep it hot. This morning, however, Nina had opened her eyes to find her husband still next to her, fully awake and waiting. Even sleepy, she had understood what that signified; had quite pleasantly discovered herself to be interested, even eager.

It had taken some time, but since the end of her cancer treatment, she and Martin had made their tentative way back into the habit of making love, first in the dark, later with Nina covered by a camisole or bra, each of them adjusting to the challenges and changes of her personal geography. *The new normal,* Dr. Tredway had called it once, and though Nina repeated the phrase, embraced it, every time Martin had slid his hands up her sides a picture had materialized in Nina's head: her former body, the way it used to be. She couldn't have said what had been different this morning—the early Pacific light, silver and forgiving; the exotic crispness of the hotel sheets; the sadness and longing etched in the lines around Martin's eyes— but when Martin's thumb had traced her collarbone and circled her left shoulder she had arched her back and raised both arms above her head. It was time. She was ready. She had lain fully naked, studying her husband as he studied her. His hands went everywhere—careful at first as they caressed her chest, the fading incision lines that disappeared beneath her right armpit—stroking her once-again flat belly, sliding through her new pubic hair, thicker and curlier than the old. "Well," he'd said, his voice thick and glottal. "Well."

Where the beach curved toward the stacked white figure of the Hyatt hotel, Martin's figure melted into an indistinguishable cluster of walking and jogging figures. Nina closed her eyes and dropped her head back against her beach chair. She yawned, her sun-warmed skin goosepimpling, giving herself over to the dull, hypnotic shushing of the waves rolling up on the beach. She drew her fingernails across her upper arms, smiling, remembering.

The trip to Hawaii had been a surprise, a celebration of the end of Nina's cancer treatment and recovery. When Martin had brought the tickets home, Nina had protested—it wasn't necessary, really; who was Audrey going to stay with when they were five thousand miles away in Maui?—but Martin had been insistent. It *was* necessary; Audrey would stay with the Rutherfords, of course, just as she had through Nina's many hospitalizations; he'd arranged the whole thing with Jenny and everything was set. He had also been right. Over the past four days, the two of them had talked more, it seemed to Nina, than they had for the previous twenty-four months combined. They'd gone into Lahaina and wandered Front Street, discussing which paintings and sculptures they'd buy from the wharf-front galleries, they'd rented a car and driven the famous Hana Highway, past waterfalls and over wooden bridges, agreeing about what parts of the trip Audrey would like, the exact point at which she would have gotten bored and asked her parents to turn the car back. The subject of cancer rarely came up, and for certain miraculous stretches of time Nina thought it might be possible to genuinely forget, for that chapter to not just end but disappear, and her life to go back to exactly what it had been before.

For all the things she had lost to cancer—her breast, her hair, a great big chunk of her memory—Nina had been surprised to discover that the loss she mourned most was that of the dull predictability of her life. In some ways, she blamed herself for her cancer: not because she thought anything she ate or wore or did had caused it, but because she had so disdained the settledness of her life that had come before. The daily walks, the garden-weeding and laundry-folding, the parent coffees at Goldengrove where she'd stood just off to the side, half-listening while she made her mental grocery list. Those tiny obligations she once regarded as tedium became the touchstones she yearned for through months of chemotherapy and radiation, hours spent in Dr. Tredway or Kennett's waiting room, in the chemo chair, in the radiation gantry, trying to talk herself out of the knot of dread that had taken over her stomach. *The chemo was working, the radiation was working, there was nothing more pressing on her mind than making sure she scheduled Audrey's dentist appointment and her Goldengrove teacher conference. The news today would be good—*

Interestingly enough, when the news *had* been good, Nina hadn't been willing to believe it at first. It had been a full year earlier, just before St. Patrick's day, at her follow-up appointment after radiation therapy ended. After mastectomy, six months of chemo, and three months of proton radiation that were somehow worse than anything that had come earlier, she had met with her cancer team in Dr. Olsen's office to hear the results of her latest tests. The radiation oncologist had been late, setting off waves of panic unsubdued by Dr. Tredway's assurances that Dr. Olsen was never on time, and when he'd finally joined the group, he had given Nina a big, goofy grin that had made her think of the bizarre, lurchy smiles she often found forming on her own face in response to bad news. He'd slapped Nina's heavy file down in the middle of the conference table, and made a declaration that took some time to compute.

"I apologize for holding you up, but I've been looking for a cancer and I can't find it anywhere." Dr. Olsen had glanced around at Dr. Tredway and Dr. Kennett. "Nina Baldwin, I have the three most beautiful letters in oncology to share with you: You are status N. E. D."

Beneath the table, Martin gripped Nina's hand and squeezed it hard. "Status N. E. D.," he repeated. "No evidence of disease."

"That is correct, Dr. Winzer."

Nina had yanked her hand away—not because she didn't want to hold Martin's, but because a sensation like electric shock jolted through her body. Her knees jumped against the table's underside. "I don't have cancer, then? I'm cured?"

Dr. Olsen's goofy smile had stayed in place. "I've brought the films, and you can see for yourself. You've had what we call a complete response to treatment. There's no detectable cancer in your body."

Nina had persisted. "But that's not the same as saying I'm cured."

"If you have any cancer left, we can't find it. Have a look."

Dr. Olsen scrolled through the scan results on a laptop computer, a series of black and white pictures of her right upper chest. Oval cross-sections of rib, dark parentheses of lung, a thin white stripe that was what remained of Nina's pectoral muscle, pathetic in its insubstantiality, the mottled incline of her left breast. Dr. Olsen turned the computer to face Nina, pointing out each landmark. Nina's heart. Nina's superior vena cava. The perfect circle of her chemotherapy port. No cancer.

When he finished, Dr. Tredway had taken over. "As I think I told you when we first met, Nina, in the world of oncology we don't really use the word 'cured.' It's just too tricky. We can't make that kind of promise, that the cancer won't ever come back again. But what I can tell you personally as well as professionally is that 'no evidence of disease' is as close to cured as you will ever hear, and it's the Holy Grail, the Academy Award and the Olympic gold medal all rolled into one. You've responded tremendously to treatment. All the tests we can run indicate that your cancer is completely gone, not just these scans, but also your blood work, your tumor markers. Everything is within normal range."

"But there's still a chance, right?"

"Yes," Dr. Tredway agreed, "there is still a chance. But there's a much greater chance that your cancer's eradicated."

Nina had nodded, retaking Martin's hand. On Dr. Olsen's laptop, the last CT scan (*slice*, she thought, a word that inevitably evoked the thought of deli meat) had morphed into a screen saver, shrinking into a smaller cube that slid across the blue screen. "Are there any more tests you're supposed to do, any more drugs I ought to take? Just to be sure, I mean, that you got everything. I'm not opposed to taking the belt-and-suspenders approach."

Oddly, at that moment Nina had felt more powerless against cancer than she had at any time during her treatment. At least before, she had been doing something, bringing weapons to bear against her enemy. Now she was faced with the prospect of doing nothing, and that seemed worse to her than every misery levied by radiation and chemo combined. Abruptly, she had laughed. "I think I might be suffering from some sort of Stockholm Syndrome or something."

Dr. Kennett had answered her. "I understand exactly what you're saying, Nina, and that Stockholm Syndrome feeling is not at all uncommon. A lot of women experience it: no matter how wretched the chemotherapy is, you know it's wretched because it's killing your cancer, and when it's over—well, who's fighting what?" Nina's oncologist gave her a sympathetic smile. "The thing to understand here is that there's nothing more for the chemo drugs to fight and the best thing you can do for your body is rebuild your strength. Eat healthy and get lots of rest. You went through a very aggressive, accelerated AC-T protocol and you handled it beautifully. We couldn't have asked for a better outcome."

For a moment, Dr. Kennett's words had brought back all the misery of her six months of chemotherapy—the queasy stomach and copper-tasting mouth, ever-present despite the battery of anti-nausea meds she'd tried; the hair that had released in the shower, not just from her head but from every part of her body (she'd tried to see the bright side in that, the time she would save on shaving; the money she would save on razors and mascara). The sores on her lips and tongue and throat. The tingling hands and the blackened fingernails and the painful joints and the crushing leadenness of fatigue. She had suffered from terrible chemo-brain, her head as fuzzy on the inside as out, but at once all those individual sufferings were again vivid; worse, somehow, in retrospect than they had been when she'd actually experienced them. *If I had known what it was going to be like—if I had to go through that again—* She shook herself. Across the table, Dr. Olsen had jogged his laptop with his elbow, reawakening the screen, and the CT scans had started over in a loop, sixty-four pictures of her thorax rising and falling like a stop-motion film of breath. "So this is a stupid question, I guess, but I don't actually know the answer," she said. "What do I do from here?"

NINA HAD BEEN AS surprised as anyone else when the answer to that question proved to be a new breast. From the beginning, Dr. Tredway had been clear with her that immediate reconstruction was not a possibility, and in the months after her mastectomy, when her chest had burned with every breath and the act of lifting something as insubstantial as a coffee cup stirred a deep, unsettling blade of pain, Nina had decided she would simply go without. The decision hadn't been as difficult as she had once imagined. On the internet and in Dr. Tredway's waiting room, she'd seen more images of reconstructed breasts than she cared to count and been utterly unpersuaded by their vigorous rigidity, the bright pink scars that bisected them, the timid eyes of their nipple tattoos. Everything about them seemed like a reminder of—a monument to—loss. No plastic surgeon could replicate the supple lushness of Nina's real breast, so why even bother? She was middle-aged now, her menopause jumpstarted by chemotherapy. Signing up for an elective surgery after all she'd been through had smacked of masochism to her.

She'd made the appointment with Dr. Levinson mostly to appease Dr. Tredway, counting the chance to say hello to the nurses in the chemo unit and bring a scone to Hector, the maroon-jacketed front desk ambassador who had welcomed her at every Boston Met visit, as good reasons to go. Slight and horn-rimmed, wearing a University of Chicago t-shirt beneath his white coat, the reconstructive surgeon had caught Nina off guard. In the exam room, when she'd opened the front of her gown for him to look at her, his eyes had gone first not to the battered blankness of her right chest, but to her left breast. Her only breast. The pervert. His green eyes had widened appreciatively.

"Wow," he'd said. "Now that is just about a perfect breast. May I?"

Nina had nodded somewhat stiffly, but Dr. Levinson's fingers had been deft and professional, prodding first her breast, then her abdomen, upper back, and the tight, numb quadrant of her missing breast, and when his eyes met Nina's they were filled with a little boy's delight and not any sort of perverse avidity. "Hell, yes," he had said, as if answering a question

Nina hadn't heard herself asking. "I can do this for you. It's going to be awesome."

Dr. Levinson had made his pitch on the white butcher paper of the exam table, sketching an hour-glass torso with a single, left breast, a football-shaped incision beneath the belly button that ran from hip to hip. He would take the football-wedge of muscle, skin, and fat and detach it from Nina's abdomen completely, mold and shape it and stitch it to the right side of her chest, connecting blood vessels no wider than a human hair. Once the transferred flesh healed in its new location, he would pinch and tuck to make an areola, add a snip of earlobe to form a nipple. When that was healed, he would tattoo the nipple to get shade and shape exactly right, and in six months' time she'd have something that was all but perfect. It would look like a breast. It would feel like a breast, warm and soft. It would move like a breast, drape and sway just like her other one.

Nina had nodded, not yet convinced. "Kind of like the fourth smokestack on the *Titanic*, I guess."

"How do you mean?"

"They put it up there for balance, right? Strictly aesthetics. It looked just like the other smokestacks only it didn't actually work."

Dr. Levinson reached for a photo album that was on his desk. "What kind of work do you need your new breast to do?" he asked. "Nurse a baby? Fill out a bathing suit? It can't do the former, no; but I can promise you it will do the latter."

He seated himself on the exam table next to Nina and opened the album across her lap. Inside the book were, of course, photos of reconstructed breasts, but these were different than the dour mug shots Nina had come across in her own computer research. These breasts actually looked real, small and large, their owners carrying them proudly. Sexily. Though none of the pictures included faces (they never did, a phenomenon Nina understood and yet still found disconcerting, the consistency of the clinical cross section: from hipbones to the underside of the jaw), a couple captured just enough mouth for Nina to realize the smiles they wore were genuine, unforced.

Closing her exam gown tighter across her own chest, Nina couldn't help but see her own photo, the way it would look if Dr. Levinson were to take it now. She often thought of her torso as a house divided against itself, like those half-angel, half-devil Halloween costumes they sold at party stores, a strange amalgamation of woman and little boy. Cover up the right side and it was the body Nina had always known—her freckled shoulder and well-defined clavicle, her sloping, supple, sensitive breast. Because Dr. Tredway had had to remove part of her pectoral muscle during surgery, the right side of her chest had been left perfectly, unsettlingly, flat, with little more than a layer of skin to cover her clearly visible ribs. Her mastectomy scar ran from the middle of her chest to her armpit, curving upward in an almost elegant swoop, stippled along its length with pinpoint holes where three dozen black stitches had been knotted into her skin. The once-livid incision was mostly faded to a silvery pink, but where it had been exposed to radiation, the section across the middle of Nina's chest had keloided into a lumpy purplish asterisk that made her think, almost every time she saw it, *missing breast here*, like some kind of entirely unneeded footnote documenting the demise of her sexuality.

"You did these?" she asked. "All of them?"

Dr. Levinson nodded and Nina peered closer.

"I'm not interested in false modesty, Mrs. Baldwin. So when I tell you that what I make is a work of art, I mean it. You can count on a week in the hospital, a good amount of pain, and at least six months' recovery time, but you won't be sorry. This time next year you'll be sitting poolside somewhere in a skimpy bathing suit, and when you are, I hope you'll think to drink a piña colada for me."

In spite of herself, Nina had laughed. "You're that good, are you?"

Dr. Levinson had grinned happily. "I am."

Eyes closed, her body lit by the relentless white of the Hawaii sun, Nina had to give it to Dr. Levinson. He had been wrong about the skimpy bathing suit (and she had known he would be; even in her pre-Audrey days she hadn't been one for string bikinis or plunging maillots) but he had been absolutely right about everything else. The surgery, the recovery, the work of art. Her new breast was a remarkable—not perfect, but remarkable— match to her "old" one; thanks to diligent applications of vitamin E oil, the curved line of her abdominal incision was already fading, the scars of the reconstruction blending into the contours of her chest. Even here in Maui, on a beach liberally sprinkled with tan twenty- and thirty-somethings, Nina found herself on the receiving end of numerous admiring appraisals, a happening for which she found herself grateful, absurdly so. On the outside she kept her cool, adjusting her sunglasses, combing her short hair back behind her ears, but her stomach plunged with the thrill of being acknowledged in a way that, a year earlier—gray skinned and steroid-bloated, the beginnings of baby bird fuzz sprouting on her head—she hadn't been able to imagine ever happening again. She patted around the sand beneath her lounge chair, feeling for her piña colada glass. Brushing off the fine grit that that clung to its sweating bottom, she raised the glass in a silent salute, swirling it to blend the melted ice before she took a sip.

"For me?"

Startled, Nina sloshed the drink a little, an icy rivulet running down her arm to her elbow. She hadn't heard Martin's footfalls on the sand but he was back from his run, his shirt stuck damply to his chest, walking in circles with his hands against his hips.

"Did you just get back?"

"I walked around a bit. I didn't want to disturb you. I thought you might be sleeping."

Nina laughed, holding the drink out to Martin. "I think I might have been. Good run?"

"Hot. Very. I now see why all the Hawaii marathons begin at six a.m." Martin lifted the the hem of his shirt to wipe his forehead, revealing a strip of flat stomach. Nina felt a small shock of desire again for the sweat-stippled skin, the curling steel-gray hairs. He seated himself on the lower half of Nina's chair and took the glass from her hand. He swallowed and then grimaced comically, pushing the drink back to Nina. "That's terrible. What is it? Coconut?"

"A piña colada."

"I had no idea that was your kind of drink."

"It isn't, really." Nina swirled the contents of the glass again. "I'm just making good on my promise to Dr. Levinson. Raising a toast to his handiwork."

"Ah, I see." Martin's voice lingered on the last word, a smile replacing the frown on his lips. "Then perhaps I should order one, myself."

Nina shifted against her lounge chair, nudging her husband with her thigh. "I'd say you've already done your part."

Martin moved his hand up Nina's leg, caressing her. This was, in some respects, Nina's favorite part of lovemaking: the intimacy that came after the fact, the playful sparring, the touches that were muscle memory and not an overture to something more. In the time between her mastectomy and the end of radiation, she and Martin hadn't made love once, and the void between them had grown almost insurmountably vast. First in pain, then ill, then repulsed by her own repulsiveness, she'd shrunk from his every touch, even knowing his intent was not—not overtly, at least— sexual. In bed at night, she'd lie rigidly still, waiting for his deep, regular breaths, wracked with guilt that turned to anger and self-disgust. Martin didn't *expect* this from her; it wasn't fair of her to blame either one of them, to hold herself on the mattress like it was a bed of nails.

At her lowest, she even wondered if she and her husband had had sex for the last time; she let herself wonder if Martin might be asking himself the same question. Did people know when that happened, other people with cancer, make a deliberate decision, perhaps, that *this was going to be it*? Too ill to miss the pleasure, she still had yearned for the proximity that came after, the aura of contentment Martin fairly radiated, the easy conversations, the unagenda-ed tangling of limbs. The fact was, even before Nina's cancer, that had become the sweetest part of their coupling, the deep satisfaction of their companionability. Nina was forty-five, now. Martin was sixty-seven. Each of their bodies knew the other's, their smells and tastes and textures, the grooves on the backs of one another's teeth. There was nothing new, nothing surprising. At least until recently there hadn't been.

"Did I, now." Martin's voice was mock-serious. His cheeks twitched with the effort of suppressing his smile. "Because I wasn't certain."

"Well, you know what they say: if you have to ask—"

Martin considered that for a moment. "I thought that phrase was particular to items that were expensive, like that gallery of atrocious paintings we looked at in Lahaina. 'If you have to ask, you probably can't afford it.' Isn't that it?"

Nina agreed that it was. "I can still see my way to making that work, though. Just ask Blue Cross if they think I'm expensive."

Martin leaned over and kissed her. "But to borrow from another cliché, you're worth it."

He removed his shoes and socks and then stood. Behind him, beige sand stretched down to the Pacific Ocean. A warm, steady cross breeze blew, making all the fronds on the palms that lined the beach stream out sideways. Two years earlier, when Nina had lost her hair to chemo, Martin had cut his own hair crew-cut short. Nina hadn't thought she would like it—one of the first things she'd been attracted to about Martin was his thick, steely hair, curling almost rebelliously against the collar of his tuxedo, and later she'd come to appreciate the ironic contrast between his outer almost-unkemptness and his absolute internal order—but rather than diminishing him, the short cut had made him look younger, more rugged. For a time after chemo ended, when Nina's hair started growing back, the two of them had matched, their hair the same texture and length and color.

Martin stretched and shook his arms loosely. "I'm going to take a quick swim, then go back inside and take a shower."

Nina nodded. "I'll come down with you." Thus far, the deepest she'd gone in was to mid-thigh, but it was hot today, the water enticingly blue. She wouldn't swim, but she could see herself out with the dozen or so others who stood ribcage deep, body surfing on the gentle rollers, ducking beneath white-crested waves and popping up on the other side.

"Will you? Very good." Martin held his hand out to Nina, his expression pleased. Behind him, a seabird skimmed along the water's edge—a petrel, Nina thought—and for a moment she had to close her eyes. It was all too much: the salty tang of the air, the roar of the waves, the heat of the sun on her skin. She wrapped her fingers around Martin's hand and pressed against the sharp ache at the back of her eyes. *I was here,* she thought, willing the moment into her memory. *I was here.*

fifteen

Back in the hotel, the red light on the room phone flashed, its staccato blinking indicating that Martin and Nina had a message. Nina heard a series of fumbling, scraping noises, then the sound of Audrey's voice saying, *no, they're not there either;* the off-stage murmur of Jenny, encouraging her to say something to the phone.

Hi, Mom. I thought you said you'd have your cell phone all the time so I could call. Anyway, it's Wednesday. Call me back, okay? Audrey's voice, flat, aggrieved, was followed by Jenny's. Nothing was wrong, she said, Audrey was missing them a little, but really she was good. They were in for the evening if Nina wanted to call.

In an instant, Nina let herself feel all the guilt she'd thus far successfully held at bay. About leaving Audrey with the Rutherfords yet again (no matter what Martin said, she didn't believe their daughter ever really got used to it), about not thinking about her, wondering how she was doing, in every minute. *We're in for the evening* had jarred her; the disconnect seemed almost impossible. She and Martin had ended up staying on the beach for several hours, then ate lunch in their bathing suits and towels at one of the hotel's poolside restaurants. It was just past one o'clock now; seven p.m. in Massachusetts, almost twilight.

Nina dug out her phone and pressed redial on the last of three missed calls from the Rutherfords' number. Audrey was begrudging but fine. She described her day, her lunch with her new Goldengrove big sister, Juliette, instead of with Willow. She wanted to know why Nina hadn't answered her phone, why they were staying away so long.

Among the many other things cancer had changed was Nina's view of her daughter—not just because Audrey had, for the most part, dealt with the past two years' many curveballs with unexpected equanimity, but also because Nina herself had come to not just recognize but appreciate something that was fundamental to her daughter: the world—or the medical world, at least—was full of Audreys. The resident who had prepped her for her first surgery, asking Nina if she was "the right mastectomy," unsmiling when she'd answered that no, she was Nina Baldwin. The ponytailed dosiometrist who had mapped out her proton treatment, impervious to small talk as he tapped away on his laptop, projecting light beam rulers across the flat side of her chest. Even Dr. Olsen himself, a little bit, who had laughed when Nina related to him how Audrey told her schoolmates her mother was bald because she'd become a Buddhist nun, and not because she had cancer. "That's awesome," he'd said, feet on his desk, fingers laced across his stomach. "How old is she—seven? Eight?"

Over the many hours Nina had spent in the chemo infusion chair and the clanging sarcophagus of the proton therapy room, she had thought about cancer, its treatment and its terms. And yet she felt she grasped only the very least part. The nature of cancer itself she got. Flawed cells reproduced themselves at breakneck speed, creating not skin and organ and bone but mush; like mold on a piece of fruit, if they weren't gotten rid of they would consume the entire entity on which they fed themselves. But the way the drugs worked? The radiation? The $C-$ Nina had received in high school physics had been pure charity; she had stumbled badly trying to explain to Audrey at the age of four how television pictures were made. She could parrot back what she'd heard from Dr. Olsen about radiation therapy—like a microwave, radiation worked by heating up cells, which killed them; protons were superior to traditional photon X-rays because they targeted tumors more precisely—but she didn't understand any of the particulars about how that worked or what all the words he used meant. How had anyone ever figured any of this out?

Maybe Audrey wouldn't have any interest in becoming a doctor, but what became clear to Nina over the days and months she spent at Boston Metropolitan was that plenty of the people there must have had an Audrey-type start. She wasn't suggesting the world didn't need its

Willows—of course she wasn't; she was pretty much a Willow herself. As were most people. Jenny and Dr. Tredway and Dr. Kennett, every Boston Met nurse Nina had encountered. But perhaps, just by virtue of who they were and how they ordered their priorities, it was more a matter of the Willows doing a better job of self-promotion than their possessing any inherent superiority. The world needed its Audreys at least as much as its Willows. The Audreys were too busy actually doing the things that mattered to be running around flogging their public worth.

Over dinner, Nina shared that thought with Martin. He lifted his water glass, taking a long swallow and arching an eyebrow at his wife above the rim, before he responded. "A world of Audreys and Willows, well. I assume I know which camp I fall into."

"You're an Audrey, of course."

"Of course." Martin gave Nina a sharp look. "And?"

"And what?" Nina leaned forward and readjusted the pair of candles in the middle of the table, white tapers in lacy votives of carved pink stone.

"And I'm imagining an extensive list of grievances related to the shortcomings associated with that designation."

Nina shook her head vigorously. "No, that's what I'm saying. Don't get me wrong; you drive me crazy sometimes. Both of you do. But I'm over thinking that Audrey has to be like something or someone else to be okay." Nina paused, trying to read Martin's face, then traced her fork through the ginger-pineapple vinaigrette left on her appetizer plate. "The only thing I do worry about, I guess, is if she's lonely."

"I don't think she is, no," Martin responded, but in such a way it was clear to Nina the question wasn't of concern to him.

"I'm thinking about, you know, like a couple of weeks ago, at the Bouchers'."

"What about the Bouchers?"

Earlier in the month, they had been invited to Easter dinner with two of Martin's colleagues and their families, and to Nina's surprise, Martin had agreed to go. After the meal, while Theresa Boucher and Erika Eklund washed the dishes, all of the children had been sent to the upstairs playroom, and Martin and Nina to keep an eye on them. The Boucher daughters had played tea party, recruiting Max Eklund into their game; Audrey had taken a book to the far side of the room and tucked herself in a corner, her long hair hanging in front of her like curtains.

"I mean, I know she loves to read, but I asked her later why she didn't play with the other kids and her answer wasn't 'because I didn't want to' or 'I was more interested in my book.' It was 'because they didn't ask me to.' I've tried to tell her a zillion times that she can't just expect everyone else to do all the work. Sometimes she has to be the one to ask the other kids to play."

Martin forked up his last bite of diver scallops and wiped the corners of his mouth with his napkin. "My recollection is that those two little girls were making Max Eklund pretend he was their dog. 'Fetch, Maxxie. Sit, Maxxie. Does a good boy need to go potty?'"

Nina smiled, in spite of herself. "Okay, maybe, but he liked it. He was having fun."

"And your point is what?"

"My point is it was the most natural thing in the world to him to just run up and join in with what they were doing. Audrey doesn't ever do that, and I worry about her missing out."

Nina and Martin's waitress, a young local in an orchid-print dress, cleared their appetizer plates while another woman refilled their water glasses. Nina watched her guide a small silver blade across the table, gathering up nonexistent crumbs. She nodded when the young woman explained their entrees would be ready shortly, then watched her retreat, her orchid-y hips swaying from side to side.

"Were you lonely?" she asked Martin. "When you were a boy, I mean."

"Was I lonely," Martin repeated. The pause that followed went on for so long that Nina wasn't sure her husband was going to say anything further. "I'm not certain I understood the feeling as such at the time. It was such a different way of life, even before the war. I had a—I suppose you'd call it a nanny—who took care of me most of the time, so that when she left and it was just me and my mother and sisters I felt it was a good thing, at first, to have so much time with my mother."

Nina rocked in her chair, her fingertips tucked beneath her thighs, pressing against the weave of the wicker seat. "But later, when you were sent to England—"

"Again, I think it's a question of terminology," Martin said, somewhat abruptly. "Not to mention of perspective. Of all the feelings I experienced then I'm not sure loneliness would have topped my list."

Nina nodded. There had been a day when she'd been particularly sick from chemo that she'd pressed Martin about his time in England, thinking it would be easier for him to talk about than Germany. She'd been well aware of his discomfort, but her own condition made her ruthless, mercenary; so weak and dehydrated she couldn't get out of bed, she'd felt then for the first time the real possibility that she might die, and not knowing had seemed intolerable. What would her life have meant if she were to die without her husband ever really sharing himself with her?

Terrified and half-delirious, she had been adamant, and he had told her, matter-of-factly. His father's cousin and her family had taken him in only grudgingly, reminding Martin at every opportunity that they were good Christian people and he was Nazi filth. At school, he was teased relentlessly for first his muteness and then his funny accent, his ratty clothes, his smell. He was beaten up, spat at, kicked. The only person who'd been kind to him was the man who ran the apothecary, Arthur Foulds, whose own wife was a Polish refugee. Mr. Foulds had given him ointment and bandages when the older boys at school would put their cigarettes out on his arms or his back.

"You were eight, right? When you went over there. How old were you when you realized you—" Nina hesitated over exactly how to say this "—that you weren't going back?"

A burst of laughter erupted from a nearby table. One of the diners, a woman with streaked blonde hair and a sunburn, stood up and flapped her napkin to the side, like a matador waving his red scarf. Her companions clapped, more laughter followed, then the sound of a man's voice. *Okay, Janice, we all get it.*

Martin stared down at the table, a muscle flexing briefly at the corner of his jaw. "I'm not exactly certain. It was after some time had passed."

"Did you ever try to find your mother and your sisters?"

The muscle flexed again. "Well, I sent several e-mails, of course," he said. "The address I had must have been bad, however, because I never heard anything back." Martin looked away for a minute, out at the churning ocean. A large white bird, coasting high above the waves on an air current, plummeted downward, hunting for its dinner. Martin shook his head, and when he spoke again the acid sarcasm that had taken over his voice was gone. "The conditions were—" he paused "—impossible. It wasn't as though I could just go back on my own. When I left them in Braunschweig, they were in refugee housing, not a place they would have stayed permanently. I didn't even know the address, if there was one, not for the barracks or the house where my mother worked. My mother had said she would send for me, and I waited—" Again Martin broke off. Nina reached across the table for his hand but he pulled it back.

"Did you ever find out what happened to them? I mean, now— wouldn't it be possible? Haven't you wanted to look?"

Martin sighed deeply, painfully. "Nina," he said. "This is not a happily-ever-after story. It's too late. Chances are they all died there, of one of the dozens of different perils we faced all the time. Malnutrition, disease, violence—" Martin broke off again. "When I first came to the United States I sometimes wondered if I might encounter my mother in one of the nice places I would go. A restaurant, perhaps, or a museum. I could see her married to an American, some G.I. she had latched on to for the purpose of rescuing her. I would be sometimes overjoyed, sometimes angry, imagining what I would say. I'm quite certain, however, that they all must have died years ago, or someone would have tried to find me." For another long moment, Martin stared down at the table, unblinking. Then he looked at Nina again. "So yes, to answer your question, I would say I was lonely."

Over Martin's shoulder, Nina saw the waitress approaching with two oversized white plates. She felt a rush of regret: surely she had ruined dinner; the rest of the evening would pass in strained conversation and long silences. The waitress swooped her plate down first and her entrée goggled up at her, a whole fish, curved limply over its bok choy bed, its upward eye cloudy and opaque. She then set down Martin's spiny lobster, lit the flame beneath a ceramic butter warmer, and retreated.

Martin busied himself with rearranging the various tools the waitress had delivered with his meal: a heavy silver claw-cracker, a long, slender fork with a matching pick, a shallow bowl for collecting the shells. Once everything was laid out to his liking, he regarded his plate itself, his head cocked to the side.

"Poor fellow," he said. He twisted a claw off, shook the juice over the bowl, and addressed himself to Nina again. "I find it's better not to think too much about these things, you know?" He indicated her plate with an upward jerk of his chin. "Once one gets started thinking about the injustices of the world, it can become impossible to do just about anything else."

Nina picked up her fork, rubbed her thumb along the beaded edge of the handle, and rolled it slowly across her palm. Delicate steam rose from the plate; pale flakes of fish were visible along the snapper's gutted dorsal edge.

"Martin—" she began.

There was so much she wanted to say. She *was* sorry, and yet at the same time she wasn't. How could Martin *not* think about these things, how could he be sure it was too late? If there was one thing cancer had taught her, it was that every single day of her life mattered, that just being here for another sunrise and sunset was a huge piece of luck. Martin, too, had been lucky, surviving his childhood; that he had made it out had no more to do with good or bad than Nina's successful cancer treatment made her good or bad. With surgery and chemo, radiation and reconstruction behind her, there were days Nina felt like the sole survivor of some terrible accident, like a person who had walked away from a bus crash or an earthquake and into another dimension where bus crashes and earthquakes only happened on TV. She knew there were others who hadn't made it; patients she saw weekly in the chemo room whose increasing frailty and dulled expression betrayed the ground they were losing to their disease, families whose sudden absence from the radiation oncology waiting room was explained by a tech's pained smile and welling eyes. Should she live less because she had made it and these others had not, honor them by constructing some straitened space for her own existence? She truly didn't think so; she understood innately the fierce desire to survive with which each of these people had, for a time, taken on their cancer, a desire that demanded you live more, not less, if you prevailed.

More than anything, what she wanted to tell Martin was that she understood. He was wrong to cling to his unearned guilt. That the two of them were sitting here, surrounded by the roar of the ocean and the calling of birds and the laughter of people whose own tragedies might be hidden just beneath the surface, was nothing short of a miracle.

Martin leaned across the table, the pink speckled tip of the lobster claw extended toward Nina between his fingers and thumb. "Eat, Nina," he said softly. "It's delicious."

The sun was down now, the candles throwing flickering light across the table as the breeze batted flames around the inside of the carved candle holders. Nina leaned forward to accept the bite of lobster from her husband, then closed her eyes. She chewed the morsel slowly, savoring the lobster's buttery flavor, the fleeting sweetness.

sixteen

In the moonlit hotel room, Martin stared at the ceiling, thinking about the lie he had told to his wife.

He remembered perfectly well how old he was when he knew his mother wasn't coming for him in England. Of course he did. He had been ten years old, exactly; the news had been his tenth birthday present, delivered to him by his father's cousin's thirteen-year-old daughter with an unfathomable smirk. *Mummy says to tell you she's had a letter from Germany. There wasn't a return address.* He could remember where he stood, what he wore, the way the sky had looked through the smog-yellowed window glass and the way the world had felt, falling away from underneath his feet. Shot through with a visceral horror, his stomach had spasmed and he had vomited on the floor, a single, bitter, watery heave that had sent his older cousin shrieking from the room. In an instant, his life had lost any last vestige of meaning it still might have held for him. His mother wasn't coming for him, not ever.

Martin had been surprised that Nina had asked him the question, but he had been just as surprised by how readily she had abandoned it. She couldn't have believed for a second that such a momentous happening was something he did not remember, and he could only assume her non-pursuit came out of a desire not to ruin the evening, the trip. But then what had compelled her to raise such a terrible subject in the first place?

After dinner they had walked the beach, Martin taking the opportunity to stretch his sore legs. It had not been late when they'd gotten back to the hotel, but they'd both agreed they were tired, and Nina had fallen almost immediately asleep. Listening to his wife's deep-sleep breaths and the steady shush of the rolling Pacific, Martin found himself alert again, his thoughts wandering back to the morning and the last time he and his wife had lain together in this particular bed. Their lovemaking had been monumental: the first time in two years he'd given himself over completely without worrying about cancer; the first time in the same interval, he was relatively sure, that Nina had climaxed. For a brief time, the various anxieties about Nina that were his indefatigable, constant companions (that he would hurt her, that he would find her reconstructed breast repugnant, that her unwillingness to show that same breast to him signified some intimacy that had developed between her and Dr. Levinson) had taken leave. Eyes closed, he could still smell the scent of sex in the sheets, conjure the feeling of being inside of her, and he felt himself stir. Nina had bared herself to Martin completely, let him look and taste and touch, and he had been stunned by how beautiful she was. Now, though, he had to wonder if there had been some sort of quid pro quo implicit in her revealing of herself, some sort of Faustian bargain he hadn't realized he had struck. Show me your most vulnerable part and I'll show you mine.

To be fair, during Nina's illness, she had asked questions about his time in England and he had answered them, if less than readily; he supposed it was possible to argue that his cooperation then suggested some sort of larger willingness to talk. But Martin was, if nothing else, a turner of pages, a closer of chapters, and both Nina's cancer and his boyhood were books that, now finished, he desired to leave shut. They were over, thank goodness. There were no lessons to be learned from leafing through them just one more time. Were he the ghost of an ancient Greek waiting to cross the river Styx into Hades, there would be no debate about what path Martin would choose: he would drink from the river of forgetting, Lethe, before he left the shore, wipe away every memory of his life.

Nina rolled in her sleep, toward Martin, and he turned to face her, propping himself up with his elbow. He studied her moonlit features: eyes shuttered and twitching with REM sleep activity, nostrils flaring with each inward breath, lips curved in a small, private smirk. Nina was a mystery to him, no question about it. He wasn't often sure what made her happy or sad, what she wanted from him, if she was even glad that they were married. After Beth, Martin had been absolutely sure that he wouldn't marry again; if it hadn't been for the accident that was Audrey—the good, wonderful accident that was Audrey—he had no doubt that he would have kept his promise. When Beth had asked him for a divorce, he had been taken completely aback; he'd had no idea that she was so very unhappy. All at once, though, she had let him have it—her anger, her sarcasm, her bitter disappointment, years' and years' worth, like a draining wound. The time he'd told her she needed to have better goals for herself. The way he never thought to buy her flowers just because, the way Kitty Provencher's husband did. Martin had never changed a diaper when the boys were little. Not one. Did Martin realize that? Beth had changed and soaked and scrubbed each one.

There had been other grievances on the list, and yet Martin had never understood what he had done that was so worthy of Beth's utter hostility. He had never cheated, hadn't even considered it, not even the time Marlene Lord had cornered him at a block party, claiming to be concerned about an irregular heartbeat. Coming out of the powder room, she had caught him by the wrist and placed his hand boldly over her substantial left breast, her lips brushing his ear as she whispered, "don't you feel that, Dr. Winzer?" He hadn't raised a hand to Beth—not ever—he rarely as much as raised his voice. He had bought the house she wanted, the car she wanted; she had permed and frosted her hair and written checks with impunity; Martin had eaten the dry, flavorless meals she cooked without complaining and took her on two vacations every year.

"That doesn't make a marriage," Beth had hissed, "that's just two people taking up space together." Somehow, Martin knew that she was telling the truth, even if he didn't understand why she was right. What did make a marriage, though? What was it that bridged the distance between taking up space together and sharing a life? After the divorce, nothing demonstrated to Martin better that he had failed in answering those questions for himself than coming across his former wife in some public space. It hadn't happened for years—Martin hadn't seen Beth since Audrey was born—but when the boys were younger there had always been events. College graduations and Peter's medical school, the occasional wedding. They spoke civilly to one another, but as little as possible, and Martin was often surprised by everything from the opinions Beth expressed to the clothing she wore. It was sad to consider that they had created children together, that their genetic coherence had given rise to three perfect boys, and yet they were, for all intents and purposes, strangers to one another, their sons firmly settled in their mother's camp as if it had been necessary for them to choose sides. As much as he disdained psychiatry, there were times Martin wished that had been the field of medicine he had chosen. What an extraordinary possibility, the idea that human behavior was learnable, quantifiable, that understanding the motivations and responses of others was achievable. Perhaps if he had studied psychiatry like that Freudian fellow he'd known in medical school, he would have been a happier person himself.

Earlier, at dinner, in a gesture of conciliation, Nina had brought the conversation back around to Audrey, and to the question of whether she was lonely. "I guess I don't think she's lonely, either," she had said. "Sometimes, though, I worry that that's because she has no idea what she's missing out on, and the thought of that isn't exactly a comfort. But of course, if there's nothing I can do for her other than make her aware that she's different…"

She had trailed off, and Martin had reminded her they'd had this discussion many, many times; there was nothing inherently wrong with being different. "Did you ever consider that perhaps you're the one who's got it all wrong? After all, assuming people are the be-all and end-all of existence is pretty narrow thinking. Maybe Audrey actually experiences more of the world because she doesn't get too hung up on its human inhabitants when there are so many other dimensions to think about. Maybe she has a truly great mind, Nina. Maybe she will change the world. You've just got to stop trying to fit a round peg into a square hole."

Nina had paused, a forkful of bok choy arrested halfway between her plate and her mouth, the expression on her face surprised and amused. Martin had asked, "What?" but she'd shaken her head and chewed the forkful of greens slowly, changing the subject when she was done. With sudden clarity, Martin understood what had happened earlier; he had gotten the idiom backwards. The phrase was *square peg in a round hole*. That Nina had chosen not to correct Martin troubled him. True, it could be she'd merely opted not to nitpick, to preserve the détente, but Martin had noted the expression on her face as she turned from him, the way her sudden amusement had faded into something much like pity. There it is, her expression said. Of course that's what you think.

There were times Martin wanted to thank Nina for putting up with him, to clutch her tight to him and beg her not to leave. He knew that Nina could have done better—he knew he was old—he knew that her cancer had given her a second chance. She had the right, now, to expect more from her marriage; she had the right to expect more from Martin. He saw these things, and yet—if there was more Nina needed from Martin, would he be able to deliver it? Companionship, comfort, material needs, physical release—what else was on the marriage grocery list?

At last, Martin felt himself drifting, his limbs like wet sand. Blades of moonlight pierced the room, turning the walls blue, slicing the sheet to ribbons. Martin stood behind a wall, enclosed, the sides of it thick and smooth all around him, impossibly tall.

seventeen

TWO DAYS BEFORE THEY left Maui, Martin got the phone call he had all but given up hoping he'd receive: Sea Life Park in Oahu had a last-minute cancellation and could offer him a dolphin-swim in the afternoon, at two-thirty, if it was possible for him to get there. Martin said he'd take it, not bothering to ask the price and not knowing whether he could actually make it happen. Hanging up, he walked out the lanai, across the Bermuda grass, and through carefully cultivated beds of ferns and oleander and hibiscus to the hotel lobby to ask the concierge about booking the short plane flight.

A conversation early in Nina's cancer treatment had been the inspiration for the entire trip. In a moment of melancholy, Nina had come out with a long list of things she'd never done but always wanted to and feared she'd never get to if her treatment didn't work. Taking a poetry class, scrapbooking Audrey's baby photos, learning French or maybe Mandarin, traveling to Egypt to see the pyramids. When she got to swimming with dolphins in Hawaii, Martin had laughed, sure she was by then poking fun at herself for her wide-ranging list, but he had been mistaken and the conversation had ended, Nina hurt. Over the following days Martin had apologized multiple times, but Nina's insistence that it was fine, he was right, it didn't matter, only made him angrier with himself, and though she had never mentioned it again, the exchange had stayed in Martin's head as something he would make right. When Harald Olsen had declared her cancer-free, it had been one of his very first thoughts; but then there

161

was Nina's reconstruction surgery—more arduous than either of them had expected—a shake-up at his office that had made taking vacation difficult, and then the holidays. He hadn't realized how difficult it was to secure a dolphin-swim reservation until he'd made the request, discreetly, when he and Nina had checked into the hotel and the young woman behind the desk had shook her head at him in dismay.

"Oh, dear, sir," she'd said. "I'm so sorry, but there's no place on Maui for doing that. You need to go to Sea Life Park over on Oahu and their reservations run months ahead of time."

She'd pushed several brochures advertising Maui dolphin boat tours in his hand, all of which prominently noted that they offered no guarantee of dolphin-sightings, and he had thanked her politely, jotting *Sea Life Park?* on the back of one. The persistence he'd shown with the Sea Life folks had surprised even him; he was, in general, accustomed to accepting *no* without an argument, and they were clearly practiced at turning people down. He'd gotten the number from directory information and made his appeal to three different people; the first two had sympathized but simply repeated what the hotel clerk had told him—they were booked months in advance—the third had told him she'd put his name on a wait-list but the chances were very slim. Now, on the way to the Maui airport, he felt immensely lucky and grateful, in spite of the shocking amount of money he'd just agreed to spend to give Nina half an hour in a swimming pool.

Martin had told Nina to pack a bathing suit and a change of clothes, he was taking her somewhere that was a surprise, and in the absence of additional details she had spent the last hour amusing herself by throwing out a range of guesses about the day's plans, everything from a luau to parasailing to a virgin sacrifice at the Halekala volcano. Now, as Martin turned the car onto the Kuihelani Highway in the direction of a sign that read *Kahului Airport, 6 miles ahead*, he told her she was getting closer to being on the right track.

"We're not staying on Maui."

"We're not?" Nina asked. "How come?"

Martin shook his head, smilingly slightly. "You'll see."

On the flight to Oahu, Nina took the window seat, silent as they taxied down the runway and lifted into the air. When the flight leveled off, she turned to Martin and resumed her guessing game.

"A Pearl Harbor tour?"

"That certainly would be an interesting choice."

"So is that a no?"

"Would you like to take a Pearl Harbor tour?"

"No, I'd just like to know what all the cloak-and-dagger secrecy is about. I've lost my taste for surprises in the last couple of years."

Martin sighed. "So I see. We're going to a place called Sea Life Park. You're going to have your dolphin swim."

For a moment, Nina didn't say anything. She turned away from Martin, staring out the window at the cumulostratus clouds and the white-capped waves they were flying low enough to see. At first glance, the white caps looked like schools of good-sized fish, thronging chaotically at the surface of the water, and on the way to Maui Martin had asked Nina, "sharks, do you think?," pretending it was a joke when she had laughed. Now she turned to face him again, squeezing his hand so hard his wedding band bit against his finger. "Really?" she asked.

"Really."

"You remembered."

Martin squeezed Nina's hand back, painfully. "I did. Shocking, I realize."

"Kind of," Nina agreed.

She released Martin's hand and reached up to touch his face. In his post-phone call haste, he hadn't shaved, and he had to fight against the impulse to pull back from her touch, reminded of the whiteness of his grizzled cheek. Her eyes held an expression Martin could only just not grasp.

"Thank you," she said. "I had no idea."

Martin nodded. "You're very welcome."

TO MARTIN'S DISAPPOINTMENT, IT wasn't a private swim—Nina was in a group with five other swimmers, including a honeymooning couple and teenage girl with brightly colored braces who stood with her shoulders curved forward and her arms folded across her torso. Each participant had his or her own dolphin, however, and Nina nodded along with everyone else as the trainer explained the way the dolphins would respond to their commands, offer their dorsal fins for a swift ride around the lagoon, and accept a snack of fish at the end of the swim.

Standing waist-deep in the turquoise pool, Nina startled slightly as her dolphin glided up to her, then gave Martin a self-conscious grin as the animal extended a flipper to shake her hand. Having finished with the teenage girl, the trainer sloshed over to join them, introducing Nina and the dolphin to one another as if they were about to embark on some sort of formally symbiotic relationship; a babysitter and child, an employee and boss.

"Calvin, this is Nina. Nina, Calvin."

The trainer gave some sort of hand signal and the dolphin reared up to nuzzle Nina's neck, just below her jaw. Nina giggled girlishly, tracing her fingertips gently over the animal's head and down its side.

"Slippery," she said to Martin. "But smooth. Like…" she thought for a second, sliding her hands across Calvin's back. "A hard-boiled egg. Do you want to touch?"

Martin shook his head, demurring, and the trainer gave the dolphin's head a familiar pat. "Hard-boiled egg, hotdog, rubber, wet inner tube—Calvin's just about heard them all, haven't you, Calvin? Dolphins shed their skin constantly, about once every two hours, to keep it smooth, and the smoothness is what allows the water to flow over them so easily."

For the next half hour, Martin watched as his wife forgot herself completely. Calvin made leaping dives and Nina cheered him on, high-fiving his flipper with her hand. He rolled over, presenting his pale belly, and Nina rubbed it, splashing back when his slapping tail splashed water into her face. At one point, Nina and the honeymooning man inadvertently traded dolphins, laughing as they realized their mistake.

Martin closed his eyes to savor the sound of Nina's laughter—genuine, uninhibited—then opened them again to check his watch. He was aware of the time passing quickly, not just in terms of this particular experience, but on this vacation, more broadly, the span from sunrise to sunset seeming to contract with each successive day. The first few days had felt disorientingly long: jet-lagged, unacclimated to the weather or the extended one-on-one proximity, they had lurched from one activity to the next dumbly, like honeymooners themselves, too exhausted to enjoy their getaway. They *had* settled in, however, and being alone together had felt the way he'd hoped it would, comfortable and right. They'd talked about Audrey, and then they'd stopped talking about her, talking instead about themselves. Nina had asked him the questions she hadn't dared to during her treatment: what he'd thought, whether he'd believed she would make it. He'd answered honestly that he had been frightened; he'd had as much trouble as she had at first believing Dr. Olsen when he'd declared her cancer-free. For months, he'd held his breath every time his private office number rang, sure it was one of Nina's doctors calling him first to break the news they'd gotten it terribly wrong.

Now, sitting lagoon-side, the whole trip felt like an oasis, a tiny, perfect, fleeting moment that he would yearn for in memory out of proportion to the actual experience of it. This time tomorrow he and Nina would be checked out of the Grand Wailea—taking a last mosey through Lahaina, perhaps, before their flight back, and already, Martin felt distinctly like it was over, felt himself suspended between the place he and Nina had been and where they soon would be. He had had no great expectations for Hawaii, but now he was pierced by a bittersweet longing to stay. Palm trees swayed around him, the sky stretched above him in a canopy of impossible blue. In addition to the dolphins, the park was home to sea turtles, sea lions, and penguins; the red-roofed bird sanctuary just down the path from the dolphin lagoon was noisy with song.

Nina and Calvin were doing their fin ride now, the dolphin towing her around the lagoon at a remarkable speed. Nina gave a couple of little shrieks, at one point losing her grip on the dolphin's fin, and Calvin circled around her, nudging her back on with his beak. At the end, the six dolphins deposited their riders in the shallow end of the lagoon, then stood up on their waving tails, executing a military-perfect pattern around the pool. As they dashed and swerved, the trainer waded down the line of humans, handing out fish. Calvin hovered in front of Nina, squeaking excitedly, and as Nina fed and thanked him, he reared out of the water one last time, this time putting his flippers around Nina in a hug. She kissed the dolphin on the nose then clambered out of the pool, pressing her face into the towel Martin held out.

She stayed that way, her expression hidden, and Martin began to grow nervous, hoping the explanation was as trivial as a bit of water in her eyes. The other members of her group were all toweling off, unbuckling their flotation vests, chattering volubly about their dolphin experience, which was making her reaction seem all the stranger by contrast.

He counted to thirty then cleared his throat. "Nina?" he asked tentatively.

She responded without moving. Her *s sssh* was towel-muffled, as were the words that followed. "Give me a minute."

Martin nodded, even though Nina wouldn't see it. When Nina finally looked at him, he was startled by the look on her face. She was smiling, but the gleam in her eye was fierce, her expression somehow more angry than glad.

"Are you all right?" he asked.

In response, Nina shook her dripping hair at him like a dog then threw her arms around him, sodden vest and all. She laughed, one note shy of hysterical. Martin held her close, hoping he understood what that meant.

eighteen

NINA AND JENNY WERE just coming around the back of the Cabot Country Club when the cell phone in Nina's windbreaker pocket rang. Without breaking her stride, Nina fished the telephone out, and for a moment, her heart seized in her chest. Instead of a phone number, the LCD screen displayed only the word 'private,' the way it did when anyone from Boston Met called. The voice in her head was instantaneous, ferocious: *Oh, no you don't. Not now. Not ever again.*

Since returning from Hawaii a week and a half earlier, Nina had taken on living with a new vengeance. The dolphin swim had been one thing, of course, the most alive moment she'd experienced in years and years, but there was also, more generally, the healthy way she felt. In the mirror, her skin's sallow color was gone, replaced by a decided South Pacific glow, despite the high-test sunscreen and old-lady straw hat she'd worn. Her hair was lightened a little also, short now by choice rather than necessity, coppery undertones to the auburn when she raked her long bangs back from her forehead. Her breast no longer hurt—it felt like it belonged to her, in fact—and neither did her abdomen; the slight fluid tightness that remained in her right arm was manageable. After a couple days of expected jet-lag, she'd awakened one morning feeling so energetic she'd called Jenny about taking a walk—a *real* walk, not another of the slow ambles around her development that had been the most she'd been able to muster for the past two years—before she could come up with a reason to talk herself out of it. That had been five days ago, and the two of them had skipped only one morning since, a day when it had rained and Jenny had declared they would be good Goldengrove mothers and take part in the Boxtops for Education clipping party Allison Silverwood had arranged. Today, for the first time, Nina had felt ready to tackle the country club loop, and as she and Jenny walked she had marveled at how long it had been, how faithfully she remembered it. Pink dogwood was in bloom all along the roads that bordered the golf course; the pair of swans who lived in the town pond paddled among the cattails. In front of the Lorings' ivy-covered brick Colonial, the postman's truck was parked half off the road and Nina had smiled to realize that this was something she remembered, too. The man who delivered the mail in that part of town was old Mrs. Loring's son-in-law, and when Nina and Jenny walked this route he was more often than not there, taking in garbage cans or fixing a broken shutter.

Taking a deep breath to steady herself, Nina flipped the phone open, gripping it tightly. "Hello?" she asked.

A male voice she didn't recognize responded. "Nina Baldwin?"

"Yes, this is Nina."

"Nina, Todd Slocum. From Goldengrove. I'm Juliette's father."

Nina stopped walking, relief flooding her so thoroughly her legs felt weak. Beside her, Jenny's face was anxious, and she put a hand out to give her friend's shoulder a reassuring pat.

"Todd Slocum, of course," she said, repeating the name for Jenny's benefit, then watching her friend's face go from worried to surprised. "Yes. Juliette is Audrey's big sister at school."

Nina closed her eyes, trying to connect a face to the name and the voice. She knew she'd met the man on the other end of the phone once or twice at Goldengrove events, a stay-at-home dad whose powerhouse wife was the subject of what seemed to Nina was an unjustified amount of scorn. He seemed friendly enough—someone who would wave hello in the parking lot or lend a hand on one of Goldengrove's more thankless community projects. Juliette was a friend of Calla Rutherford's, and for one disoriented moment Nina wondered if she was meant to hand the phone over to Jenny. Perhaps there was some eighth grade matter Jenny and Todd Slocum needed to discuss.

"I apologize for taking so long to call, but Juliette told me you and your husband were away and I didn't want to disturb your vacation, no matter how important Juliette thought it was that I get through to you as soon as possible."

"Oh?" Nina frowned into the phone, a shade of the unease she had felt when Audrey described the Goldengrove big sister program to her in Maui returning. Jenny had confirmed it was a school-wide thing (Willow had been assigned to Courtney Morrison, in spite of her protests that she already had a *real* eighth grade sister and didn't need another one), but it didn't seem out of the question for the thoughtful, deliberate Goldengrove staff to create an entire program for one child's benefit. She didn't know a thing about this Juliette, but she could imagine Audrey's teacher hand-picking for her daughter someone with a special ability to deal with odd duck younger kids.

Todd Slocum laughed, however. "I suppose you've heard from Audrey all about the great horseback plan of 2005. Juliette wants to bring Audrey over to the barn to meet Sunny and maybe even get her up on him, and I promised I wouldn't show my face at school today until I had a plan in place for when it was going to happen. We were wondering if Friday afternoon might work for you."

"Friday," Nina echoed.

She had not, in fact, heard the first word about the great horseback plan of 2005, though she had noted with some interest the stack of horse-related books Audrey had checked out of the library while her parents were gone. "I didn't know you were interested in horses," she'd commented to her daughter, and Audrey had looked offended, responding, "Of course I am." Apparently, Nina should have pressed further. When Audrey had responded negatively to her question about whether she and Willow had been scheming about taking riding lessons, Nina had let the subject drop.

"Or next week, if that doesn't work for you," Todd continued. "I know Friday afternoons don't work for everyone. We're at the barn every Monday, Wednesday, and Friday, so I was thinking I could pick up the girls from school, bring them by the house for a quick snack, and if Audrey wants to wear jeans and some sort of boots with a heel we could get her right up on Sunny, if she wanted. We could feed her dinner after or I'd be happy to run her back home."

Nina shook her head, not sure she was keeping up with the flood of information and options being presented to her. Jenny, clearly trying not to snoop, meandered a little ahead of her, bending to move a broken pine branch away from the road.

"I'm sorry, could you catch me up? I think I've heard a little less about this great plan from my side than you have from yours. I take it Juliette has a horse, and has been talking with Audrey about coming out to meet her. Him."

"Him," Todd said. "That's right. I'm sorry; I just assumed. Apparently Juliette and Audrey have been bonding over horses. Juliette's been riding since she was five, and we've owned Sunny since she was ten. Audrey's been telling Juliette she'd like to try to get up on him and I told her I'd make it work."

Still a little off-balance, Nina heard herself say okay, Friday would be great, but she didn't want Todd to go to all the trouble of driving Audrey around. She'd be happy to meet him at school and follow him over. When he said it wasn't a problem, she insisted, explaining that their house was a good twenty minutes the opposite direction from school, meaning close to an hour's trip each way if he were to drive Audrey home.

He finally got it. "Right, I wasn't thinking. She doesn't know me from Adam, and neither do you, for that matter."

"Well, no." Nina felt herself flush. "It's just that Audrey's a little high-strung. She takes a while to warm up to new people. I just can't see her getting in a car with someone she doesn't know."

"And I guess I have to keep in mind that she's eight, not thirteen." Nina thought she could hear the smile in Todd's voice. "But I promise you both that I'm harmless."

"Good to know." Nina nodded as Todd told her he'd be at Goldengrove a few minutes early on Friday and then hung up, thanking him for the invitation almost as an afterthought. She grimaced apologetically to Jenny, now double-knotting her tied shoelaces, and tucked her phone away.

"Well that was unexpected," she said.

"Should I ask?"

"Apparently Audrey and Juliette Slocum have been working on some grand scheme for Juliette to take Audrey horseback riding, which is, quite frankly, about the last activity I would have imagined my daughter doing."

Jenny nodded in agreement, resuming the brisk pace she had set for herself and Nina before the phone had interrupted them. "No offense, but…yeah."

"None taken. I mean—" Nina paused. "She can barely keep from tripping over her feet on a perfectly level surface. I'm not sure I want to think about her on the back of a horse. Sunny," she added, as if it was relevant.

Jenny squinted. It had, indeed, become sunny out in the last five minutes of the walk, and Nina wondered if her friend thought that she was making some sort of non-sequitur observation about the weather. "Well," she said, "at least you're going to be there so you can step in if things aren't going well. But who knows? We're talking girls and horses. And it's good that Audrey got Juliette Slocum for her big sister. Willow will be green with envy."

"Ahhhh." This was making sense to Nina now. "So Willow's into horses, too? I guess I missed more than I thought in Hawaii."

An emotion Nina couldn't read flickered on Jenny's face. "No, Willow's into the social pecking order—learning from only the best, of course. She informed me that Juliette's the most popular girl in school and I'm sure she's envious that Audrey gets to be her little sister."

Nina and Jenny were coming into the back of their loop now, where the road bordered a vast stretch of woodlands owned by Cabot College. They both fell silent, and Nina took in the scenery as if she'd never seen it before. Trees that had only begun to bud when she and Martin left for Hawaii were now in full green leaf; tightly scrolled fiddleheads had opened into lacy ferns; squirrels and robins hopped busily through heavy undergrowth. High above the road in a slender birch tree, a male cardinal *chew-chew*ed noisily. Nina tilted her head back, scanning the canopy for his drab mate.

She had always loved the spring—the explosion of scent and sight and sound that rushed to fill the emptiness of winter—and had never been able to fathom why her brothers had moved to California and Arizona, places where the season didn't exist. (One time, she'd asked Neal the question, and in a way that was much more big brotherly than introspective he'd told her it had to do with inherent disposition: some people didn't need to lose something—in this case, nice weather—in order to appreciate its return.) The past two years, Nina had suffered the feeling of missing the spring acutely. Pain-fogged, sick to her stomach, she'd spent most of the season inside while the world had gone on in callous disregard for her misery. Right after her mastectomy, watching Martin and Audrey from the porch as they planted her garden, had been the most self-pitying she had allowed herself to feel. While she focused on holding down the smallest sips of water *(don't throw up, don't throw up,* a relentless chant in her head), they had dug and furrowed, sprinkled and mounded and watered. The first turn through the garden had always been her favorite, the thrill of waiting until it was almost too late to clear away last year's dead growth and winter leaves, finding the tight new sprouts already there, fighting their way up like sturdy green fingers, certain that they would find the sun even when all indicators suggested otherwise. Martin and Audrey's voices floated over to her beneath the drone of the O'Bryans' lawnmower and the insistent calling of an eastern phoebe and the metronomic barking of the Turcottes' dog, and she had thought, *So this is what it will be like: The world without me.* It wasn't that she begrudged her husband and daughter their happy industry. It was more the shock at seeing with absolute clarity exactly the way in which life would go on.

The sun was fully out now, burning the last of the overnight rain off the pavement, and Nina breathed in deeply, loving even the creosote-y smell of the hot asphalt. Ever since Dr. Olsen had declared her cancer-free she'd felt a strange pressure—an obligation of sorts—to prove herself worthy of her tremendous luck; only recently had she felt genuinely capable of holding up her end of the deal. Getting her exercise, being a good wife and mother and friend…it seemed there should be more on the list, a great deal more, a daunting complement of kindnesses and gifts and selfless acts she needed to deliver.

What, to take just the least of it, of the list of regrets she'd shared with Martin? In Hawaii, he'd turned himself inside out to deliver the dolphin swim he'd ridiculed a year before, and she'd been moved beyond words that he'd remembered, but she'd been strangely frightened, too. She owed it to someone—Him? Dr. Tredway? Her parents?—for the things she wanted from her second chance to be more than a frantic, random grab at whatever was in front of her. She was the lucky contest winner who got five minutes in the toy store to fill her cart for free. She needed to fill it with things she actually wanted.

And yet at the same time, there was a part of her that wanted to simply resume the story, continuing on with her life as if the last two years hadn't happened. It was almost possible, too: she had her new breast, a real-enough replica that she could let her husband look at it—at her— sexually. She was out walking the same route she'd always walked with her best friend, passing the same house with the garish, rusted sculpture in the front yard, crossing the same shuddering footbridge with its length marked in spray-painted increments.

And Audrey had a play date, of sorts. For now, Nina wasn't going to go looking for the potential trouble in that, no matter how unlikely it seemed that an eighth grade girl would genuinely befriend anyone five years younger. There was no point to overthinking it; Juliette Slocum had invited Audrey to meet her horse, and on her daughter's behalf Nina had accepted the invitation. If she was way off the mark she would know the moment she brought the conversation up with Audrey and she would make her apologies to Todd Slocum tomorrow morning. Otherwise, she would learn in a little more than forty-eight hours whether she and Audrey had bitten off more than they could chew.

nineteen

JULIETTE SLOCUM WAS LOVELY.

On Friday afternoon, much to Nina's surprise, Juliette asked to ride with her and Audrey over to the barn instead of in her own car ("In case my dad loses us; he drives like a maniac," she'd explained cheerfully), eschewing the passenger's seat to sit next to Audrey in the back. Nina had planned to pick up a snack for the girls on the way, but Juliette announced she already had something in her backpack: oatmeal raisin cookies she and her father had made the previous night. Nina shot Audrey a warning look in the rearview mirror, mentally urging her to accept a cookie without sharing her feelings with her Goldengrove big sister about either oatmeal or raisins, and to her great relief her daughter did just that. Audrey's first bite was tentative and followed by an almost comical expression of disbelief that the taste in her mouth was actually *good*. A second bite followed, then a long slurp on the juice box Nina had handed over from the front seat. Juliette leaned her head over and said something Nina didn't quite catch and then Audrey erupted into laughter.

"What's so funny back there?"

Audrey gave her mother a guilty look. "I'm not going to tell."

"You're not?" Nina asked lightly. "Why not?"

"It's okay," Juliette told Audrey, "It's not a secret."

"Sunny eats oatmeal raisin cookies, too. Isn't that so weird? She said I could give him one when we get to the barn."

Juliette hadn't been kidding about her father's driving—though Nina

175

managed to keep up with him, when she pulled in next to his black pickup truck at the Royal River Equestrian Center, the trip had taken her fully ten minutes fewer than her MapQuest directions had indicated. Todd was indeed the man she'd pictured in her mind, tall and boyish, perpetually baseball capped to cover a thinning hairline. In the sunlight, his eyes were vividly blue, crinkled at the corners. He looked like someone who spent his time on boats, though Juliette had just finished telling Nina that she wasn't the only Slocum who rode; her father had a horse at Royal River, too.

While Juliette went inside the barn to change, Todd gave Nina and Audrey a quick tour of their surroundings: grassy paddocks for the thirty-odd horses who lived at the barn, white-fenced rings for dressage and stadium jumping, a rolling meadow full of logs and other obstacles he explained were for something called cross country. Nina nodded along; growing up, she had never been a real horse girl, unlike some of her friends, though looking around now she could see some of the appeal to the animals. There were two horses in the paddock closest to them, a brown and a gray. The gray horse had its head down, its tail swishing side-to-side as it grazed. The brown one stood by the fence, its ears pricked forward, watching Nina with an expression of eager curiosity.

"So, are you excited?" Todd turned to Audrey, crouching so his face was level with hers. Nina cringed, waiting for her daughter to pull herself back, but Audrey nodded. She actually made eye contact as she agreed that she was.

"Well, I know Juliette's excited that you could come today. She was up half the night last night trying to find some old pair of half chaps she was sure she still had that she thought you could wear. I had to threaten her with cleaning her room from top to bottom before she'd accept that we consigned them at the tack shop years ago."

"You know, Daddy, I'm still not completely convinced."

Juliette emerged from the barn wearing riding pants and a lightweight vest over her t-shirt. She had changed from her sneakers to a pair of black boots with what looked like black suede legwarmers zippered over them. She shot a teasing glare at her father and pointed at one of the leg warmers for Audrey's benefit.

"These are half chaps," she explained. "They help protect your legs when you're riding. I had some really cute purple ones when I was your age, and I thought they would be perfect for you. Unfortunately…" she shrugged. "Are you ready to come meet Sunny? He's all ready for you."

The inside of the barn was laid out in an H, with two long rows of stalls connected by a central aisle. Sunny's stall was on the far leg of the H, and as Nina walked through she took a couple of deep breaths, almost involuntarily, pulling the smell of leather and hay and horse into her lungs. Over the half-doors of a handful of stalls, horses stuck their heads out into the aisle and Juliette greeted each of them by name. "Hey, Flash; hi, Sterlin'. How you doing, Jack?" The horses nickered at her in return.

"Why are these guys inside when it's so nice out?" Nina asked.

"Show horses," Todd explained, repeating the same greetings to the horses his daughter had just made, pausing to scratch one animal on the forehead and to pat another on the side of the neck. "Most of them got turned out for a couple of hours this morning but they spend most of their time in their stalls. Sunny's usually out this time of day but we had the barn manager bring him in early to save us a little time."

Juliette stopped at the second stall from the end and put her hands on either side of a chestnut-colored horse's face, kissing him on the muzzle. "Hello, sweety face," she crooned. "Audrey, this is Sunny. Sunny, say hello to my friend Audrey."

Audrey approached the stall shyly, holding out her flat hand so Sunny could sniff. The horse's nostrils flared as he inspected her palm thoroughly, exhaling with little whuffling, trilling noises, and then his tongue came out. Audrey giggled but didn't pull her hand away, her voice scaling an octave in hasty steps as she said, "He's licking me!"

"I told you, he's just like a gigantic puppy. You've got cookie taste still on your hands. Watch this."

Nina watched as Juliette rolled back Sunny's stall door and led him into the aisle, clipping his halter to a pair of ropes that hung from the walls. She tried to recall the way Todd had described the horse to her two mornings earlier on the phone—had he mentioned the word huge, or the word gorgeous? Sunny's orangey red coat gleamed; his muscular haunches rippled when Juliette pivoted him around so he faced into the long side of the aisle. The horse towered over her, bending his big neck forward to shove at her abdomen with his head so hard that Juliette stumbled to the side, but neither the girl nor her father seemed the slightest bit concerned.

"Knock it off, you big pig," Juliette laughed. "Audrey, are you looking? He knows I've got cookies in my pocket."

"Seriously?" Nina asked.

"Yep." Juliette held her arm away from her body and Nina watched in amazement as Sunny nosed at the girl's waist, finally grasping the pull-tab of her pocket zipper with his big lips.

"You have got to be kidding me," Nina laughed as the horse successfully extracted the treat from Juliette's pocket. "You must go through a coat a week like that."

Nina stood to the side as Juliette showed Audrey how she readied herself and Sunny to ride. She handed Audrey a flat rubber oval with rows of rubber teeth and moved her hand through quick, scrubbing circles to lift the dirt from the horse's coat, then lighter, flicking motions next to whisk the dirt and loose hairs away with a stiff brush that reminded Nina of the one her own mother had used on the linoleum of their kitchen floor. Juliette followed with a third, softer brush and handed Audrey still another, a much smaller one the older girl explained was for Sunny's face. When Audrey had finished (Sunny had closed his eyes, his ears drooping to the sides in a way Juliette said meant he was happy), Juliette lifted Sunny's big feet one after the other, showing Audrey how she cleaned the shallow underside of them out with a small metal pick.

"You know what this part is called, don't you?" Sunny stood patiently while Juliette cradled his bent foreleg in her hands, pointing the metal pick at the upturned foot she had just finished cleaning out.

"Um, the frog, right?"

Juliette laughed. "Actually, I was just looking for 'hoof,' but yes, you're correct. That V-shaped part is called the frog, for whatever reason. You've been studying. Do you know what the frog does?"

Audrey peered closer, as if the frog's function might be written on it. "I think it's like a shock-absorber, right? It's supposed to touch the ground. It also has something to do with blood-circulation in the legs."

"That's exactly right. You probably also know that it's super-sensitive, so when we pick the hooves out, we're careful to go on either side of it. We only want to pick out this part, which is called what?"

Audrey smiled. "That's the sole."

The two girls worked together to saddle and bridle Sunny, settling a brightly colored rectangular pad across his back and then the saddle, running a complicated series of straps from the bridle to the saddle underneath the horse's chest. Nina marveled at how at ease her daughter looked, reaching under Sunny's massive ribcage to buckle the Y-shaped straps with Juliette's guidance, pulling his forelock out from underneath the browband of his bridle, running her fingers over the strip of white hair on his forehead that ran down to his nose.

"Juliette's so good at this," she said quietly, leaning into Todd.

Todd smiled proudly. "She loves it. Her trainer does riding camps every summer and last year she got to help out with the beginner kids. This year Deanna's actually paying her, officially, to work. She can't wait."

Nina thought about that. She didn't have the impression that Juliette needed a summer job. The home address Todd had given her Wednesday was in Standish, one of the most expensive of Boston's many prohibitive suburbs. And while Nina may not have known much about horses, it was evident even to her that Sunny was not some SPCA rescue backyard pony. Everything about the barn screamed expensive, from the brass nameplates on the horses' stalls (another case in point; Sunny's read *Ryde the Sky*, with *Sunny*—obviously just a nickname—beneath it in quotation marks) to the herringbone-patterned red-bricked floors.

Juliette asked Audrey if she still was interested in getting up on Sunny and Audrey nodded vigorously. "After you ride him, though," she said.

"That's just what I was thinking. We'll let him get any mischief out of his system before you get up."

Juliette led Sunny to the big indoor arena attached to their leg of the H, and Todd boosted her up into the saddle, slapping Sunny's back end lightly as he walked away. Juliette rode for close to an hour, circling her horse one way around and around the arena and then changing directions, riding him over a series of jumps set up in the middle of the ring over and over again. A couple of times, his back hooves clipped one of the jumps, sending the top white pole tumbling and Todd into the middle of the ring to set it back up. Once, he skittered sideways as another horse reared, bellowing angrily.

When they were finished, Sunny's arched neck was dark with sweat, and damp strands of hair clung to Juliette's flushed cheeks. Still in the saddle, she leaned forward to give the horse a hug and then guided him over to the wall where Todd, Nina, and Audrey waited.

"Ready?" she asked Audrey.

Juliette swung her right leg over Sunny's back and slid down his left side. Todd joined her in the ring, adjusting the saddle for Audrey, and then beckoned her in.

"How long have you been riding?" Nina asked him.

"Since I was twelve or thirteen, I guess. There was a farm where I worked after school and when the owner was short, he'd pay me by letting me ride one of his nags. He was short a lot of the time, so eventually I got pretty good."

"Aha." Nina had pegged Todd for the private-high-school, polo-team type. She gestured toward Sunny. "When you say nags, I take it you don't mean horses like this?"

"Noooo," Todd laughed. "We're talking one step away from the glue factory."

Todd tightened Juliette's helmet on Audrey's head and lifted her onto Sunny's back. He clipped a long rope to the horse's bridle and Juliette walked alongside Audrey. Audrey sat up tall, her expression fixed with concentration, pointing her stirrupped toes up at her shins the way Juliette had told her. A quick spasm of fear gripped her face and vanished as Sunny started to move. Nina watched as Todd concentrated on Audrey, orbiting around him in big, slow circles. After a few minutes he nodded, then looked back over to Nina to pick up the thread of their conversation.

"How about you?" he asked. "You ever ridden?"

"A horse?" Nina shook her head. "No. I did ride a dolphin recently, however."

Audrey scowled without looking over. "Ha, ha, Mom. Very funny."

Todd grinned at Nina. "We'll have to get you up here next."

"Me? I don't think so."

"Why not?"

Nina looked around. There were five other riders in the ring with Audrey and the Slocums, three teenage girls and a pair of women who were probably in their mid-twenties. To a one they were tall and lithe, long-legged, as if their body type had dictated their decision to pursue a sport that involved wearing form-fitting breeches. "Well, for starters, I'm too old."

"Not true. Next?"

Nina thought for a minute and then allowed as how that was pretty much her sole argument. "Does your wife ride?" she asked.

Todd and Juliette exchanged a look that suggested Nina had stumbled on an inside joke. "She did, for a while…"

"Until Dad talked her into riding Little John ("my horse," Todd interjected, though Nina had figured that) and he bolted and threw her into the wall over there." Juliette pointed.

Nina spread her hands. "I rest my case."

"That's too bad," Todd said. "Audrey's looking right at home on old Sunny, here. It's always nicer to ride with someone else."

Todd unclipped the rope he'd been using to lead Sunny and showed Audrey how to steer the horse herself, pulling on one rein and pressing the opposite leg against his side to get him to turn. Audrey gave it a try as the big horse plodded along, and Sunny turned obligingly first left and then right. Todd crossed back over to where Nina stood and pulled himself up onto the half wall, so close to Nina she could smell the scent of sawdust and horse on his clothes.

Audrey and Sunny made two slow circuits around the arena and then a smaller loop just around the far side, Juliette a couple of steps behind them. At the wall, Sunny turned right; a few steps later the horse turned again, reversing direction. Enamored of the new trick she had learned, Audrey pointed Sunny back toward the middle of the arena and then turned him a couple more times, weaving back and forth like the two of them couldn't agree about which way they should be headed. "Easy on him, honey," Nina called.

Todd stayed Nina with a hand on her forearm. "She's okay."

"I just don't want her driving the poor horse crazy, yanking him around like that."

"He's humoring her. Believe me, if he didn't want to play along, all the kicking and pulling she wanted to do wouldn't make a lick of difference. He's perfectly happy."

Todd's hand still rested against Nina's forearm. She glanced at him, but his gaze was focused on the girls in the ring. He smiled, his cheek lifting, revealing the errant dimple Nina remembered from the Goldengrove reception two years earlier. Her eyes noted his angular jaw, a small white scar just beneath his bottom lip, a tear in the collar of his t-shirt. Red-gold light slanted across him, startling Nina with the realization it was late, the drive back to Cabot an hour long. She lifted her arm away from Todd's hand to check her watch.

"Yikes! I didn't realize it had gotten so late. I'm so sorry. We must be holding you and Juliette up."

"It isn't that late, is it?" Todd asked. "Fridays we usually take our time around here. But if you and Audrey have to go…"

"I think we should," Nina said. "I'm sorry. I really didn't think we'd taken up so much of your time."

"Really, you didn't. Now I'm just feeling bad that Audrey didn't get more of a chance to ride."

Todd gestured to Juliette to lead Audrey over and Nina watched her daughter's face fall as she told her it was time to finish up. *But Mo-om*, she complained. As Juliette had earlier, Audrey leaned forward and wrapped her arms around Sunny's neck. "Already?" she whined. "But I just got started."

"It's been twenty minutes, actually," Nina responded. Unwisely, she found herself promising they'd come back again; she'd get the name of Juliette's trainer and find out about maybe taking a couple of lessons. Audrey slid down from Sunny's back, still glaring balefully at her mother.

"You had fun, right?"

"Not just fun, Mom," Audrey said. "I had the best time *ever*."

Juliette turned to Nina. "Can Audrey stay long enough to help me untack Sunny and give him his dinner?"

"Of course." Nina nodded. "It seems like that's part of the package." She rapped the top of Audrey's still helmeted head. "In fact, I think you should probably help shovel out Sunny's stall."

Audrey gave Nina a cluck of disgust. "It's called *mucking* out, Mom. Not shoveling."

Juliette handed Audrey the reins to lead Sunny back down to his stall and Nina resolved not to follow them, slightly awed by the sight of the massive animal next to her daughter, clopping along with his head nearly touching her shoulder, as docile as a dog. She went in search of the bathroom she'd spotted earlier and then afterward, gathered Audrey's backpack and discarded sweatshirt to take out to her car. She found Todd in the driveway, apparently on a similar mission, Juliette's school bag slung across his shoulder. He lifted a hand in greeting as Nina approached, in conversation now with a woman who stood next to a silver sedan, one hand on the still-open driver's door.

"There she is," he said. "We were just talking about you. Nina, this is my wife, Susan. Turns out you just saved my hide, calling an end to the riding lesson. It seems I forgot we have dinner guests coming tonight."

"I *did* tell you," Susan responded, "and it's on the calendar." The other woman's smile, when she turned to Nina, was tight. "Hello, Nina. Susan Slocum. I'm sorry to come in here with my hair on fire. I know Juliette was so excited to bring your daughter to the barn."

Nina nodded mutely. Susan Slocum was startlingly beautiful. She had chin length hair, the same dark blond as Juliette's, which framed her face in a careful tumble of loose curls. She wore no makeup except a sheer mauve lipstick; her eyes were a vivid aquamarine against her tan skin. Nina thought she remembered Carolyn Hadley saying Susan Slocum was a banker or lawyer in Boston and she dressed the part, in a beige linen dress with a wide crocodile belt and a cream-colored sweater draped across her shoulders. Though Susan was the one not dressed for the location, Nina felt suddenly out of place in her jeans and scuffed clogs, large and awkward though she and the other woman were nearly the same height. Nina shook the hand Susan Slocum offered, glad she'd just washed up in a sink she hadn't been sure was meant for that purpose. She noted the other woman's French manicure, the gold bracelets that jangled on her wrist.

"I'm so sorry," Nina said. "I had no idea we were messing your evening up."

"That's not your fault," Susan replied. "It would be nobody's fault, in fact, if someone could remember to bring his cell phone into the barn."

Todd shrugged. "It's only Patrice and Gabriel. It's not like we don't get to their house half the time and the oven isn't even turned on."

Susan Slocum's tone was icy. "You know perfectly well that's not the point."

"No, I suppose it's not," Todd countered. "The point always seems to be to have too many cocktails while the girls watch movies and then trash-talk all our so-called friends."

As the Slocums squared off, Nina found herself backing away, unwilling to surrender the flush of happiness she'd been feeling only minutes earlier. She tossed Audrey's things into her passenger's seat and hurried back into the barn to collect her daughter, noting the brief flicker of distress that crossed Juliette's face when she told the girl her mother was outside. Sunny was in his stall already, working noisily on a rubber bucket of grain. His saddle and bridle had been put away, and Juliette was just finishing up sweeping the immaculate brick aisle. Nina took a last, deep, horsey breath. Impulsively, she gave Juliette a hug and thanked her for showing Audrey such a good time. Outside, Susan Slocum was in the driver's seat of her car, and Todd had his hands braced on her open window, the expression on his face intense. Nina honked and waved as she pulled out and was halfway to Cabot before she realized she hadn't thanked Todd for his time, or asked him if she owed him anything for Audrey's ride.

twenty

It was almost a full week later when Nina stopped Todd Slocum in the Goldengrove parking lot. After debating all weekend whether it had been more rude for her to leave the barn without saying good bye or for Susan Slocum to pick a fight in front of her, she had eventually settled on the latter, but concluded her own conduct wasn't entirely above reproach. She'd hoped to find an email address in the Goldengrove handbook so she could apologize without having to face Todd directly, but the only listing was Susan's, clearly an office address, and that wouldn't do. On Monday, she'd passed the black pickup truck on Route 117 heading away from school; Tuesday she had waited for almost ten minutes after dropping Audrey off before concluding that Todd had already come and gone. Wednesday Jenny had driven; on Thursday she was just about to pull back onto Bunganuc Road when she saw him in her rearview mirror, exiting the Upper School building.

"Hey there," she called. "I've been meaning to catch up with you. I wanted to thank you again for last week. I really think Audrey meant it when she said it was the best day of her life. She hasn't stopped talking about it yet."

"Fantastic." Todd smiled. "She's welcome any time. Both of you."

Nina twisted a little section of hair behind her ear uneasily. "I also wanted to apologize for just taking off at the end, there. It looked like you had a lot going on is all."

"No worries." Todd made a dismissive gesture. "I didn't think you'd bailed on us or anything. Everything worked out fine. Susan has a different view of our social obligations than I do."

Two girls who looked about Audrey's age stepped out of the Lower School building, carrying a United States flag and the Goldengrove flag in a flat wicker basket. Nina squinted, trying to identify them, then decided they were probably fifth or sixth graders. Their faces were more angular than Audrey's, their bodies longer, the first hint of new breasts pressing against their shirts. She watched them for a minute, setting down the wicker basket, flapping open the American flag first. They turned themselves and then the flag around, careful to not let it touch the ground, until the flag was oriented to hang properly from the pole.

"I think Audrey is serious about wanting to take riding lessons," she said, her eyes still on the flag-hanging girls. "If there's a riding teacher you'd recommend, I told her I'd make a couple of calls."

"I can give you Deanna's number right now. She's been teaching Juliette since she started riding, and she's terrific. Strict but not scary, great with younger kids. I don't remember her number off the top of my head, but it's in my cell phone—"Todd patted his jeans pockets and his t-shirt, then gave Nina an embarrassed grin "—which, I believe, is still sitting in my truck. Right this way."

The bed of Todd's truck held a load of yellow two-by-fours, several large boxes of nails, and a squat, red cylinder that Nina thought was an air compressor. On Friday, Todd had mentioned that he did some carpentry work for Royal River—not as a full time job, but enough to cover monthly expenses for Sunny and LJ. She arched an eyebrow at him. "On your way to the barn now?"

"The Hallowell Community Center actually. I'm building an outdoor shelter for their play area."

"Good for you," Nina answered. She knew the place Todd was talking about, a low brick building on Route 117 that housed a low-income dental clinic, a childcare center, social services, and the county welfare offices. She had seen children out playing in the cyclone-fenced yard with its tire swing and single, off-kilter slide and felt her conscience nag at her. More than once, she'd thought of stopping to offer the bright plastic play set Audrey had outgrown years earlier, but had always come up with one reason or another to keep driving. "I really need to do more stuff like that.

Not building things, necessarily, but volunteering."

Todd thumped his fist on the hood of the truck. "Come on down. I could use an extra set of hands."

"What? You mean now?"

"Something else you need to be doing?"

"Only five or six loads of laundry, for starters, finding a birthday present for my nephew in California, baking cupcakes for the third grade spring picnic…" Nina gestured back toward Goldengrove's Lower School building, into which the flag-hanging girls had disappeared. She let her voice trail off, realizing how weak and self-centered her list sounded. Was. It occurred to her that Todd Slocum would probably bring store-bought cupcakes and not lose a minute's sleep over their lack of hand-craftedness; would tease Carolyn Hadley to her face about Goldengrove students' purported preference for healthy snacks and get away with it. "Okay," she said abruptly. "Why not?"

Todd gave her shoulder a little, big-brotherly slug. "All right, then. I'll even throw in a cup of coffee. My treat. I promise to have you back at school for pickup time."

Nina walked around to the passenger side of the truck, a little bewildered by what had just taken place. She rubbed her shoulder, which didn't really hurt, but which reminded her she needed to be clear with Todd. Dr. Levinson had okayed her to carry grocery bags and resume her regular work around the house, but she was pretty certain he didn't expect that to include light construction. She was getting the distinct impression that Todd was someone whose enthusiasm ran well ahead of his common sense and could see herself getting into something way over her head if she didn't make her limits clear.

They'd picked up Starbucks and were on their way to the community center when Nina finally, reluctantly, brought the subject up. She wasn't eager to share any more of her story than she had to but figured it wasn't going to take very much.

"So, listen," she started. "You may already know this through the Goldengrove grapevine, but I was sick for kind of a while and probably can't do anything too taxing, here. I mean, I can hold a box of nails or prop some boards up but I shouldn't be raising walls on my own."

Todd handed Nina a napkin for her latte without looking over. "I do know. Breast cancer, right?"

Nina agreed, startled by the matter-of-fact way Todd had said the words. Most people took great pains not to say cancer, referring to it as "the c-word" or "the big C." And even rarer than those who used the word *cancer* were people who dared to mention the anatomy with which Nina's was affiliated. They'd gesture in the direction of her mastectomy (as if that was somehow preferable) or point at their own chests.

"One of my sisters had it, infiltrating ductal carcinoma. Julia. She's the one we named Juliette for."

Nina rolled the napkin between her finger and thumb. *Had it* could mean she'd been cured, but it also could mean that she had died. From Todd's words, she was relatively certain that he had meant the latter.

"I'm sorry to hear that."

"It was very late when they found it. She was only thirty-eight. No children, thankfully, if you know what I mean."

"I do," Nina said. "Thirty-eight. Holy cow."

"Thirty-five when she was diagnosed. And yet I remember one of the first things she told me was she just really wasn't that young. There were women in her doctor's office in their twenties, one girl who had just gotten engaged."

Nina nodded, a little surprised to be having this conversation after all this time, and with such an unlikely partner. There had been one woman at Dr. Kennett's office who had always haunted her, a young mother who brought her daughter to her appointments, a somber, tow-headed toddler who could have passed for Audrey at the age of three. She remembered trying to tell Martin about this little girl—unlike any other child Nina had ever seen at any doctor's office, she had sat quietly, unmoving except to shift against her face a pink blanket she was chewing, covered with bald spots where velvety fabric had been gnawed off—remembered, too, the way Martin had turned away from her. He didn't want to think about the suffering of another young mother, a child.

"That blew my mind, too. Before my own diagnosis, I really thought breast cancer happened to older women, grandmother-aged. It definitely makes it a little harder to feel sorry for yourself when you know there are women fifteen and twenty years younger than you fighting the same thing."

after

Todd glanced at his rearview mirror, changing lanes. "Self-pity sucks, doesn't it? Julia always said that was one of the worst parts about having cancer. That, plus the way certain people started treating her like a leper or something. They'd either avoid her completely or just give her one of these—" Todd turned to Nina with a remarkably genuine look of pity on his face, shaking his head at her with a combination of sadness and disappointment she remembered all too well. After her hair fell out, she'd gotten it a lot: in the grocery store, walking with Audrey through the mall.

Nina looked out the window at Route 117 sliding past. Corrugated metal buildings, a roadside farm-stand advertising fresh eggs and early lettuce, bundles of yellow forsythia and pussy willows, a chiropractor's office with a sign that riffed on a popular dairy industry slogan: *Got pain?*

"I remember that face very well," she said. "I try to be a little generous about it. I think cancer is just something people get stupid-scared thinking about, and it's way too easy for anyone to put themselves in your place. It's is like one of those myths from childhood, like the boogeyman, only it actually turns out to be real and there's not a lot you can do to keep it from making a grab for you. I don't think there's anything that scares people more than that."

Todd took a drink of his coffee and frowned. "I'd say that's more than a *little* generous of you. I'd say that's very generous."

"Either that, or it's my highly evolved capacity for denial." Nina lifted her own coffee cup, slurping off the milk-foam that had bubbled through the little hole in the lid. "You said she was *one* of your sisters, yes? How many are there?"

"Counting Julia, five. All older."

"*Five?* Your poor mother. So you were the long-awaited heir, I take it?"

Todd grinned. "The baby."

They came up on the community center, and before Todd had even turned the truck off a middle-aged woman with an orangey perm was hurrying to unchain the cyclone fence. Todd introduced Nina to the woman, Annette Geeslin, the director of the community center, and busied himself unloading supplies while Annette held forth on how much she appreciated Todd's help. There was a long row arbor vitae that Todd had planted along the back of the property, providing some privacy from the pharmacy parking lot behind it. In front of the trees there were several pallets of rubber tiles that would become new footing for the play area once the shelter was up. As she pointed the latter out to Nina, Todd turned to the two of them. "My next project, right, Annette?" Flustered, the permed woman exclaimed that—goodness!—she wasn't hinting. He winked at Nina as he hoisted another stack of two-by-fours out of his truck.

For a while, Todd worked without saying much of anything, setting up a pair of sawhorses and lining his tools along a low concrete wall, handing Nina an extension cord to plug in to a covered outlet beneath the center's peeling clapboards. He scowled as he measured and cut all the boards for the back wall of the shelter, assembling the sides of the frame with a series of efficient punches of the nail gun. After the final sides of the rectangle came together, he pushed his baseball cap back off his head, passed a hand across his forehead in a now-familiar gesture, and resettled the cap, tugging down on the bill.

"So." He laid a sheet of just-cut plywood over one side of the frame. "Now I'm thinking I'm the one who owes you an apology."

"An apology." Nina repeated. "For what?"

"For being a thoughtless asshole. You bring up your cancer and I start talking about my sister who died."

"No," Nina said. "Not at all." She pulled off the pair of work gloves Todd had produced for her earlier, wiping her sweaty hands on her jeans. "I'm glad that you told me. I mean, it's not a secret that a lot of people die from cancer." She paused. "Everyone is so frantic to tell you about all the people they know who were diagnosed with something worse than yours and beat it that you start to feel like some sort of pathetic mental midget for worrying that you might die. I appreciate you actually *talking* to me about cancer, if you know what I mean. It's a whole lot better than the 'hey, buck up, on to the next' pep talks I usually get."

Todd squatted on his heels in the grass. He took his gloves off, too, laying them across the plywood. "The tyranny of positive thinking," he said.

Nina frowned. "The what?"

"One of Julia's doctors had a term for that buck-up pep talk thing: he called it the tyranny of positive thinking. The obligation you and everyone else have to think positive and say optimistic things, like that determines whether or not you get better, when in reality it has nothing to do with it."

A shadow passed over Todd's face. "But maybe that's not what you were talking about."

Nina shook her head. "That's just what I was talking about."

It was something she wrestled with daily, the question of whether her attitude could be the minute difference that tipped the scales for her toward cure. As much as her logical brain knew it was ridiculous, there was a part of her that hadn't been able to dismiss the idea entirely; it was hard to go through cancer and not engage in some amount of magical thinking. If I meditate, if I swear off red meat, if I feel positivity coursing through my body—when the arsenal of weapons was finite and the enemy was invisible, what harm could it do? There were a number of times she'd questioned her chances, only to feel an immediate, internal reproach for her pessimism. What if there *was* a mind-body connection; what if her moment of weakness and doubt had provided fuel for her cancer cells, cells that had been *this close* to surrendering? It was the very definition of insult added to injury: not only did you have to have cancer, but you had to walk around pretending it was some sort of challenge you took on enthusiastically, like a contestant on one of those TV shows where people volunteered to live on an island eating bugs.

Todd shifted the rectangle of plywood over the frame until all the corners were flush. He asked Nina to check her end and she gave it a look and a quick thumbs-up.

"It's a crappy thing to do to people," she said. "Right now, I'm considered cancer-free, which is as close as anyone's going to come to telling me I'm cured, and there's not a lot I can do about it except eat well and exercise and maybe not take up smoking or anything like that. It's amazing, but it's also…" She trailed off.

"You're still aware that there's a sword hanging over your head," Todd suggested.

"Exactly. So if I get sick again, does that mean it's my fault?"

"Of course it doesn't."

The look Todd gave Nina was so frank and so direct it almost frightened her. Unconsciously, she found herself imagining Martin's response to the same question—the almost-anger that would cross his face, then the professional, clinical blankness that would come down. She knew it had everything to do with the strength of her husband's feelings for her—he loved her so deeply that to even suggest such an idea would be intolerable—and yet there were times she needed to get the words out, to release them into the atmosphere where they could dissipate, rendered inert by the sheer quantity of nitrogen and oxygen molecules that stood ready to bind to them. Almost instantly, asking the question of Todd seemed like a silly thing to do, childish and naïve. Of course if her cancer recurred it wouldn't have anything to do with the way she'd *thought* about it; it wasn't like she had been obsessed with getting cancer for years and then her worst fears had been realized. If anything it had been the opposite: she had strolled along whistling in the dark while her cancer had dug itself in.

Nina glanced away, unable to hold Todd's gaze any longer. "Sorry," she said. "It's been a while since I've talked about all of this with anyone. As you can see, it doesn't take me long at all to get deep in the weeds."

"You're hardly deep in the weeds. Don't stop on my account."

"Even I get tired of looking at my own navel eventually." Nina smiled slightly. "I appreciate you listening, though. You're a good sounding board."

Todd smiled back, but with a certain restraint that made Nina wonder if she had said something wrong. "Any time," he said.

He picked up the nail gun again and nailed the frame and the wall together with a rapid series of blows. The hydraulic reports slapped against Nina's eardrums and she took a deep breath. She was kneeling in the grass, which still had tracks from a recent mowing—one of the first of the season—running through it. The sky overhead was a piercing blue, hung with fat white clouds. It was a beautiful day, much too beautiful to be discussing cancer or any of her petty grievances. What Nina had meant to tell Todd was that she felt lucky, incredibly lucky. She was alive. The air smelled like warm dirt and cut grass and fresh sawdust. The sun felt hot, good, against her bare arms. She was happy to be outside, doing something for someone other than herself.

After the second piece of plywood was fastened to the frame, Todd nailed together a pair of triangular supports that he added to the base, screwing them in at right angles to the corners. He then stood the wall up, holding it as far away from himself as possible to get a look.

"Wow," Nina said.

"Wow, what?"

"Did you mean for it to be like a foot higher on one end than the other?"

Todd did a double-take at the perfectly level structure and then at Nina. He laid the wall back down carefully then reached for his empty coffee cup and threw it at her. Nina caught it and threw it right back.

BY EARLY AFTERNOON TODD had all three sides of the shelter assembled, the two peaked walls joined to the back. Her lower back stiff and the first subterranean heat of sunburn rising on her arms and neck, Nina readily accepted Todd's suggestion that they knock off and grab a quick lunch before collecting their daughters from Goldengrove. While he transferred all of his tools back into his truck, she scoured the grass for errant nails and sharp splinters of plywood; the orange-permed Annette reappeared just as they were about to leave. Nina accepted both an exuberant hug and a chocolate brownie from the woman, wrapping the latter in a Starbucks napkin to share with Audrey on the trip home from school. She and Todd arrived back at Goldengrove in plenty of time for pickup, just as he had promised, but on the ride from Goldengrove, Audrey ate her half-brownie distractedly, not even interested in guessing how her mother had spent her day.

"What's the matter, honey?" Nina asked, trying to catch her daughter's eye in the rearview. "You seem kind of down."

"It's nothing," Audrey said glumly. "It's stupid."

"Did you have an okay day at school?"

Audrey had brownie crumbs on her shirt, a smear of chocolate on her cheek. "Not really." She looked out the window then asked Nina, "Mom, do you know how to play Concentration?"

"The card game? Sure I do. I loved it when I was little." Nina thought she was younger than Audrey when she'd played it, but she could still see the square red and white checkered cards in her mind, feel their substantial heft in her hand.

"It's not a *card* game, Mom. It's a clapping game." Apparently one that Audrey was not good at; you picked categories (animals, for example, or girls' names, or things that started with the letter *R*) and tried to name as many words as you could without pausing for too long or messing up the clapping pattern. Willow had taught it to her, then teased her when she named the same words over and over again every time they played. "It's really hard, though. I can't think and move my hands at the same time."

"That *is* a serious problem." Nina bit her lower lip, painfully. She had meant for her tone to be lighthearted, but the words had come out glib, sarcastic. "I'm sorry, honey."

The day she'd spent outside had left her energized, on the verge of giddiness. Everything around her seemed better: the air fresher, the birdsong sharper, Audrey's problems more ordinary. At lunch, Todd had looked at her like she was crazy when she'd told him how grateful she was for the kindness Juliette had shown to Audrey. "Why wouldn't she be kind?" he'd asked. "She thinks she's lucky to be Audrey's big sister. Audrey's a remarkable kid."

Audrey pressed her fingers to the window glass, making prints that vanished rapidly in the air-conditioned enclosure of the car. "And anyway, it's not fair. Calla taught it to Willow so she's already gotten to practice."

"Maybe you could get Juliette Slocum to practice with you."

"Maybe," Audrey responded, her tone doubtful.

"When do you have a big sister lunch with her again?"

"Next week."

Nina nodded. Perfect. She would ask Todd to help her set it up.

At home, she brooked no arguments when she asked Audrey to help her make the cupcakes for the next evening's picnic. They were cooled and frosted and Audrey bathed and put to bed before Martin came home. He was in the middle of four days of being on call and deep lines of exhaustion etched his face.

"Hey there," Nina said. "Are you home for the evening?"

Martin rubbed his face with both his hands, slapping his cheeks. "Hopefully. Though we both know how Murphy's Law works."

"Ah, right. Quiet day, so chances are something will explode around midnight, yes?"

Nina followed Martin into the kitchen and watched him extract a tub of chicken salad from the refrigerator, reaching over to the dish drain for a clean fork. "I'm sorry," she said. "I figured you'd eaten at the hospital. I'd have saved you a plate if I had known."

"I did. I had a roast beef sandwich about an hour ago. It just didn't do the trick." Martin opened the container and, most un-Martin-ly, speared a chunk of chicken from it directly. He took a couple of forkfuls before answering Nina's earlier question.

"Yes, something very much like that: unremarkable day, which could mean a busy night or nothing of the sort." He put the hand with the fork to his lower back, stretching against it with a grimace. "More than anything, I'm reminded that I'm getting too old for this."

Nina nodded; she hadn't really expected Martin to talk in any great detail about his day. He was scrupulously discreet about his patients—years earlier, Nina had discovered that her childhood piano teacher had been a patient of his only when they'd encountered Mrs. Velardi, ancient by then, in downtown Cabot—but sometimes he'd talk about procedures he'd done or diagnoses he had made, share funny stories like the recent one about an older man who'd complained of shortness of breath then taken exception when Martin had jotted down *patient SOB*. Even when she hadn't understood half of it, she'd always enjoyed the stories, imagining her brilliant, life-saving husband moving through the halls of St. Serafin in his suit and white coat. Even her own patient experience had not diminished the pleasure she took in that.

"How about you?" he asked. "How was your day? I see you made cupcakes."

"For the third-grade picnic tomorrow night, but I'm sure Audrey wouldn't mind if you helped yourself to one."

"What time is the picnic?"

"Are you planning to come?" Nina heard the incredulity in her own voice. She hadn't even mentioned the picnic to Martin on the assumption he'd still be at work. "It's from five to six-thirty at school."

"No, you go without me. I have a big stack of dictations to catch up on." Martin reached for a cupcake, setting the half-eaten tub of chicken salad aside. He flashed Nina a sardonic smile. "I just wanted to be sure I had a good excuse for missing it."

Perhaps it was because she was tired, too, but for once Nina didn't find her husband's cynicism particularly amusing. She looked over his shoulder at the granite countertop behind him, the drain board filled with pots and pans. "You know, it wouldn't kill you to show up at these things every once in a while, hang out with the unwashed masses a bit."

"It might," he countered, peeling the paper wrapper off the cupcake.

"And then wouldn't you be sorry."

"Not too sorry," Nina answered. "You've got a good insurance policy."

Martin considered his naked cupcake and then arched an eyebrow at Nina. "I'm almost afraid to eat this now."

UPSTAIRS IN THEIR BATHROOM, after Nina had brushed her teeth and hair, she pulled off her t-shirt to put her nightgown on. The sunburn she'd felt earlier in the day had declared itself definitively, with a deep red V of skin on her chest and bright pink upper arms. At first, Martin was concerned— Nina hadn't burned like this in Hawaii; didn't she realize she needed to be careful with her skin, still vulnerable from nine months of chemotherapy and radiation? His expression changed when Nina explained how it had happened.

"So it was just the two of you, you and this Todd Slocum fellow, the same one you were out with last Friday night?"

"You make it sound like I was on a date or something," Nina said. "I wasn't *out* with him. We were at the horse barn, remember? With our daughters?" Nina felt a new surge of irritation. "And yes, I was helping him with a volunteer project. He needed a second set of hands and I offered. He's building a play shelter at the Hallowell Community Center."

"How very noble." Martin folded his arms across his chest. "I don't like it. I don't like you hanging out with this man."

"My God, Martin, are you kidding me? It's just friendly. His daughter is Audrey's big sister."

Martin didn't respond, and Nina knew she should wait him out, but she was too annoyed to hold her tongue. "And it *is* noble, by the way. There's nothing sinister going on. It's been good for me to change my routine a little, get out of the house and do something useful with myself. He's married, for Pete's sake. Just like I am."

Martin's expression remained stony. "Being married doesn't make a man safe. You know better than that. Especially if he's out of work. A man without a job is going to be looking for another way to fill his time and his ego."

Nina grabbed her dirty clothes and tossed them in the laundry hamper next to the shower, slamming down the flimsy lid in a way that wasn't close to satisfying. "So, what? Would you rather I not tell you what I'm doing, how I'm spending my time? How can you be suspicious when I'm *telling* you exactly what's going on?"

"No," Martin said calmly. "I'd rather you weren't spending your time with this guy. It's not you that I'm suspicious of."

"I can't believe you." Nina looked around the bathroom: the double sink, the brushed nickel sconces with their frosted shades, the tiled walk-in shower, its glass door peppered with water spots. For a minute, she hated all of it, the manner in which she had come to have it, with an irrational intensity that frightened her. Had it ever been worth it, marrying Martin? He was old, the skin on his stomach folding over in loose pleats despite the rock-hard muscles beneath it. He was condescending, authoritarian. Too often to be an accident, he treated Nina like a child, as if their marriage was not a partnership of equals but the unbalanced scale of father and child.

"I'm going back next week to help him finish this project, whether you like it or not. It's insulting that you don't trust me."

Briefly, Martin closed his eyes, pinching the bridge of his nose between two fingers. Something flickered in his expression—pain? sadness?—but then the familiar mask settled into place. He left the bathroom, closing the door behind him, and Nina listened to the sound of him moving around in the walk-in closet, the squeak of his shoes going down the stairs. A minute later, there was the low hum of the garage door opening, the roar of Martin's car as he pulled out of the driveway and into the cul-de-sac. Nina stared at her reflection in the mirror, lips slightly parted, eyes wide with disbelief.

"It's not my fault," she said out loud. Martin had taken one of the best, most innocent, days she'd had in a very long time and ruined it. Though she and Todd had talked about cancer, she'd felt less like a cancer patient than she had since her diagnosis. They'd talked about Audrey, and Todd's praise for Nina's daughter had echoed for hours in her head. Why shouldn't Juliette be kind? Audrey was *remarkable*. Temporarily, at least, the two biggest burdens Nina carried daily had been magically lifted, just by talking about them, and she'd felt herself nearly shaking with possibility. And now— Let Martin be angry with her. Let him sleep on the couch in his office or in the cramped, uncomfortable quarters of the call room. How dare he doubt her trustworthiness, question her right to have friends?

Nina splashed cold water on her face and then pressed her palms against the hot V of skin below her neck. She opened the middle drawer of the vanity and pulled out a tube of aloe vera gel, spreading the slippery liquid on the burn. Very deliberately, she screwed the cap back on and put the gel away, wiped her sink and then the countertop with a tissue. She turned the light off, crossed the darkened bedroom, and padded barefoot down the hallway to kiss Audrey good night, the same way she'd done every night since her daughter was a toddler. "Sleep tight, baby girl. Mommy loves you," she whispered. Audrey was sweaty, her face damp.

When Audrey was younger, on nights when Martin wasn't home, Nina sometimes would curl herself up in her sleeping daughter's bed. She wouldn't stay, but for a while she would listen to the deep, regular rhythm of Audrey's breaths, stroke her thumb against the palm of her daughter's open hand, marvel at how relentless the march of the growing divide between them was. Only an eye-blink ago, her daughter had been a newborn, a nursing infant, a toddler clinging to her with all her might. Another eye-blink and she would be a teenager, disavowing her connection to her mother in some shopping mall, a college student, out in the world. It had been as if the still-countable minutes of Audrey's life were cards from a deck, being flipped away altogether too freely by a callous dealer, and Nina was helpless to gather them back no matter how she tried. The thought had been excruciating, but Nina had been compelled to push herself through it, a form of labor that yielded not the start of her identity as a mother but the end. When she found out she had cancer, those nighttime visits had taken on a new urgency. *Remember me,* she would whisper, *remember me. Please know how much I loved you.*

Back in her own room, Nina slid between the sheets and pulled the covers up to her chin with both hands. She lay in the dark with her eyes open, stunned by the realization that for the first time since her cancer, she and Martin were having a fight.

twenty-one

THE SHRILL NOTE OF the ringing telephone bore a hole through the pitch dark, jerking Martin from sleep. Ivan was coming, just like the schoolteacher from Bad Freienwalde had warned everyone, the heavy tanks so close to the city they were ringing the telephones that had been silent for months, shaking the mirrors and pictures from the wall. It was time to go, go, go! But to where—? To what—? Martin was halfway across the room before he remembered himself: It was 2005; it was one-thirty in the morning, and the phone was ringing because he was on call. He was in his office at St. Serafin Hospital because he and Nina had had a fight. He had walked out on her where she stood in the bathroom—so angry and terrified at once it was all he could do to keep from breaking into a run—and driven away.

Martin shuddered, willing his heart to stop hammering in his throat, and blew out one long, hissing breath. On the phone, a junior attending from the emergency department identified herself apologetically. One of Martin's patients was being admitted to the intensive care unit with an acute MI, a Mrs. Hebert, ninety-one years old, a good candidate for percutaneous coronary intervention but refusing treatment. The attending had tried his pager and then his home number and his wife had suggested she try his office. Since he was the cardiologist on call and was already so close by, did he want to come down to the ICU?

Focused now, Martin grimaced at the way the younger doctor put the question. The way the junior staff spoke often reminded him of the way the teachers at Audrey's school delivered their requests ("You *may* use your words," he'd heard one teacher saying to an angry child who was wielding a branch; "You *may* put the stick down." Or he may crack you one with it, Martin had thought). Of course he didn't *want* to come down; coming down was his job, and as he fumbled around his desk for the light switch he asked a few questions about Mrs. Hebert. She was ninety-one? What time had she been brought in to the emergency department? Who brought her in, and did whoever it was know what time she'd suffered her MI? What were her vitals right now? The phone pinned to his ear with a shrugged shoulder, Martin slipped on his pants and fastened his belt. In his right front pocket, his pager. He squinted at its tiny screen in the dim light, wondering why the piercing beep hadn't awakened him. The screen was blank, the unit's battery dead.

Mrs. Hebert, Mrs. Hebert...as Martin hurried out of the office and toward the elevator bank, he rummaged through his mental files, trying to summon any particulars about his patient, shrugging off the last unpleasant filaments of the disorientation with which he had been roused. It had been happening more again lately—the nightmares, the strange, liquid moments in which he felt himself out of place and time—and he worried that his memory was beginning to fail him, just the slightest bit. To allay the fear he often found himself demanding more of his conscious brain, conducting little mental tests to prove himself: naming all the bones in the wrist or the innervations of the cervical spine, rote lists he hadn't needed to use since he was a resident. *Ninety-one years old,* he reminded himself now; *Mrs. Hebert.* Still carrying a caseload of some 400 patients, he couldn't expect himself to recall each one perfectly, but something in the attending physician's description had nagged at him. Was Mrs. Hebert one of his unstable anginas, maybe an aortic stenosis, patients whose outcome was not a question of what, but when? He doubted it; most patients fitting that description were desperate for any sort of intervention offered to them. It sounded like she was a non-compliant, a smoker, maybe, or a dementia.

As the elevator shuddered slowly downward, Martin pressed both hands into his stiff lower back, thinking almost longingly of the high-tech, multi-thousand-dollar bed in which he would find his patient in short order. Once upon a time, the middle of the night had been his favorite time to be on his way to work, the way it made him feel that he was the only person paying attention to a game with tremendous stakes.

Tonight, however, as was more and more the case of late, he felt tired by the weight of his responsibility, his senses dulled by the repetition and years of shortchanged sleep. He and Nina had been back from Hawaii for only a matter of weeks, but already the vacation felt like it had happened a lifetime ago.

The elevator reached the ground floor with a thud, and suddenly it was there for him: Mrs. Hebert was a repeat MI, the old Eastern European woman who'd waggled a scolding finger in Martin's face when he had tried to talk to her about putting a pacemaker in. Ruta Hebert. Martin swallowed a sour taste in his mouth. He hadn't seen Mrs. Hebert in almost two years; Barton Eldredge had taken over her care while Nina had been sick. He knew he had been lucky avoiding her this long, but still—there were few things he would relish less than walking into the ICU tonight and resuming any sort of negotiation about her right to suffer a preventable cardiac death.

The first floor of the hospital was eerily quiet—the outpatient x-ray and day surgery waiting areas dark, the gift shop and coffee stand shuttered, the only sounds Martin's brisk strides on the polished floor and the far-off whine of a vacuum cleaner in another office suite. He rounded corners, the blackened windows turned to mirrors under the occasional low-energy light, took the stairs to the intensive care unit two at a time. On the critical care floor, there were more signs of life, lit nursing stations populated by night-shift nurses and aides, the sounds of several querulous patients calling *nurse, nurse.* In the ICU itself, the transition from night to day became complete—lights blazing, a metallic menagerie of ventilators hissing and monitors bleating, doctors and nurses speaking in conversation-level voices about patients and medications and what they were going to do on their next day off. As a young medical student, the mundane exchanges of the ICU had seemed callous, called to mind nothing so much as a favorite poem from his university days. After all these years, he was inured to it, but there were still times the opening lines of W.H. Auden's *Musee des Beaux Arts* would unfurl inside his head: *About suffering they were never wrong/ The Old Masters; how well, they understood/ Its human position; how it takes place/While someone else is eating or opening a window or just walking dully along—*

Mrs. Hebert was in the back corner of the unit, barely conscious, her hands moving ineffectively around an oxygen mask. No surprise, Martin thought, that she wasn't intubated; that too was surely an intervention she would resist. He looked at the monitor that showed her blood oxygen level wavering between eighty-six and eighty-three percent. Mrs. Hebert's cardiac tracing showed abnormalities in the entire QRS complex; her heart was beating in a dangerous and ragged ventricular tachycardia. He greeted his patient's nurse, a woman named Tracey, who was adding another bag to the already susbstantial collection hanging from Mrs. Hebert's IV pole, and shook his head.

"Not good, I know," Tracey answered. "The family's in the hallway if you want to try your luck with them on at least getting us an airway, but Mom here is in no shape to cooperate."

"You've tried to talk to her? She's non-responsive?" Without waiting for an answer, Martin turned to his patient. "Mrs. Hebert, it's Dr. Winzer, your cardiologist. Can you understand me?"

Mrs. Hebert's half-opened eyes rolled in response to Martin's voice but there was no light of recognition, nothing but an oxygen-starved blankness in them. The tip of her nose and her lips were turning livid, the cyanotic tissues tinged an ominous purple. Mrs. Hebert needed to be intubated, and soon. Martin turned back to the ICU nurse.

"Does she have a DNR?"

Tracey shook her head. "Just a health care proxy. Her son is her agent."

"Does he know what her wishes are?"

Tracey made a cynical face that reminded Martin, painfully, of an expression Nina would use. "Wouldn't that be nice?"

Martin scowled as he scanned the ER attending's notes. He told the nurse he'd speak with Mrs. Hebert's family ("The son, his name, it's…?" he asked; "Robert," she said, "No, wait: Richard."); ordered an increase in her medications. Thrombolytics, pressors, heparin. There was nothing in her chart that ruled out pain relief, so he ordered morphine added to her IV, just a little, as well. Automatically, he laid his hand briefly on his patient's before he left her bedside. Ruta Hebert's skin was as he expected it would be, in spite of the warmed blankets that covered the lower half of her body. Her hand was ice cold, the beds of her fingernails blue.

Richard Hebert sat with his wife in the overlit hallway. He looked exhausted, gray and rumpled, his loose-skinned face ready for a morning shave. He stood and put his hand out to Martin, walked to meet him in the middle of the hall.

"Dr. Winzer. You told her two years ago it would come to this, but I'm not sure any of us believed it."

Martin shook the other man's hand and told him the obvious: his mother's condition was very serious. The rhythm of her heart was life-threatening.

Richard Hebert nodded and rubbed his mouth with his hand. "That other doctor in the emergency room, Dr. Lim, she told us there's some procedure you can do that will get blood back into the area of her heart that isn't getting any. Mom said no when they brought her in but if it's my call at this point then I'm going to tell you to do everything you can."

Martin shook his head. "I'm sorry. The procedure Dr. Lim mentioned, percutaneous coronary intervention, might have been a possibility when your mother first came in, but at this point I'm afraid it's longer an option. What time did you say your mother's heart attack happened?"

"It was just a little past eleven o'clock. Linda and I were both sound asleep and we heard a crash. Mom must have been on her way to the toilet."

Martin glanced again at his watch. It was a quarter of two now; after almost three hours of ischemia, a large area of Ruta Hebert's left ventricle was dead, lusty red muscle now turned to waxy yellow.

"Mr. Hebert, the tests that were done after your mother's first heart attack showed areas of decreased blood-flow across almost all the arteries that provide blood to the heart, and the EKG that was done when you came in tonight indicates that one of them, the left anterior descending artery, is almost completely blocked." Martin did not tell the other man the name cardiologists gave to an occluded LAD: a widowmaker. "There's a very small window of time for doing any kind of coronary intervention after an acute heart attack, particularly for a patient as fragile as your mother. At this point, even if your mother consented, the damage is irreversible."

Richard Hebert's eyes filled with tears. "So you're telling me this is it?" he asked. A decade earlier, the doctor who took a growth off his mother's nose said it was melanoma and they should be prepared for it to spread aggressively; four years ago it was pneumonia in both of her lungs. "This is a woman who was widowed twice," Richard Hebert said, his voice catching. "My mother survived the death camps in Yugoslavia, Dr. Winzer. Did you know that?"

There it was, the tiny snippet of biography that Martin knew had been lurking. An icy thread of fear circled the nape of his neck. "I'm very sorry," he managed. "I'm sure your mother has lived a remarkable life."

Linda Hebert rose to put her arms around her husband and Martin turned away, giving the couple a moment of privacy, relieved to have the excuse. He was preparing to turn back, to recommend to Richard that he spend what time he could with his mother, when he saw Tracey starting toward him down the hall. The nurse didn't move with particular urgency; in her face or her body language Martin couldn't read bad news or good. He stepped toward her, but Tracey spoke around him, a hand extended to his patient's son.

"Mr. Hebert," she said, "Your mother is conscious and she's trying to talk, but I don't think she's speaking in English."

There was panic in Richard Hebert's voice when he explained that his mother spoke Serbian into her late twenties but never wanted him to learn it. He knew a phrase or two but it was his sister, Eva, who understood more. Martin led the way back to Ruta Hebert's bed, where she had pulled the oxygen mask away from her face. Her saturation numbers blinked in red. Eighty-two, eighty-one, seventy-eight…Tracey tried to fasten the mask back over Mrs. Hebert's nose and mouth and Martin marveled that his patient was still conscious. The numbers blipped, lower and lower; it had to be a matter of seconds before the oxygen level in her brain was so low higher functionings were shut down, like a bank of lights switching off.

"Mrs. Hebert," Martin said loudly, "can you hear me?"

The elderly woman's eyelids fluttered. Tracey stepped forward and briskly twisted her knuckles against the patient's bony sternum. "Mrs. Hebert," she said, "we'd like permission to put a breathing tube down your throat now."

With no indication that she could hear him, Martin explained to his patient that without the tube she would fall unconscious and her heart would stop. "If that happens, you will suffer brain damage and you will die, very soon."

The death sequelae were logical, reliable; nothing more or less than the final pattern in the dance every living thing was involuntarily dancing. In Mrs. Hebert's case, the pattern was not so much a chain of events but a spiral; because her heart couldn't pump blood properly her lungs were filling with fluid; because her lungs couldn't deliver oxygen to her brain, her spasmodically jerking ventricle would finally surrender and stop altogether. Mrs. Hebert's blood would be drained of its oxygen and glucose reserves and turn acidic; her muscles would spasm, her sightless pupils would dilate, no longer able to record the light.

In medical school, Martin's professors had called this sequence—organ failure, the cessation of heartbeat and breath, the clenching of starving muscles, even in the voicebox sometimes, the source of the otherworldly death-rattle—the agonal phase; agonal for *agon*, the Greek word for struggle. "That's because the end is agony," a classmate had joked, and the room had filled with nervous laughter. But Martin had been secretly thrilled, had gotten it, agreed. There again was the truth and the beauty of medicine, the frank admission of what so many other human constructs sought to deny: the end was agony.

Once more, Tracey gave Mrs. Hebert a sternal rub. A bird-claw hand against her chest to stop the painful stimulus, Ruta Hebert opened her eyes. She looked directly at Martin. "*Docktor*," she said. "*Molim. Pomagati molim, docktor.*"

Next to Martin, Richard Hebert spoke excitedly. "Help me. She said, 'please help,' Dr. Winzer. Go ahead, now. Put the tube in."

Martin held his hand up. "Just a minute, please. Help you *how*, Mrs. Hebert? Are you asking me to put the breathing tube in?"

He spoke loudly, but Mrs. Hebert was done. The oxygen monitor went off, a sustained keening note. Richard Hebert's voice was agitated as he said, "Of course she is! That's what she just said. Please. Do it now!"

Martin knew all the nurses were watching him, but he didn't need to be reminded. Ruta Hebert had no DNR, and from the moment the family had arrived in the ER her son had become legally empowered to make his mother's treatment decisions. There was no medical or legal reason that he could not—should not—put his patient on life support. For a moment, he looked around. A half-dozen beds each surrounded by two or three monitors; plastic chairs hastily mounded with shoes and clothing and pocketbooks; Styrofoam cups of cafeteria coffee that was minutes or hours old. The patients were all in hospital gowns, wreathed with wires like life-sized marionettes; two other families, summoned unexpectedly like the Heberts, were dressed just like them: wrinkled slacks and unmatching pullovers, bare ankles showing where feet had been thrust hastily into shoes. The nurses were the only ones who had planned on being here, and they looked like it, dressed in Dansko clogs and pale green scrubs, perfectly made up despite the fact that it was—Martin glanced briefly at the clock on the wall—2:03 a.m. Exhaustion washed over him.

He rubbed his face and walked around to the head of Mrs. Hebert's bed. He lifted her mandible and peered into her mouth. This, too, was automatic to him. Press apart the lips, remove any dental work, move the tongue to the left with the blade of the laryngoscope. Slide the blade past the hypopharynx, lift the epiglottis to expose the vocal cords, pass the endotracheal tube along the scope and into the trachea. If he hit his mark, both sides of Mrs. Hebert's thorax would lift equally, the two boggy oblongs of her lungs reluctantly filling with 100% oxygen. Without looking, he extended a hand behind him, to Tracey. A size seven endotracheal tube should do.

Please help.

•

PLEASE HELP.

Helfen Sie, bitte!

Martin's mother's voice was the blackest hole, rimmed with ice, her screams coming from somewhere on the first floor. Martin raced down the stairs on shaky legs, following the sound, then stopped in the doorway of his father's library like he was rooted to the earth, seeing without understanding the scene in front of him. His father, sprawled on the carpet and gathered halfway in his mother's lap, pants of herringbone wool and his head flung back. A dark inky puddle beneath his mother's skirt and bright red blood on her bodice. She was hurt. Mutti was hurt! Martin cried out and his mother looked at him with wild eyes, her voice an icicle again, shattering in his ears—*get out! don't look!* Rough hands on his shoulders as

Sieghilde, the cook, pulled him into the hallway and pressed him against the wall. *Go and get help*, she said to Martin. *Take your sisters and go. Do you understand?* Martin nodded, terror-struck, watching as the cook entered the library and pulled the paneled doors shut. Behind Sieghilde in the closing rectangle: a faint ghost of smoke in the air, a glint of light off the glossy black pistol near the toe of one of Martin's father's splayed feet. Drops of blood and something heavier fell from a spattered circle on the ceiling, an exploded crimson star, hitting the Oriental carpet with a steady, wet *thock*.

ALONGSIDE HIS BODY, MARTIN'S father had left a note instructing Mutti to flee west with Martin and his sisters; there were relatives in Penrith, England, who would take them in. Through his father's burial and into the days and weeks that followed Martin waited, but Mutti did nothing, asked no one in particular why she would leave Berlin when the worst already had happened. Soon, families and single women, women in pairs, starting coming through the Winzers' stone wall, still standing in a city of rubble. They knocked on the Winzers' back door and Martin's mother let them in. Pulling carts and dragging steamer trunks, their presence was a comfort, filling the echoing house once again with noise. While Martin's mother smoked cigarettes, staring out unseeingly, the refugee families busied themselves with building fires and hauling buckets of water and patching broken windows, scrubbing clothes on the back patio, scraping together meals of watery soup and stale bread and ersatz coffee. A pair of sisters whose apartment house in the east of Berlin had been bombed took Martin to stand in the ration lines, arguing on his behalf when the grocer measuring flour put his thumb on the scale. A teacher from Bad Freienwalde helped Martin when another of the refugees—a grown man with a beard—tried to take Martin's bicycle away to trade at the butchers, pushing it down the road while Martin clung to the handlebars, the soles of his shoes scraping against stone.

At night, the families gathered around the Winzers' massive dining table for their meager meals or filed to the basement to wait out yet another interminable air raid. The whooping of the sirens came almost constantly now, and in the musty dark, different people would offer in whispers what news they'd heard about how close the Russian army was to the German border, the little towns of Peitz and Beeskow, the eastern outskirts of Berlin. When his father was alive, Martin had heard plenty about the Russians, listening as he and his business acquaintances disparaged the Red Army over drinks and dinner, chuckling disdainfully about the Ivans' inferior weaponry, but the stories shared in the basement were riddled with fear: Russian soldiers shooting civilians on the spot, Russian soldiers burning houses to the ground. "They're raping German women, sometimes three or four of them at a turn," a woman from Sagan announced one night. "Young or old, it doesn't matter." Martin didn't know the word rape—*Vergewaltigung*—but he saw the tight clenching of his mother's jaw, the lightning glare she flashed before reaching a hand toward his sister Brigid. "My sister in Frankfurt said in one village near her they were killing babies. Took them right by the ankles and swung against whatever was closest. Rocks or trees, the side of a house."

The morning Martin was awakened by the sound of thunder, he ran to his window to check the sky, but the air was silver, striped with pink clouds. It was the schoolteacher from Bad Freienwalde who explained to him that the sound he was hearing was Ivan, the rumbling of their tanks rolling through the city. The Russian army would be on the Ulmenstrasse in hours and there wasn't time to waste. Several of the refugee families took the schoolteacher's advice and fled, heading west on foot with no other plan than to put as many kilometers as possible between themselves and Ivan. Martin packed his own bag, ready to go, and the teacher smiled at him sadly before disappearing around the stone wall with the other refugees. Mutti had told the man she wasn't leaving; the Russians weren't going to come up the Ulmenstrasse, not today. Why would she run if she didn't have any place to run to?

All day long, the families who had decided to stay worked to prepare the house, carrying sacks of barley and potatoes to the basement and lugging buckets from the water pump two blocks up the street. Doors that had gaped open for weeks were nailed shut with broken sticks of furniture. Slabs of mahogany armoire blocked off the patio and the cold cellar and the servants' entrance; the Winzer's piano, heavy and upright, was rolled in front of the arched oak entry door. *There*, Martin's mother said at one point; *see?* At suppertime, she spread hard pieces of bread with a thin scraping of lard and turned her head away when Martin broke his in half to share with her, though her dress hung loosely and the blades of her collarbone were so sharp they looked like they hurt her skin. Another of the women asked Martin's mother, "Shall we make ourselves ugly, just in case?" and in response Mutti laughed bitterly; there was no need. "Just in case what?" Hedy asked. "No need for what?" No one answered her, and Mutti spoke angrily when Martin's sister asked her question again. After they were finished eating, Martin and Hedy were sent to their rooms to stay out of trouble. Brigid collected the dishes off the table and stacked them in the soapstone sink. Up in his room, Martin flipped through a book left behind by the schoolteacher, a Latin text full of mysterious masculine nouns. *Rex, puer, vis.*

Just when it seemed that Mutti was right, the Russians weren't going to come, the low rumbling sound that had surrounded the house all day poured through the walls and filled Martin's bedroom with a menacing roar. It vibrated in his ears, it rattled the windowpanes, it set off the hallway telephone that had been silent for months. Out in the garden, Martin heard the sound of men's voices, the horrible bark of words he didn't understand. He pressed his face to the window, watching as three soldiers hoisted a piece of garden statuary, stayed put as Mutti had ordered him to even as he heard the firework noise of the statue going through the glass-paned solarium wall. The three men disappeared below him, followed by half a dozen others whose terrifying shouts soon spread across the first floor.

Please help.

Helfen Sie, bitte!

It was the woman from Sagan, the woman who had used the strange word *Vergewaltigung* in the basement, who burst into Martin's room first, crying out and shaking with fear. *Helfen Sie, helfen Sie, kleiner Junge!* Behind her came the stomp of booted feet, a sharp, animal odor like nothing Martin had ever smelled before. The woman pulled Martin to his feet, wrapping her arms around his torso to hold him in front of her like a shield, and words poured from her in a frantic tumble—a child, please, a baby, you can't, not with him here to see everything. Martin looked up at the blank, filthy face of the man to whom she was making her wild entreaties: Ivan himself, no older than twenty, reeking of sweat and alcohol. His beard was stringy, his uniform stained and tattered; one of his front teeth was missing. The soldier glanced at Martin, his face registering nothing, and took another step toward the woman from Sagan. She locked an arm around Martin's neck with a shrill scream and all at once, his voice came, as well: Mutti! he screamed. *Mutti!*

The worst had already happened. The first time he had heard Mutti say those words, they had frightened Martin, their flatness and despair. But as the soldier in his bedroom grasped his shirtfront and pulled him from the Sagan woman's grip, throwing him into his bookcase like something weightless, Martin thought of them again, wrapped them around himself like a cloak. Books and toys and his collection of model airplanes fell down around him; the sharp wing of a Messerschmitt hit above his eye. The woman's cries turned to sobs as she spilled backward onto Martin's bed, Please no, please. Martin saw a shocking flash of pale skin, heard the hiss of ripping fabric and the thud of something heavy (a belt? a rifle?) hitting the floor. The soldier moved over the woman like a hammer, rabid breaths bursting out from him with each violent jerk of his hips.

The cut above his eye didn't hurt, not much at least, but Martin cried silently, his face against the hardwood floor. All around him, the house echoed with the sounds of chaos—running feet, slamming doors, the war noises outside that had threatened the house for months finally internalized. There were screams, and at one point, Martin had heard Brigid's voice saying no—not shouting, but speaking the words of someone fighting her way out of a nightmare, slow and muffled, insistent. No, no. No. Martin's own lips formed the same word, moving uselessly against the cold floorboard. After that, he didn't remember anything at all.

twenty-two

NINA KNEW IT WAS childish—even cowardly—to pin her actions on her husband, but as she looked out the passenger window of Todd Slocum's pickup truck, she found herself thinking, *Well, Martin, is this better than construction work?*

The previous afternoon she had encountered Todd at Royal River while Audrey was having her riding lesson with Deanna—a now-weekly undertaking Audrey was not yet ready for her mother to watch. While her daughter rode inside, Nina had wandered around the property and discovered Todd in one of the outdoor rings on the back of his own horse, a foaming black creature who snorted and pawed the ground impatiently when Todd guided him over to the fence so he and Nina could talk. Somehow, as they visited, Todd managed to convince Nina to get on Little John's back and walk around on him, a questionable idea that hadn't seemed any less so when Nina had slipped between the fence rails and sized up the horse. Little John's name didn't seem any more accurate from up close than it had from ten feet away.

"Isn't this the one that ran your wife into a wall?" she had asked.

"It is," Todd agreed, "but Susan was wearing spurs and old LJ here hadn't been ridden in a week and was pretty full of himself. I ran him off his legs today. He needs to walk for a bit one way or another to cool off." Todd jumped down and patted the horse's huge chest affectionately. "I'll keep him on a lead line and you'll be fine."

Biding for time, Nina had held her hand out for the horse to sniff.

"Who's the wise guy who named him Little John, anyway?" she asked. "Or did he put on an unexpected growth spurt recently?"

Todd laughed. "I bet Audrey would get it—he's named after the character in the *Robin Hood* stories. He's a gentle giant, I swear. Up you go."

Nina had pressed Todd's sweaty riding helmet on her own head reluctantly, but the instant she'd mounted LJ and he had started moving, she understood the pairing of terror and thrill that had flashed across Audrey's face at the beginning of her first ride. The sensation of moving under a power other than your own was utterly unnatural—her thighs clutched the saddle involuntarily, her fingers clenched tight around the reins. The big gelding walked slowly, though, with an easy, rolling stride, and as Nina looked ahead between his forward-pricked ears, she relaxed. Her fingers uncurled; of their own accord, her hips swayed in a gentle back and forth. At the age of forty-five, she was riding a horse for the first time. Being led like a child at a birthday party, yes, and only walking, but still. Todd unclipped the lead line, and she was *riding*, just like that. She wondered what else she'd been missing out on, like skydiving, maybe, or getting a tattoo.

She had dismounted fifteen minutes later already saddle sore but surprisingly energized; she accepted eagerly when Todd told her he could show her a couple more basics and she'd be out trail riding before she knew it. There were paths in the woods all around Royal River that were beautiful this time of year and she could ride Sunny, who was as quiet on them as a thirty-year-old ranch horse. This morning, when he had pulled up next to her in the Goldengrove parking lot and told her to hop in, they were going to head to the tack shop and buy her some riding gear, she had said okay as if that had been her plan for the day all along.

"So, you don't need too much to start out," he said now. "Some paddock boots and a pair of riding pants, for sure. A helmet if you're picky about hygiene, though there's a bunch of lesson helmets kicking around the barn."

"I can probably manage," she answered, already thinking about Martin's reaction to her potential purchases. "What about one of those vest-type things you were wearing yesterday, though?"

Todd shook his head. "That's for jumping, which I don't see us having you do for some time."

Glancing over at Nina again, he frowned. "Then again, maybe that wouldn't be such a terrible idea. Not for jumping, I mean. Just for…you know. General protection."

"That's kind of what I was thinking." Nina's heart pounded in her throat. There was no reason to bring this up with Todd and yet it seemed important for him to understand. "After everything that went into it I'm not sure who would be the most likely to kill me if I fell off a horse face-first, my husband, my insurance company, or my reconstructive surgeon."

Todd looked straight ahead. "Jumping vests are expensive, though. Almost three hundred bucks. You can just borrow mine for now if you want."

The tack shop was just across the Massachusetts border into New Hampshire, a forest green barn-like building with wide wooden doors and the smell of leather on the air. On the main floor, there were displays of riding clothes—gleaming black boots and tailored jackets, crisp pastel shirts and leather gloves—that looked like they belonged at Hermès or at least Nordstrom, a wall of monogrammed horse blankets, a bank of riding helmets with velvet covers. By the stairs to the second floor, a fully turned-out mannequin posed beside a polished wooden trunk with brass fittings, one hand resting on a caramel-colored saddle. Nina groaned. She could easily see herself spending a thousand dollars without even trying.

"Awesome, right?" Todd said. "I didn't want to give you too much time to think about it. This store is just about the most dangerous place in the world."

Nina walked over to a rack of riding coats and picked one up, looking at the price tag. $519. "You can say that again. It's like somebody took all my childhood middle-class insecurities and turned them into a store."

"Huh," Todd replied. "That's pretty much Susan's take on my shopping forays here. *Who do you think you're impressing buying all this stuff?*" He delivered a pinched imitation of his wife. "Then again, I'm not the one paying the credit card bills." He shrugged, and his Susan-face was replaced with a sheepish grin. "Speaking of which, let's get to it."

An hour later they were done, piling a small mountain of bags in Todd's truck. Todd held the door open for Nina, then glanced at his watch before he swung it shut again. "Probably not enough time to try your new toys out before we're due at school," he said. "Do you want to stop and grab something to eat, though? There's a place just before the highway that serves breakfast all day."

The restaurant was a 1950s-style diner, a narrow, stainless steel building with a turquoise neon sign and a black and white checkerboard floor. Todd pointed Nina to a booth, steering her with one hand on the small of her back, and handed her a menu in a maroon vinyl folder. The name of the diner, *Not That Mickey's*, was stamped on the folder in gold foil.

"Wow, I'm having flashbacks," Nina said. "My dad used to take me and my brothers to a place up in Maine that looked just like this."

Todd opened his menu and then closed it again without looking, pushing it away from him toward the napkin holder. "I thought I remembered you saying you grew up in Cabot."

"I did. My dad was a professor at the college and he had summers off. We used to go up to the place where he lived as a boy, this little island called Aggamassic Reach, just north of Bar Harbor. He'd do a little observing of the fauna and call it research."

"So, let's see." Todd drummed his fingers against the tabletop. "You grew up in Cabot, summered on Vinalhaven Lite—I'm not getting the middle-class insecurities you mentioned earlier."

A waitress set down water glasses and Nina took a long drink from hers, turning the ice cubes around with her straw. "Well, not when you put it that way, I suppose not. I grew up in the faculty neighborhood, though, which was barely a step up from the graduate student housing. And Aggamassic Reach was hardly Vinalhaven. We lived with my grandparents in a little three-bedroom, one-and-a-half story cape. The island itself was just a little fishing village, half a dozen houses, no stores or cars or anything. My grandfather was a lobsterman."

"But you liked it there."

"I did." Nina nodded. "It was my favorite place in the world. It's been close to thirty years since I've been there, though, so I'm probably romanticizing it."

"Thirty years? How come?"

"My grandfather died when I was a sophomore in high school and my grandmother had Alzheimer's so she couldn't stay there by herself, so my parents moved her into a nursing home in Bangor. My dad was an only child and knew he wouldn't be getting back up there much so he sold the house to pay for her nursing care."

"It's still there, though? The house?"

"As far as I know."

"You should take Audrey up there sometime."

Nina smiled. "I actually thought about it a lot a year or so ago, when I was going through chemo and I was just so incredibly sick. It was one of those bargaining things I did with myself: if I made it through chemo, if I made it into remission—"

"Which you did," Todd prompted.

"And then I did the reconstruction thing a year ago and spent all of last summer recovering from that."

"So this summer, then."

The waitress had returned to take their order and Nina was relieved for the interruption, not only because Todd appeared to be fully prepared to commit her to a plan she hadn't had a chance to think through. Perhaps it was just the power of suggestion (again, fairly or not, Martin's fault), but she couldn't deny a certain intimacy developing between the two of them. It was the conversation—Todd had seemed to understand, almost innately, how much Charlotte Harbor once meant to her; try as she might she couldn't help but imagine a similar conversation with Martin and how quickly he would seek to change the topic, agree it was foolishness to romanticize the past. But it was something else, as well: the confidence with which Todd had taken control of the day's agenda, the easy way he moved with and around her. She didn't think of herself as the kind of woman who craved that sort of ownership (even now, to be conscious of it gave her a little disgusted shiver) but wasn't that what had drawn her to Martin early on? The age difference, the aloofness she had taken for wisdom, the professional confidence she had assumed extended to all aspects of his life. Now, sitting across from Todd, she was aware of the space between their hands on the table, the way their knees fit underneath it, alternating his and hers.

Nina hadn't looked at the menu yet, and she apologized to the waitress, scanning it quickly.

"Take your time, hon." The waitress gave Nina and Todd a wink. "You folks out playing hooky while the kids are in school?"

Nina jumped a little. "No," she said, more sharply than she had intended. "We're just coming from the tack shop. Our daughters ride together. Well not together, exactly. His daughter is my daughter's big sister at school."

The waitress nodded, clearly disinterested. Nina gripped the menu more tightly, feeling heat flood to her face. Beneath the table Todd's left knee gave hers a little accidental bump. He looked at her for a long minute—his head cocked to the side, the barest suggestion of a smirk on his lips—then shifted his attention to the waitress. "Sorry," he said. "Seems we're not quite as ready here as I thought."

twenty-three

OUT THE FRONT WINDOW of the Java Pot, Nina and Jenny watched as a familiar scene played itself out. Cabot College's spring semester was over, and Center Street was lined with SUVs and station wagons angled up onto the sidewalk, trunks open and hazard lights flashing. Tanned girls in tiny shorts with Greek letters emblazoned across the seats embraced one another weepily; boys whose bleary eyes fairly shouted *hangover* dragged plastic hampers and net bags jammed with laundry; a duo who perhaps were staying around for the summer fired a football back and forth over a hamper-dragging friend's head. Commencement had been the day before, another 800 Cabot graduates dispatched into the world. Just a few more hours and the town would be transformed into its sleepy summer self.

"Ugh." Jenny took a swallow of her coffee and then made a sour face at the window. "Get this over with, already. Wall to wall traffic, and all the pushy parents double-parking and taking the handicapped spaces. No wonder their kids are all so self-centered. At least in fall they all come in and out of here in one fell swoop instead of dragging it out for two weeks."

Nina actually liked this time of year, the students lugging their mini-refrigerators and hot-plates to the sidewalk, the music thumping from open dorm windows, the voices edged with year-end euphoria. She liked it the same way she liked the change of seasons, the perpetual reminder that the world was constantly in motion, but in a way that was predictable. It helped her remember what it felt like to be twenty-one years old.

"I don't know, Jen," she said. "It's not that bad. It always seems so quiet when they're all gone."

"Yes. Exactly."

"Don't you remember how depressing it was when we were in high school? You'd wake up one morning and suddenly we lived in Dullsville again." Nina jutted her chin toward a bemused-looking mother outside, fists on her hips as her son sprinted in the direction of the dormitories one more time. "And anyway, that's going to be you before you know it."

Jenny's son Silas was in tenth grade now, taller than Jenny by a head and almost as tall as Jim. Rather than softening, however, Jenny scowled in response to Nina's comment. "Ha," she said flatly. "I'm not holding my breath." Jenny stretched in her seat, raising both arms above her head. "We got a call from school the other day letting us know Silas is going to flunk both chemistry and French, but he *doesn't care*." Jenny dropped her voice to a surly teenage snarl on the last two words. "I had to go in there and make a royal pain of myself getting him into the summer classes and now he tells me he isn't going. I'm ready to strangle him."

"Oh, no! But he's so bright." Guiltily, Nina wondered for a moment if her dismay was for Silas or for the inevitable comparison to Audrey any mention of his academic achievement brought about. He had always been Audrey's counterpoint, a walking, breathing example of the one comfort Nina could always take in regard to her daughter's other quirks: she would never have to worry about how she was faring academically.

"Yes, apparently that's his argument. He doesn't do his homework— or attend half of his classes, from the sounds of it—because he's *bored.*"

"Oh, no," Nina said again.

"Oh yes, unfortunately."

Jenny gave a single, unhappy laugh and then continued. "Here's one funny thing, though. Do you remember Madame Desmarais, the fourth-year French teacher? It turns out she's still there. I bet she looks just the same. She probably still has the same single pair of panty hose with the run up the calf."

"Well, it might not be such a bad thing for Silas to avoid tangling with Madame Desmarais," Nina said. "She was tough."

"Seriously?" Jenny raised her eyebrows at Nina. "I don't know, I think tough is pretty much what the doctor has ordered, here. He's telling us it doesn't matter if he has to repeat the tenth grade. He's not even sure he's going to go to college. I think he needs someone to give him a good kick in the pants."

Out on the sidewalk, the not-Silas boy was back, trotting toward his mother with a terrarium tucked underneath one arm. Jenny wiped her mouth with the back of her hand then gestured toward Nina's legs.

"Speaking of pants, can I ask what you have on today? It's supposed to hit eighty degrees this afternoon."

Nina uncrossed her legs and lifted the left one straight out, turning her ankle from side to side. She was wearing her new tack shop purchases—proudly, she would argue, though she had waited until Martin left the house to get dressed. "They're riding pants."

"*Horseback* riding pants? You're taking lessons now, too?"

"Not lessons, really. I'm just learning some basics so I can go trail riding with Audrey, assuming she ever gets to the point she'll as much as let me watch."

"Where? With whom?"

"Same place as Audrey. The Slocums have two horses and Todd's letting me ride Juliette's."

Jenny looked from Nina's wagging ankle back out at Center Street, her expression possibly even unhappier now.

"What?" Nina asked.

"Are you sure that's such a good idea?"

"It's perfectly safe. I'm only walking, and even then I'm wearing a protective vest. It's made of Kevlar or something. I'm more likely to trip over the sidewalk out there than I am to fall off a horse."

Jenny frowned out the window at the sidewalk in question before turning back to Nina again. "That isn't what I mean. Weren't you telling me not too long ago that you and Martin had some big blowout about this guy?"

"We did," Nina said evenly.

"So…"

"So I should give in to his completely unfounded insecurities by denying myself something I really want to do?"

"*Is* it something you really want to do?"

"Well, yes," Nina said, trying to keep the defensiveness out of her voice. "I like it. It's incredibly freeing. The whole atmosphere, the way it smells, there are little birds darting in the rafters—" Nina realized whatever argument she was trying to make was coming out not only unconvincing but incoherent. "It's something I can do with Audrey, something I thought the two of us could learn together. She's really loving it, and I think it's good for her. The responsibility, the physical exercise."

Jenny took another sip of her coffee, blowing a tendril of hair from her face. She'd cut her hair short when Nina had lost hers two years ago, but her curls now were almost shoulder-length again. The errant ringlet settled against her cheek again and she coiled it around her finger, looking at it instead of Nina as she spoke.

"But you could do all that at another barn, correct? It's not like you *have* to drive all the way up to Standish to take riding lessons with Audrey. So what would be the harm in making your husband feel better by taking riding lessons somewhere around here? Rumor has it they even have barns right here in Cabot."

A handful of arguments came immediately to mind: because riding was something Audrey was doing with Juliette; because she knew the horses there now, and trusted them; because she wasn't paying Todd for her own lessons and riding somewhere else with Audrey would cost twice as much. She didn't bother trying them on Jenny, however, because she knew none of them were the real reason she wanted to ride at Royal River and she understood, somehow, that Jenny knew that, too.

Instead, she nodded and sipped her own coffee. "I've heard that, too," she said.

"Which is not the same thing as saying you're going to do it."

"Jenny, what do you want to hear me say? I'm not cheating on Martin. I'm learning how to ride a horse."

"I'm just saying your husband is a good man. If Jim was upset about something I was doing, if I was in your position…"

Out the window, Nina watched the Cabot College mother and son climb into their station wagon, a white Volvo with Connecticut vanity plates that read *OUT2C*.

"But you aren't in my position," she said, hoping that would be enough to put an end to the discussion.

"I know I'm not. But I'm your friend, aren't I? I don't have anything at stake but your best interests."

Nina was aware of the stubborn jut of her chin, the belligerence of her words when she responded. "Todd is my friend, too. His daughter is Audrey's big sister at school, and spending time with her has done more for Audrey's self esteem in the last month than Martin and I and Goldengrove have done in the last eight years put together. If Martin can't get over that, it's his problem."

If she had had any thoughts at all of how her friend might respond to this argument, it certainly wasn't with what happened next. Jenny slumped in her seat, her expression defeated. "Really?" she asked. "Is that what this is all about?"

Nina frowned. "What do you mean?"

"Willow and Audrey."

For a moment, the world outside the window seemed to tilt and slide. "Jenny, what are you talking about?"

Jenny sighed in a way that seemed more aggrieved than anything else. "Willow said she and Audrey weren't getting along but I figured it was just usual third-grader stuff. Calla and her friends used to go through it all the time. Audrey hasn't said anything to you?"

"What do *you* think, Jenny? Of course she hasn't." Jesus. If there was a problem between Willow and Audrey, why hadn't Jenny said anything to Nina before now?

"It's nothing, probably." Jenny sat up again. Looking out the window, she continued. "I don't know. I said something to Willow the other day about how we hadn't seen Audrey in a bit and she told me they've been hanging out with other people, playing with other girls who are more interested in the same things as they are. You didn't mention it, so I thought maybe I was making a big deal out of nothing." She paused again, and when she resumed speaking her words came faster. "I probably am. If Audrey hasn't said anything to you…"

Nina shook her head. Jenny knew as well as she did that Audrey's silence on the subject didn't signify anything, and she couldn't help but think the *they* her friend had so deliberately used in relating Willow's explanation was really *she*. *Willow* was hanging out with other people. *Willow* was playing with other girls who were interested in the same things she was. A picture flashed in front of her: Audrey at drop-off the morning earlier, her exit from Nina's car slower than usual perhaps, her head tipped forward as she had moved toward school. Nina had watched her disappear through the front door, feeling a pang of love for her daughter's rounded shoulders and her no-nonsense navy blue backpack, unadorned with the multiple stuffed-animal keychains and plastic gimp braids that seemed to clutter all the other childrens' bags. Now, a sharper pain arrowed through her chest.

"Jenny," she said. Her voice caught. For the first time in a long time, she was aware of the fragile, hothouse nature of Audrey's friendship with Willow, the tenuousness of her daughter's place in the world. Over the past few years, she'd let down her guard. She'd brushed off every concern voiced by Audrey's teachers regarding her overdependence on Willow, mentally chastised herself on the rare occasion she allowed herself to doubt. A few weeks back, Jenny had mentioned that the girls had a couple of tiffs while she and Martin were in Hawaii, but Nina had been willing to think that was a good thing, "normal" girl stuff that any pair of eight-year-olds would go through. Then, she hadn't thought to question Jenny further; the questions that she had now she had too much pride to ask: Who was Willow *hanging out with* instead of Audrey? Callie Burke? Heather Moran? How many playdates had they had, giggling over some Disney Channel show while Audrey sat alone in her room reading *The Hobbit*—or even worse, the encyclopedia? And most importantly, *Why?* She couldn't even bring herself to wonder what kind of mother it made her that she hadn't picked up on Audrey's unhappiness until now.

Jenny put her hand on Nina's. "I'm sorry. I should have said something sooner. I know it's different for Audrey, but it's probably just a rough spot. Girls are just like that. Like I said before, Calla and her friends went through all this stuff at the same age."

The shrill, digital ring of Nina's cellphone somewhere deep inside her purse spared her from having to say anything else. She dug the phone out and glanced at the display. *Private.* It was rude, she knew, but she flipped the phone open and pressed talk, a small, ironic smile quirking her lips as she thought, *Todd.*

twenty-four

MARTIN STOOD JUST OUTSIDE the glass doors of the ICU, not quite ready to take the half dozen steps required to enter the unit and confront the group gathered just beyond the closest bed. In addition to Richard Hebert and his wife, Linda, there was a woman who so resembled Martin's patient he was certain it had to be her Lake George-based daughter, Eva, and a tall figure in green scrubs and rubber clogs that he recognized as Bobby Lansford, a young cardiac surgeon who had recently joined the staff. The three Heberts were ringed around the surgeon, Richard and Linda's faces wearing such expressions of rapt, hopeful attention Martin experienced a moment of actual dread. Lansford had been at St. Serafin for less than two months, but was already secure in his reputation as a cowboy, a surgeon willing to take on complicated cases others wouldn't. Martin couldn't imagine what business Lansford would have with his patient's family if not to discuss some sort of risky procedure that would do little more than further prolong her misery.

It had been a week since the disorienting middle-of-the-night phone call from the Emergency Department, six days since Martin had stopped in the ICU at the end of a long workday to learn that Mrs. Hebert was hanging on. That she was had left him more regretful than surprised; after he had intubated her, Richard Hebert had exercised his right as health care agent and authorized every medical and mechanical intervention available—an automatic external defibrillator to stabilize her heartbeat, a full complement of beta blockers and vasodilators, blood thinners and diuretics to keep it working—Martin's warnings that none of these measures would reverse the damage that had already been done to her heart muscle falling on deaf ears. Two days ago Mrs. Hebert had begun to show signs of overbreathing her ventilator; yesterday, Martin had extubated her, watching with some amazement as, following an initial drop, her oxygen saturation levels climbed slowly toward ninety on just an oxygen mask. Her blue eyes were open but, still sedated, her face remained expressionless, and she had yet to respond to Martin with anything more than a slow blink. It was difficult to say if her lack of responsiveness was due to the medication or something else, but the truth was Martin had little desire to find out.

Over the past week, Martin had come to understand that he felt accountable to Ruta Hebert in a way he rarely did with his patients. He felt guilty, as if his actions in the ICU had fallen short of serving her best interests, regardless of their medical expedience. It was all well and good to hide behind technicalities—true enough, she had no DNR; and true enough, her son had the legal right to order continued treatment. But those technicalities failed to serve him in the many moments his patient's deadened gaze and gasping-fish mouth intruded on his thoughts. *Pomagati molim, Doktor.* Martin had gone so far as to look up a translation of the words his patient had uttered that first night, not expecting them to be other than what her son had told him they were. What of Martin's moral obligations? He felt certain he knew, he had known, what it was that she had wanted that night in the ICU. It had not been the sequence of events that had brought her to today.

Inside the unit, Martin saw Bobby Lansford extend his right hand to Richard Hebert while making a show of checking the beeper he held in his left. Steeling himself, Martin pushed open the double doors, fixing what he hoped was a genuine-looking smile on his face as the surgeon turned his direction, clearly intent on making a quick getaway from the ICU.

"Speak of the devil!" Lansford said, striding toward him. "Dr. Winzer, were your ears burning? The Heberts here and I were just talking about you."

Instinctively, Martin touched the top of his left ear. "Well, I'm glad I caught you then," he said.

Grinning, the younger doctor waved his beeper at Martin. "Actually,

I just got word from OR 3 that my quadruple bypass is under, so I am going to need to catch you up later. But the bottom line is the Herberts here would like to put Mom on an LVAD. We'll consent them after you all have had a chance to talk."

For a moment, Martin was sure the surgeon was joking. He followed him out into the hallway, past the Heberts. "An LVAD? You can't be serious."

The surgeon stopped at the elevator bank, punching the down button with his index finger. "Of course I'm serious," he said.

"To what end?"

"More time, of course. Quality of life."

"Quality of life?" With an effort, Martin kept his voice low. It was a matter of courtesy, but it was all he could do to keep from grabbing Bobby Lansford by the arm and shaking him like a child. "Are you aware this is a patient who wanted no interventions, who refused a pacemaker because she didn't want to be—" in the two years since their first conversation, Martin had forgotten his patient's exact phrasing, but he remembered the gist of Ruta Hebert's objection to a pacemaker "—hooked up like a toy?"

The elevator door chimed and Bobby Lansford turned, spreading his hands supplicatingly. "In the end, everyone changes their mind, don't they? You and I have both seen it hundreds of times."

Lansford stepped into the crowded elevator, the doors closing before Martin could retort: it wasn't true; it wasn't Mrs. Hebert who had changed her mind. Martin steadied himself before turning back for the ICU. LVAD was short for *left ventricular assist device,* a battery-powered pump that took over some of the work of a patient's failing heart, and Ruta Hebert's heart was failing, for sure. Each day the physical exam Martin gave his patient was incrementally worse: when he listened to her chest, instead of a healthy lub-dub, he heard her heart beat with a series of feeble shuffling noises (the sloshy third beat of an overfilled left ventricle; an occasional hypertrophic fourth beat, as well); when she breathed, her lungs made little bubbling noises, her waterlogged alveoli struggling to siphon what oxygen they could from the fluid-filled lobes. Assuming she could even survive the surgery, an LVAD would fix all that, circulating her blood with the powerful pulses required to push it through all those miles of blood vessels, but Mrs. Hebert would be stuck inside a hospital, stuck with a pump orders of magnitude more significant than the pacemaker she had refused two years earlier, and what would happen then? Martin wondered who had suggested the idea of an LVAD to the Heberts; someone would have had to put them in touch with Dr. Lansford. Cowboy or no, he didn't see Lansford trolling the ICU for cases. *Goddammit,* he thought, taking a deep breath.

Inside the unit, Richard and Linda Hebert were still standing where Martin had left them. The woman he assumed was his patient's daughter, Eva, however, had moved to the older woman's bedside and was bent over her, stroking one of her limp, swollen hands.

Martin walked around the other side of the bed until he was sure he was in the woman's field of vision. "Hello. You must be Eva," he said. "I'm Martin Winzer, your mother's cardiologist."

The younger woman lifted her head, startling Martin with the intensity of her expression, the piercing blue of her eyes. "Yes, hello," she said. "Eva Sorrentino."

Martin nodded. "I'm glad you could be here. I'm sure it means a great deal to your mother."

Eva Sorrentino glanced over at her mother. Ruta Hebert's eyes were closed now, her immobile face turned to the side. "I'm not sure my mother knows I'm here."

Richard Hebert, who had followed Martin to his mother's bedside, responded to his sister before Martin could. "Mom knows you're here, Eva. Of course she does. Don't you, Mom?"

Ignoring her brother, Eva addressed herself to Martin again. "When I got here this morning, the nurse who was caring for my mother said she was oxygen-deprived for a long time. Doesn't that mean there's a good chance of brain damage?"

Martin nodded again. "It does. Right now it would be difficult to evaluate." Martin saw Richard and Linda Hebert exchange a look. "Why don't we all go to the family lounge where we can talk with a bit more privacy? We can discuss your mother's prognosis and you can tell me about your conversation with Dr. Lansford."

In the lounge, Richard Hebert explained that he had contacted Dr. Lansford directly; two days earlier, he had looked up congestive heart failure on the internet and read about left ventricle assist devices. The first surgeon he tried said he wouldn't do the surgery and the second hadn't bothered to return his call. When he'd called Richard back yesterday, Dr. Lansford had been very convincing.

"Dr. Lansford said it can make a huge difference to a patient's outlook." Richard Hebert's tone was defensive, as if he was responding to an argument Martin hadn't yet served up. "He said that sometimes it's patients not getting enough oxygen to their brains that makes them refuse treatment. It makes them frightened, and on some subconscious level they already feel like they're dying and there's nothing they can do about it. If Mom gets this LVAD and starts feeling better, she could very well change her mind about the whole thing."

Martin folded his arms across his waist and looked around the room. Behind Richard Hebert, on the muted lounge television, a young, telegenic newscaster filled the screen. He appeared to be providing an update about the war in Iraq, his brow knit with consternation while images of rolling tanks and fires played in the upper right corner. "Did Dr. Lansford also explain to you that the only patients who ever come off the LVAD are ones who receive a new heart, and at the age of ninety-one your mother is not a candidate for transplant?"

Richard Hebert scowled, but Martin pressed on. Even before he had arrived in the ICU this morning he had known he had to have this discussion with the Heberts. Part of him had been hoping he could pass it off on one of the nurses—they were always better than the doctors at these things, and to say this part of the work was not his strong suit was an understatement—but there wasn't time for that now, not with Bobby Lansford already calculating when he could fit an LVAD surgery into his busy schedule.

"Mr. Hebert, I realize this is all a difficult, emotional experience, and I am sorry for that. I truly am. But your mother was very clear when she came into my office two years ago, and she was clear when she came into the hospital last week. You told me yourself that she said she didn't want to be hooked up to any machines."

Unsurprisingly, the other man's expression darkened further. "And then my mother changed her mind. She said help me, Doctor."

Martin pressed his folded his arms more tightly across his midsection, frowning down at the scuffed brown toe of his shoe. "As I told you at the time, I am not sure I know how your mother wanted me to help."

Richard Hebert gave a short, incredulous laugh. "What's not to know? You're a doctor. She wanted you to save her life."

"Two years ago, your mother was well aware that she was at risk for a second heart attack and refused to undertake even a minor procedure to guard against that. At that time, what she wanted was for me to understand why it was her preference to let nature take its course."

Eva Sorrentino leaned forward in her peach vinyl lounge chair. "So what are you suggesting, Dr. Winzer? Are you saying that we should just stop treating her?"

"I am suggesting that the three of you sit down and have an honest conversation about what your mother would want to happen at this point. I am not trying to say that I know what's best for her. I'm just trying to offer an objective perspective."

Eva Sorrentino nodded. "What would happen if we stopped treatment?" she asked. "What would that look like?"

Choosing his words carefully, Martin again described the various medications and interventions supporting Ruta Hebert, explaining how they were helping her heart pump and decreasing the demands it would otherwise face. Acknowledging that the medications were having some beneficial effect, he explained that their efficacy was already limited and would become more so as the cascade of symptoms from her heart failure continued. If they withdrew all medications, her liver and her kidneys would shut down and she would slip into a coma rather quickly. She could last a while, or she could die in a matter of days.

"The nurse I spoke to earlier said heart failure feels like drowning from the inside out," Eva persisted. "She said as your lungs fill with fluid it's like trying to breathe through a straw."

"Yes," Martin agreed. "The effects of congestive heart failure are extremely unpleasant. The sedation we've given her takes the edge off that drowning sensation and also helps with the pain."

Eva Sorrentino frowned. "Why would she be in pain?"

"Your mother's heart sustained a great deal of damage. I will be absolutely blunt with you here. Whether or not she shows it, right now, your mother is suffering."

To Martin's astonishment, Richard Hebert laughed. It was a

humorless laugh, harsh and alarming, punctuated with raw gulps of breath. Linda Hebert put a hand on her husband's back. "Well, Dr. Winzer, there you have it," he said. "We can all get what we want here. My mother wants to be suffering."

"Not like this."

"So this is your expertise, too, all of a sudden? You know my mother better than me?" Richard Hebert raked his hands across his bald head and stood. "Let me tell you something, Dr. Winzer: my mother has been ready to die as long as I can remember. If I'm not ready to give in to her just yet I think it's my own goddamn business and none of yours."

Richard Hebert jabbed a thick finger at the air in front of Martin and then turned from the room. His wife and sister hurried after him, and Martin sat for a minute in the suddenly empty lounge, his face flushed with an emotion he couldn't quite put his finger on. The TV had finished its Iraq coverage and the screen now showed an exhausted-looking middle-aged couple holding a photo of a young, heavily pregnant woman. Martin reached for the television remote, pressing buttons until the sound that accompanied the picture flooded back. The man on screen was explaining his pregnant daughter hadn't been heard from in several days; less than a week ago the father of her unborn baby had threatened to take a chainsaw and cut her into pieces and she'd been trying to get a restraining order from the police. The baby's father couldn't be located, either, but a home improvement store had just uncovered surveillance footage from last Friday that showed him walking out with a Husqvarna box in his hands. Martin shook his head, pressed the channel button until a cartoon of a talking yellow sponge appeared on the screen in place of the news. *Much better,* he thought. Could anyone blame Ruta Hebert if she had had enough of living in this world?

twenty-five

It was the end of the day when Eva Sorrentino caught up with Martin outside the ICU. He had been planning to stop in only quickly on his way out the door, and when he spied her daughter in the hallway he allowed himself an inward sigh. Though he had apologized to Nina for the argument about Todd Slocum, he was well aware their marital truce was tenuous, Nina's forgiveness incomplete; delivering on a promise like the one he'd made this morning to be home for dinner still mattered disproportionately. In Eva Sorrentino's expression he could see the determination to have a conversation of some consequence, and it was important, but still. Martin's patient's daughter stood, brushing imaginary wrinkles from her cotton pants, and gave him a weary smile.

"Dr. Winzer," she said. "I was hoping to catch you. The nurses said you'd be up to see my mother before you left for the night."

"Yes, of course," Martin said. "Have you been in with her? How do you think she's doing?"

Eva Sorrentino lifted her hands. "I think it's pretty much what you told us this morning. My mother is on her way out."

Martin nodded, glancing down at the floor. Eva Sorrentino was wearing sneakers, and impulsively, he heard himself ask her, "Would you be willing to walk me to my car? I'm guessing you've been up here all day, and I'm afraid I'm rather short on time. This hospital air is terrible for you, you know."

If Eva was surprised by Martin's suggestion she didn't show it, waiting at the door of her mother's cubicle while he checked her over and conferred with her nurse, following him silently to the elevator bank. Outside, it was humid, the early evening air hazy with orange sunset. Martin had been inside all day himself, juggling office visits, other hospitalized patients, and an emergency catheterization no one else could cover. An ambulance wailed down Railroad Avenue, its lights flashing; some sort of heavy machinery at the under-construction St. Serafin Cancer Center hammered away with regular, percussive thuds.

"So." Eva Sorrentino swung her purse across her body and held it there, matching her strides to Martin's. "It seems a bit absurd to be apologizing for a sixty-year-old man, but I wanted to say I was sorry for my brother's outburst this morning. I don't get the feeling we made the progress we needed to about my mother's care."

Martin nodded. "There's no need to apologize. This is an extremely emotional experience. Your mother is in the most difficult place we find ourselves in medicine, where there are things we can do to prolong her life without being able to cure her disease. It's not a question of whether we can continue to keep her alive but what the quality of that life will be, and the answer to that is subjective. It's a question of values. It's much easier when you're weighing issues of science."

A car rounded the corner, music flooding from its open windows, and Martin grimaced. The little speech he had just given Eva Sorrentino was exactly that, a tidy spiel for the Hebert family he had rehearsed in his head all day long, polishing and refining the various turns of phrase until it sounded just so. It was all he had, however, and he realized now that it sounded too packaged, too pat. What was it he really wanted to say to this woman, now that he had the opportunity? *This would be a hell of a lot simpler if your mother had just written a DNR order. You need to talk your brother out of this foolish LVAD idea.*

Eva squinted ahead. "My brother's relationship with our mother has always been more complicated than mine. I don't know what he's told you, or what she might have told you, for that matter, but she had another family in Yugoslavia before Richard and I were born. They were killed in the Ustashi death camps in World War II, her entire family, her husband and son, both of her parents, her two sisters. She had insisted on staying in Yugoslavia even when her husband wanted to flee. He had a cousin in

Albania, I guess, with Muslim friends who could hide them, but she didn't want to leave her mother and her sisters behind."

Of course. The same afternoon Martin had looked up the Serbian words Ruta Hebert had gasped to him, he had searched "Yugoslavia in World War II" on his computer, Richard Hebert's brief, fraught biography still vivid in his mind. She wasn't necessarily Jewish, Martin concluded, but it was likely; had more than a handful of Serbian Jews survived the war? The truth was Martin's grasp of World War II had never been as comprehensive as it should have been. Before he went to England, he had known the war only as a thing that had affected innocent Germans; as a schoolboy in Penrith, his lessons to the contrary had been delivered with two fists. By the time he was in medical school, Martin had assembled enough of the pieces to construct a terrible picture; did it really require explanation that he had left that picture unfinished? It was one thing to realize the mosaic of history was full of monsters. It was quite another to discover the piece in the very center was a mirror.

An article he found suggested his limited understanding had been correct: the Serbian Jewish population had been nearly wiped out. A small mercy, the Yugoslav death camps had been run by Croatian fascists, the Ustashi, operating under Nazi protection, but still. The words and pictures were familiar, and yet Martin had made himself look: emaciated men and women, trenches full of corpses, piles of suitcases and shoes and human hair. As he read, Martin had become more curious about how his patient had made it through the war. She would have been barely out of her teens during the early years, in her mid-twenties when the Nazi genocide in Yugoslavia really picked up steam. Had she been married? Had she had a family? Well, now he knew.

"She never forgave herself, as I'm sure you can imagine, and Richard always thought that when she looked at him, she saw the son who died, Danijel, and she couldn't love him because of that. She always denied it, of course. It was easier for me, being a girl." Eva smiled ruefully. "Poor Richard. I probably took advantage more than I should."

Martin and Eva were rounding the back of the hospital now, the physician's parking lot just ahead of them on the left. The wailing ambulance had reached the emergency bay, and in his mind's eye Martin followed the choreographed dance taking place just out of public view. Inside the ED, a team in scrubs was ready for the EMTs; in just a moment the back doors of the rig would fly open, the patient would be transferred into one of the trauma bays, and the team would set to work. Unlike many of his peers, Martin had never loved the energy of the emergency department—the grim, aggressive pace brought back flashes of air raid siren drills, the sight of his father's splayed legs and a pool of dark blood…He shook himself.

"In retrospect," Eva Sorrentino continued, "I probably should have been the one in charge of her medical decisions. I think Richard's been hanging on hoping for some sort of confession or apology she was never going to make."

Martin knew he needed to say something. "I'm sure your mother's past was difficult for her to talk about," he managed. *Very* sure, he thought, and not difficult—impossible.

Eva smiled again. "She talked about her past all the time. I think she was desperate for someone to understand what she experienced. What a pathetic thing, when you think about it, to be holding on that long in the hopes of finding something so basic and yet impossible. And now—all that suffering for nothing."

The two of them had reached the entrance to the parking lot, and Eva stopped walking, touching Martin on the sleeve. "I was down in North Carolina last week visiting my daughter and her family. I just got here last night. The first I heard about this whole LVAD thing was about five minutes before you came in this morning and Dr. Lansford made it sound like he could fix my mother. What would you do? If it was your mother, I mean?"

Images flashed through Martin's mind—his mother pinching her lips shut with her fingers as if not trusting her volitional ability to refuse his proffered bread; his mother sitting in the shattered solarium the morning after Ivan, her gray, drawn face so utterly absent he had cried out to be sure she wasn't dead. His mother receding from him one final time in the bitter predawn dark, an expression of despair crossing her face so quickly Martin couldn't be sure he hadn't made it up.

Martin found his car keys in his pocket, and he closed his fist around them before he answered. He blinked twice then forced himself to look his patient's daughter in the eye. "If it was my mother," he said, "I wouldn't want her to suffer. If I knew it was what she wanted, I would let her go."

after

•

I<small>F</small> N<small>INA WAS SURPRISED</small> to see Martin home in time for dinner as promised, she didn't show it. She was in the dining room when he arrived, laying out a trio of placemats on the cherry table. The air smelled of garlic and roasting chicken, and breathing in the scent, Martin couldn't help but ask, "Special occasion?" They hardly ever ate in the dining room, and if it weren't for the unchanged expression on Nina's face when he had walked into the room, he would have wondered if she hadn't been expecting someone else.

Nina shrugged. "In a sense, I guess. It's not often you're home at—" she consulted her watch "—six-twenty on a Monday." She inclined her head toward the kitchen and continued, "Audrey has a bunch of stuff for a school project spread all over the table in there and I didn't want to disrupt the flow she seems to have going."

Martin reached for the pile of silverware on the buffet, nodding. "I can see the sense in that. It smells delicious."

"Thanks. Audrey's in her room. I'll let her know you're home. I didn't tell her you were eating with us, just in case."

Nina turned, but Martin stayed her with his hand. "Wait a minute, if you would. I'm realizing I'm not done telling you I'm sorry."

Nina swung back around, and now her expression *was* surprised. "Wow," she said. "I don't think I know quite what to say."

"Well, I suppose that's better than if you did. I've been imagining any number of things you might be preparing to say to me." Martin pulled out a chair, gesturing for Nina to sit, and then seated himself next to her. "I think we can both agree I'm not all that well versed in what it means to be a modern husband."

"No, I suppose you're not. But thank you for saying so."

Nina pressed her right thumb against her left palm, rubbing her hand with slow strokes, and for a minute she rocked herself. Martin waited, and Nina shook her head. "I just—" she started. "It's the strangest thing. In some ways, this is harder than when I had cancer, this 'being cured' business. I don't know what I'm supposed to do with myself."

"I don't know that there's anything in particular you're supposed to be doing."

"But there is." Nina frowned. "I mean, I got lucky. I really did. And I feel like I've been given notice that life is really...finite. Mine could be over now, but it isn't. And so I should be *doing* something with myself, something significant, like going back to school or doing—I don't know, some sort of thing that helps someone."

"Like riding horses?"

From upstairs, Martin heard the sound of Audrey's feet thumping down the hallway, and then a door slam, the muted shush of the bathroom faucet running.

"Like charity work. Like volunteering. You know, if this is your idea of apologizing, you might as well not even bother."

Martin sighed. "I'm sorry, Nina. I am trying."

"Very," she said, and then it was Martin's turn to frown as she repeated herself. "Sometimes you are very trying."

After another pause, she gave him a sad smile. "You know, I'm only a little more than ten years younger than my mother was when she died. At the time, I tried to convince myself it was okay. She'd lived a long, full life; had a good marriage; seen her children grow up. But now, fifty-seven seems so young to me. Impossibly young. She had so much living left to do."

Nina was staring off, and Martin followed the direction of her gaze to the glass-doored china cabinet on the other side of the room. In the late afternoon light, he could see the fine layer of dust that coated the shelves, a small constellation of greasy fingerprints surrounding the silver knob. When was the last time that cabinet had been opened, he wondered, never mind anything inside of it used? It was full of vases and decanters, several crystal bowls in the shapes of different animals (a turkey for Thanksgiving, a rabbit for Easter), a dozen fragile and impractically undersized china cups.

"It's interesting, isn't it? The way your perspective changes over time. My mother was in her middle thirties when we left Berlin. And to me, as a boy of seven, she was a rock. She knew just what she was doing. I look back on it now and I realize how terrified she must have been."

For a moment, Nina didn't respond, and Martin could sense the careful stillness that had overtaken her. In nearly a decade together, Martin had never once *volunteered* information about his childhood, as clear as

Nina had made it that she wanted to know, and they both were well aware that was the case.

"Do you?" she finally asked. "Do you think about it?"

"Of course I do."

"What was it like?"

"Well—" Martin looked down at the table, adjusting the knife and spoon in front of him until the tip of the blade was lined up with the top of the bowl. "It's difficult for me to describe. At first, I didn't understand why we were leaving. There was a Russian officer who essentially took up residence in our house, and for a time we were well provided for, with foods we had not had for a long time, canned fish and vegetables and such. Then one day he was gone, and not long after that my mother woke me up in the middle of the night." Martin's voice was tight as he spoke, and his fingers pressed against the table, but he continued. There had been a man with a horse-cart; but they had to hurry; Martin had had only a few minutes to fill a single bag. Still dazed with sleep, he'd watched his half-timbered house recede behind its stone wall as the horse had clopped the cart away over the cobblestone road, not suspecting he'd never see it—or any of Berlin—again.

He didn't know how long they'd stayed with the horse-cart or how far they'd gotten, but the roads had been full of people like themselves, refugees, all shuffling blindly westward from towns like Zossen and Mittenwalde and Teltow. Martin's mother had packed a box full of food, but after a time, the last tin of fatty pork had been opened; Brigid had let Martin lick the salty oil from the last packet of sardines. They'd stood in the ration lines in strange Marketplatzes, begged at farmhouses where weary fraus had already heard a dozen times that day the same story of hardship they told. Some days they got lucky and the frau would give them some root vegetables or even a couple of eggs; others it would be Martin's job to crawl under the fence and see what he could take without getting caught. Every night, however, he had fallen asleep thinking about the pear trees and raspberry bushes that had surrounded number 20 Ulmenstrasse, replaying in his mind again and again the times he'd crushed the berries between his fingers just to feel the tiny globelets of fruit pop or taken a single bite of a pear before discarding it as too mealy or displeasingly bruised. He forced himself to remember again and again until the flavor no longer haunted his tongue.

"Where did you sleep?" Nina asked.

"Different places," Martin said. "Most places there were people who were willing to let *Flutchlinge*—refugees—stay. Sometimes, we'd find an empty house for a time. You have to understand, the whole of Germany was a nation of hermit crabs, people crawling into abandoned houses for a while and moving on."

Nina nodded. "Where were you all going to?"

"Away from the Russians. Germany was occupied for quite some time, you know, following the war. Some of the occupiers were more merciful than others. The British and American occupation zones were to the west and in general, if you were under rule, you would rather it was one of theirs. Particularly if you were a war prisoner turning yourself in."

"I don't think I ever understood that. I guess I've only thought of that type of exodus as happening in African countries, all those civil wars."

"Right." Martin nodded. "There are plenty of examples through history. I'd be hard-pressed to think of a war that wasn't followed by some kind of mass displacement."

"But where you were—there must have been some people who stayed."

"There were plenty. She waited too late, but as you know, my mother was trying to get us to England, where my father's relatives were. Once the Russians occupied East Berlin it was no longer possible to take the trains west, so we had to find another way to get to the British zone."

"And…Braunschweig?" Nina said the name tentatively. "That's where you ended up?"

"Yes, in the spring of 1946, after we spent the winter in an internment camp outside of Wolfenbuttel. We had two rooms in a barracks there. My mother had a job in town and my sisters and I went to school."

"A job?" The look Nina gave Martin was incredulous. "I don't mean to sound like an idiot, but I always kind of had this picture of refugees as *persona non grata*, sitting around waiting to be—I don't know—*not* refugees."

Martin was silent for a moment, leaning his weight slightly forward against his still-braced fingertips. "Well, you're right about the *persona non grata* part," he said. "But no, people held jobs and they went to school and they had rations cards, just like everyone else. There was a complete infrastructure built by the occupying countries, a bit like what the U.S. is attempting in Iraq today. There was a real investment in enabling the refugees to support themselves."

Nina nodded. "What did she do?"

"My mother? She worked in the house of an upper-level English officer, as a kind of hostess, I suppose. She spoke excellent English and of course she had had a great deal of experience entertaining senior members of the Nazi party."

"In Braunschweig," Nina said again. "And you left…?"

"In the autumn. November of 1946. Before he killed himself, my father had made arrangements for all of us to go. His cousin's fortunes had changed with the war, however, just like everyone else's, and by the time my mother was able to write they could take only me."

"You must have felt terrible. Guilty, I mean."

"How do you figure that?"

"I guess—I just figured you were desperate to go, to get away from everything Germany had become."

Martin closed his eyes, feeling the terribly futility of the conversation close in around him. What had he been thinking, imagining Nina might understand, that telling her might make a difference? *How foolish.* He had allowed his exchange with Eva Sorrentino to get to him.

"Actually," he said. "No. I was desperate to stay." Abruptly, then, he stood. A chiming noise had been coming from the kitchen for several minutes, the stove timer, Nina's willingness to ignore it a sign of how invested in their conversation she was. "I'll go pull that chicken from the oven for you and then let Audrey know that dinner is ready. It would be a shame to let it dry out and ruin all your hard work."

Nina blinked. "Wait, Martin. What did I just say wrong?"

Halfway across the room, Martin paused, his face composed, but effortfully so. "Nothing," he said. "You didn't say anything wrong." He patted his stomach to pantomime being hungry, though for the moment he was anything but. "All that talk of food made me ready to eat."

Martin knew Nina didn't believe him, but that couldn't be helped. He had spent his whole day talking—Jesus God, nothing but *talking*—and it hadn't made a bit of difference at all.

twenty-six

MORE THAN EVER, MARTIN understood there was no way to tell Nina the truth: He had loved Germany, mourned his lost country long after he had known that he shouldn't. He'd done all the right things—learned English, lost his accent, forsook his homeland for American citizenship, but still. On some level, all of that was window dressing; *wanting* to want to be something other than German didn't make it so. The nights he awoke with a gasp weren't always because he was having a nightmare. There were times the nightmare was awakening to the realization that it was only a dream.

In the mornings, Martin would be roused by the smell of coffee brewing in the kitchen, the clatter of heavy dishware as Sieghilde set the long oak table in the dining room, the insistent barks of Fritzi beneath his bedroom window as the little dog chased a bird or a squirrel. He would pull his eiderdown around his ears and watch the wavery sunlight through the diamond-shaped panes, try to recapture the vaporous snippets of his dreams. He had been riding the street car, the limestone face of his father's office building sliding past him, his brown-suited father just glimpsed as the building went out of sight. He was standing on the Schlossbrücke with his friend Ernst, tossing handfuls of small pebbles into the Spree. They turned into his favorite toys, shattering when they hit.

Martin's house was heavy and quiet, and he loved the way he felt so small moving through it, not always sure who else was at home. He would creep down the dark wood stairs, his footsteps swallowed by the thick Oriental runner, press his face through the banister to watch Ulla dust the lamps in the solarium, his breathing louder than the *tick, tick, tick* of the grandfather clock in the downstairs hall. If Ulla moved to his father's library, pulling the carved door shut behind her, he might slide down the railing, putting his hand behind him to cushion the impact against the newel post. In the dining room he would look at the antlered chandelier, run his fingers against the sharp table edge. Cut crystal decanters on the sideboard held thrilling, jewel-colored liquids, ruby and topaz and citrine. Martin's seat was right across from the row of decanters, and he liked to imagine the liquids' taste when his parents poured out glasses for themselves and their guests. The ruby one would be cherries, the topaz butterscotch, the citrine wintergreen. Ulla cleaned the crystal bottles once a week, using a tiny, soft brush to get between all the little crevasses, often sighing noisily as she worked.

One time, when they caught him touching the bottles, Martin's sisters had taken turns pinching the tops of his ears, but today was a school day, Brigid and Hedy in starched dresses and in the car with Mutti half an hour ago. Sieghilde was in the kitchen; Martin could hear her through the swinging door, humming happily to herself. Another year and Martin would go to school, too, carry a large paper cone full of candies and cookies and apples to his first day of class. He'd wear long pants, like his father did, and a crisp, collared shirt. He would shine his shoes himself the night before.

The kitchen door swung open and Sieghilde caught him standing next to the sideboard, one hand dangerously close to the decanter of topaz liquid. She clucked, swatting him on the shoulder with her dishcloth.

"You know better than that," she said. "What are you doing in here all by yourself?"

"I don't know," Martin answered.

"You come with me."

In the kitchen, Sieghilde was making sausage, chopping slabs of pink pork into little cubes, mixing the cubes with some of the herbs from the kitchen garden, sage and thyme and summer savory, grinding the meat and spices into ribbons like spaetzle. When all the meat was ground up, she would stuff the mixture into long, slippery tubes of casing, just the right amount to make a sausage that was neither too skinny nor so fat that it would burst when it was smoked, tie each sausage off from the next with a twist.

"You can grind for me for a while," she said. "My arm gets tired."

Martin climbed on a stool and grasped the wooden handle, eager to prove himself worthy of the task. Sometimes, when she got to the bottom of the bowl, Sieghilde would give him a little taste of the meat, let him put his fingers into the soft pink mixture. Martin liked his pork sausage best this way, raw, even better than when it had hung in the cold room for a month to cure.

Martin turned the meat grinder, watching the spice-flecked cubes of pork tumble over one another before they fell into the neck of the funnel, easing the thick pink ribbons into the bowl when they came out the other side. Sieghilde's plump arm brushed against his as she reached over, scooped up a perfect sausage's worth of meat without even looking, slid it into the casing, and gave it a sharp twist. A heavy coil of sausages already lay on the table; Martin wondered how long the rope of links would stretch if he unspooled it. It was longer than the table, he thought. Would it stretch from the sink to the stove?

The limp, cloudy skin of the sausage casing was in another bowl, one filled with warm water to keep it moist. "What is that?" Martin asked.

"*Es ist die Darm,* the casing," Sieghilde said.

"But where does it come from?"

The cook looked at him severely. "It comes from the same place the sausage does. You know that."

Martin did, in fact. "It's the pig's intestine," he announced, pointing at a spot just beneath his own belly button. "Just like mine, right here. It's where the food goes after it's been digested by the stomach."

Sieghilde nodded. "*Ja,*" she said. "Do your sisters teach these things to you?"

Martin shook his head vigorously. They most certainly did not.

"What, then?"

Martin had seen the pictures in a book in his father's library one time, the whole network of tubes that ran from his mouth to his stomach and then out—horrifyingly, thrillingly—his bottom; after he had seen them, he had resolved for three whole days to hold his bowel movements in. There had been other drawings, too, describing the much smaller tube that led to the slit at the tip of his penis where his urine came out, the mysterious, exclusive workings inside women and girls. A little upside-down gourd with skinny arms and curved fists. Two plump, puffy circles where Martin's *pfennig*-sized nipples were. Breasts. Martin knew better than to say more, however. One time he had rolled Fritzi over and parted the coarse hair of the dog's stomach to count the nipples there—eight! When he'd asked Mutti about them—why did Fritzi have so many breasts?—she had slapped him on both cheeks and sent him up to his room.

Sieghilde's nodding head now shook back and forth. "Mister Smarty-pants," she said. "Why is it that you always ask questions you know the answer to?"

Martin swung his feet. Lately, it seemed all the questions he asked were met with anger. What had happened to Gerlinde, the housekeeper who had come before Ulla, and what about the Jacobsohn family who used to own the fancy apartment building down the road? What of the puzzling statement he'd heard one of his father's business friends make when he'd been listening at the library door, *It's been difficult since the Fuhrer suspended Aktion T4*—? His nursemaid's face had gone white when he'd asked what *Aktion T4* was—it sounded like a type of plane to him!—and that night Martin's father had strapped him, hard. The red marks on his back had been tender for weeks. Asking questions he knew the answer to seemed like the safe thing to do, and better than not asking questions at all.

The sound of a car came through the open kitchen window and Sieghilde peered out, wiping her hands with a white cloth. "Your mother's home," she said. "She's early. Let me finish up here so I can get started on supper."

Martin slid from his stool, disappointed, but the cook turned back to the table again and took a fat pinch of sausage meat in her clean fingers, staying him with her other hand.

"Here," she said, and Martin opened obediently, chewing the warm, savory mouthful as slowly as he could. "Now take one of the white bowls on the lower shelf and go outside. If you can fill it all the way with raspberries I might have time to make a pie."

AND MARTIN HAD LOVED Berlin specifically, had not understood for a long time that all the things he loved it for were wrong. His family's home was just northeast of the city proper, the Ulmenstrasse a wide boulevard lined with linden trees and a cobblestone sidewalk. As a boy of four or five, as a special treat his father would sometimes take him to his office. He would dress in his best clothes and they would leave the house early, when the stone streets smelled like snapped chalk and there was a strange, shimmery quality to the light. They would take his father's big black car to his office building, ride the elevator to the fourth floor, an agonizing stretch of minutes in which Martin would stare at the accordioned metal of the cage door, revel in every shudder and lurch. While his father spoke to other men in suits, Martin would be given a glass of milk to drink and if he was hungry some bread with jam; he would have a picture book to look at until his father was ready to go. They would walk to lunch or take a trolley ride; Martin liked to eat at the fancy department stores along the *Liepziger Platz* so he could look in the big glass windows as they passed. He would order the same meal as his father: calf's liver with bacon and onions, a Coca-Cola, pumpernickel bread spread with creamy white butter. Sometimes after they ate his father would go shopping for his mother, picking out a silky blouse or a pair of stockings that would make her flush and say, "It's beautiful, Josef. You shouldn't have."

In later years, Martin would replay his memories of Berlin like a film, scouring each individual frame for some recollection of the suffering and privation that must have been all around him. At the age of five, he knew there was a war, but knew it as a good thing, a heroic thing, handsome Luftwaffe officers in the newspapers and *Hitlerjugend* marching up and down the streets, waving their flags and singing their songs. Hitler was a good man, his cause just. To the end, there were clothes in the windows at Wertheim and Hermann Tietz and Kafhaus de Westens; right up until the Russian tanks rumbled in, the announcements had blared at noon and night: *the German army has Ivan at the brink, the hour is upon us!* All hands were needed and traitors would be shot.

The first time Martin had seen bodies hanging from lampposts near the Brandenburg gate, he had been certain that they were Russians—spies, perhaps. The bodies were dressed in a variety of uniforms, faded Wehrmacht costumes and homemade fatigues and even a street-car conductor's outfit, drooping pants and shirts as if the figures inside them were skeletons already, or little boys playing dress-up. All of them, however, had the Volkssturm armband around one sleeve, a strip of red-bordered black, the words *Deutscher Volkssturm Wehrmacht* printed in white. Martin had been with Mutti to the Marketplatz—though Sieghilde had stayed longer than any of the other servants, she, too, had finally gone—and he was helping to carry back the spoils of their Class-Two ration card, the same staples they'd been receiving for weeks, turnips and potatoes and a large sack of barley. The smell had reached him first, then the macabre display itself: blackened faces, grossly protruding tongues. Flies swarmed around a spatter of excrement on the sidewalk beneath one of the bodies, and Martin had cried out, gagging.

"Don't look!" Mutti had cried. "For God's sake!" She'd hurried him to a side street, a rubble-filled courtyard where a woman hung dripping laundry between the trunks of two blackened plane trees. Hydrangea and forsythia were in wild bloom, in spite of everything else.

"But why, Mutti?" he had cried. "What happened?"

"Their own fault," she had hissed angrily. "Men who refused to fight."

"But why did they hang them from the light posts?"

"Because— Because—" Mutti looked around wildly. The despair on her face made Martin think that perhaps she was seeing the devastation that surrounded them for the first time, too. Guns on the bridges, antiaircraft artillery at the train station. While their own neighborhood remained largely unscathed, this one had borne the brunt of heavy bombing, entire buildings reduced to piles of bricks and broken furniture. Across the street from where they stood, an apartment building had been cut seemingly in half, perfectly intact rooms framed by ragged walls open to the street, like the dollhouse that Hedy used to have. Martin saw the kitchen, its table still set, a room of heavy furniture frosted with a layer of white dust. What had happened, he wondered, to the people who had been living there? The Americans bombed in the daytime, he'd heard, planning their drops for particular locations. Had the occupants of this apartment heard the air raid siren, gotten up from their breakfasts? Had they decided not to come back? Checkered curtains flapped around an empty window, filling Martin with a pain he didn't understand. Where would those people have gone?

Mutti had dragged Martin home without answering his question about the hangings, and he'd known better than to ask her again. When he'd told Brigid later about what he had seen, his eldest sister's eyes had filled with tears.

"Not spies, Martin," she had whispered, "those were German boys. Boys," she had said again. "My age."

"Did the Russians hang them up there?" Martin wasn't sure how this would have happened. The refugees who filled their house were talking about the Russians now—Ivan, the enemy—but the only Russians he had seen had been prisoners, working for the Volkssturm at gunpoint. He'd seen them digging wide dirt trenches, ragged men barely able to lift their empty shovels, he'd seen them collecting American bombs that had been dropped and not gone off.

Brigid had chewed her lip a long time before she'd answered, looking at her own hands instead of Martin's face.

"I don't think so," she said.

"Who, then?" Martin wondered. "The French? The Americans?"

It was late afternoon, almost sunset, and Brigid had crossed the room to look out the window. Martin followed, kneeling on the velvet sofa beside his sister to follow her gaze. Tiny white snowdrops carpeted their lawn, horse chestnut trees spread their broad leaves. Through the branches of one of them, Martin saw layers of orange clouds, purple above them, strips of colorless sky. He could hear the faint sound of evening frogs, calling from the banks of the Spree.

"It's hard to believe, isn't it?" she asked. "How can there be a war coming here when all of this is still so beautiful?" Brigid had looked at Martin then. "You love Germany, don't you?"

Martin had nodded, not sure he understood the question.

"Then say it," his sister urged him. "Say it out loud."

"*Ich liebe Deutschland*," Martin said, and the words somehow frightened him. It was less than a week until the Russian army would take over his home.

twenty-seven

THE PRIVATE CALL THAT had ended Nina's painful conversation at the Java Pot hadn't been from Todd, after all. It had been the Boston Metropolitan Hospital Breast Imaging Center, calling to remind Nina about her upcoming CT scan. It was routine, the latest in a series of regular scans Dr. Tredway had told her to expect for several years to come, but knowing that didn't make her shaky hands any steadier, her thudding heart beat any less anxiously as she sat across from the intake nurse going through the registration routine. An hour earlier, in an anxious hurry to get to Boston Met on time, she had clipped the side of the garage door with her car. The car appeared to be fine, but the wood framing that ran all along the length of the door had torn loose. Swearing at herself, she had dialed Jenny, her newfound reluctance to be in the presence of her best friend trumped in a splintering of wood by her lack of faith in her ability to make her way to the hospital safely. Now, she could hear a high-pitched ringing in her ears, like a drill buried inside her brain.

"One-fifty-eight over one-oh-five," the nurse said, unhooking her stethoscope from her ears. She looked at Nina's chart. "It looks like Dr. Tredway wrote an order here for Xanax."

"I don't want it." Nina shook her head. "I'm fine." There was no point in explaining to the nurse that the CT was only partly to blame for her state. She had been in a panic for days now, replaying her conversation with Jenny, coming up with her own answers to the questions she'd refused to ask, scrutininzing Audrey's every expression for despair. The tension with Martin wasn't helping, either; the almost-breakthrough conversation that had ended as badly as the one with Jenny had. Was it all just her? Needless to say, Nina hadn't followed up her ill-considered observations about Germany by sharing the latest Willow-Audrey drama with her spouse.

The nurse frowned, jotting Nina's vitals on her chart. "You know you won't get your results right away." She looked at her watch. "Probably not for a couple of days."

Nina thought about that for a minute, picturing her upper body in the claustrophobic tunnel of the CT scanner; picturing herself heading home for two or three days of waiting for the phone to ring. Jenny sat out in the waiting room, pretending to be interested in one of the many brochures about various Boston Met services or perhaps eyeballing the tray of chocolate croissants. One Xanax wouldn't hurt. Martin would never do it, of course. She held her hand out to the nurse, palm up. "Okay, then. Why not."

Back out front, waiting for the little white tablet to kick in, Nina fingered the paper bracelet the nurse had fastened around her wrist, sliding the familiar shackle up to her hand and back down. Every time she'd ever had to have anything done, whether it was a simple blood draw or a major surgery, she'd had to wear one, provide her name and date of birth to every medical person who looked at her wrist. Far more than the procedure itself, *this* was what pushed her heart right to the top of her throat: the dreadful familiarity of the rituals, having her vitals taken and offering out her wrist for the bracelet and putting on the flimsy johnny stamped with the BMH logo. It might be a routine check-up, and chances were excellent she would leave the hospital today and not be back again for another three months, but it looked and smelled and felt like every other appointment she had ever had. She could be waiting to be called into surgery; she could be biding her time before her turn in the gantry room at the Proton Therapy center.

She could be setting the stage to get a call from Dr. Tredway, requesting that she come in as soon as possible with Martin in tow.

The only difference now was the barium contrast agent one of the radiology techs had given her to drink in the waiting room, a plastic cylinder with a picture of fruit on the front and an overly optimistic label that called it a berry smoothie. Nina held the cylinder up when Jenny asked her if she needed anything; held her nose and drank the contents in three big gulps as she waited to be called. In the CT room itself, she climbed onto the narrow platform that would bear her, bier-like, into the white ring of the machine. The lights went down and the disembodied voice of the tech came through the headphones on her ears. Nina closed her eyes, waiting for the Xanax to take effect.

To her surprise, the radiation phase of her cancer treatment had been orders of magnitude harder for her than chemotherapy had. Despite the inherent grimness of the chemo infusion room's *raison d'etre* (it had given Nina pause the first time she'd spied an actual skull and crossbones on her IV bag), there had been something pleasant, almost comfortable, about the place. The nurses were terrific, each one of them exquisitely attuned to whether Nina's mood was chatty or introspective or irreverent. The other patients were, for the most part, Nina's fellows-at-arms, asking about each others' lives and families. There had been Mrs. Gomez, an older woman who was on the same treatment schedule as Nina and a nearly identical regimen; there had been Trevor Molloy, a gruff construction worker from Southie who referred to his chemo cocktail as Unhappy Hour. While they shared their greetings, the nurse would clean and prep Nina's chemo port, ask her if she was ready before she started to let the treatment run. In addition to making her nauseous and killing her hair cells, six months of chemo had turned Nina into a temporary country music junkie, and so as a taste like zinc filled her mouth she would put her headphones on and visualize, the way she had learned to from her guided imagery tape. Chemo good, cancer bad. Somewhere along the line, too, she had appropriated the imagery of one of those household cleaning product ads for her treatment. Her chemo drugs became scrubbing bubbles, little fat white Casper ghosts merrily dispatching green, glowering cancer cells, zipping hither and thither on their whiskbroom feet. Pop, pop, pop. After each infusion was completed, Nina would pay a visit to Dr. Kennett, who would review her bloodwork and praise her white-cell counts like a parent admiring her child's straight-A report card. The oncologist would send her home with Zofran to dampen her nausea and orders to sit on the couch and watch a movie, eat Chinese take out from the carton while she could.

This was not her life, not any more, this place, but in the moment,

Nina found that fact difficult to hold onto. Over the past two years, how many CT and PET and MRI scans had she had, for how many hours had she lain with her eyes pressed shut, trying to pretend the classical music coming through her headphones was relaxing, trying not to think about the fact that she was *here*, alone, while everyone else was *there*? When she'd had her bone cancer scare as a twelve-year-old, she'd had a series of full body X-rays at Children's Hospital, a mustard-yellow machine with a cannon-barrel head training its crosshairs on every inch of her from the top of her skull to her toes. She'd been in the X-ray room for more than an hour, alone except for the occasional appearance of a tech who'd moved her this way or that on the metal bed or swapped out the big black plates of X-ray film. There had been a water stain on the ceiling tiles above the mustard-colored machine, coming more and more into view as the cannon-barrel moved down Nina's torso and legs. It looked like a woman, an hourglass figure without a head, and Nina couldn't help but imagine that it was a sign. As the machine buzzed and the table jerked, she had begun to cry. She wanted her mother, waiting far down the hallway for her in an orange chair, probably still reading the *Good Housekeeping* she'd been flipping through when Nina left. Tears had puddled in her ears and salty snot coated her upper lip as she lay obediently still against the table, struggling to fathom the fact that she wasn't going to grow up.

This time, it was all over in thirty minutes. She kept her eyes closed, her awareness of the curved wall of the scanner inches away from her nose growing ever more abstract as the Xanax went to work, equally interested in the piano music coming through her headphones and the mechanical howls of the CT machine they weren't quite able to block. Halfway through Chopin's *Piano Concerto No. 1*, the technician's voice interrupted to tell her she was finished; the music resumed and the table slid back out of the tube. The lights came on, and Nina peeled her sticky thighs from the vinyl surface. In the little changing area just off the scan room, she shed her gown and her paper slippers, shook out her capri pants, buttoned her blouse with tingling fingers. As she walked back out to the waiting room, she slid the paper bracelet off her wrist, crumpling it into a little ball at the bottom of her pocket.

Jenny glanced up at her. "All set?"

Nina nodded, leading the way out of the hospital, past the elevator banks and the first-floor cafe and the glass wall that overlooked the Boston Metropolitan courtyard. It was over. It would be August before she had to do any of this again. She was in the Boston Met parking lot, one hand on Jenny's passenger-side door, before her stomach heaved, spattering the remnants of her berry smoothie all over the concrete beneath her shoes.

twenty-eight

MARTIN STOOD IN THE doorway of cardiac unit patient room 23E, not quite sure at first what he felt. The room was almost empty, almost quiet, a single mylar balloon tied to the guest chair the only evidence the sterile space was occupied. Just beyond the pastel privacy curtain, Mrs. Hebert lay in a nearly upright position, eyes shuttered, her unseeing face turned toward the window like a sun-starved plant straining to reach a few meager rays of light. There was an IV in her hand to provide hydration and a cannula in her nose for oxygen. A tube snaked beneath the sheets to collect her urine, a monitor above her head continued to record her faltering heartbeats, a glowing clip on her index finger offered up her oxygen saturation level. All the other lines and wires that had hung over her in the ICU, however, were gone—the feeding tube and the multiple bags for a battery of medications, the automatic external defibrillator Richard Hebert had insisted on—and without the machinery, without the hustle and bustle of caregivers and family members, the sense of absence was almost tangible. Martin picked up his patient's chart and brushed his fingers across the bright yellow sticker affixed to its front, as if not quite believing it was really there: *DNR*.

The previous afternoon, he had watched Richard Hebert sign his mother's order not to resuscitate with a shaking hand, countersigned his own name with a flourish he hoped conveyed his confidence that enacting the order was the right thing to do. When it was finished, Eva Sorrentino had started crying, but Martin had pretended not to see her tears, not wanting to open up whatever conversation had led, after several days of tense negotiation, to Richard's change of mind about the LVAD—or to learn, for that matter, what sort of role he himself might have played. Instead, he had focused on the things that had to happen next, taking Ruta Hebert off everything except pain relief and supplemental oxygen; moving her to a regular patient room on the cardiac floor so the Heberts could have some privacy for their final goodbyes.

For a moment Martin wondered if something had gone wrong: it was almost eleven o'clock in the morning, and according to the floor nurse, neither Eva Sorrentino nor Richard Hebert had yet been in. The quiet of the room was uncanny, Martin's temptation to fill it with the sound of his own voice immense. From the hallway he heard the squeak of rubber-soled shoes on linoleum, the *sssssshhh* of something (a shopping bag? a child's hand?) scraping against the wall. He bumped the guest chair and the balloon tethered to it spun, revealing itself as a castoff from the room's prior occupant: *So Glad You're On The Mend!*

Drawing the curtain around the bed, Martin set down Mrs. Hebert's chart and unfolded his stethoscope to listen to her heart and lungs. Against his ears, the shuffle of Ruta Hebert's heartbeat was ever more dim, the crackling of her chest rales like popcorn bursting in a pan. He pressed his fingers to his patient's right carotid artery, digging to find it in her swollen neck; he lifted her foley bag to examine her urine output, scant and brown. It wouldn't be long at all now, and Martin patted his patient's swollen legs, hard and cool beneath the hospital sheet, feeling a small moment of satisfaction, reassurance, relief. It *was* the right thing to do.

Martin tucked Mrs. Hebert's sheet in tight across her lap, then stepped back out into the corridor, closing the door behind him. Richard Hebert and Eva Sorrentino would be in later; they were probably busy meeting with a funeral home director, picking out a casket, deciding on readings and a venue for their mother's service. Of course they were. Mrs. Hebert was in her final slide to death and it would all be over in another day or two.

twenty-nine

THE EXPRESSION OF SURPRISE and then pleasure that crossed Todd's face when he spotted Nina across the disco-lit Goldengrove gymnasium sent a jolt through her stomach and she looked away quickly, afraid of what her own face might show. He was here, just as she had wondered if he would be—had *hoped* he would be, if she was honest with herself—of course he was. It was the eighth grade formal, after all, the leading event in a two-week whirlwind of activities that marked the end of Goldengrove's eldest students' careers, an occasion Juliette had brought up at least in passing every time Nina had seen her over the last six weeks. The only one out of place tonight was Nina herself, overseeing a table of desserts and sherbet-flavored punch alongside Jenny Rutherford, admiring the dresses of girls she recognized as Juliette and Calla's classmates, joking with boys whose pimpled complexions and gangly bodies inspired a maternal sort of pity in her.

Pity, Nina was fairly certain, was the emotion that had compelled Jenny to ask her to come along tonight. A week earlier, as Nina had stood in the Boston Met parking lot staring down at her vomit-splashed shoes, her friend had run around to the passenger side of the car, crouching down and dabbing at Nina like she was a small child. "Oh, Nina!" Jenny had cried, ignoring her weak attempts to wave her off, "Oh, my gosh!" Nina had been fine—really, she'd assured Jenny, it was just the barium drink on her empty stomach—but there had been something about the moment, so graphic and visceral, that had disloged the awkwardness that had grown

257

up between them ever since the coffee shop. Jenny had made Nina sit in the car while she ran back to the hospital café for a bottle of ginger ale; she'd glanced over nervously, repeatedly, as she'd maneuvered through the Boston traffic and onto the Mass Pike. They had been back in Cabot when Jenny had pulled her car over on the side of the road, flashers on, and announced that she had a plan. If Nina would be interested in helping chaperone the eighth grade dance, Audrey could come for a sleepover with Willow and Nina could be her date instead of Jim; probably all the girls really needed was to find themselves in the same place without any other distractions and everything between them would be fine. Nina had wanted to feel indignant—she wasn't a charity case; *Audrey* wasn't a charity case. But then she had seen again all the evidence she'd willed herself to ignore up until her conversation with Jenny at the Java Pot—the defeated curve of her daughter's back, disappearing through the doors of Goldengrove, the quiet that now attended even her drives to the barn—and she'd kept her eyes on the dashboard as she said okay.

When Nina had dropped Audrey off at the Rutherford's house earlier, her daughter's expression had been joyful, and when Willow had run to greet her, any uncharitable thoughts she had entertained about the bribery the evening's arrangement might have required evaporated, replaced by gratitude and elation of her own. Maybe Jenny was right; all the girls needed was a little coaxing; maybe over popcorn and *Old Yeller* (Audrey's choice, Nina's suggestion to choose something a little more contemporary brushed off with the assurance that the movie was also one of Willow's favorites) they would remember how much they enjoyed one another's company. Entering the gym with her own best friend, Nina had been able to think about her daughter without that cold lump of fear forming in her throat. It wouldn't be long before Audrey and Willow were among the clusters of girls who hovered nearby now, whispering in each others' ears between cupped hands and darting glances at the boys, giggling a bit too obviously. It wouldn't be long at all, and what was more, Nina would be here to see it. She'd gotten her CT results from Dr. Tredway's office on Monday, and the surgeon herself had been the one to call Nina with the news. Dr. Olsen had given the films a look and they were negative. The only thing showing up on the studies of her chest was scar.

"Well, well, if it isn't Nina Baldwin." Todd had crossed the room and now stood in front of Nina. He gave her a broad grin and helped himself to a plastic cup of sherbet punch. "Let me guess: Audrey decided to go ahead and graduate this year with the eighth grade."

Nina picked up a cup herself and gestured toward Jenny, who stood in the doorway with Bonnie Mason, engaged in an unusually intense-looking conversation. Bonnie was gesturing around the room and frowning, her upper arms flapping dangerously beneath a sleeveless top of vivid scarlet. Jenny was nodding along, mirroring the other woman's expression of concern. "Thank God no. I'm here with Jenny. I'm being Jim Rutherford."

"I see," Todd grinned. "A definite improvement over the original model, I have to say."

Nina laughed, but her face went hot and she felt a surge of schoolgirl giddiness. "Is Susan here?"

"She's traveling." Todd's easy smile disappeared. "On her way back from San Francisco. Don't get me started on that. Juliette was beside herself. What about Martin? Home with Audrey I guess."

"Audrey's at the Rutherfords' with Willow. Martin's at the hospital. As usual. On call."

Bonnie Mason's dance-related concerns apparently addressed, Jenny made her way back over to the refreshment table, her disapproving expression unrelieved by the sight of Nina and Todd. If Todd noticed, he pretended not to, greeting Jenny with the same wide smile he'd given Nina a minute before.

"Evening, Jenny," he said. "I've been hanging with your new husband, here. Everything okay in Bonnie's world?"

Jenny addressed the air in between Todd and Nina. "She felt it was a little darker in here than it ought to be. *We're not a public school, you know. It might be okay at other middle schools for eighth graders to sneak off into the corners and make out, but here at Goldengrove—*" Jenny offered up a fairly accurate Bonnie Mason impression.

"Well, of course, she's got a point." Todd nodded his head. "Our kids would prefer to dance under a searchlight, if possible, maybe with Mom and Dad on either side to make sure nothing unseemly is going on."

Jenny's expression relented. "Seriously, right?" she said. "Calla has me on strict orders to not so much as look her direction. She made me *pinky swear*. If she needs something from me, she'll let me know."

Todd came around to Nina and Jenny's side of the table and the three of them were busy for a bit, serving nervous eighth graders who were finding mass consumption of brownies and punch a preferable activity to tackling the dance floor, which stood empty through a run of songs Nina thought seemed oddly dated and out of place. Finally, something by Madonna started and a girl in a purple dress with a sweetheart front dragged a tall boy into the middle of the gym, a small crowd following in their wake. The girl spun and Nina saw that it was Courtney Morrison, Willow's Goldengrove big sister, her partner a boy named Justin whose father taught philosophy at Cabot College.

"Ah, Madonna," Todd said. "Favorite of teenagers for many generations."

Nina nodded, making sure her response included Jenny and Todd alike. "Indeed. Think your kids have any idea that this particular song is actually from about twenty years ago?"

"I *do* think so," Todd replied. "Juliette informed me on the ride over here that The Eighties was the theme of tonight's dance. She thought I might have some pointers about what was cool *way back then*."

"Ouch." Nina laughed. "She probably meant that as a compliment." Once again, Nina looked at both Todd and Jenny. "Whatever happened to—I don't know, *A Night to Remember,* or *Under the Sea?*"

"*A Night to Remember?*" Jenny said. "I think you've maybe gone back an extra generation or two. Our prom theme was, what? Something by Styx, I'm pretty sure."

The Madonna song ended and Michael Jackson came on, bringing another wave of eighth graders to the dance floor. The playlist was making sense to Nina now. "I wouldn't know," she said. "I didn't go to prom."

"You didn't? Really?"

"Nope." Nina shrugged.

"How come?"

"I was on the prom committee that tried unsuccessfully to get *Paradise by the Dashboard Light* for our theme," Todd volunteered. "Unfortunately, the vice principal was cooler than we imagined and actually knew the song. We ended up going with *Hotel California* instead. Apparently addiction and insanity and making deals with the devil were more thematically acceptable than teenagers having sex in a car."

The three of them were deep in a discussion of that irony when a red-faced Calla Rutherford rushed up to the table, grabbing Jenny by the wrist. Jenny excused herself, and Todd and Nina watched the twosome disappear through the lobby doors, Todd wondering out loud if the distressed expression on Calla's face had been verging on angry or tearful. Nina wasn't sure.

"Oh well, I'm sure we'll find out." Todd helped himself to a brownie and took a bite. "So. No prom for you, huh? Too cool for that?"

"Hardly." Nina shook her head, scanning the now-full dance floor curiously. "Nobody asked me."

"I find that hard to believe."

"I'd just broken up with Mister Popular, captain of the soccer team, and none of his friends would ask me out. I guess at the time I really didn't want to go, but later I was sorry. Not that there was much I could do about it. Things weren't so liberated in Cabot in 1978 that it would have even occurred to me to ask someone myself." Remarkably, Nina felt a wave of self-pity pass over her.

"Aaw, poor Nina," Todd held his hands out. "How about now?"

"Dance? To this?" Nina felt a little leap of panic. "I don't think so."

The Michael Jackson song had just ended, replaced by a ballad by a British band Nina remembered as having enormous, spiky hairdos and lots of eyeliner, and the roomful of thirteen- and fourteen-year-olds were now trying to figure out how closely to hold each other. Around the edges of the gym, a handful of the husband-and-wife chaperones were dancing, but that was something else altogether. When she had spied him at the evening's start, Nina had noticed right away how handsome Todd looked, wearing an expensive-looking pair of jeans and an open-collared shirt the color of a cloudless sky. As he had crossed the room to her, his eyes had covered her appreciatively—tailored black pants and a wrap-front blouse that emphasized her real-and-fake breasts—a small smile on his lips. It was a game they were playing, both of them. Her heart pounded, half terror and half thrill.

"Suit yourself," he said. He finished his brownie, crushing its paper wrapper in his fist, and gave Nina a roguish grin. "But later."

"We'll see about that," she said. She ticked her chin at Janet Smith and Bonnie Mason, manning a table of finger sandwiches and fruit on the opposite wall, matching frowns on their faces as they watched their children slow dance. "I'm kind of worried some of the Goldengrove elders' heads would explode."

Todd's solution was to dance with Bonnie Mason first, taking her hand across the sandwich table when the first brassy notes of a Cyndi Lauper song began. Nina found herself pitying poor Bonnie for the embarrassed, delighted smile on her face. They skirted clumps of dancing teens, making little hiccuppy hops to the *oh! oh! oh!*s of the song, and over to Juliette, who seemed much less appalled than Nina imagined Audrey would be if presented with a comparable scene. Todd danced with his daughter once, to "Whip It," and then with Linda Staley, a single mother with a lower-back tattoo whose daughter Petra had come to Goldengrove the same time as Juliette. When he finally made his way back over to Nina at the punch table he was breathing audibly, smiling enormously, unabashedly pleased with himself.

"I can't imagine that you need to dance with me now," she said. "You've clearly gotten your quota."

Todd's mischievous expression turned serious. "But I do need to dance with you," he said.

"And why would that be?" Nina asked as casually as she could.

Todd shrugged, looking away. "Do I have to have a reason? I just do."

For a while, the tempo shifted and the DJ played a string of hard-thumping arena rock songs. Most of the girls filtered away from the gymnasium as Bon Jovi bled into Poison and then Van Halen and the boys lined up along the walls, jerking their heads up and down. A number of the parent chaperones stood with their arms crossed and Nina scanned the lineup for Jenny. Todd hummed along to the music, occasionally breaking into snippets of one song or another. The massive disco ball that had been hung from one of the rafters threw handfuls of sparkly magenta light over the half-dozen couples still out on the dance floor.

Nina put her hand on Todd's arm. "I'm going to go look for Jenny, I think. Make sure everything's okay."

Todd nodded. "I'll go with you."

"You probably shouldn't. Someone should keep an eye on things here."

Todd raised an eyebrow at the phalanx of full punch cups ranged across the table. "You mean in case there's a massive run on punch and none of these almost-high-school-students can figure out how to use a ladle to serve up more?"

There was no sign of Jenny or Calla in the atrium, the girls' bathroom, or the main hallway. It wasn't until she stepped outside and saw that Jenny's car was gone that Nina thought to check her cell phone, and sure enough, there was an apologetic, *sotto voce* message. Calla had gotten her period and hadn't realized it; she had bled on her white dress and Courtney Morrison had pointed it out to her in front of a group of kids that included Elijah Reid, the boy Calla liked, and Calla had insisted on going home. Jenny had hoped she could convince her to change into a different dress and come back but it didn't look like that was going to happen; she would try once more and one way or another she'd be back at the end of the dance to bring Nina back.

"God." Nina flipped her phone shut. "Girls can be so mean."

Without providing too much detail, she related to Todd what had happened with Calla. He grimaced, chewing on the side of his thumb. "Damn. You know, this is exactly why I steer clear of mares."

Nina snorted, feeling a sudden, unwelcome flash of hostility. "Because they embarrass each other, and make fun of each other's dresses?"

"Because they're mean to each other, the second they hit puberty. Juliette's been on the receiving end of plenty of it here."

For the thousandth time, Nina thought of Audrey, her sad shoulders, the shy delight that had animated every fiber of her being when Willow had flung her arms around her two hours earlier. She started walking, skirting the building to enter the gym from the back, where the doors were open to let in air. Out front, there were several small clusters of eighth graders on the steps, boys scuffing their shoes on the pavement, fists in pockets; girls giggling and whispering. Nina didn't want to encounter Courtney Morrison among them, afraid of what she might say to her.

At the back of the building, Nina stopped. "I'm not sure boys are any less mean, but at least they're more straightforward about it," she finally said. "It seems like they just tell each other they suck and then move on. But girls...for all of Audrey's smarts, she just doesn't get the way girls interact. There's part of me that's kind of okay with that, but there's a bigger part that realizes it's a huge handicap, like she's missing the most fundamental thing she needs to get along in the world. Even her friendship with Willow, after all these years—"

Nina swallowed around the hard knot starting to rise in her throat. It was dark behind the gym, darker still in the fields that surrounded the school, bordered with the stands of skeletal birches she'd imagined Audrey spending so many happy recesstimes climbing. Peepers sang in the tall grass and fireflies lit the dark and disappeared.

Todd touched Nina's arm. "That just isn't true," he said. "Audrey's a great kid. She's different because she's exceptional. By the time she graduates, she's going to be ready to take it all on. You'll see."

Nina gave another hollow laugh, not quite able to put a name to the enervating weight that settled in the pit of her stomach. "You sound like Martin now," she said.

They were at the gymnasium doors, and without waiting for Todd's response Nina stepped through them, inside. At the other end of the room, Mary Chisholm was mounting the stage to say that the dance was winding down.

"Well, it's not exactly the jungle, boys and girls, but we're going to have just one more song here before we all go back to the world outside the eighth grade dance," she said. "I hope you've had a wonderful time tonight, and that you remember to thank your parents for all the work they put into this special event, providing the refreshments and the decorations. For those of you whose parents didn't stay, please remember to thank them for driving you back and forth. Moms and Dads, if you'd like to join us on the dance floor, I think you'll find this last song is something we all can handle."

There was some half-hearted applause. Nina followed the clapping around the room and stopped at the refreshment table she and Todd had abandoned earlier. Jenny was back, glaring across the room at her with a mixture of censure and shock she might have found amusing under other circumstances. Instead, it was Jenny's expression that decided it. Nina turned and pulled Todd by the forearm in the direction of the dance floor.

"Alrighty," she said. "Last song."

If Todd was surprised he didn't let on. The song was a slow one— "Sailing," by Christopher Cross—and almost immediately Nina realized her mistake. Todd pulled her against him in a way that made her excruciatingly aware of every point where their bodies made contact, and the song took her suddenly back to the summer after her first year of college, a time when she had known so much more than her mother. She had been seeing a couple of different boys that year, and she remembered the way she would stretch the long cord on the first floor telephone to make her plans with them from the privacy of the den. Once, she opened the door to find her mother in the hallway, waiting for her. *I hope you know what you're doing. You know you can always come to me if you have any questions.* Nina had laughed in her mother's face. She was nineteen years old, ripe; her middle-aged mother an object of her disdain. What could she have to teach Nina about pleasure, lust, with her pilly sweaters and her cheap-permed hair, married to Nina's hopelessly dorky father? Her mother had made some sort of nasty rejoinder—*You won't be laughing when you get crabs or worse from one of those boys*—but Nina had seen the hurt on her face as she had turned away.

Nina and her mother had never really fought, but there had been a tangible distance between them from the time she reached puberty into her early twenties at least. *Why?* she wondered now. What had been so objectionable about Nina's nascent womanhood that for years, it seemed, her mother regarded her with no expression other than a critical scowl on her face? What ugly secret had she known about Nina that Nina herself had not understood?

Heat rose from Todd's skin and streams of colored light rippled over the tired bodies swaying around them. Nina felt herself melting into him as she gave herself over to her guilt and grief, her longing for the irretrievable past. She closed her eyes and breathed in deeply, the scent of sweat and stale gymnasium air evoking pain as sharp and sweet as the feeling of her reconstructed breast pressing up against his chest.

thirty

EVEN AS SHE SET about ignoring it, Nina knew that her first reaction to the sight of Todd's truck Monday morning was the right one. She was still in her sweatpants, unshowered, when she looked through the living room window to place the sound of the engine in her driveway. Watching Todd unfold himself from the driver's seat and run his hands over the top of his head, she went to the front door and pressed her own hands against the panels. She stared at her splayed fingers on the painted wood and told herself, "No."

Nina's second reaction, however, was to flip the deadbolt and open the door. Up the street, Linda O'Bryan and Sara Vanderweghe were beginning their morning circuit, marching briskly down Vaughn Circle, brightly colored dumbbells in their hands, the Vanderweghes' bulldog plodding along behind, and the familiar sight triggered a cascade of emotions that, in the bleak morning light, surprised her more than perhaps they should. Shame, envy, disdain, despair.

"Hello, Todd," she said. "In the neighborhood, were you?"

Todd pushed his hands into his pockets and gave Nina a half-smile. "Not really. I just thought I'd check on you, make sure everything was okay. After Friday night, I mean."

Nina half-smiled back at him. "Okay enough, I guess. I suppose you'd better come inside."

Friday night, after the music had ended and the gymnasium lights had come up, Jenny Rutherford had crossed over to where Nina and Todd were still extricating themselves from their "Sailing" embrace. Jenny had addressed Nina without acknowledging Todd at all, her lips trembling for reasons Nina had only at first thought she understood. If Nina was quite finished, they really needed to go; Audrey was in the car and she had promised her she'd only be gone for a minute. She and Willow had had a fight and she wanted her mother to take her home.

"A fight?" Nina had echoed. "What happened?"

Evidently Willow hadn't wanted to watch *Old Yeller*, that dumb movie about a dumb dog who gets rabies, after all; her plan had been for the two of them to watch *American Idol* and call in votes for some singer named Bo Bice. Jim had tried to help out and suggested the girls flip a coin to decide which thing to do; both Willow and Audrey had agreed to that but when Willow won Audrey had gotten upset and the whole thing had snowballed from there.

"By the time I got there with Calla—" Jenny had trailed off. "She wouldn't even stay in the house while I came back to pick you up. She was already out in your car."

Nina didn't think she was imagining the anger in Jenny's voice, and she'd hurried out the door without another glance at Todd, her legs rubbery with fear and guilt. Todd had called her cell phone Saturday and again yesterday; she'd ignored his messages as well as the pair Jenny had left, her voice pitched low, asking if they could get together and talk. She'd planned on calling both of them back eventually—just not today, when she had a backache from sleeping badly two nights in a row and her head was feeling wooly from the Vicodin she'd swallowed at breakfast to blunt it. With Nina's luck, Jenny would be pulling up behind Todd's truck any minute now, bearing a plate of fresh-baked strawberry scones or some other sort of peace offering. She glanced quickly past the advancing figures of Sara Vanderweghe and Linda O'Bryan before shutting the door and Todd inside.

"I saw you on 117 after you dropped Audrey off this morning but you didn't see me," Todd said now. "Seemed like a good sign that Audrey was game to go to school."

Nina folded her arms across her body, gripping her elbows with her hands. "I'm not sure I'd say she was game to go, I just didn't give her any choice. She told me yesterday that she wanted to be homeschooled."

"Poor kid." Todd stepped toward Nina. "At that age, the things they fight about."

Nina took a corresponding step back. She knew Todd was only trying to make her feel better, but the devil was in the details. When Audrey had lost the coin toss she'd demanded that Jim do it again. She'd *locked* herself inside Nina's car while Jim and Silas—*Silas!*— tried to cajole her back into the house. And then there was *Old Yeller*...Nina had tried to warn her daughter that a movie filmed in 1957 might not go over with Willow quite the way she imagined. Frankly, after at least a dozen viewings, she wasn't all that nuts about that corny, *gee-whiz, ma* video herself.

"And let's face it, Jim Rutherford was in the wrong there, flipping a coin," Todd continued. "What happened to all that Goldengrove grace and courtesy stuff, like letting your guests choose?"

Nina sighed, looking around her foyer at the crooked throw rug and the rain-speckled sidelights, a trio of ladybugs huddled in the corner where the ceiling met the wall. What was there, really, that she could say? The grace and courtesy part of the Goldengrove curriculum had never been Audrey's strong suit, seemingly as mystifying to her as multivariate calculus was to Nina. Todd was right, but she could easily imagine Martin making the same mistake as Jim, and what did it matter, given how it had played out? It wasn't the kind of situation where you could assert your superiority on the principle of the thing.

She supposed she should invite Todd to sit down somewhere, offer to make him him a cup of coffee, but she was tired and her back hurt. All weekend, she'd moved around in a daze that was part her own indiscretion and part Audrey; Martin hadn't asked why Audrey had come home on Friday night and she hadn't offered, sure if she told him about the girls' contretemps his response would be the same as always. Willow was bossy; Audrey wasn't in the wrong; Audrey could do without a friend like Willow, after all. Whenever Martin had looked at her, Nina had felt her face snap into the manic rictus of a housewife on the brink, selling Tupperware door-to-door.

"As for the whole Bo Bice, *American Idol* thing—"

Nina waved him off. "Yeah, I know. If you ask Mary Chisholm or Bonnie Mason or whoever, Goldengrove kids would rather read a book than watch TV."

"That too, I suppose." Todd shrugged. "I was just going to say that anyone with any brains at all knows Carrie Underwood is the real deal this season. Jim Rutherford should have told his daughter to get a grip."

Nina hadn't expected to laugh. She wasn't even sure, for that matter, that she thought Todd was funny. But she burst out laughing until tears started in her eyes, and then she was laughing and sobbing both, covering her face with her hands. This time, when Todd closed the space between them, his arms going around her shaking body, she didn't step away.

"Hey, Nina, hey," he murmured. "It's okay."

Todd's hand rubbed Nina's back. After a minute she lifted her wet face, her nose running now, and answered him. "No, Todd. It isn't." Then she wiped her arm across her face like a child and pulled Todd's head down to hers.

Todd kissed her back, tentatively at first and then more hungrily. Nina pressed herself against him insistently, attacking the unfamiliarity of his teeth and tongue and the taste of his mouth. Todd tightened his arms around Nina's torso, pinning her body to his own as if he understood just how far she was falling

•

FOR A LONG TIME after it happened, it continued to shock Nina how easy it was to tumble into transgression. Up to the very moment that she was, she didn't believe herself capable of being an unfaithful wife. She had been the child who never cheated in school—not once, more afraid of getting caught than of failing; the adult who hurried back into the grocery store with apologies if a roll of mints or a birthday card had slipped through the checkout process in the corner of her cart. Being married had seemed like the same kind of absolute, a tautology; if you were married, you didn't cheat. The wedding vows that bound her to Martin were the links in the strongest of chains, connected to a stake that held her securely to the earth. She'd never realized that marriage's power to keep her faithful was purely illusory; she hadn't wanted to know, in fact—what was sure about falling other than the fact that you landed, scraped and bruised at best? Take that first unshackled step, and all bets would be off.

From the living room, Nina and Todd had moved upstairs to the guest room, pulling at each other's buttons and buckles and zippers with fevered haste. Nina left her bra on. Todd shucked his jeans and boxer shorts, then took his erection in his hand and pushed himself against Nina. She pulled him down onto the guest bed and locked her legs around his waist. He hovered over her, hesitating.

"I don't have any— I wasn't expecting— Do we need to—"

Nina squeezed her eyes shut and shook her head.

"No," she said tightly. "The chemotherapy. Chemical menopause."

"I'm sorry."

Nina pressed her forehead into Todd's collarbone until it hurt. "No," she said again. "I'm not."

He thrust himself inside her then, and as Nina lifted her pelvis to meet him, neither of them was sorry any longer. She dug her fingernails into his back and ran her teeth along the salty sweat of his shoulder and for a stretch of exquisitely mindless minutes neither one of them was sorry at all.

thirty-one

MARTIN SAT INSIDE HIS locked office until all the workday sounds faded away—his partners' voices, the bleating of the front desk telephone, the throaty hum of shelves moving on mechanical wheels down the hall in the filing room. Barton Eldredge knocked on his door, but only to call a good evening as he made his way out; Elaine, who was used to his late-night hours and closed door, e-mailed him before she left. *Here's your schedule for tomorrow. I rebooked this morning's urgent patients from noon to one so you can skip the lunch with the pharma reps ;-).* When he heard the photocopier turn itself off down the hallway he got up to put on his running clothes.

The outfit he kept in his credenza drawer was a spare, and as he pulled the shirt over his head he realized that it hadn't been washed since it had last been worn a month earlier. The sour musk that surrounded him reminded him of his boys as teenagers, though none of them had run; Jonathan had gone out for baseball and Peter and Christian played hockey. All-American games, which had suited Martin just fine. He always suspected a tacit criticism behind his sons' rejection of the athletic pursuits that interested him, but nothing could have made him happier than to have such apple-pie evidence that they were Americans, New Englanders. As he bent to lace his running shoes, Martin felt a stabbing pain beneath his ribcage. He straightened up again, extending both arms above his head, hands together, palms up. He was getting old. He was getting soft, sentimental. He braced himself against his office wall to stretch his tight quadriceps and calves.

It was cool, the evening air dry for the first time in days, and Martin started at a slow jog. Making his way down the same heaved sidewalks he and Eva Sorrentino had walked almost two weeks earlier, he checked the construction progress of the cancer center. The building was being named after a former St. Serafin oncology chief who had died, ironically enough, of melanoma, and the sight of it made him wonder, as he often did, where cancer doctors placed their particular terrible knowledge of mortality. As a cardiologist, Martin could still delude himself into thinking himself protected from his patients' vulnerabilities—by eating well; by controlling cholesterol and blood pressure with medications, if need be; by running. But oncologists and the radiologists and surgeons who dealt in cancers must have to employ a different form of magical thinking; there were so few preventive measures to be applied. They could do their self-exams obsessively, eat their leafy greens for colon health and still. The variables were too many, too impossible to control. Just look at Nina if you needed a case in point. She had done all the right things and her reward had been an aggressive tumor, two of them.

Martin had never told his wife, but early into her treatment, he had cornered one of St. Serafin's younger oncologists to ask his opinion of Nina's care plan. The man had told Martin it sounded like an outstanding approach: the chemo the same regimen he would recommend, the proton treatment head and shoulders above anything St. Serafin would have been able to offer her. But the look on Dr. Jain's face had told him more. An estrogen-receptor-negative tumor with chest wall infiltration and lymph node involvement? Martin still felt the tightness in his own chest when he thought about the oncologist's expression. *I hope you're not kidding yourself into thinking your wife will survive.*

A motorcycle revved past Martin and weaved side to side on the mostly open avenue, its rider in shirtsleeves, bareheaded. *An organ donor,* the name physicians gave to motorcyclists who rode without the proper gear. Nina *had* survived. Wasn't that the point? Martin's conversation with Dr. Jain had been nearly two years ago; Nina had been status N.E.D. for almost a full year now and her most recent CT scan had come up clean. Even Martin got it: Nina's outcome was a miracle, what every person with cancer hoped for but very few got. She was lucky. He was lucky. Martin picked up his foot turnover slightly and allowed himself a moment's flight of fancy. Maybe Nina herself was the answer, the intangible factor that allowed cancer doctors to do the work they did. The patient for whom there was a happy ending when all data indicated otherwise.

Ruta Hebert had finally died today.

When the floor nurse had called in the morning to let Martin know that Mrs. Hebert was at the end, she was apneic and her blood pressure was bottoming, he had frozen at first. He'd asked if her family was there, already sure he knew what the answer was. Richard Hebert hadn't been to the hospital since he signed his mother's DNR; Eva Sorrentino had been over from New York for the weekend but had gone home to Lake George yesterday afternoon, almost four hours away. If by some chance the answer had been different—Richard Hebert had come around and was in his mother's room; Eva Sorrentino had experienced a moment of intuition and decided to stay an extra day—Martin probably would have left it at that, ordered an increase in morphine PRN, paid his last respects to his patient later when he was paged to pronounce her and sign her death certificate. But Ruta Hebert was alone, her daughter speeding down I-87 just as fast as she could, her son's answering machine blinking with half a dozen messages from the hospital, and as he gripped the phone a picture had flashed in Martin's mind: Ruta Hebert's tiny, bloated figure, the bright white braids that had crisscrossed the top of her head the first time he had met her. She was nearly the age his own mother would have been now, just a couple of years younger. He'd asked Elaine to reschedule any patients who couldn't wait and walked across the street to the main hospital.

Of course, there had been nothing he could do; Mrs. Hebert was in multi-system organ failure. Her skin was deeply yellow, evidence her liver was no longer functioning, she was breathing in Cheyne-Stokes cycles, pulling deeper and deeper before fading into stretches of stillness. Martin listened to her heart, patted the swollen hand she clenched to her chest, greeted her by name. She was in hepatic coma, but she might still be able to hear.

"Hello, Mrs. Hebert, it's Dr. Winzer," he told her. "It's almost over now. Your children have been called and they will be here as fast as they can."

Across her bed, a nurse named Gretchen gave Martin a look, and he glanced down at Ruta Hebert's chart, wondering about the half-truth he had just told. Should he have told his patient just her daughter was on her way? The words he had said weren't dishonest, strictly speaking; both of Ruta Hebert's children *had* been called, and if Martin were to give Richard the benefit of the doubt and say his failure to visit over the past few days were because he truly *couldn't* witness his mother's dying, the statement was technically accurate. But Martin knew his intent had been to suggest to Mrs. Hebert that both of her children were on their way to her, to provide that tiniest shred of comfort in her final moments. Richard and Eva would be there. She wouldn't die alone.

Ruta Hebert's chest gave a heave, kicking off a new cycle of Cheyne-Stokes breaths, and Martin tapped her chart against his palm, feeling the terrible helplessness of death's happening. Gretchen had given Mrs. Hebert morphine twenty minutes earlier, per his telephone orders; he was sure she wasn't in any pain. For a moment, Martin thought of a pediatric nurse, a woman named Patty, who had worked on the medical floor many years ago. Her expertise had been sitting with patients—children—and their families in their final moments. It didn't happen often, but from time to time she would be called to the emergency department to be with a patient who had been in a motor vehicle accident or some other trauma, alone because his or her parents were also injured or simply couldn't summon whatever unthinkable strength it would take to sit and watch their child die. Martin had never seen it himself, but one of his colleagues had once described the way she would do something she called The Chant: she would stroke the patient's forehead, if it was possible to, and whisper over and over in his or her ear: *You're not alone, I'm right here with you, you are loved, don't be afraid.* Hearing was the last of the senses to go.

Martin walked to the head of Ruta Hebert's bed, bent the slightest bit toward her and then pulled himself away. The mylar balloon attached to the guest chair, half-deflated now, skittered in circles as Martin backed into it. It was absolutely out of the question, even if he had wanted to try.

He cleared his throat. "Any word from Richard Hebert?"

Gretchen shook her head, and Martin felt the weight of it in his limbs: how, after all the drama of the last month—the last six decades, from what he understood—could Richard Hebert stay away for his mother's final moments? It was not Martin's job to be in this room, not at all; this process was the very antithesis of everything he had ever trained for. Doctors plied the interventions, set themselves against the challenge of holding off the inevitable for hours or days or years, and when every end had been exhausted, it became someone else's task, that of priest or parent or nurse. Richard Hebert had made him lie to his patient. Martin had told her that her son was coming. He pressed his folded arms against his sides, squeezing his hands against his ribs.

"She's agonal now," he said. "Neither of them are going to make it in time."

Gretchen nodded. "I know."

For a few more minutes, the nurse busied herself around Mrs. Hebert, straightening the bedclothes and unhooking and rehanging half-full bags of saline. Mrs. Hebert took another jerking breath and Gretchen smoothed a gloved hand across the old woman's hair, as if to quiet both of them. "Almost there, Mrs. Hebert," she murmured. "You're doing fine."

Martin came around beside the nurse and the two of them watched Mrs. Hebert breathe, the intervals lengthening between each run of breaths, the cycles of deepening inspirations much shallower now. Out in the hallway voices approached, and for a moment Martin felt a flare of hope, sure he heard Richard Hebert's edgy tenor, the miracle of Eva Sorrentino's soothing alto. The voices fell away, and Martin shook himself, ridiculous. Ruta Hebert's head arched back and her chest gave a final heave.

A small purring noise came from the old woman's parted lips and Martin clutched his hand around her curled fist, the taut skin cold already, like marble. "It's okay, Mrs. Hebert," he said. "You know I understand."

Ruta Hebert's eyes opened, and the corners of her empty mouth lifted in the slightest possible suggestion of a smile. Martin was so startled it took him a moment to realize that he had been correct, she was done. The lines of her faint smile were already turned to wood, the curve of her unseeing eyeballs had gone flat. He pulled his stethoscope from his pocket and pressed the bell against her chest, hearing the absolute, unearthly silence of the truly dead. He held it there much longer than was necessary, then looked at the clock and said the words: time of death eleven-seventeen a.m. Gretchen looked at the clock, too, and agreed.

"Poor woman," the nurse said. "She sure hung in there longer than any of us thought she would. We'll keep her up here as long as possible, and maybe her daughter will be able to make it in to say goodbye before we take her downstairs."

"Probably best if you can," Martin agreed.

If Gretchen noticed the roughness in his voice when he spoke she didn't show it. She shook out a yellow paper gown and pushed her arms through the narrow sleeves, opened a plastic eye shield and set it on her face, ready to start the business of preparing Ruta Hebert for the morgue.

•

AT HOME, MARTIN FOUND Audrey alone at the kitchen table, a heaping bowl of ice cream in front of her. Chocolate, judging by the dark line of it around her lips, the little beard that ended in the dimple of her chin. She started as her father entered the room, giving him an anxious, guilty look.

"Mom said I could make myself some ice cream," she said.

Martin lowered himself into the chair to her right, suppressing a grin. "And so you have," he said. The bowl Audrey had chosen was a soup plate, mounded with easily twice the amount of ice cream her mother ever served her. There was chocolate syrup and the milky remnants of what Martin assumed was once a large quantity of whipped cream. A few colored sprinkles clung to the side of the bowl, their bright pinks and greens and yellows leaching out of them in little penumbrae. "A sundae."

Audrey nodded, scooping up another mouthful. "Mom didn't say I couldn't."

Martin looked around the kitchen. The ice cream carton still sat on the counter, a large silver hostess spoon leaking chocolate beside it. The whipped cream canister lay on its side in a little bed of sprinkles. An unopened jar of maraschino cherries sat apart from the rest. New, Martin figured; the lid too tight for Audrey's small hands to untwist.

"Where *is* your mother?" he asked.

"Upstairs, I think. She said she had a headache and was going to lie down for a while."

Martin picked up a spoon, leftover from dinner, he supposed, and turned it from side to side, idly noting his inverted image. "Well, your mother's been pushing herself very hard lately. I think she sometimes forgets everything she's been through in the last two years. We'll let her rest a bit."

Audrey wiped her mouth with the back of her hand, smearing chocolate across her cheek. Martin raised his spoon above her soup plate. "May I?"

"I could make you your own," she offered.

"I think—" Martin began and then stopped. He'd been about to tell Audrey she had more than enough ice cream in her bowl to share, but then he'd caught the expression of reluctance on her face. There was no harm in letting her eat her whole dessert herself—or at least letting her try to. "I think that sounds like a splendid idea," he said instead. "Just as long as you promise not to tell your mom I had ice cream for dinner."

While Audrey spooned the now-soupy ice cream into her father's dish, squirted the whipped cream and added sprinkles ("I finished the chocolate syrup," she confessed, her expression contrite), Martin tidied up the detritus of her efforts. He threw out the empty ice cream carton and wiped the counter and picked up the jar of cherries to put them back. The lid came off with a little effort. Audrey nodded happily when Martin asked if she thought they should add some to their sundaes.

"You know why they're called sundaes, don't you?" Martin asked his daughter when they were seated again.

"I think so," Audrey said slowly, tipping her head to the side. "Actually, no."

"The story I learned was that it was the way ice cream shops in the Midwest served ice cream sodas on Sundays, when soda water couldn't be sold."

"It couldn't? Why not?"

"It was considered sinful." Martin wiggled his eyebrows at his daughter. "Water with carbonation was much too wicked to be served on the Sabbath."

"That's funny." Audrey licked the back of her spoon. "I guess it makes sense." She thought a minute then added, "So many words are weird, though."

"How so?"

"Well, like right at dinner. I asked Mom if I was going to keep going to Royal River over the summer and she said she was still on the fence about it. I figured that meant something good, because fences and riding pretty much go together, but she said it meant she hadn't decided."

Martin nodded, surprised and pleased to hear that Nina was considering giving up on that barn, the thought of which he still didn't like. "When you're on the fence, it means you could climb off one side or the other. One side is yes, the other side is no." Martin suddenly found himself feeling terribly magnanimous. "I'm sure we can find a place right around here where you can ride if your mother decides that other one is too far a drive."

"But I *like* Royal River." Audrey scowled. "I like Deanna, my riding teacher. Tinkertoy would miss me."

Martin realized he had miscalculated. "That saying," he continued quickly, "*on the fence,* is something called an idiom. It's a colorful way of saying something that could be said in plainer words and that can't be figured out just by the words' literal meaning.

"When I first was learning English, I tried to memorize all the idioms, but there were too many and I found that after a while I was able to figure them out from their context. I won't forget though, the first one I encountered; someone told me I had a chip on my shoulder and I actually turned and looked." Martin could laugh about that now. "To make things worse, I was coming from England and then Canada, where chip meant French fry. So I thought someone was telling me that I had somehow gotten a French fry on my shoulder."

Audrey erupted into giggles, clapping both hands against her mouth to hold them back. "Oh, *Dad,*" she said, "you did not."

Martin spread his hands wide. "I did."

"So what does it actually mean?"

"It means to be angry or argumentative, which I apparently was."

"*Chip on my shoulder,*" Audrey murmured softly, rocking herself in her seat. "So, have a cow? Is that one too?"

"It is," Martin agreed. "Can you guess what it means?"

Audrey turned her spoon around and around in her almost-empty ice cream bowl, her face scrunched up with effort. "Don't be such a baby?" she finally guessed. "Willow sat with Heather Moran instead of me at lunch again today and when I tried to get her to change her mind she told me, 'don't have a cow, it's only lunch.'"

"You were close," Martin said. "It means don't get so upset."

Audrey sighed and Martin pushed his ice cream bowl away. "Don't be discouraged," he told his daughter. "Some of them are hard. But you'll figure it out. Some of them actually make sense, though, when you take them apart a little bit, and it can be like a puzzle decoding them."

"Really?" Audrey eyed her father skeptically. "Like what?"

"Well—" Martin extended his legs out underneath the table, buying time while he thought. His left knee was stiff. "To continue with the example of cows: *chew on it.* That's a phrase you'll often hear people use: let me chew on it and get back to you. It means to think something over."

"I've heard that one. Mom uses it sometimes, and so does Jenny. But I don't see what it has to do with cows."

"Well, not yet you don't. But listen to this: the big word that means to think something over or reflect on it is ruminate. And do you know what the name is for animals that have multi-part stomachs for digesting, like cows and camels and deer? They're called ruminants, or ruminators. They eat their food partway, in essence, then regurgitate it and chew it over again to make it easier for their digestive system to absorb. So to ruminate is to chew something over, turn a thought over and over again the way a cow processes its food." Martin rubbed his hands together, absurdly pleased with himself. That was one he had figured out on his own in medical school, the connection between the phrase and the Latin root word *ruminare* like a light had shined down on him.

Audrey blew out her breath noisily, however, and glared down at the table.

"That is not easy, either. Just because you know everything doesn't mean I do, too, you know. I'll never figure them all out."

Martin understood his daughter's frustration, imagined the intimidation she felt. It was a feeling he knew all too well. "You don't have to learn them all. You just have to make a little note to yourself, in your head, when something someone says sounds a bit off to you."

Martin gave a little chuckle. "What's more, I'd like to correct the notion that I know everything. One time years ago, when my three boys were little, I asked their mother if she would fix some smash for dinner, because I loved it so. It took a while for all of us to figure out that what I'd meant to say was squash. It was summertime and I wanted to eat some squash. I'd mistranslated the word I knew in German, and boy did my sons not let me forget it. For months they'd say, 'hey, Dad, how about tonight we have some smash?'"

Audrey looked up at her father, her face serious. It sometimes shocked him, how much she looked like childhood pictures of him: the same light hair, the same dimple, the same blue eyes. And right now, the same mind, too, as she took her father's hand across the table. "Poor you," she said. "I don't think that's so funny."

"Well, thank you, Audrey. I appreciate your sympathy."

"You're welcome, Dad," she said. Absently, she twirled one long lock of blonde hair in a spiral and let it go. "You know," she added, "I think I might be German, too."

thirty-two

SWEATY AND SPENT, TODD turned to kiss the side of Nina's head. "Our timing is terrible, you know," he said.

As he spoke, his lips brushed against Nina's cheek. She rolled her head against the pillow, away from him, and looked out the window. "Our timing?" she repeated. "Is that what the problem is?"

Todd tucked his knees up behind Nina's and pulled her naked body back against his so his deflated penis nestled in between her buttocks. He buried his face into the nape of her neck and breathed out. "For starters, I guess."

His point, Nina knew perfectly well, was that the two of them had been doing this for more than a week now, and school was going to be over in less than two. After graduation and a trip to Cape Cod, Juliette would be working for Deanna at Royal River for the better part of July and August, but Audrey would be home with Nina the entire summer break. Goldengrove's last day was next Thursday; after that, the only possibility for Todd and Nina to be together would be if Nina changed her mind and signed Audrey up for the beginner's riding camps Juliette was helping teach, something for which Audrey had been campaigning relentlessly. Todd, naturally, thought it was an excellent idea.

The truth, however, was that Nina privately hoped the circumstances of summer would put an end to her affair—not because she *wanted* to end it, precisely, but because she couldn't tolerate the guilt of going on. After Todd had left on Monday, she had stripped the guest bed and run the sheets through her washer's sanitary cycle, then did the same to herself, scrubbing until the shower ran cold. She had gone through the motions of being with Audrey after school—her gratitude for her daughter's obliviousness painfully reminiscent of the way she'd felt moving in a similar fog after her cancer diagnosis—and later sat on her bedroom floor in the dark, her spine pressed against the wall and the knuckle of her forefinger clamped in her teeth, listening to fragments of Martin and Audrey's conversation drift up from downstairs. On Tuesday, Todd had come over again, this time bringing tools to fix Nina's splintered garage door, and for the rest of the week they had gone to the Slocums' house after Nina had rejected Todd's suggestion of a hotel. Every night, Nina had gone to bed early, exhausted by the charade, and Martin had worked obligingly late; the one day they had spent as a family—Sunday—Nina had been on eggshells, a fragment of T.S. Eliot chasing itself over and over in her brain. *Prepare a face to meet the faces that you meet—*

Even before her own infidelity, she'd been unable to imagine how people who were cheating on their spouses could simply walk around, buy their groceries and exercise their dogs and fill their car tanks with gas as if they were doing nothing wrong. She couldn't do it, couldn't turn off the deep current of shame in constant motion underneath her skin, and she supposed that was something, at least. It couldn't continue. It *wouldn't* continue, and she hoped a summer home with Audrey would break her new compulsion, the way having your wisdom teeth out could help you quit smoking, or a broken arm could make a thumb sucker stop.

"What are you thinking about?" Todd trailed his hand down Nina's side, from her shoulder to her elbow and then along the curve of her ribs. In the interest of equity, they were back at Nina's house, in her guest bed, and she fought the urge to pull away.

"I'm thinking that you're right," she said. "Our timing is terrible."

Todd's finger continued its travels, tracing Nina's forehead, the curve of her ear, the underside of her jaw. "We could leave them, you know."

"And—what? Live at the barn with Sunny and LJ? No, we couldn't."

"Yes, we could," Todd countered. "Not live at the barn, of course, but...I don't understand. What's to keep you from leaving him?"

Nina sat up in the bed. The ache in her lower back from more than a week ago hadn't quite gone away—because of all the sex she was having, no doubt—and she stretched against it, folding herself forward around her knees.

"Todd, you can't be serious. Do you want the complete list, or just the top one hundred reasons? There's Audrey, obviously, for numbers one through ninety-nine, and I couldn't do that to Martin. I couldn't. He would be devastated." As soon as the words were out of Nina's mouth she realized the truth of them. Martin would be devastated.

Todd sat up, too. "Martin, devastated? That doesn't sound like anything I've heard you say about him before."

"I know it doesn't. It isn't. Martin can be prickly." Nina smiled ruefully. "He can be a downright prick. But he's a good person. An… *absolute* person. For as smart and complicated as he is, I sometimes think there's something that's—naïve, I guess, something really innocent about him." She stopped. Talking this way to Todd about Martin was almost more of a betrayal than having sex was. "He would never cheat on me. It would crush him to know I was doing this."

"But you don't love him."

Nina laid her cheek against her knees, facing Todd. "Todd," she said quietly, "I do love him."

"You do." The words, not a question, hung in the air.

"I do." For a second, Nina felt relieved. It made it seem better, somehow, that she still loved her husband, even if it was in a way that was diminished, conciliatory. At the very least, she loved him enough to want to spare him from getting hurt.

Todd rubbed his palm against his cheek, making a loud, sandpaper sound. "Then what are we doing here?"

"I'm not exactly sure. I've been asking myself that question since we started this." Tears filled Nina's eyes. "Before, actually. I think I started asking myself that first time we met at Royal River with the girls. It's—it's incredibly selfish. It's having your cake and eating it, too."

"You're being too hard on yourself, Nina. I don't believe either one of us is just scratching an itch. We haven't killed anybody."

Nina rocked herself a little before she responded. "I wish you were right, but if anything I'm not being hard enough on myself. I've had this argument with myself from every angle imaginable. What kind of person does this? What kind of people are we?"

Sometimes, she felt she deserved this affair, that it was *owed* to her, that having cancer and beating it was a challenge to live her life as fully—as happily—as she could. Other times she felt her obligation was to do a better job of honoring the commitment she'd already made. She thought of her own parents' marriage, the seemingly inexplicable adoration her father had continued to feel for her mother long after her stomach sagged with the aftereffects of bearing three children and the little crease beneath her jaw became an outright jowl. Was the way she loved Martin enough—for either one of them? Had she made a mistake she needed to be brave enough to fix (what was the final straw, she found herself wondering after so many years, that had driven Beth Winzer to file for divorce)? What if she left Martin for Todd, only to find her feelings for him eventually change? There was no part of her that felt she and Todd were simply destined for one another, that they were, in fact, *meant* to do this. All her past crushes had abated sooner or later; there were a thousand people out there you could reasonably argue were your destiny. Marriage was about discipline, about valuing all the things that compelled you to build a life with someone above your attraction to anyone else, about respecting not the strength but the fragility of your bond. Nina had failed at that, was failing at that.

"Don't do this," Todd said. "Really." He climbed out of the bed and pulled his boxers on, then held a hand out to Nina. "Come on, I think what we need here is a change of scenery."

Nina waved his hand away and he sat back down on the side of the bed.

"Okay, then," he said, "What do you want to do?"

"I don't know."

Nina looked around her guest room. When was the last time she and Martin had even *had* guests? His son Peter and Peter's wife, Leanne, had stayed with them once or twice before they had kids, but that was years ago; on the rare occasion one or the other of Nina's brothers were in town they stayed in a hotel. At one point, Nina had thought maybe she would have a second child, and that this room would then become his or hers, but Martin had rejected the idea out of hand. Surely Nina knew he was too old for fatherhood again; it was bad enough being mistaken regularly for Audrey's grandfather.

"I think what I really want is to turn back the clock."

Todd folded his arms and scowled down at his feet. "So none of this ever happened, you mean."

Nina had meant something even more absurd: so that she and he could have met in an alternate universe where they had Audrey and Juliette but not their spouses, so they could be together without anyone getting hurt. Todd's assumption, though, and the tone in which he asserted it, stopped her cold. He sounded pouty, like a little boy, his arms clamped sullenly across his naked chest. Nina hadn't noticed before the soft fold of skin just above his waistband, the sprinkling of old acne scars on his shoulders. Suddenly, she wasn't sure what she wanted. A little wave of panic washed across her abdomen.

"It would be easier, don't you think?" she said.

Todd uncrossed his arms and leaned his forearms on his thighs, studying his upturned palms as he answered. "Just because something's easier doesn't mean it's better, you know."

"Sure it is. After the last couple of years I've given up my taste for hard."

The silence between them grew, finalizing itself, and then Todd slowly pushed himself away from the bed, moving around the room to gather his clothes. He shook out his t-shirt before he put it on, checked all his pockets for cell phone and wallet and keys before stepping into his jeans. Nina knew he was stalling for time, waiting for her to take back the words she'd just said.

When she didn't, he gave her a crooked smile. "I have to say," he said, "this isn't quite how I imagined this conversation going."

Nina knew it wasn't; it wasn't how she would have imagined it herself. What *was* it that she'd thought she wanted when she'd started this affair, though? What other way had she imagined it going? For a moment, she would have settled for a clock she could turn just five minutes back.

"I'm sorry, Todd. I'm really not feeling very well today." It was true; the receding panic had left a light film of nausea behind, and she felt achy and stiff, as if she might be coming down with the flu.

"Sure," Todd said lightly. He paused in the doorway, frowning. "You do look a little tired, actually."

Nina nodded, feeling the tears she'd blinked back earlier threaten again. "I'm really sorry," she repeated. "I'm just not any good at all of this."

"I'd be worried if you were."

Through the window, Nina heard the sound of a lawnmower and the faraway hum of traffic. There were roofers at the Crandalls' house, four doors down, their nail guns a dull *thunk-thunk-thunk*.

"Are you going to be at the barn tomorrow?" she asked. "Because I was thinking—maybe, if you were, I could come ride Sunny for a little bit, if…" she trailed off.

"Is that what you want to do?"

"I think so." Nina smiled unsteadily. "Maybe. I don't know. I obviously don't have the first clue what I want at the moment."

Todd nodded for what seemed like a long time, tapping his fingers against the doorframe. "Why don't you call me in the morning, when you've had a chance to think it over a bit."

Nina nodded back, swallowing the knot in her throat, and said, "I will."

·

SHE WOULDN'T, THOUGH.

The next morning, when Nina woke up, her backache had taken on a new intensity, and when she went to the bathroom, there was blood in the toilet. She stared at the pink-stained water in horror, wondering if she'd developed a bladder infection like some twenty-year-old from having too much sex. When she called Dr. Raab, the primary care physician told her to come into the office to give a urine sample, and said she was going to set up a CT scan for Nina, just in case.

"Just in case what? I just had a CT scan with Dr. Tredway two weeks ago and everything was normal."

Dr. Raab sounded relieved when she'd told Nina it was probably just a urinary tract infection and she'd prescribe her a course of antibiotics. She was going to check in with Dr. Tredway, however, on the outside chance the breast surgeon wanted to see Nina herself. Nina was fairly certain that the pain she was having wasn't because a new breast was growing out of her back.

She was on her way out the door an hour later when the telephone rang, a pair of calls that came in such quick succession she had brief reason to hope the second was an apology, a reversal of the first. The first was from Mary Chisholm at Goldengrove, calling to say she was very sorry to report that there had been an incident on the playground with Audrey, who had lost her temper and punched Willow Rutherford in the stomach, and though there was only a week left in the school year, a meeting was going to be required.

The second was from Boston Metropolitan Hospital, equally sorry to be telling Nina that Dr. Tredway needed her to come in as soon as possible for some tests. It was probably nothing, but after speaking with Dr. Raab about Nina's back pain Dr. Tredway had pulled Nina's CT films again and thought they should take some more pictures of her lower abdomen, just to be safe. The studies they'd taken in May didn't include a full series of Nina's kidneys and after going through what they had with a fine-toothed comb, Dr. Tredway had asked Dr. Olsen to take a peek at what looked like a funny spot just below Nina's left adrenal gland. It was probably nothing, maybe a cyst or even a flaw on the X-ray, but there was no point, given her history, in being anything other than absolutely sure.

Fall 2005

thirty-three

SOME DAY, THE SUN was going to go out.

The anchor of the solar system, the Earth's sun was a star, an exploding ball of hydrogen and helium so powerful the light and heat it gave off had made life ninety-three million miles away possible for the last three and a half billion years. Not just human life, of course, but plants and animals, protozoa and trilobites, the bacteria that started it all in the Archean period. People never thought about that. When they thought about life on Earth they thought only about other people, or maybe the first creatures that had crawled from the oceans and grew legs. Or dinosaurs. That's where all the boys from school thought life had begun.

Audrey had needed her father's help to do the math, but the two of them had figured out one time that it took almost eight and a half minutes—500 seconds—for the light from the sun's rays to reach the Earth. Some scientists thought that sixty-five million years ago there was a terrible ice age that had turned the planet into a giant snowball, and that it happened because an asteroid or meteor had come crashing though the atmosphere. Continents had collided and volcanoes had exploded, burning the forests, sending clouds of ash in the air so thick that none of those rays of light, 11,000 degrees Fahrenheit traveling 186 thousand miles per second, could get through. *Penetrate* was the word all the books used, a sharp and terrifying word almost as heart-stopping as the thought of that terrible black cloud snuffing out all of the light. Without the sun's rays, no plants, nothing green could grow, and water from the earth couldn't get pulled back up into the air. It had grown colder and colder, the water had risen higher, drowning everything, and before long the ice had covered the entire planet, miles deep. Millions of years of evolution wiped out just like that. The Cryogenian Period, they called it, part of the Proterozoic Eon, and it had lasted thousands of years, until enough cloud dust had settled to let the hot rays of the sun again shine through. When the ice had melted the atmosphere had been filled with oxygen and life had developed rapidly, the Cambrian Explosion, mollusks and plants and gigantic mammals, then the earliest human beings. The world that began had ended and then begun again.

But here was the point: when Audrey was five or six, she had thought the sun would go out like a flashlight, burning dimmer and dimmer in millions of light years of blackness until it faded into permanent dark, leaving the Earth to turn into another never-ending ball of ice. The thought of that had been terrible, but nothing compared to what was really going to happen, which was that Earth was going to get burned up. As the sun used up its supply of hydrogen it would actually get bigger, hundreds of times bigger, expanding like a balloon before it collapsed. All the planets that were close to it—Mercury, Venus, Earth—would be burned to blackened lumps, like squares of charcoal. On Earth, all the water was going to boil away, and the atmosphere was going to escape into outer space, the only evidence, if anyone was out there looking for it, that the planet had ever even *been*. Billions and billions of years of existence would simply disappear.

Audrey didn't understand why no one else she knew was bothered—was ripped inside into a trillion tiny pieces—by the fact that their sun was just out there waiting, a ticking time bomb, to grow into a giant monster and cook the planet until there was nothing left. The kids at school just thought she was crazy, and even her mother had told her once, "But sweetheart, you're talking about something that will happen billions of years from now, you just told me that yourself," as if it no longer had anything to do with her. Her mother had bit her lip not to make the argument Audrey knew that she had meant to (you'll be long dead then, so what will it matter?), but it *did* matter. It made Audrey feel helpless in a way that actually, physically hurt. Her own death she could somehow handle now; there were even times she felt some relief to think that some day all of this would be over. But even dead she still pictured herself *here*, somehow, her body anchored to the Earth, becoming bones and then dirt and then perhaps the roots of a new tree. If there was no Earth, there was no anything. None of the things she thought or felt or said or did had any meaning at all.

AUDREY'S MOTHER'S CANCER HAD spread to her kidney and bones. Right after third grade ended, Dr. Tredway had found a tumor the size of a quarter on her mother's left kidney and had sent her to another surgeon to have it taken out. At the time, Audrey's father had told her everything was still okay, Dr. Hsang was going to use a special piece of equipment that used radio waves to basically cook the tumor—*ablate* it, a word that coated Audrey's tongue like cream cheese when she said it—and her mother would probably be able to go home the same day. Between her first CT scan and the surgery, though, the tumor had grown bigger than a golf ball, too big to *ablate,* and when Dr. Hsang went to take the whole kidney out he found that it was stuck to Audrey's mother's intestines and her colon, and that made it impossible to remove. She started on a new medicine, Sutent, which didn't sound to Audrey like chemotherapy at all, and then in August when her back started to hurt a lot and Dr. Hsang thought it was another tumor in her kidney, it turned out to be new cancer on her spine. Audrey had been scared, of course, but she hadn't been surprised. Two years ago, Audrey's father had explained to her that to cure a cancer completely you had to kill every last single cell of it, and there were approximately ten trillion cells in an adult human's body. The job of chemotherapy had been to find a hundred million needles in a hundred million haystacks; leave even one and they'd divide and divide until there were thousands of them again before you had time to stop and think. At the time, that had sounded impossible to Audrey; last year, she hadn't been able to understand how her father could just accept the doctors saying her mother had No Evidence of Disease.

"Don't you remember how sick the chemo made her?" he'd asked. "That was all those cancer cells being poisoned. The poison was so strong it killed a lot of healthy cells, too."

Obviously, the chemotherapy had missed a lot of haystacks; the doctors were now telling Audrey's mother that her cancer had grown resistant, which meant it had figured out how to survive the chemo drugs. There were other things they could try, different chemotherapy, more radiation, a different medicine that could strengthen her bones. It was still breast cancer, somehow, even though it wasn't in her breast anymore.

"But they can't do surgery to take your spine out, can they?"

When Audrey asked her parents that question the day they told her about the new cancer they had looked at one another, and for a minute, she thought they were going to lie to her. She knew the answer, of course; of course they couldn't.

Her father had said they could try to use the ablation to break the tumors up because they were just tiny spots, then fill the holes with a special bone glue. Her mother had added, "Kind of like the way they fill a cavity at the dentist," but Audrey hadn't been comforted by that.

"What kind of bone glue?" she had asked instead.

Her father had said it was probably some kind of acrylic and her mother had joked, "Maybe it's Elmer's." Audrey hadn't laughed. It wasn't a joke, and she didn't appreciate her mother pretending it was.

"But we just *did* this, don't you realize that?" Audrey was packing to stay with her father's son, Peter—her brother, she supposed, though she hardly knew him—and his wife, Leanne, who had moved in September to a house fifteen minutes from Cabot. She didn't want to go. She didn't want her mother to be in the hospital again. "You told me Dr. Olsen said you had No Evidence of Disease. How come the doctors said your cancer was gone and now it's not?"

The truth was that Audrey was angry with her mother, even though she knew it wasn't fair. But everything that was wrong right now seemed to be her mother's fault. The same day her mother told Audrey she was sick again, she also had told her she couldn't ride at Royal River any more, but if she wanted to they could look for a barn that was close to home. Audrey hadn't wanted that at all—"but what about Tinkertoy?" she'd asked, "what about Juliette?"—but that hadn't changed anything. Her mother had said she was sorry, and she had cried, which hadn't made Audrey feel any better. She was riding at Broadacre Stables now, a gray Connemara pony named Lady, and it was fine, but it wasn't the same.

Audrey wasn't friends with Willow anymore, either, and that was a change that seemed like her mother's fault, too. Lucy Sweet's mother was fat and had skin on her upper arms that flopped over her elbows and Teagan Lester's mother smoked cigarettes, but nobody else's mother had cancer in her kidney and spine. After Audrey had gotten angry and punched Willow in the stomach, her mother had asked her if she wanted to go to another school. She'd said OF COURSE she didn't; she loved Goldengrove and she would DIE if she had to ride the school bus and sit at a regular desk and have homework the way they did in public school. Her mother had asked her to explain, then, why she'd punched Willow, but Audrey had been too upset, too humiliated to try to put it in words. It was about a finger rhyme, and Willow teasing her, but it hadn't been about those things at all. This year, she'd been put in a different class from Willow for the first time since kindergarten, and though she cried every day for the first week straight, she'd stayed in Mrs. Saller's class and Willow and Heather and Callie had all stayed with Mrs. Ross. It was November now, and Mrs. Saller was the best teacher she'd ever had, but it still didn't make up for not having Willow in her class. Mrs. Saller was short, not much taller than Audrey, and she gave Audrey hugs when she came into class in the morning. Students from all over the Lower School came to her classroom to get their teeth pulled and have a white Tic Tac put in the hole that got left. Mrs. Saller's first name was Flor and Audrey loved that. Flor was Spanish for flower. She would ask her teacher to say it sometimes for her and Mrs. Saller would, *Florrrrr*, ticking the *R* with a long soft purring of her tongue. She was teaching Audrey Spanish during reading time, because Audrey had finished the Lower School reading program the year before. She had her own Composition book with a black marbled cover, full of nouns and verbs and phrases like *¿Cómo estás?*

At school when she got upset, Mrs. Saller squished her tight and would sometimes rattle off a long string of Spanish words she didn't understand, the big ups and downs of syllables like a rollercoaster, and if anyone tried to push Audrey too hard Mrs. Saller would say they mustn't rock Audrey's boat. Audrey had told Mrs. Saller once that she knew that was an idiom (that one was easy; Audrey didn't have a boat) and Mrs. Saller kissed her forehead and said that was exactly right, *Pobre chica*. When Audrey asked what that meant, *pobre chica,* Mrs. Saller had looked away and said she would write it down sometime in Audrey's book.

On lots and lots of nights, after her parents fell asleep, Audrey would wake herself up. She'd done it for as long as she could remember, not on purpose, and she didn't know why it happened, except now it was kind of a habit. When she was little, she would sometimes call her mother to keep her company, but even before she'd gotten cancer, Audrey had stopped doing that. The truth was, she didn't mind being by herself most of the time. The dark house hummed with the furnace in the winter and the air conditioner in the summer and her father snored, just loud enough for her to hear. Her closet had soft blue carpeting and a bookcase along the back wall and Audrey would take the pillows from her bed, turn the light on, and shut the door. There were favorite books she read again and again, *Little House in the Big Woods, Charlotte's Web, A Children's Book of Greek Mythology*. She would set the pillows in a square around herself, put her book up on her knees and disappear for hours inside one story that would melt into another and then another. Daedalus and Icarus, building their wings from feathers and wax; Theseus unspooling his string to find his way back out of the Minotaur's labyrinth; Charlotte weaving her fragile, word-filled webs, launching her spinners, attaching, starting again. The fluorescent light buzzed and the knobs of her spine would start to hurt but some nights she would read until the morning, surprised and confused when her mother opened the closet door, smelling of sweat and sleep, gray-white light filling the rectangle all around her.

"Oh, Audrey," she sometimes said, "you didn't read all night again, did you? What time did you wake up?"

Audrey would guess three or four, although she never actually checked; her mother would tell her she was going to be a wreck at school today, but so what? She was a wreck every day, even when she stayed asleep; she'd be so much better if she could stay up every night and never go to school.

Lately, when she'd been waking up, Audrey didn't let herself get straight out of bed. She would make herself lie in the dark for a while, imagining she was the last human being left on the planet, letting her absolute aloneness eat into her bones just like her mother's cancer was doing to hers. She was more alone than when she overheard the other kids in her class talk about a birthday party they all were going to (Mrs. Saller made a rule that the class could only talk about outside activities everyone had been included in, but it didn't make any difference); more alone than she was at recess, in the birch grove, watching Willow and Lydia and Callie and a new girl, Miranda, play.

The first week of school, she'd followed Willow to the water fountain and had asked the question she'd wondered for months and months. "Why don't you like me any more?"

Willow had answered her right away. "Because you're weird, that's why."

"Weird how?" Audrey had asked.

Willow pointed to Audrey's shirt, a souvenir from the butterfly exhibit at the Museum of Science, and her navy pants (soft pants, because she couldn't stand the hard feel of denim against her stomach and the backs of her legs). "You dress weird. Your hair is too long." Willow was wearing a jeans skirt with three sequined hearts stitched on the back pocket and a ruffly blouse with thin straps that showed her shoulders. "I just got tired of having to help you all the time. It's like the whole world is purple, everything, and you aren't. You're this spot of orange."

That night in bed, and the night after, and after and after, Audrey lay with her eyes open, trying to understand how orange she was. *Orange, I am orange,* she whispered to herself, feeling the heat of it radiate from her skin. When her mother was taking the Sutent, it had turned her skin a little bit yellow, and even though she knew Willow didn't know that, she couldn't help wondering. Purple was a royal color, made in ancient times by crushing snail shells that were more rare and more expensive than gold. Orange wasn't the color of anything special—a sharp-tasting fruit that coated your fingers with sticky white stuff when you peeled it, traffic cones, Halloween. Audrey had a new friend now, a girl named Una Curran who liked math and classical music and some of the same things that Audrey did, but in the dark she could still see herself, alone, a glowing speck in a sea of violet that stretched out in all directions as far as she could see.

OUTSIDE, A DOG WAS barking—the Crandalls' terrier, Audrey thought; the sound was too high-pitched to be Princess, the Vanderweghes' bulldog; everybody in the neighborhood had a dog but them. Downstairs, the grandfather clock in the living room ticked. Audrey folded her covers back and slid her hand across the wall for the closet light, bypassing Laura Ingalls and Charlotte and Wilbur for her silver-covered encyclopedia. She ran her thumb across the edges of the color-coded pages, sections on history, science and technology, people and places, the Earth. The encyclopedia was at once Audrey's favorite book and the one that terrified her the most. So many facts, so comforting in their solidity; too many facts with the terrifying ability to become real. In the Weather section alone: the amazing white spiral of a hurricane could become an actual storm, blowing roofs off of houses and tearing trees from their roots. Earthquakes ripped the ground like it was nothing more than tissue paper, actually cracking continents apart. Audrey saw the news stories. Last year, the day after Christmas, an earthquake deep in the Indian Ocean had created a giant tsunami with waves almost one hundred feet tall, killing 230,000 people in eleven different countries. Entire families and cities had been swept away, children had been pulled right out of their mothers' arms. Even now, almost a year later, there were people who were sick or hurt who didn't have a place to live, who had nothing at all. Every day something horrible happened, somewhere, something catastrophic. How could she be the only one who constantly shook from the fear of such news?

Audrey flipped past Geology, full of words that fizzed and foamed in her mouth—*obsidian, basalt, schist*—to her favorite section, Science and Technology. As she always did, she turned first to the paragraphs about time, her eyes going over the explanation of Einstein's theory of relativity again and again. It should be easy, it should make perfect sense, and yet every time she stopped to think about what the words on the page really meant, it hurt her stomach so much she thought she might throw up. Time didn't pass at the same speed for everyone, depending on how fast you were traveling through space. Time began with the Big Bang, the universe was still expanding. If the universe expanded forever, time would continue infinitely; if the universe collapsed time would stop.

When she was younger, Audrey had found the thought of the universe collapsing on itself—a massive black bellows slamming shut— terrifying beyond all words. What would be out there if the universe disappeared? She'd imagined screaming winds, a never-ending whirlpool of howling darkness turning over and over on itself. Now, though, she thought it would solve everything: the sun consuming the Earth before it subsided into a dead lump of coal; Willow not being friends with her anymore; the horrible things that happened every day, not just earthquakes and tsunamis and hurricanes but car accidents and fires. Children getting kidnapped and molested (she'd looked that word up once, when nobody would tell her what it meant). Crazy people putting their own babies in microwave ovens. Other crazy people flying airplanes into skyscrapers or strapping bombs to their bodies and blowing up entire city blocks. Cancer eating her mother up from the inside out.

Audrey knew her mother was going to die. Nobody was admitting it just yet, but when the cancer spread to her mother's spine, her father had stopped saying everything was still fine. Her parents had started talking more in their room at night (she could hear the low hum of their voices through her closet wall); they went back to having downstairs conversations that stopped when she walked in the room. Sometimes, she would catch little snatches of what they were talking about; her father using phrases like *chronic but controllable,* her mother worrying about her, Audrey, and saying *I'm sorry* about all sorts of things that weren't her fault. (What, for starters, did Juliette Slocum—who had promised to send her a letter when she started high school but never did—have to do with anything?) She never said so, but Audrey knew the cancer she had now hurt the way the breast cancer hadn't. She took big, white pain pills and sometimes a see-through patch of a drug called fentanyl that made her so sleepy she spent the whole day in bed and Audrey's father was the one who had to drive her to school and back, which was something he had never done before. After Christmas, he was going to retire, he said, which meant he'd be at home even when Audrey was at school. That would be strange, but not in a way that was bad.

BACK WHEN SHE HAD first learned that she herself was going to die someday, Audrey had let herself believe in heaven. It had been the only thought that stopped her elevator-lurchy stomach or the sound of ringing in her ears: after her body ended, she would go to a place where she would be reunited with her mother and father again, get to meet her grandparents, spend her whole days doing only the things she liked to do. It only seemed *fair,* but after a while, it hadn't made a lot of sense. How would it work, for example, if the only thing she wanted to do was spend the day in the garden with her mother, but the only thing her mother wanted to do was to be with her own parents, playing at the beach as a little girl? If you got to choose the age you wanted to be forever in heaven, how would it work if she wanted to be ten and her father wanted to be five? She used to ask her mother where heaven was and her mother would say, "It's all around us, pumpkin." *But how close to the ground?* she still wanted to know. Were they breathing in people's souls right now without even knowing it, did birds and airplanes rip them apart? One time, her mother had pointed out the evening sky, showing Audrey a strip of dark blue cloud with a pink glow rising from it. "Right there," she had told her. "I think that's heaven right there."

In first grade, when Audrey received her silver encyclopedia as a Christmas present, she had stopped asking her mother about heaven. She knew for sure then it couldn't exist. Space scientists had found black holes and invisible objects and quasars; her encyclopedia had pictures taken by the Hubble telescope of the Horsehead Nebula, thousands of light years away from Earth. If heaven existed, it wouldn't be out there beyond that; anyone who knew anything about the Bible knew it said God created heaven and Earth together, so why would He put heaven 1,500 light years outside of the solar system? The answer was that He wouldn't. If heaven existed, there was no way astronomers wouldn't have found it by now.

Audrey loved the thought of space, the enormous, turning planets made of feldspar and magnesium, hydrogen and methane. The knowledge that the light she saw from the stars had traveled for years before it made its way to her was almost enough to make Einstein's ideas make sense. What she couldn't abide, however, was a different thought. If the universe was always expanding, wasn't it possible that her mother's soul would be sucked out to the very edge of it, traveling ever, infinitely farther away? If that was the case, Audrey would try to chase her, dive after her like a silver minnow darting off in a bottomless pool. But in the impossible expanse of all that emptiness, how would she ever figure out which direction to go?

Part Three

Summer 2006

thirty-four

IN THE EARLY MORNING, Charlotte Harbor was leached of all its color, the rocks and water and sky all pale versions of themselves, even the bright colored sailboats tipped with different shades of silver-gray. By eight o'clock, the sun was high enough for all the objects in the harbor to reclaim their true hues: the water in the cove a deep sapphire, the boat hulls forest green and cinnamon and turquoise, the sky cerulean, hung with perfect white cumulus clouds. At that hour, the lobster boats were long gone, tailed by crowds of hectoring seagulls, the morning ferry maneuvering up to the commercial dock to collect its first load of passengers heading farther out into Frenchman Bay. Through the window, Nina could hear parents calling their children over, the heavy thump of hawsers landing on the weathered boards, the deep guttering noise of the diesel engine shutting off. The world wavered—fentanyl, the rippled window glass, the ruffled harbor lit with coruscating diamonds of sunlight—and Nina turned her cheek against the cool pillow, closed her eyes to fold every sensation into herself. Down the hallway, the clatter of dishware as Martin and Audrey busied themselves in the kitchen making breakfast, pancakes with applesauce and cinnamon sugar. Nina wasn't hungry, of course, but she would do her best to take a couple of bites.

It was the middle of July, more than a year since her kidney metastasis had been discovered, and a month since Martin had spent a full day packing the car in Cabot before driving them all five hours north to Charlotte Harbor. At first, Audrey had fought the notion: she didn't *want* to spend the summer up on some island in Maine; she didn't *care* if it was the place where her mother had spent her childhood summers. It hadn't taken her long, though, to settle in, waking up early to ride her bike to Schoodic Point with Martin for homemade donuts at the Schoodic Country Store; discovering the Schoodic Point free library and its vast collection of marine biology references.

Nina had fantasized about renting her grandparents' house, but when she reached the woman she and her brothers had sold it to a decade earlier, she learned the property had just recently been sold again. The family who bought it wasn't there this summer, but they were undertaking extensive renovations and wouldn't be able to let Martin and Nina stay there. The house they'd eventually found was not on Aggamassic Reach but on McKittrick Rock, on the opposite side of the harbor, and while Nina had been disappointed at first, she'd eventually decided this arrangement was better. Every morning she awoke to a literal view of the place that loomed larger than any other in her memory, the folded gray rocks fringed with brown-green kelp, the long, low waves that would throw themselves against the Cedar Island breakwater in an explosion of white. A farmer's porch ran across the front of the house, and Martin had dragged out a reclining chair onto it so Nina could sit and watch the wheeling gulls, listen to their looping cries, take in deep breaths of the salty air. When she'd said the ocean air would ruin the fabric, Martin shook his head. "We'll buy them a new chair," he had said. "That old recliner is the last thing I'm worried about."

In the past year, Nina had learned something new about pain. The cancer in her bones was excruciating, orders of magnitude more painful than anything she'd ever experienced. Dr. Kennett had tried all sorts of things to manage it—hypnotherapy, acupuncture, a variety of medications that left her so foggy she couldn't even grasp the words on the back of a cereal box—with only limited success. Strangely enough, the thing that had finally worked best for her had been concentrating on it as hard as she could, trying to pinpoint its exact physical location, determine its quality and size and shape in her mind's eye. It didn't make any sense, Nina realized, but the proof was in the results. If she focused all of her thoughts on a particular pain, it often lessened—not completely or permanently, but enough to give her an hour's respite. A pulsing, spiked mass of bone-snapping agony would shrink to the size of a musket ball, still sharp-clawed, but manageable, small enough to close inside a box. Concentrating on the pain reminded her of childbirth, the steady breaths she had willed of herself, the way she'd envisioned each contraction as a thin white blade that cut her in two. *Life before motherhood, life after*, she'd chanted, over and over in her head.

More reluctantly, Nina had taken the same approach to her other pain, as well, gritting her teeth and stepping into the truth. The affair with Todd had ended the moment she'd taken the phone call from Dr. Tredway's office asking her to come in for another CT scan of her abdomen—not the day she had the test, not the day that Dr. Tredway, her own face drawn and white as she took Nina's hand across the table, told her the results of her kidney biopsy were unequivocal. It might, in fact, have ended two minutes earlier, as Nina had listened to Mrs. Chisholm say that Audrey had punched Willow, hearing not just the woman's words but the message that there was no magic, no matter how much she might have hoped, to Audrey's friendship with Juliette Slocum, nor Jenny's efforts to bring Audrey and Willow together again. It was over, instantly more than irrevocable; impossible. In a heartbeat, she had once again become the woman she had thought she'd transcended. Breast cancer patient. Mother of a damaged child.

Telling Todd had been hard, telling Martin harder, and when it came to the latter, Nina had been able to rationalize for a while why she should not. There were other dramas to focus on—talking to Audrey about her relapse and kidney surgery, the blow of learning surgery wasn't possible, the *coup de grace* of metastases on her spine. Confessing an act so selfish as her affair with Todd seemed nothing more than cruelty. What, after all, would it accomplish beyond transferring the burden of the truth from her to Martin?

In the end, however, Martin had surprised her. She finally told him in late August, on one of the first nights that the air turned cold, the day she'd spotted a swath of red in the backyard maple tree. Time had already started passing much too fast. She'd sat on the side of the bed and told Martin she had something terrible to tell him, something worse than cancer, and he'd closed his eyes and shook his head. "I already know."

"You do?" she'd asked.

"I have a pretty good idea."

Nina had seen in her husband's face that he hadn't wanted her to put it into words, but she couldn't leave it unsaid, couldn't be anything but one hundred percent clear about it. Only days earlier, she'd stood in the bathroom looking at her naked body, and it had seemed preposterous. The scar from her aborted kidney surgery, livid pink and as thick as a pencil. The faded smile marking the spot where her breast reconstruction tissue had been harvested, now stretched across her edema-swollen abdomen. Her foolish, perfect breast, a first-rate decoy that should be doing justice to someone else's body. The two things were linked in her mind, somehow, her infidelity and the return of her cancer, and it felt like coming clean was her only hope. She let down her guard, loosened her grip on her marriage, and this was what had happened. If only she could reclaim her marriage, make amends, make it better, maybe, just maybe— She had forgotten the vigilance with which she had to protect the things that she had.

"I had an affair," she said, the words barely a whisper. "I'm so sorry. I cheated on you, Martin."

Martin had nodded. He'd brushed his hands together, slowly, as if he was rubbing off dirt from the garden. "With Todd Slocum," he said.

"Yes," Nina answered. "It was only a week." *As if that somehow made it better.* "It ended in June."

"When your cancer came back."

"Just before."

For a moment, the two of them had sat side by side without speaking, and then Martin had turned to her.

"But it wasn't really just a week, was it? The physical part, perhaps. But in terms of intimacy—"

He'd trailed off and it had been Nina's turn to nod. "I guess you're right. I didn't think that part would matter to you."

Pain crossed Martin's face then. "I suppose you didn't," he said. "So that's where this is my fault."

Nina had protested, but her husband had held her off. "The truth is, Nina, we've always both made the assumption you'd outlive me, and that once I was gone you'd find a better match. It wasn't an easy idea, necessarily, but at least it occasionally lessened my guilt about claiming all your best years for myself." A smile appeared and vanished from Martin's face. "Does it make a difference, really, if it happened before rather than after I'm gone? I've been trying to convince myself it doesn't. At least this way I get to know who the fellow is, try to undertand what you need that I don't give you."

The part that Martin had left unsaid was the inevitability, now, of Nina being the one who would be gone first, and that was another of the pains that had to be taken head-on. Through the spring, her team at Boston Met had treated her recurrence aggressively, trying a number of different chemotherapies for her kidney and radiation for her spine, but it was a losing battle. No sooner would one spot begin to shrink than another would appear, in her ribs, in both iliac bones, in—ironically enough—her left femur. Nina found herself thinking about cancer treatment like a game of Whac-a-Mole. The chemo left her exhausted, depleted; Dr. Kennett stopped talking about trying to achieve remission and instead peppered her comments with references to *extending Nina's quality of life*. There were still a couple of tricks left in the chemo bag, treatments that would require weeks of hospitalization and might—just might—give Nina a couple more months. But when Nina saw her chemo scrubbing bubbles now they were no match for cancer, green-black cells lurking at every turn, reaching out with their sticky arms to inhale the bubbles whole. Like a video game, hapless bubbles zipped by pockets of cancer cells and the cancer cells streamed out after them, pouring down the new pathways the bubbles had opened up into the farthest corners of Nina's body. The cancer was eating her bones, driving spikes into her hips and back; her failing kidneys were pumping liters of fluid into her abdomen. She was dying. There were nights the thought of it woke her up, her heart gripped with a terror so absolute it was all she could do to keep from wailing like a child. There were days she said the words in her head over and over again until they no longer meant anything to her at all.

Nina had been sure of her decision to end treatment, but what to do with the unknown amount of time she had left had not been immediately obvious. She knew for certain she didn't want to die in the hospital, but she'd worried what harm it might do to Audrey to have her mother die at home. Would the house be haunted—ruined—would Martin and Audrey have to move somewhere else to escape from Nina's ghost? She had suggested Charlotte Harbor as a week's vacation before she became too ill to travel; Martin was the one who proposed staying for a month. He was a doctor, after all, and there wasn't anything to Nina's care at this point he couldn't handle himself. They'd said their goodbyes in Cabot without really saying them—Nina telling Jenny she'd consider her request to come visit, promising her she'd be back in August, in any event. It had been last August when, after a summer of radio silence, she had finally picked up the phone and apologized to Jenny for whatever pain her affair with Todd had caused, listened to Jenny apologize for the painful, permanent abruption of the once-invincible bond between their girls. Over the past eleven months she and Jenny had found their feet again, a new kind of friendship. Nina was grateful they'd done so, of course, but the two of them had told each other everything they needed to say.

The truly impossible conversation was the one with Audrey, and even as she heard her daughter's voice in the hallway, explaining that she was going to let Mom know that the pancakes were ready, Nina wondered again how much longer she'd be able to put it off. Audrey understood what was happening, but what were the things that Nina wanted to be certain got said? She had been an adult when her own mother died; if she'd had the chance she might have wanted to talk about the differences they'd had when she was a teenager or asked if it was okay if she didn't keep her collection of souvenir spoons, but she couldn't imagine what other unresolved questions between the two of them her mother would have been able to answer. Audrey had turned ten in February and was on the cusp now of puberty, shockingly ripe after a sweaty day at the beach or on her bicycle, the first hint of breasts swelling out from her little-girl chest. Already, she locked the bathroom door when she showered at night, turned her back if she changed her clothes in Nina's presence, and for that Nina was strangely, fiercely glad. There was a loss that was happening as it was meant to; a loss that had nothing to do with Nina's cancer. Audrey's body would have been gone to Nina soon whether or not she was around to experience its going away.

Her daughter's fingers wrapped themselves around the jamb of the open door. Audrey's expression was serious as she looked into her mother's room.

"Boo," Nina whispered.

"I wasn't sure you were awake. Dad and I made pancakes. Do you want me to bring you some?"

Nina pushed herself into a sitting position, the spikes in her bones and back pounding dully, fentanyl-blunted. "Are you eating in the kitchen, or on the porch?"

"The porch, of course." Audrey drifted into the room, picking up items from the bedside table and setting them back down, a head scarf, an almost-empty water bottle, a small blue pot of lip moisturizer. The hairs of her arm were light gold against her tanned skin; her fingernails were bitten short but clean.

"Give me a minute and I'll join you."

Nina watched her daughter struggle to suppress a smile of pleasure at the news. "Okay," she said. "I'll go tell Dad." She paused again in the doorway, swinging herself around again. "Do you want coffee or apple juice?"

OUTSIDE, BREAKFAST OVER. WARM sun on her face, a blanket across her legs. Nina tipped her head back against the nubby fabric of the reclining chair, bright galaxies exploding behind her closed eyelids as she listened to Martin and Audrey discuss the human circulatory system. There was a time—indeed, a not too distant time—when the exchange would have aggravated Nina: why did Martin insist on encouraging Audrey's different-drummer fascinations? Was there any other ten-year-old girl who was interested in her heart as anything other than the vessel for her latest crush? But now, in this place, she remembered her interest in her own father's work at about the same age; remembered her sincere if less-than-successful efforts to grasp the thrill occasioned by an uptick in the native population of bladderwrack. It was a connection, a vital connection; it wasn't her place to judge the quality of it. Especially not now.

"So what would happen if someone held their breath while they were running?"

Audrey's voice came to Nina in a burst of magenta and bottle green—color-wheel opposites, if Nina recalled correctly. Martin's words spread like liquid indigo, filling the cracks and the valleys inside Nina's head when he spoke back.

"Someone who held their breath while they were running would be foolish to do so."

"I *know* that, Dad." Behind Audrey, the mournful, steady toll of the buoy out in the channel. "I'm just saying, what would happen if they did?"

"More than likely, they would lose consciousness and begin to breathe normally again."

"That's all?"

"That's all," Martin's inky voice assented firmly. "And don't let me catch you trying it out when we go jogging or that will be the end of that."

As a little girl, Nina had loved the playground carousel that spun you round and round like a ride at the carnival, would tip her chin to her chest and fling her head back at the last second just to see if she could make herself pass out. "You two are running together?" she asked. "Since when?"

"Since today." Audrey chewed her lower lip, guilt on her face. She came to sit on the arm of Nina's chair, her tanned thigh flattening against the fabric. Golden hairs on her legs, too. How old had Nina been when she'd begun to shave? Eleven or twelve, maybe; she remembered long, flat scabs on her ankles where she'd pressed a rusting razor blade too hard against the thinly cushioned skin, scabs that would curl up and catch on her socks, tear open again, as they began to heal. Her mother's hard edged voice, *So you thought you'd just use my razor and not ask?*

"I think that's nice, honey." Nina reached her hand out for her daughter's warm leg. Strong from riding, knowledge Nina recalled dimly from the few times she herself had tried posting, pushing herself up from the stirrups in time to Sunny's trot until her thighs and stomach muscles screamed. "Don't work your dad too hard."

Across the table, Martin laughed. "You only think you're joking. As Peter and his brothers used to like to say, I think she'll make me eat her dust."

Martin's eyes moved from Nina to Audrey. "That's an idiom, of course, *eat my dust.*"

"I can tell," Audrey said, looking around. "I don't get it, though."

Nina explained that it was the title of a movie that had come out when she was a girl. "There's a car chase, and the car in front churns up dust all over the chasing car. So I guess it's about being disrespectful to someone you're already beating. Kind of like adding insult to injury." She closed her eyes again, out of breath. If she could have, she would have added that the movie starred Richie Cunningham from *Happy Days*, and that she'd seen it in the little Cabot theater that had closed years ago, a place where you were allowed to smoke and the cool kids sat in the balcony seats, dropping popcorn on the people sitting below.

She felt Audrey push herself away from the arm of the reclining chair, her daughter's footfalls impatient slaps against the wooden deck. "That sounds boring," she announced. "Dad, let me know when it's time to go for our jog."

"In a little bit." Martin patted his stomach. "After I digest. I'm going to sit here with your mother for a while."

"I'm going inside to read."

One seagull's call separated from the rest, a high-pitched, keening trill, and from the shell-lined path that ran in front of the house Nina heard a pair of women's voices, felt one small, nostalgic trill of pain. A pair of girlfriends out for a morning walk, just like the people Nina and Jenny once had been.

thirty-five

Audrey ran stiffly, her foot turnovers jerky but quick, her elbows angling sharply from her sides. Martin had already told her twice to relax her frame, and it took an effort now not to repeat the exhortation once more; both times before she had scowled at him and said, "Dad, I *am* relaxed." Notwithstanding her interest, Martin wasn't convinced his daughter was meant to be a runner, though she seemed not to tire and had the perfect build for the sport: long, lean legs, a shorter torso, a slender frame. Martin himself was built precisely opposite, and precisely the wrong way to be a natural for track and field, his legs not only short but slightly mismatched in length, a defect that became more relevant the older he got, pains in the knee of the shorter leg now answered by pains in the opposite hip. It was like the old saw about the bumblebee not being able to fly because of its aerodynamically impossible wing-to-body ratio; did Martin run because he was simply unaware that he shouldn't, anatomically speaking, be able to? He occasionally pondered what it signified that the single act that gave him the most pleasure in life (aside from sex, of course, but that was now a thing of the past) was the one to which he was least inherently disposed.

Since coming to Charlotte Harbor, Martin had found himself wondering what his life would have been like had he been a lobsterman instead of a cardiologist. A ludicrous fantasy, of course, but in the early morning hours when he was the only one up he would often sit out on the deck and watch the boats in the harbor prepare for their day. There were the lobstermen in their short sleeves and yellow rain pants, two or three of them to a boat. While one readied the wheelhouse the others would tie on long black aprons and drop open the back of the boat to haul up the nearby traps. Out would come undersized lobsters and ribbons of seaweed, tossed back into the water under a cloud of circling gulls, and back into the water would go the fish-baited, empty traps. Shouting voices as one aproned man banged on the wheelhouse, the anchor winch groaned to reluctant life, the deep shudder of the boat engine filled the predawn air.

As he watched one boat after another conduct the same routine and then head for the open water, a satisfying languor would overcome Martin, his muscles aching with the weight of hauling the heavy traps, the salty ocean spray needling his face with a thousand invisible bites. There was something to the simplicity, the pattern, of the work; the obligations that were entirely unlike making decisions about another human being's heart. What if he had been wrong, all this time? What if he had been meant to be a lobsterman living in some broken-down house at the edge of the sea? It wasn't necessarily as laughable as it sounded. Growing up, he'd never been to the ocean, and as a younger adult, his frame of reference had been a string of disastrous family trips to the beach: crowded and hot, his food bitter and gritty with sand, the boys sunburned in spite of the repeated layers of white cream Beth slathered on their shoulders, necks, and ears. Here, there were lichen-covered rocks, folded and gray and veined with white quartz; here were fried clam strips and sweet lobster rolls served at a tiny beachside shack on Schoodic Point. When all of this was over, might Audrey decide she wanted to stay?

For a time, after Nina's cancer came back and Martin's suspicions about her affair with Todd Slocum had begun to cohere into actual facts, he had thought about leaving her. While he had known he couldn't—affair or no, what kind of a man would he be to leave his wife when her cancer had come back in incurable form?—it had given him some satisfaction to imagine it: taking his retirement and packing his bags, moving to a place that conjured up absolutely nothing about his old life.

Like so many other things, Nina's confession had been at once both more and less painful than he had imagined. Less, because it was over, the words he'd desperately wanted Nina not to say to him said. More, because in their own way, the words had been somehow worse than the event itself. Selfish, and too long past to be met with any dignity. He hadn't needed his wife's infidelity articulated; for months, the truth had radiated from the slump of her shoulders and the stunned, bewildered look he often caught on her unguarded face, a despair he knew had to do with her cancer, but something else as well. Had she planned to leave him, had this Slocum fellow spurned her once her cancer had recurred? Martin perfectly understood that the appeal of an affair was the absence of reality, the quotidian cares of paying bills and parenting and falling asleep with no more intercourse than a chaste peck on the cheek.

The truth was, Martin had been angry—much angrier than he'd ever let on to Nina, because what kind of man would he be to hold a grudge against his terminally ill wife? He had tried to believe what he had told her once, that her romance had simply happened out of order, but that was too easy. She had lied, disregarded his feelings—even now he sometimes felt sick with anger, imagining Nina naked in another man's arms as he had plodded along at the hospital, completing dictations and reviewing EKGs. Was he allowed, even in the privacy of his own mind, to resent his wife for cheating on him, to struggle for forgiveness? Nina hadn't planned any of it, he knew; not the affair, not the wildfire spread of her cancer. But the last time they'd talked about her infidelity, she'd responded to the question about what Todd had given her that he himself had not with an answer that cut him to the core: Todd had given her stories, the stories of a life. His childhood, his family anecdotes, all the nonsense of birthday parties and Thanksgiving dinners and the family dog. It was the most fundamental human transaction, Nina had told him, not food or even sex, but my truth for yours.

Half a dozen strides ahead of him, Audrey was running a little slower now, weaving from side to side as they crossed the metal bridge—the Singing Bridge, the locals called it, for the sound cars' tires made when traveling across it—that connected Cedar Island, the next small settlement out from McKittrick Rock on the south curve of the harbor, to Whaleback, the easternmost. A trio of teenage boys were jumping from the bridge, egging each other on to balance their long feet on the railing and leap down into the cold, swift-moving water below. Dangerous, in Martin's opinion, but no one had asked him. A boy in baggy, surf-style bathing shorts climbed up, steadied himself momentarily, and pushed off into the air, howling a note Martin suspected he only *hoped* his friends would think was mock-scared.

"You doing all right?" he asked Audrey.

"Mmm-hmm," his daughter answered, pressing her right hand against her side.

"Side-stitch?"

Audrey grunted again, this time in the negative.

"Take a couple of deep breaths, that should help. We might not have waited long enough after we ate our breakfast."

"I told you, it's not a side-stitch," Audrey gasped.

Martin nodded, though his daughter couldn't see him. "Okay, then." He checked his watch: 10:38. They'd probably gone close to two miles at this point, their pace slow, but brisk enough that Martin had to wipe his sweaty forehead with his arm. Behind him, another boy launched himself over the railing with a yell.

It was a beautiful morning, as nearly every morning since their arrival here had been, even the foggiest days typically burning off to full sun. Today the sky was a deep blue, full of mare's tail clouds whipped by the wind into feathery V's. Small clusters of hungry gulls surrounded the lobster boats still in sight of the harbor. From here, their raucous calls sounded like the voices of children on a playground, a high-pitched blur of nonsense, but nonsense passionately felt. Martin was much more favorably inclined toward Charlotte Harbor's cormorants, big black birds that would slap their wings against the water with a comical *wap-wap-wap-wap* and then dive to catch whatever meal their efforts had churned up, tossing thrashing fish in their pointed beaks like a cat with a ball of yarn until they were ready to gulp them down. When they finished their meal, they'd perch on seaweed-covered rocks at the edge of the water and stretch their wings out to dry. Martin had heard the locals call them shithawks, for the way they sprayed the ledges and piers with their droppings, he presumed, and maybe he'd feel differently about them had he a dock to hose off every morning, but there was an innocuousness to them that—while he was surely anthropomorphizing—he found appealing. The first day he and Audrey had taken a picnic lunch to the beach, a seagull had swooped down and plucked Audrey's sandwich, still in its plastic baggie, right from her hand, prompting a startled shriek and a short-lived, futile chase. While the two of them had shared Martin's sandwich, half a dozen other seagulls had hovered nearby, watching their every movement through small, obsidian eyes.

Audrey's weaving steps slowed to a walk, and Martin pulled up beside her. "Nice job," he said, giving his daughter's ponytail a gentle tug. "I think that was just about two miles."

A breathless Audrey bent over her knees and shook her head. "I just want to stop for a minute, then we can start again." Her face was deep red, with a faint pale line around the edge of her lips.

"I don't think so," Martin said. "That's already a lot for your first time out. You don't want to push yourself so hard that you're discouraged from going back out there again."

"But I'm not discouraged," Audrey protested. "I wanted to run the whole way out to the mermaid statue and back."

"Next time." Martin looked at his watch. "I think it's time we get back to your mom, now."

Alarm lit Audrey's flushed face. "Why? What's wrong?"

Martin reached a hand out to stay his daughter. "Nothing's wrong. I just think it's time for the two of us to get back. I bet she's missing us."

Immediately, Audrey was upright. She pivoted to retrace their steps toward the Singing Bridge and Cedar Island, stumbling into a panicky trot. "Come on, Dad," she said, "hurry up. You shouldn't have let us go out this far."

Martin caught Audrey in one quick stride and put his arm around her. "Audrey, sweetheart, your mother's fine. I'm just worried about you overdoing it and think we should get back. You could get heat stroke, even on a day like this." Warm, but not yet hot, the steady ocean breeze taking the edge off the oblique heat of the sun. Audrey relented, reluctantly, eyeing her father mistrustfully, and even Martin had to cringe at the imprecision of his words. Nina wasn't fine, at all, of course, nor would she ever be again. As absurd as it sounded, the part he hadn't realized until this moment was just how acutely attuned to this truth his daughter was. When Audrey broke into a run again just before the gas station/bait shop that marked the boundary between Cedar Island and McKittrick Rock, he didn't try to stop her, but picked up his own pace to match her suddenly racing feet.

thirty-six

THERE WAS MUCH OF the story of Martin's life he no longer remembered—
how his mother had settled on Braunschweig as the end of their flight,
for example; how she had secured their barracks housing from the British
government; how he had come to attend the large primary school many
kilometers' walk through the Harz forest from their living quarters instead
of the smaller one Brigid and Hedy went to just blocks away. What he did
remember vividly was his first impression of the place: the hopeful leap
in his chest at the thought of a real bed after a year of frozen ground and
scratchy bales of hay; the sight of pale gray smoke curling from the many
stovepipes that jutted through the barracks buildings' black roofs. The
claustrophobic narrowness of the dark staircases, the sound of more voices
than Martin would have ever imagined coming from such a small space.

The barracks had been arranged in a U, three low stone buildings
facing in on an earthen courtyard. Each apartment was made up of a pair of
small rooms, a wood stove and pump-driven sink in one and a windowless
space for sleeping in the other. The bathrooms were in a separate building,
set a little bit away from the rest, but no matter: to Martin, after months of
shivering in the animal barn that had served as the Wolfenbuttel internment
camp, the idea of a roof and a source of warmth made the barracks seem as
grand as a castle. There was even electricity, a thin wire that connected naked
light bulbs to the ceiling in both of the rooms. The kitchen was furnished
with a mismatched table and chairs the previous occupants had left behind,
and there were camp beds folded up in the corner of the sleeping room. The

yellow pine walls wept beads of sticky sap and around the stove-pipe that
ran from the wood stove to the roof the ceiling boards were dangerously
black; there were cracks in the walls that let in wind and snow and through
the thin wood it was possible to hear every movement and word from the
apartment adjacent, but still—Mutti had been decisive when she'd looked
around. Martin would be in charge of gathering firewood, Hedy and Brigid
would be the ones to go to the Marketplatz. Mutti's new employer, Herr
Davies, was a high-ranking RAF officer and he would help her post a letter
to Martin's father's cousin; they would be here only a short time. None of
them mentioned their grand old house at number 20 Ulmenstrasse; Martin
suspected that, like him, his sisters didn't dare let themselves think about
where their lives had once been.

It was the end of winter when they arrived, the trees surrounding the
barracks bare of buds, the muddy square of the center courtyard frozen
into hillocks and troughs. Mutti brought home a heavy skillet from Herr
Davies' house for frying their unrelenting ration of potatoes, paired every
so often with a loaf of soft white bread. Springtime came, and the man in
the next apartment laughed at Martin's efforts to plant a tiny garden plot
in the viscid courtyard earth; a girl Hedy's age who lived down the hall
went to the hospital with hepatitis and never returned. In the summer,
flies arrived to swarm the foul mud, and entire apartments went empty
as barracks occupants died by the dozens from cholera. The heat from
the cooking stove made the tiny apartment unbearable. One day Martin
burned his arm on the flimsy stove-pipe, stumbling over the stack of
branches he had brought to keep the thing going. The burn made a large
oval scab that cracked and bled and finally left a purple scar.

By August, Martin woke up with imagined words from his father's
cousin's letter in his head almost every morning: *Liebling Trudi, please come
with the children to England at once. We have been waiting anxiously to hear
from you and have plenty of room!* The letter that arrived in October had
held a different tone entirely. *Gertrud Winzer, we did not expect to hear from
you after all this time. What you ask is impossible. Even those of us who left
Germany long ago have suffered by your war. We will respect Josef's wishes to
the best of our ability and take the boy alone. Write when you will send him by
train to Penrith and we will see that he is picked up. Margaret Thompson (I do
not go by Margrit any more)*

Martin had learned that he was to go by himself on a school afternoon, when he came home, as he frequently did, bleeding from a fight. He'd dropped his wood bag and his school slate on the front room floor with a loud thud, surprised and alarmed to see his mother already home. She had risen from the table hastily, stuffing the thin sheet of blue paper up her sleeve, fussing over Martin's split lip and the blood drying to brown on the collar of his last good shirt and the way his right eye was swollen almost shut.

"You're hurt!" she cried. "How does this keep happening?" She'd pressed Martin into one of the room's rickety seats, trying to hold a wet dishcloth against his lip and his eye at the same time.

"I don't know, Mutti," Martin had responded, his voice muffled by the weight of the cloth, and it was the truth. From the start, the boys in his class had teased him: for being smart, for his clothing that was somehow too fancy even as it was threadbare and outgrown. They made fun of the fact that he lived in the barracks where most of them were Braunschweig natives, living in real houses near the center of town. At first, he'd tried to make friends with them, offering to help them with their schoolwork, telling them about his former home to persuade them that he, too, had once had his own bedroom and a ball for playing soccer and a small dog to whom he fed bits of his dinner underneath the table. For reasons he didn't understand, however, that had only seemed to make things worse, elevating his torment from words and shoving to punches and hard-shoed kicks in the play yard. He'd begged and pleaded, he'd tried making himself inconspicuous; after a while, he had resorted to lying outright. None of it had worked.

One day, on his way home from school, he had been cornered in the Harz forest by one of his schoolmates, a bigger boy who had stepped into his path and showed him the rock in his fist. Martin had tried to run, but the boy had caught the back of his jacket and thrown him to the ground. In a panic, Martin had shouted: his father was an important member of the Nazi party, a close friend of the *Führer's*; his mother had received word only yesterday that he was on his way to rescue them. If the boy let Martin go on his way Martin would see that he got a reward.

Rather than frightening the bigger boy, Martin's words had spurred him to deliver a beating more severe than any he had suffered at school.

He'd struck Martin's face with the fisted rock until Martin could feel the blood from his nose run down the back of his throat. He'd lifted Martin by his jacket and then dropped him to the ground again, knocking the wind from his lungs. Martin had curled himself up in a ball, and the boy had aimed powerful kicks at the exposed curve of his back. Just before he'd lost consciousness, Martin had felt a horrible, hot wetness and realized the other boy was urinating on him. The stream had spattered his neck and chest as the boy had spat words at him. "This is what I think of your Nazi father."

The moon was out and Martin's soaked clothes were frozen to him in spots when, hours later, he had finally come to. Mutti had cried over him that night, but only until he repeated the words he'd said to scare off the older boy. Then, her face had gone white and her lips had come together in a hard line. "You must never speak like that," she told him. "Not to anyone. Not for any reason."

Martin had asked why not, on the verge of tears himself, and she had shaken him all over again. "Because I said so!" she had shouted. "You mustn't talk about your family to anyone. Not ever." After that, she'd gone back to cleaning his wounds, but her hands had pressed with hard, angry strokes.

After, Martin knew better than to ask questions, not even when the boys at school taunted him for living in a building full of *Dirnen,* a word that wasn't in his dictionary but that made them all laugh and thrust their hips when their ringleader said it; not even when they called him Devil spawn and told him they would turn him in to the British police. If Mutti hadn't been home at this unusual hour, he would have done what he usually did and cleaned himself up without ever mentioning the fight. Martin knew she would see the cuts and bruises; her eyes always looked at them, but his sisters were the only ones who ever asked.

Mutti continued dabbing at the blood beneath Martin's lip. "Well," she said, "it's not going to happen much longer. We've had a letter from your father's cousin."

"We're going to England?"

When his mother hesitated, Martin had seen the paleness of her cheeks and the redness of her puffy eyes. "Not all of us. Just you. You are to go on ahead." She bit her lip and stared over the top of Martin's head.

"In a matter of months, I expect, your sisters and I will be able to come."

For a moment, Martin had the wild idea that this news was his punishment for allowing himself to get beaten up so frequently. "No," he said. "I won't go. Please. Not until we can all go together."

"You will go," his mother said simply. "The letter's already been sent."

"Then send another one!" Martin started to cry in earnest, though eight was much too old, and waited for Mutti to slap his face for talking back. "What about my school? Who will collect the firewood?"

"Hedy will collect the firewood." Mutti sat down at the battered kitchen table and looked at her red, chapped hands. "You will go to school in England, just as your father did as a boy. Before he—" Her raw hands clenched and uncurled and she pressed her fingers hard against the tabletop. "It was always in the plans for you. You are meant to go to university, something that is impossible for me to make happen here."

Martin sobbed openly, hot tears squeezing out of his throbbing right eye, salty mucus sliding into the split on his lip. "H-how long?" he finally asked.

He had meant how long would it be before Mutti and his sisters would come to England, but his mother answered a different question. Herr Davies said he'd help her to make arrangements and they should know by the end of the week. Martin would have to take a train from Hannover to Belgium and probably a different one from Brugge to Oostende, on the coast. There was a ferry from Oostende to Dover, in England; Mutti wasn't sure if it was one train or two from there to Penrith but she guessed the journey itself would take at least five days. They'd buy a ticket as soon as Margrit wrote back to say which date would be best. It might be a matter of weeks from here, but Martin should be over and settled inside of a month.

"A month!" Martin cried. Mutti left the table and Martin followed her, throwing his arms around her middle the way he had not done since he was very little. "I can't!" he sobbed. "You can't!"

Mutti unlatched Martin's hands from her waist and put them back in front of him. Her voice was calm when she told him there was no point in crying about it, his tears weren't going to change anything. The decision was made and it was time for him to stop broadcasting his cowardice for the entire barracks to hear.

KRISTIN WATERFIELD DUISBERG

•

THE DATE OF MARTIN'S departure was set for late November and his train tickets to Brugge and Oostende were purchased with Herr Davies' help, but a week before he was scheduled to leave, his eldest sister fell ill. Brigid's already pallid face turned gray, she developed a fever, and a speckled red rash appeared on her hands and arms. One morning, Martin looked to where she sat across the table from him, slumped, and realized her hair had gotten so thin he could see her scalp; even her eyebrows and lashes seemed to be falling out. Shamefully, he found himself rejoicing: if Brigid was *this* sick there was no way Mutti would make him leave. What if he were to come down with the same illness on his way to Penrith? When he wasn't at school or finding firewood, Martin spent as much time as possible by his sister's bed, sure that the first sign of his fever or red rash would shut the door on his journey for good.

The days passed, however, and Mutti continued making preparations, just as Martin remained in solid health. She brought home a pair of undyed leather boots, brand new, that were only a little too large for Martin's feet, darned the holes in his shirts and his underclothing. One night, she cut his hair with kitchen scissors and scrubbed his head beneath the sink with hard brown soap. "You have lice," she told him, almost accusingly. "You'll have to keep your cap on and hope the inspectors aren't too careful." Martin nodded his head numbly, vowing to himself that he wouldn't wear a cap but instead would scratch until great, raw patches of skin showed.

Martin turned in his slate at school and said farewell to the barracks neighbor who had laughed at his efforts to garden, still not believing his mother would make him leave until she woke him up in the dark hours the morning he was supposed to go.

"Martin," she had said. "You must listen to me. I need to take Brigid to the hospital. Herr Kappel is taking us in his wagon now. Your train leaves Hannover at half past five o'clock. Herr Kappel has agreed to come back and take you. I will meet you at the station, but if I'm delayed for some reason—" Martin felt, more than heard, his mother hesitate "—you must get on without waiting for me. Is that understood?"

Martin had cried no—he couldn't!—and his mother shook his

shoulders. In the harsh light her face looked weathered and old. There were deep lines on her forehead and around the sides of her mouth. Brigid sat just behind Mutti on her cot, staring blankly, a sheen of sweat on her sallow face. "You can. You will. We'll—" Mutti's fingers gripped his shoulders spasmodically. "We'll come for you, *Bärchen*. When things are better here, you can come back."

Martin's mother gave the top of his shorn head a glancing kiss and busied herself with half-carrying Brigid out the door. She left without turning around again, ignoring Martin's desperate questions. What did she mean, come back? Wasn't the plan for everyone to go to England, for Martin to some day go to university? Martin followed his mother down the hallway and outside in his bare feet, shivering in the brittle November night as Herr Kappel hoisted Brigid in the wagon as if she were nothing more than a pile of empty clothes and Mutti clambered up. Herr Kappel snapped the reins and his horses took off with a jolt, moving much too fast for Martin to keep pace. He shouted one last time before he fell back. He saw the white flash of Mutti's turned face before the wagon disappeared in the dark.

HOURS LATER, HE ARRIVED at the Hannover Bahnhof in a daze, the air thick with the sound of voices and the exhaust from a hundred Army jeeps. Herr Kappel pulled his horses up short of the railway station and Martin's legs shook as he climbed down from the wagon bench, aching and stiff after seven frigid hours of jolting over rutted roads. Wordlessly, Herr Kappel handed Martin his suitcase and the bag of butter sandwiches Mutti had left on the table, then nodded straight ahead as he clucked to his team, melting into the crowd of carts and cars before Martin understood what was happening. *Wait!* he tried to cry, but his dry tongue cleaved to the roof of his dry mouth. *Herr Kappel!* Numb with fear, he let himself be carried along in the throng of bodies moving toward the low brick train station. *Inside*, he whispered to himself. *Mutti is waiting inside for me.*

The station smelled of urine and coal and heavy steam clung to Martin's face like a spider's web. His eyes swept the crowded concourse even as his feet moved him toward the ticket window, his own voice loud in his head, *Mutti, please…* There was the station restaurant and men in

RAF uniforms. A number of surprisingly well-dressed civilians looked at him. He stood at the ticket window, mute, elbowed aside by one impatient traveler after another before he was finally able to stammer out his request. Clutching his ticket and a handful of banknotes he stumbled away from the window and stood at the base of the platform clock, watching its uncaring hands moving closer and closer to five. His lips moved soundlessly as he asked the hands of the clock to stop, his mother to come.

Five o'clock came and went with no train and Martin felt a moment's elation: it hadn't happened! He wasn't going to leave! But the clock passed six and then seven and panic set in. It was dark now and he was freezing cold; the platform was crowded with bodies. Mutti wasn't going to come and he couldn't go back. He didn't know where the hospital Mutti took Brigid was, and Herr Kappel had taken so many twists and turns on the long drive. A few feet away, an exhausted mother held her own two children and their cardboard suitcases and Martin inched his way toward her, hoping. The mother gave him a hard, tired look and he inched back.

It was almost nine at night when the train to Brugge finally arrived, a big, black locomotive pulling a long string of passenger cars. Martin's stomach lunged. He had always loved to ride the train, thrilled even at the prospect of taking the Berlin streetcar with his father when he was younger, but now the cars seemed to bear down on him menacingly, the locomotive hissing hot steam, the smokestack blowing coal soot that swirled and stung in his eyes. A scream of metal on metal as the train slid to a stop and the doors opened; bodies around him surged forward while Martin stood as if rooted. A uniformed conductor called out the next stop, *Münster*.

Through the fogged-over train windows, Martin saw the people who had been standing beside him only moments earlier settling their suitcases and peeling off hats and coats. How could that be? A blade of wind blew across the platform, punctuated with bursts of wet snow. The locomotive's whistle hooted and Martin felt the platform vibrate beneath his frozen feet as the train shuddered back to life, the smell of coal filling his nostrils as clouds of damp, hot steam enveloped him. Metal wheels howled against steel tracks. Martin's empty stomach growled. His suitcase knocked against his shins as he stumbled toward the train.

The carriage doors closed behind Martin with a *thock* and for a moment he felt the pressure in his ears, as if he had plunged into a lake. He shuffled down the aisle in search of an open seat, listening to the wheels beneath him as the train began to move in earnest, *clackety-clack. Clackety-clack. Clackety-clack.* He slid past a man in a shabby brown suit and into a window seat, his body wracked with shudders as he struggled to comprehend what he'd just done. He was on the train, by himself, speeding away from his home and his family. He imagined Mutti running through the station, wailing his name, collapsing at the platform's edge as the train became a tiny speck of light. He saw Brigid in a hospital bed; Hedy home alone, wrestling with the stiff latch on the wood stove's hinged door. He touched his fingers to his face, patting his cheeks as if to confirm the surprising fact that he wasn't crying.

•

IT HAD HAPPENED A lifetime ago. As Martin lay in bed listening to the sound of Nina's slumbering breaths, he could almost imagine himself telling her all of it, and even more. Not far from Braunschweig, his mother had killed a starving dog and cooked it for their supper, taking a sobbing Martin by the jaw and forcing the stringy meat into his mouth. Studying infectious disease in medical school, he had finally understood the ailment that had laid claim to his beautiful eldest sister: syphilis, no doubt contracted when the Russians had invaded their Berlin home. He could almost tell Nina, yes, but to what end? These were the stories of his life, but they weren't the legacy he wanted to leave. Sharing them with Nina would not be a kindness. What comfort would it give his dying wife to know the permanent wound that was created when a child's mother tore a hole in the fabric of his very existence and then stepped through?

It had been a while since Martin had last slipped out for a predawn run, but he knew there was no way he was going to go back to sleep. He'd hardly gotten out at all in the month they'd been in Charlotte Harbor (reluctance to leave Nina under Audrey's care, though the likelihood of something happening was small; guilt over flaunting his health, when Nina's was forever gone) but the easy miles he'd done with Audrey the day before had left his muscles as awake as his brain. He didn't need to be particularly quiet—the morphine Nina took at bedtime pulled her into a heavy, subterranean sleep—but he felt around carefully for his running shorts, still damp with sweat, laced his sneakers blindly in the dark. Outside he stood for a minute, getting his bearings. Then he set off on the road that led away from the muttering ocean and toward the few and distant lights of Schoodic Point.

FIVE DAYS AFTER MARTIN boarded the train at Hannover station he'd begun the final leg of his journey, another train from London's Euston Station to Penrith. Five days had passed since he had said good-bye to Hedy in the front room of their tiny Braunschweig barracks apartment, five days since Mutti had awakened him in the dark with her unforgiving hands and voice. He felt only emptiness inside as he was pushed and jostled into the third-class train car and then from one hard seat to another. He knew he smelled bad—he hadn't bathed since the last time Mutti had scrubbed him with her hard brown soap—he knew he still had lice on his head, in spite of his bristle-short hair. What did it matter, any of it? He unfolded the paper from his last sandwich, the butter rancid now, and saw the way the family across the aisle looked at him, scooting tighter in their seats toward the soot-streaked window. His fingernails were rimmed with dirt, chipped and ragged; his hands left blackish prints on the sandwich paper and on the stale yellow bread.

"Mummy," the little girl sitting closest to him said loudly. "That boy is eating on the train with dirty fingers."

"That's not very good manners, is it?" the mother replied.

"No it isn't. Don't you think someone should tell him to stop?"

Martin stared straight ahead, letting the British voices flow over him like the countryside sliding by outside. It was late autumn here, just like in Braunschweig, the gray city giving way to bare, yellow hills and dead leaves pushed up in piles along the sides of rutted roads. The train passed a sprawling farm, belted Galloway cows and dark squares of earth strung with frost-blackened vines. It stopped at a village station where a little boy ran along the platform as the steam engine heaved itself back to life.

A discarded newspaper lay on the seat next to Martin and he reached for it, thinking the puzzle of the words might be something to fill his echoing head. It was folded open to a story about the government taking over the British Coal Mines, an advertisement for Raleigh cigarettes in the lower corner of the page. A woman with a bared stomach beamed out from the page at him, a military-looking cap of some sort perched on her dark curls.

A man who'd boarded the train at the village stop gestured to the cigarette ad. He smiled as he said something that Martin didn't quite understand.

"Sorry?"

"I said, You look like more of a Lucky Strike lad, to me."

"Oh." Martin struggled to put the words in his head together in English. "I'm not smoking any cigarettes. I have—" he stumbled—"I have not enough years."

The friendly smile on the man's face faded. *Sie Deutsch?*

Martin nodded. The man squinted at Martin's dirty face, then took the newspaper from him. He turned the pages so the front showed and, rising, slapped it down on Martin's lap. Martin grasped some but not all of the words the man said as he made his way to the back of the train.

"I don't know why they didn't round up every last one of you and kill you all."

The headline of the paper was a single word, in large type, an English past-tense construction Martin didn't recognize: *Hanged!* Beneath the word there were ten small square photographs, an eleventh set off from the rest in a box of dense type, pictures of men in military uniforms or business suits. For a moment, Martin felt an ache in his chest so intense he could hardly breathe. The men in their business suits reminded him of his father, their stern expressions, their slicked-back hair. He read the names— Wilhelm Frick, Alfred Jodl, Ernst Kaltenbrunner, Wilhelm Keitel. The picture set off to the side gave Martin a start: he recognized the face; it was that of a man he'd once seen for himself, Hermann Göring. Three years ago, Martin had watched his father walk up on a stage and shake *Reischmarschall* Göring's hand when he'd come to Berlin to inspect the SS troops. Göring had been a large man, his own father slight next to his uniformed bulk; he had been jolly and made jokes with the crowd. Hundreds of people had waved posters with a picture of his eagle-sharp face.

Martin clutched the newspaper, holding it close to his eyes as if that would help him better understand the English words. *Luftwaffe commander Hermann Göring, chief of the 4-Year Plan and architect of some of the Nazi party's most heinous crimes, was found dead in his cell the night before he was to be hanged, a cowardly suicide. The third-highest ranking Nazi official convicted at Nuremberg behind Reich President Karl Dönitz and Deputy Führer Rudolf Hess, Göring is believed to have poisoned himself with cyanide.*

As the train rolled on through the English countryside, Martin grappled with the newspaper, his mind reeling with the words he recognized, the grisly, blurry photos on the inside pages. It wasn't true; it couldn't be true. All the men who had come to his house when he was little, men who had brought him comic books and metal airplanes—they had been good men. They had been his father's friends. A group of skeletal children stared at Martin from one grainy newsprint picture and he saw more words he knew: Jew, Sachsenhausen.

Aloud, he said the word *no*. These were lies in the newspaper. This wasn't possible. People weren't capable of such cruelty. But then he thought of his father once more, his splayed legs and dark blood in the study; he tasted again the stringy dog meat his mother had forced him to eat in the forest outside of Helmstedt. His mind reeled with the things he thought he'd always known. His home. His family. His own suffering, meaningless now next to the haunted, skeletal figures whose empty eyes burned holes in him from the newspaper page. It was possible. It certainly was possible.

It was nighttime when the whistle of the train signaled its arrival at Penrith Station. A row of grim-looking people lined the platform, haloed under the yellow sodium lights, each of their faces as unfamiliar and as unwelcoming as the next. For the first time in hours, Martin had stood, his legs shaking with fear and hunger and the weight of a question it was much too soon for him to understand he would carry for every day of the sixty years and more that stretched ahead of him, a question he would wait far too long to try and answer:

What shall I do with my second chance?

thirty-seven

BECAUSE OF THE AMOUNT of pain medicine she was taking now, Nina no longer fell to sleep but slid in and out of it, as if consciousness were a drawer that opened and shut with her inside. She didn't like the feeling—the perpetual fogginess, the inexorable detachment of her brain from her body that now seemed well underway—but the bone pain was a constant, grinding presence now, white-hot talons sinking into her legs and back and sides if she backed off the fentanyl too much. When the decision had been made to stay in Charlotte Harbor, Martin had been kind enough to pretend it was because he loved the place too much to leave, but even if that were true, Nina knew it was only one piece of the puzzle. It was too late for her now; the only way she could make the trip to back Cabot would be by ambulance. She worried about Audrey's isolation here, and Martin had suggested recently they might stay indefinitely, but what sort of say was she going to have in the future, after all? She had no choice but to trust that Martin would know what was right for Audrey. Next week, a year from now, when Audrey was ready for college—

In the early evening the waves around the island sounded like a giant heartbeat, and Nina imagined not that she was dying but being born.

"I remember that," Audrey said. She curled up with her mother sometimes now, her fingers active on the plastic frame of the hospital bed or the wrinkles in the soap-smelling sheets.

Nina hadn't realized she'd spoken out loud. "You remember what?"

"Being inside you. Waiting to be born. It does sound like that, only with muffled voices behind the heart sounds."

"Oh, honey…" For a second, Nina struggled to compose a coherent argument against her daughter's claim. But what was the upside to doing so? The idea of a beforelife was no crazier than that of an afterlife; if anything, it had greater—not lesser—validity. Maybe Audrey *did* remember what it was like before she was born.

"You do?" she asked. "What do you remember?"

"Not a lot. Just what it felt like. What it sounded like. It wasn't like I could *see* anything." Audrey thought a moment and then added, "It was warm."

"Warm," Nina murmured. "I suppose it would be."

"Warm and squishy, like a bath only different."

Nina stroked her daughter's head, running her fingers through the tangles in Audrey's long, sun-streaked hair. Over the past year or so, the wheat color had started to darken, and while Nina had been saddened by that, the thick swaths of near-white laid over dark blond were even more striking than the undifferentiated yellow had been. Her thick, curving lashes, her full, red lips…Audrey was going to be a beauty, no doubt about it. She would need someone—Jenny, maybe? Martin's daughter-in-law, Leanne?—to help her fathom potentially unwanted attentions. Nina hoped no one would break her daughter's heart.

"Did you know me, know I was there, even if you couldn't see me?"

"Uh-huh."

"And so you'll know I'm there, even after I'm gone?"

All around the house, waves rolled in and out with a steady shushing sound. Martin, who had been folding laundry on the couch, glanced up sharply, pain raw on his face. There was no reason not to continue this conversation, though, not at this point. Nina was going to do the best that she could.

"I think so," Audrey said softly.

"I think so, too." Nina worked her fingers through a knot at the end of Audrey's hair, careful not to tug on the strands as she pulled them apart. "Is there anything you want to ask me?"

Audrey shrugged. "I guess so." She was quiet after that, though, and Nina asked her if she was thinking. "I was wondering, I guess," she said, "what it feels like."

"Having cancer, you mean? Or dying?"

"The second one."

"So far, it's not too bad. It doesn't hurt too much."

"But that's because you're taking pain medication."

"That's true."

Audrey's fingers traced the lettering embossed on the bed rail just beneath the control panel. *Hill-Rom.* "Do people always know it? When they're dying?"

"I'm not sure," Nina said, as lightly as she could. "I think probably most of the time."

"Is it scary?"

Nina hesitated before answering. "No, it's not scary. I'm sad about leaving you and Dad, though. I'm sad about missing out."

Audrey nodded her head. "I'm sad about that, too." She rolled away from her mother and picked up the flashlight on Nina's bedside table.

"I know you are, sweetheart. We all are."

At once, a boiling red arrow of pain sliced through Nina's torso, angling from her lower left back between her ribs and out through her right lung. Waves of nausea rolled over her, and her face, her armpits, the backs of her knees were sticky with sweat. She gave a small, involuntary gasp. She took a ragged breath and the arrow slowly receded, leaving a pulsing afterimage in its place.

"What, Mom?" Audrey sat up in the bed.

Martin started over, a t-shirt of Audrey's still in his hand. "Are you all right?"

Nina shook her head. Already the pain was lessening, the edges blurring, a puffy, salmon-pink contrail from a long-passed airplane. These spikes were coming more frequently now, but Nina knew from experience it could be hours or days, even, before another leapt at her like that. She wondered what they were, what they meant, what additional territory her body was giving up.

"I'm fine," she said weakly. "Just a little surprise."

"Do you need something for it?"

Martin meant a morphine shot, one of the little glass vials he kept in the back of the guest room closet for the times the pain became too much. On top of the fentanyl, morphine would knock out the pain, but it would also drag Nina under a thick, gray sleep. She shook her head, not wanting that at all. "Just give me a minute."

Beside her, Audrey twisted a section of Nina's sheet around her finger. "Does it hurt a lot?"

"Not really," Nina said, mostly truthfully. The pain was gone now, a throbbing emptiness describing the place where it had been.

"That's good."

Another minute passed and Audrey settled herself back down again. "Sometimes," she said, after a pause, "I wish I was going with you."

"Oh, honey," Nina said. "I'm glad— It's not—" There were words in her head, and she reached for them helplessly, but trying to catch them was like trying to catch smoke. "It's okay for you to miss me," she managed. "But I wouldn't want you to be only sad forever. It's okay for you to stop missing me, too. I'm glad to know you're going to be staying."

Audrey aimed the beam of the flashlight up at the ceiling, clicking the black rubber button on and off, her slight frown suggesting her mother's words weren't having their intended effect.

"I'm sorry," Nina said. "I wish there was something I could say to make you feel better."

"Do you think—" Audrey hesitated, biting her lip. "Do you think we're going to see each other again?"

"I hope so," Nina whispered. "And I know you'll always carry a piece of me. Do you know that? Because you came from me, my cells."

Audrey nodded, watching the wavering, elongated circle the light from her flashlight made on the white ceiling. She shook the flashlight a little, and for a second the edges of the circle burst into ripples, like a pool of water someone had poked with a finger.

"Do you think you'd be able to go outside? If Dad carries you?"

"Right now?"

"Yes," Audrey answered. "It will only take a minute."

"Audrey, sweetheart, I don't think that's such a good idea." Martin moved a pile of towels he'd gone back to folding and seated himself at the foot of Nina's bed "Your mother's tired. It's probably time for her to get a new fentanyl patch."

"But—please?" Audrey's face looked pained, desperate. "It's just— that—I had this idea—"

"Martin," Nina said softly. "It's fine." Their eyes met and she knew he understood her expression. It wasn't like they were going to have that many more chances for it.

Martin wrapped two blankets around Nina and carried her out onto the farmer's porch. "Here?" he asked, pausing at the reclining chair.

"No," Audrey answered. "Out on the lawn."

Audrey was still clutching her mother's flashlight, and Martin watched as she lifted the seat on the porch bench and pulled out a second torch. In the dark, she clattered a pair of beach chairs onto the grass and gestured to her father to carry her mother over. As Martin knelt to set Nina down in it, she lifted her face to him.

"I'm sorry, Martin," she whispered.

His heart pounded against her cheek, loud, robust. She felt him stop, his arms tremble. "I know, sweetheart. I'm sorry, too."

Nina tilted her head against the chair back and took in the inky night. The stars seemed heavy, low, and she briefly felt the stupefaction she'd felt as a young girl, trying to connect the cold, white pinpricks of light into the magical figures of the constellations the Greeks had imagined sprawling across the sky. Cassiopeia, Sagittarius, Ursa Major, Perseus—she'd only ever been able to make out Orion's Belt and the Big and Little Dipper—which her brothers had been happy to tell her weren't constellations at all. The Dippers were *asterisms*, a fact that Audrey likely knew, too. Nina's father had told her once about an aboriginal tribe that believed the sky was a gigantic black cloth, the stars a thousand little holes that let light from beyond it shine through. As a child whose stomach knotted at the thought of infinity, that explanation had appealed to her: a universe bound up in black velvet, suspended by magic in a vast sea of brilliant, blazing white. She closed her eyes, feeling an aching, inchoate connection to the vast emptiness. The stars were dead, the light that shined from them mere illusion. *Very soon—*

"Here, Mom." Audrey put one of the flashlights into Nina's hand and pointed it up at the sky. She held her own the same way and said, "When I say three, push the button to turn your flashlight on, okay? One, two, three—"

Nina clicked and the two torches went on simultaneously, their twin cones of yellow light almost immediately dispersed into the cloudless sky.

She waited, but Audrey kept pointing her flashlight straight upward, not aiming it back at the house or toward the beach where the waves shushed in and out.

"Why are we doing this?" Nina finally asked.

"Because the light will keep on traveling forever. Then, when I miss you, I can look up at the sky and know your light is still out there."

Nina's throat closed. The idea was lovely; it was absolutely lovely. But it was also—wasn't it?—entirely wrong. The light had gone only a couple of feet before being swallowed up by the darkness, conquered effortlessly. For a moment, she focused on the surprise of that, all the possible implications of her daughter's fallibility, to distract herself from the exquisite pain now closing around her heart. She closed her eyes, and her lids pressed hot tears out from the corners and over her cheeks. "It would be nice if it worked that way, wouldn't it?" she said.

"But it *does* work that way," Audrey replied. "It's physics. I'm not saying I'm going to be able to see it or anything. The production part is finished, but the photons are still traveling. Unless they hit an asteroid or something, the light waves we just made will travel on and on into the universe."

Nina laughed—her daughter was now not only smarter than her, but also a bit of a mind reader, as well—but the sound that came from her mouth was a wet, snorting sob.

"Don't be sad, Mom," Audrey said, her tone alarmed.

Nina pivoted her flashlight until its yellow beam met the light still shining from Audrey's lamp, the two streams of—photons, was it?—merging into one. She tried to picture the individual particles of light soaring outward, intertwined, spiraling around one another endlessly like the pictures she remembered from high school science of the double-helix shape of DNA. "I'm not sad, sweetheart," she said. "I'm—" There wasn't a word to describe how she felt right now. She took a gulping breath. "I'm glad."

She paused again, surprised by the word that had come to her. She *was* glad. She felt a fluttering in her chest that she recognized as a form of contentment—of happiness, even. Her beautiful, extraordinary, remarkable daughter. Her daughter's uncommon, exceptional brain. She stared straight upward, trying to comprehend not the emptiness but the fullness of the sky spread above them, her photons and Audrey's soaring out into it. She repeated the words. "I'm just so glad I got to be your mom."

thirty-eight

WHEN SHE WAS PREGNANT with Audrey, Nina had taken a class called childbirth preparedness—a Lamaze lite, she had joked, that emphasized birthing plans and the importance of breastfeeding and strategies for getting the lone St. Serafin labor room with a whirlpool tub. After the four-week course ended, she'd realized her most pressing question was one that had never been answered satisfactorily: how was she going to know when she was really in labor? Forget breathing and back labor and understanding how an epidural was administered; what could be more essential to *preparedness* than knowing that? The answer that first Martin and then her instructor had given her hadn't been reassuring to someone as anxious as Nina was about the process—both had told her that when the time came, she simply was going to know. "But know how?" she'd persisted. "Know by what?" She'd been having Braxton-Hicks contractions for weeks and they certainly felt real enough to her. The night the thin, wringing cramps at the base of her taut stomach had pulled her from her sleep, she realized Martin and her instructor had been right: This was it, she was in labor. She did just know. Hours of wrenching pain and anxiety and exhaustion lay ahead of her, but the greatest love affair of her life was about to commence.

DYING WAS EXACTLY the same.

Nina had awakened at sunrise, the scent of lilacs so heavy in the air

341

she realized somehow she had ended up back in Cabot on a May morning, running barefoot in the garden behind her childhood home. The sky was pink and the air was dense with the cries of gulls and in another breath she was back in Charlotte Harbor, her ten-year-old daughter curled against her side. She kissed Audrey's bare shoulder, breathing her daughter in as hard as she could, and summoned her strength to focus on where Martin lay sprawled across the couch. "Martin," she whispered. That was all. Two days ago, she had watched Audrey and Martin build a makeshift tent of blankets and sheets in the yard, and last night Martin had taken her on the porch to see a lightning storm so far out over the ocean the shocks that lit the clouds with white and purple seemed to never stop. For a fleeting instant, she had been sitting at the hand of God, witnessing the birth of a new universe, and when the storm had faded to flickers and then nothingness a strange sadness had gripped her, a terrible sense of loss. It was Wednesday, August 9, 2006, five-forty a.m. She knew.

Martin crossed the silvery room and bent low over her hospital bed. His warm fingers pressed against her wrist (her pulse, she realized); *my arms,* she thought, *my arms*—he lifted her forearm and laid it across Audrey's curled, still sleeping form and she relaxed. He understood.

"Do you need morphine?" he whispered. "Squeeze my hand if you do." No, she didn't. She wasn't in pain, and she wanted her head to be clear. *I love you,* she thought with all her might. *I love you, I love you.* "I'm going to get my stethoscope."

Martin returned, pressed the cool disc of his stethoscope against Nina's back. She was still breathing, she knew, felt Martin's hand stroke her forehead, her hair. "You're doing just fine, my love," he told her and inside her head, at least, Nina smiled. Fine was good. It was one of the things she'd worried about: dying well.

Time stretched. Nina thought of molten glass, the sun rose enough to touch her eyelids and again Martin understood, opening the window to let the salty air blow in. Audrey moved and from somewhere Nina heard her ask her father *Is she*—? her tone just a couple notes sharp, and he answered her, "Not yet, sweetheart. But soon." *It's okay, Mom,* Audrey said a little later. *You know I love you.*

Rings of Technicolor brightness folded in behind her eyelids. Nina remembered a glass blowing demonstration she had seen one time, the metal pole the man had withdrawn from the roaring mouth of the oven, near-liquid glass glowing on the end of it like a giant lollipop she'd been desperate to touch, to poke, even as her insides had curdled with primitive fear. Martin's voice was close to her ear now, saying *I'm with you, we're here and we love you,* and Nina thought calmly, So this is it, then. It was happening now. Had she ever told Audrey how one of the messages in a bottle she and her brothers had launched from Aggamassic Reach had been found, years afterward? A man from Turks and Caicos Islands had sent them a note: *My name is Marcus Robidoux and I found your bottle here on Salt Cay on 17th May, 1984.* The glass blower had done more turning than blowing, she remembered, rolling the metal pole across a steel table of sorts with the glowing orb of glass, elongated now, hanging over the end. She was driving a convertible down an empty highway, somewhere where the fields on either side rippled and swayed with Queen Anne's lace and purple loosestrife and milkweed heavy with fat, green pods. Monarch butterflies rose in waves and it was so beautiful Nina ached. My God, she thought, the world— Pools of water shimmered on the blacktop then disappeared.

Blackness, then, nothing but perfect darkness; everyone wrong all along and no one to tell it to. Nina knew that it was over, her breathing stilled, her heartbeat stopped. She began a gorgeous falling, arms outstretched, a liquid spiraling around a fireman's pole, the whorled inside curves of a Nautilus shell. *You're not alone, we're both here with you, Mom. We love you. Nina, ninanina*— She was inside the shell, sounds distorted, circling with inexorable languid speed for the very point, a pinhole of perfect, blinding white. It rose up to meet her, opening, illumining, the rise of the sun as seen from outer space, but still, she was gorgeous-falling too fast. She'd never make it, never make it! Put her hands out against the impact, the hole, the wall of electric white, blinding, stunning, not yet—not. Yet—

Oh, Audrey!

After

thirty-nine

FOR A FULL WEEK after her mother died, Audrey didn't speak a word. She couldn't. She was afraid that if she opened her mouth and filled her ears with her own speech, she would lose the sound of her mother's voice in her head. There were people who had something called perfect pitch, the ability to hear a note of music and know whether it was an A or a B flat or an F as automatically as other people could look at a color and say if it was green or orange or blue, and while Audrey didn't have perfect pitch herself, it was what she thought of when she thought of her mother's voice. A timbre, a tone, that only she could recognize, that she knew in the millisecond before thought, that she'd never hear again. She played words and phrases her mother had said to her—*could you hand me that, sweetie?; what are you thinking about?*—over and over, as if by doing so she could burn them permanently into her brain. *Carefully, please. My beautiful girl—*

After her father took out his stethoscope, listened to her mother's chest and slowly nodded his head, Audrey had stayed in the room only a few minutes more. The two of them had talked about it the night before: how quickly things would begin to change, how it wouldn't take long at all before her mother wouldn't look like herself anymore. Audrey could stay if she wanted, but on the other hand, she might want to remember her mother the way she had been, alive. Her mother's cheek was still warm when she touched it with her fingertips; she walked from the room as her father began to do all the things he'd told her he would once everything was over: disconnect the hissing oxygen that had helped her mother breathe for the last couple of weeks, call the hospital and then the funeral home, arrange an ambulance to come for the body. Audrey was outside sitting on a long, flat rock as the truck rolled slowly up the road, its lights flashing but its sirens turned off. It seemed like such a strange thing now, an ambulance without an emergency, the pounding heat of the sun on her skin and the bawling cries of seagulls in her ears now that her mother was gone. Her mother was dead.

At the funeral, back in Cabot, Audrey wore the bright orange earplugs her mother had bought her years earlier, muffling the voices of the lipsticked strangers who told her, *Your mother was such a lovely woman, I knew her when she was younger than you are now, did you know that?;* silencing the neighbors who looked at her from the sides of their eyes and said things to each other like, "The poor thing," and, "I can't imagine what will become of the two of them." Hundreds of people showed up, packing the high-ceilinged rooms of Cabot's Victorian funeral home with their perfume and powder and body heat, nurses from Boston Metropolitan and doctors from St. Serafin and a whole bunch of parents from Goldengrove. Audrey's father did all of the talking for both of them, shaking hands and accepting hugs, telling even Willow Rutherford *thank you for coming* when she stood with her mother in front of Audrey, twisting the hem of her black polka-dotted skirt. Though Audrey had seen the moment in her head many times, imagined the words she might say to Willow as her former best friend begged for her forgiveness, she found herself looking beyond Willow, wondering if Una Curran might come with her parents to pay their respects. She didn't see them, but the Slocums came, Juliette's mom and dad but not Juliette, and Audrey's father seemed to sense her disappointment when they introduced themselves, his grip on her shoulders tightening before he held a hand out to Juliette's father. "Todd Slocum, of course. It was good of you to come."

Audrey spent most of her time in her room, but every now and then she would pause in the hall on her way to or from the bathroom and catch little bits of conversation from downstairs: her half-brother Peter and his wife, Leanne, who stopped in almost every day to check on her and her father; Jenny Rutherford, who came without Willow; her uncle Neal, who told Audrey he'd met her as a baby but wasn't surprised she didn't remember, patting her head as if he thought his own unfamiliarity was the reason she didn't speak. The first couple of days there was another uncle—Roger—her mother's oldest brother, a tall, thin man who had flown all the way to Boston from California. His wife had bothered Audrey, trying to coax her into eating the disgusting casseroles the neighbors brought, aluminum pans of noodles with tuna fish and soggy mushroom bits or deviled ham and breadcrumbs, but Roger, like Audrey, had been quiet. When his wife suggested in Audrey's hearing that her father ought to be taking her to a psychiatrist, Roger had come to Audrey's defense. "She just lost her mother and she's ten years old," he said. "Why in the world would you think she'd want to talk?"

"I'm not saying she has to talk about her mother," the wife replied. "I'm just saying it's worrisome that she doesn't talk at all. And the father isn't exactly what I'd call a pillar of comfort."

"I think Martin's doing remarkably well under the circumstances. And I'm sure Audrey will talk when she's ready to."

Audrey wasn't sure that she would ever be ready, but she did know that at some point she would start to talk again. Earlier in the summer, she had found a magazine article at the Schoodic Point free library about the Georgia Guidestones, an enormous set of six granite slabs, almost a quarter of a million pounds in weight, inscribed with instructions for how to rebuild the world if there was some sort of catastrophic event that left only a small number of survivors behind. In the periodicals room, Audrey had read the article all the way through twice, and then, knowing it was against the rules, she had torn the pages out of the magazine, folded them into a small, thick square, and tucked them into the pocket of her shorts. Back at the house on McKittrick Rock, she had hidden the article in her top dresser drawer, retrieving it from beneath a stack of pajamas almost every night to read over again. It was like a science fiction story, thrilling and beautiful and eerie all at once. Four of the giant stones were inscribed with a list of ten instructions in eight different languages, English, Spanish, Swahili, Hindi, Hebrew, Arabic, Chinese, and Russian; a fifth giant slab lay across the four, its ends carved with a different message in Babylonian cuneiform, Classical Greek, Sanskrit, and Egyptian hieroglyphs. The slab in the middle didn't have any adornments, but there was hole drilled in it at eye level so that people standing on the south side could look through it at night and find the North Star.

No one knew the identity of the person who had commissioned the gigantic monument or why he or she wanted to build it, and reading about it had filled Audrey's head with questions: why Georgia, why these particular ten instructions (*maintain humanity under 500,000,000 in perpetual balance with nature*, read the first, *avoid petty laws and useless officials*, read another), why the eight—twelve—languages that had been chosen? When she had read the article back in her room in Charlotte Harbor, Audrey had felt comforted by the notion that someone had thought things through so thoroughly, had felt so sure they knew the answers for how to reassemble the world after it had fallen apart. But now, taking it out once again while her father said good night downstairs to the last of their daily guests, the words terrified her more than they provided consolation. What information did these mystery builders have about the end of the world that everyone else did not? How could they be sure the instructions were the right ones, written in the right languages? The only survivors might be children; hundreds of years might pass before any civilization stumbled onto the guidestones. If the world began again, it seemed to Audrey it might do so in a brand new language altogether, the words on the stones as strange and unknowable as the clicks of whales and chirps of birds were to her.

Audrey heard her father's footsteps on the stairs and folded the article in half as he knocked on her closed door and then let himself in without waiting for a response. He sat next to Audrey on the bed, the mattress sinking beneath his weight.

"What have you got there?"

Guiltily, Audrey slid the pages across her quilt. The top half of an ad for a minivan faced up at her, a blond family and their white dog beaming out from the page. While her father read, Audrey traced the stitching of the quilt with her pointer finger, following the raised lines of thread that outlined jumping horses and stout ponies, stirrups and saddles and riding helmets. The bedding had been a gift from her mother the summer before, shortly after her cancer had come back and Audrey had been made to stop riding at Royal River. It had come from an expensive catalog and Audrey had begged for it, knowing the price was ridiculous. By the time the box had arrived and her mother had called her into the living room, *Come see what I have for you*, she hadn't wanted it, unable to look at the quilt without seeing all the losses it represented.

"*Life Magazine*, hmm. I don't recall that we subscribe to this. Did this come from the house in Charlotte Harbor?"

Audrey gave her head the tiniest twitch, *no*.

"From the library?"

Tracing a stirrup, Audrey tipped her head forward once, *yes*.

"I see. The one here, or the one in Schoodic Point? I suppose it doesn't actually make a difference."

Audrey closed her eyes, trying to summon the words her mother would have said to her next, reminding her of the importance of respecting others' property, or asking her how she would feel if someone tore something from a magazine that was hers. The answer was angry of course; probably outraged. It hadn't made a difference at the time.

"You know, when I was a boy, shortly after my mother told me I was going to be sent to England by myself, one of the things I did was steal a comic book from another boy who lived in the barracks."

Audrey's father paused.

"It was called *The Beano Comic*, *beano* being British slang for having a party, having a bean feast. It was one of two British comic papers that were popular when I was a boy, *The Beano* and *The Dandy*. They printed on alternate weeks, because of paper and ink rationing."

Audrey heard the crackle of paper turning over, and then her father continued. "At any rate, I wasn't sure why I was doing it—taking the comic, I mean—and I certainly knew that stealing from someone who had even less than me was wrong. The soldiers gave them out sometimes, comic books and gum, and if you were the lucky boy or girl who was given one you paraded it around so everyone else could see. I asked this boy if I could borrow it, and then later, when he asked for it back, I told him someone had stolen it, that I'd left it outside the latrine and when I was finished it was gone. I don't think he believed me, but there wasn't anything he could do. He was younger than me, and I rationalized that he probably didn't read English well enough to appreciate it anyway."

For a minute, night sounds filled Audrey's room, crickets and katydids trilling in the back yard, a moth bumping against the window screen, futilely drawn from outside to the light beside Audrey's bed. In Charlotte Harbor, night had sounded completely different, shushing waves and the lonely, clear note of the channel buoy, the steady murmur of her parents' voices from the farmer's porch. Audrey felt an aching at the back of her eyes and her dry, hollow throat. Her mother was dead. She would never see her again. *It's okay, Audrey. Oh, goosey. I'm just glad—*

"I guess I just was upset, and felt like I was entitled to something. Why should this other boy get a comic book if he was going to stay with his family in a place where soldiers handed them out? I think I already knew in my heart that I wasn't ever going to see my mother and sisters again." Audrey's father stopped, clearing his throat again. "Of course, the irony was that when I got to England you could get *The Beano Comic* anywhere. They even sold it at the pharmacy where I had an afternoon job."

Audrey's father turned the creased article over once more and then slid it back across the comforter to her.

"Your choice was much better. The comics really were pretty foolish. This at least has some educational value."

Audrey nodded. She stared down at the paper in front of her, the photograph at the top of the page she had all but memorized. The massive gray slabs of the Georgia Guidestones rose from the earth in a star pattern, silently waiting for the time when they would be needed. Words swelled in her stomach. She practiced them in her head a few times before she said them, afraid, knowing that as soon as she spoke, the *now* she had clung to for the past week would be replaced with *after*. After her mother's life. After her own life as a girl who had a mother.

"Dad?" she whispered. She swallowed, her throat hard and reluctant. "What— What's it going to be like?"

Audrey raised her eyes to her father, who seemed to be waiting for this very question. His hands trembled a little as he brushed them together, but when he put his arms around her shoulders they were warm and sure.

"Well, then," he said. "Where shall I begin?"

Acknowledgments

First, my heartfelt and humble thanks to two extraordinary women who believed as much as I did that this story had a place in the world. Rachel Sussman, my agent, saw me through multiple drafts and proved herself both patient and relentless when it came to submissions. I couldn't have asked for a better partner over the last three years. Editor Victoria Barrett has been a writer's dream, bringing insight and inspiration that not only made this a much better book, but helped me fall in love with it all over again.

For both the medical and historical content in these pages, I drew on a variety of resources. Invaluable to my understanding of the German experience in and after World War II were *Laughter Was Never Rationed,* by Dorothea von Schwanenfluegel Lawson; *German Boy: A Child in War,* by Wolfgang W.E. Samuel; the anonymous autobiography *A German Woman in Berlin; My Father's Keeper,* by Stephan and Norbert Lebert; and *Tearing the Silence: On Being German in America* by Ursula Hegi. To better understand the emotional and physical dimensions of breast cancer and treatment, I turned to *Why I Wore Lipstick to my Mastectomy,* by Geralyn Lucas; *The Victoria's Secret Catalog Never Stops Coming,* by Jennie Nash; *Living Beyond Breast Cancer,* by Marisa Weiss; and more extraordinary, raw, and insightful blogs than I can list. The internet isn't all bad. Speaking of the internet, most of the additional medical information here—about cardiology, breast cancer, and autism spectrum disorders—comes from my own online research, for better or worse. Any and all factual inaccuracies are mine.

For their support and generous feedback on earlier drafts, thanks to Eve Bridburg, Christopher Castellani, Michelle Chalfoun, and Mary Evans. An extra hug for Eve, who renewed my faith in myself as a writer when I needed it most. For their flexibility and encouragement, thanks to my colleagues at the University of New Hampshire. Thanks, too, to the many caregivers and patients at Massachusetts General Hospital with whom I crossed paths in my previous professional life. While this book is a work of fiction, the courage, dignity, and integrity I encountered at every turn are in many ways the inspiration for the story here.

Much love to the friends and family members who cheered me through the many years of this novel's incubation, especially Gayle Cooper, Mike Norberg, Sara Norberg, Lance Waterfield, and Ruthe Waterfield. Extra shoutouts to Amanda Brodkin, who provided expert proofreading; Allan Waterfield, who has probably bought more copies of this book and my previous one than the rest of America put together; and Elizabeth Dodge and Elizabeth Whaley, former high school English teachers and too infrequent lunch companions who provided feedback and encouragement on this project from the earliest draft. A debt of gratitude to Peter Duisberg, who shared enough of his own story with me to plant the seed for Martin's.

At the very heart of it all, of course, are my husband and children. Grace and Henry, thank you for bringing joy to my life, and thank you also for allowing Audrey to borrow some of your brilliance for this book. You are truly two individuals greater than the sum of your parts. And Erik, once again—I'm awed by your belief in me, your exceptional Patience Man-ness, your unconditional support and willingness to put my writing first. The words thanks and love aren't nearly enough.

About the Author

Kristin Waterfield Duisberg received her undergraduate degree from Bowdoin College and her master's degree in creative writing from Boston University. She has taught creative writing at Boston University and the Boston-based Grub Street Writers' Workshop and worked as a writer for J.P Morgan and Massachusetts General Hospital. Having spent most of her life in New England, she returned recently to the seacoast New Hampshire college town where she grew up and currently serves as editor of the University of New Hampshire magazine. She lives with her husband, two children, and two exceedingly hairy golden retrievers. *After* is her second novel; she is also the author of *The Good Patient* (St. Martin's Press).